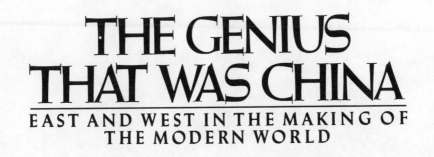

THE GENIUS THAT WAS CHINA

EAST AND WEST IN THE MAKING OF THE MODERN WORLD

THE GENIUS
THAT WAS CHINA

Bodleian Library, Oxford

EAST AND WEST IN THE MAKING OF
THE MODERN WORLD

JOHN MERSON

The Overlook Press

Woodstock, New York

For Gwynned, Emily and Francis

First published in 1990 by
The Overlook Press
Lewis Hollow Road
Woodstock, New York 12498

Library of Congress Cataloging-in-Publication Data

Merson, John
   The Genius of China

1. China – Civilization – 20th century. 2. Technology – China – History – 20th century.
3. Science – China – History – 20th century. I. Title.
DS775.2.M47   1990   951.05   89-26569

ISBN 0-87951-397-7

Produced by Weldon Owen Pty Limited
43 Victoria Street, McMahon's Point, NSW 2011, Australia
Telex 23038; Fax (02) 929 8352
A member of the Weldon International Group of Companies
Sydney • Hong Kong • London • Chicago • San Francisco

Editor: Lesley Dow
Designer: Warren Penney

First published as "Roads to Xanadu", the book accompanied a four-part film series produced by Film Australia. We gratefully acknowledge their assistance.

Printed in Australia by
The Griffin Press

Page 2: Wang Hui (1632-1717) and his assistants, *From Tsinan to Tai-an, with Performance of Ceremony at Mount Tai.* (Detail no 4 "Arrival at Mount Tai.") Handscroll: The K'ang-hsi Emperor's Second Tour of the South. Scroll no 3 from series of 12. Ink and colors on silk, Ch'ing Dynasty (1691-98).
The Metropolitan Museum of Art, Ourchasem The Dillon Fund Gift, 1979

Page 3: In response to China's growing wealth and power, the merchant-adventurer Marco Polo left his native Venice in the late thirteenth century and travelled to Kublai Khan's summer retreat, known in the west as Xanadu.
Bodleian Library, Oxford

CONTENTS

PREFACE

During the past decade, some scholars and journalists have asked if the shift of economic power from the Atlantic to the Pacific would continue and would change the shape of the world in the twenty-first century. The question is not as speculative today as it was ten years ago. And thirty years ago, the question itself would have been considered absurd. But asking the question of the present will yield little profit if we do not go further and ask a few questions of the past, even though these may seem old, familiar ones. For example, why did a scientific civilization not emerge in the Pacific in the first place? After all, China had a brilliant start and remained creative for two thousand years. And why did this scientific revolution occur in a corner of Western Europe? That was a most remarkable circumstance, which made it possible for the west to transform and dominate the world. Yet, less than two centuries later, there are new questions about how long that dominance will last.

Of the old questions, one still baffles us. Why did China succumb so easily to the aggressive drives of the upstart powers of northwestern Europe in the nineteenth century? Another old question remains important. Why did Japan succeed in responding to the western challenge where China failed? Now, surprisingly, the question is, will China follow the rest of East Asia into new forms of capitalism, and will this usher in "the Pacific century" in a few decades' time?

John Merson has set out to bring both old and new questions together in a fresh way. He has asked similar questions before. As an experienced science journalist and historian he has personally pursued answers to these questions for several years. Those about China intrigued him most of all. They aroused his curiosity and led him, not only into China's scientific past, but also into history, culture and the nature of Chinese society. He produced a major series for the Australian Broadcasting Corporation and published a book, *Culture and Science in China,* in 1981. But China continued to change after 1981, so too did Japan's position as an economic superpower, and even more so the "four small dragons" of East Asia, which glowed like satellites around the brightest star. So questions were reframed and reexamined. Advances in the region's economy, and new attitudes in China towards science and progress were recorded on film. And, not least, John Merson wrote this book to capture his odyssey through world history and through the events that mark the latest shifts in technology and culture.

I have known John Merson for more than ten years. His keen and retentive mind, his infectious enthusiasm and his feel for the adventures in science that the Chinese people have experienced qualify him to tell this imaginative and fast-moving story. I commend this book to all who enjoy the sweep of history and love the juxtaposition of chance and genius, discovery and loss, catastrophe and rebirth that make the human condition so enduringly interesting. Today this story has become increasingly important.

WANG GUNGWU

Vice Chancellor
University of Hong Kong
September 1988

Unidentified artist, *Family Group,* Hanging scroll, colors on silk. Late Ming Dynasty (1368–1644).

INTRODUCTION

In Xanadu did Kubla Khan
A stately pleasure-dome decree:
Where Alph, the sacred river, ran
Through caverns measureless to man
Down to a sunless sea.
So twice five miles of fertile ground
With walls and towers were girdled round:
And there were gardens bright with sinuous rills
Where blossom'd many an incense-bearing tree;
And here were forests ancient as the hills,
Enfolding sunny spots of greenery.

Samuel Taylor Coleridge

On a summer evening in 1797 the English poet Samuel Coleridge took his regular draft of laudanum, a mixture of opium and alcohol. He had been reading of Kublai Khan and the palace he commanded to be built. In the drug-induced reverie that followed, he composed his poem on Xanadu (Shangdu), the summer retreat of the Emperor of China. First described by Marco Polo in his account of his journey to the Far East in the late thirteenth century, Xanadu became an ideal place of mythic wealth, beauty and harmony. Ironically, it was opium, smuggled illegally into China by the same European merchants who were supporting Coleridge's habit, that led in 1839 to a devastating war between Britain and China; a war in which the Chinese were to see the return, on board British gunboats, of gunpowder and the cannon, which they had invented a thousand years earlier, their destructive power now tempered and refined in the highly competitive industrial environment of nineteenth century Europe. The obvious superiority of British military technology revealed China's profound vulnerability and, by 1900, the Celestial Empire was in ruins.

In the thirteenth century, however, China was not only the richest and most powerful country in the world but, according to Marco Polo, the most civilized as well.

> ...equally opposite to preconceived ideas, was the polish, courtesy, and respectful familiarity, which distinguished their social intercourse. Quarrels, blows, combats, and bloodshed, then so frequent in Europe, were not witnessed, even amid their deepest potations. Honesty was everywhere conspicuous: their wagons and other property were secure without locks or guards. Notwithstanding the frequent scarcity of victuals, they were generous in relieving those in greater want than themselves.

From Marco Polo's time until the late eighteenth century the stability and wealth of the Chinese empire were regarded with awe and envy by the tiny nation-states of Europe. The thirteenth-century empire of the Great Khan, which stretched from the Mediterranean to the China Sea, had enabled direct links to be made between the civilizations of the Far East and those of Europe. Along the fabled Silk Road and sea routes from the Persian Gulf, European and Arab merchants shipped the exquisite products of Chinese civilization. Silks and porcelain of such refinement that few, if any, European craftsman could match them until well into the eighteenth century. But China's influence on the development of Europe came not only from the export of luxury goods; its technology also had a profound influence.

In the sixteenth century the English philosopher and statesman Francis Bacon, reflecting on the forces that were transforming European society on the eve of the scientific and industrial revolutions, identified three inventions that he believed had changed the world — paper and printing, gunpowder and the compass. Paper and printing rapidly expanded access to scientific and technical knowledge. The compass enabled merchants to navigate the globe and to bring back to Europe the riches of the east. Gunpowder, and the arms race it spawned, allowed the highly competitive European nation-states to inflict their will upon the rest of the world. At the time when these key innovations were introduced in Europe, few Europeans had any idea that they had been invented in China, or that they had been in common use there for at least five hundred years. This raises some interesting questions. If these technologies were already available in China, why did the Chinese not sail their junks, bristling with guns, into European ports and demand trade? This they could easily have done in the early fifteenth century, for not only was the Chinese navy the largest in the world but China's trading and financial networks were as extensive as those of European merchants. The Chinese were trading with paper money as early as the eleventh century, using mechanical clockwork in the twelfth century, and spinning with water-power-driven machines in the fourteenth century. Yet these inventions did not have the significant social and economic impact in China that they later had in Europe.

In the modern industrialized world we have come to regard technological and social change as linear and driven by inexorable economic forces. Once an invention has proved its usefulness it will continue to develop irrespective of the cultural context. For example, the European matchlock rifle, introduced in Japan in the sixteenth century, was widely used and developed to a high level of technological sophistication; yet it had virtually disappeared from Japanese society by the early seventeenth century and did not reappear until the nineteenth century. Computer-controlled industrial technology and robotics were developed in the United States in the 1950s but this technology was taken up and developed more effectively by the Japanese in the 1960s and 1970s so that, by the 1980s, Japan had eclipsed the United States in key industrial fields to become one of the world's leading economic powers.

The Genius That Was China explores why the full potential of scientific discovery and technological invention, now regarded as the source of wealth and power, is often not realized in its country of origin. The reason, paradoxically, lies not in failure but in success — in the tendency of cultures and civilizations to ossify around those economic institutions and ideologies that, at some stage, provided maximum stability and wealth. These institutional structures are often retained by bureaucracies and the power elites who are their beneficiaries long after they have become redundant. Economic growth and cultural development do not stem merely from technological innovation but from social and political change. However, the motivation for such change rarely comes from within. Often, it has been the competitive threat from outside that has forced societies to come up with new and innovative social, economic and political structures.

This book is a journey through world history, and follows the different roads taken by nations to achieve their wealth and power. It traces the transfer of technology, ideas and even social institutions from east to west and west to east. In the process it explores some of the reasons why the centers of economic power, intellectual creativity and technological innovation have shifted in the course of the last thousand years from China to Europe and the United States and now perhaps to Asia again .

JOHN MERSON
November 1988

9

U.S.S.R.

□ Urumqi

XINJIANG

PAKISTAN

KUNLUN MOUNTAINS

QINGHAI

GANSU

Xining □

Lanzhou

XIZANG

Nu Jiang
(Salween R.)

SICHUAN

Lancang Jiang

Chengdu □

NEPAL

□ Lhasa

Zigong

BHUTAN

(Meekong R.)

INDIA

Kunming

BANGLADESH

YUNNAN

BURMA

VIETNAM
(CHAMP

LAOS

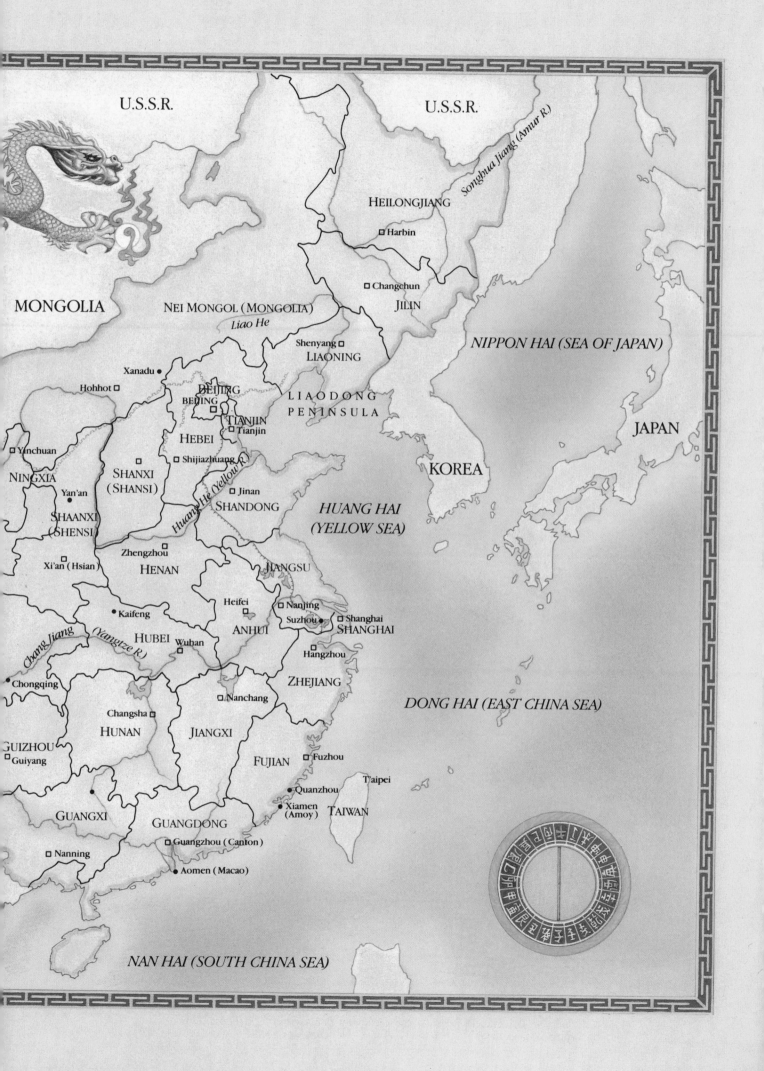

One of the most important ritual functions of the emperors of China was to begin the agricultural year by turning the first sod of earth, as shown in this painting by Guiseppe Castiglione.

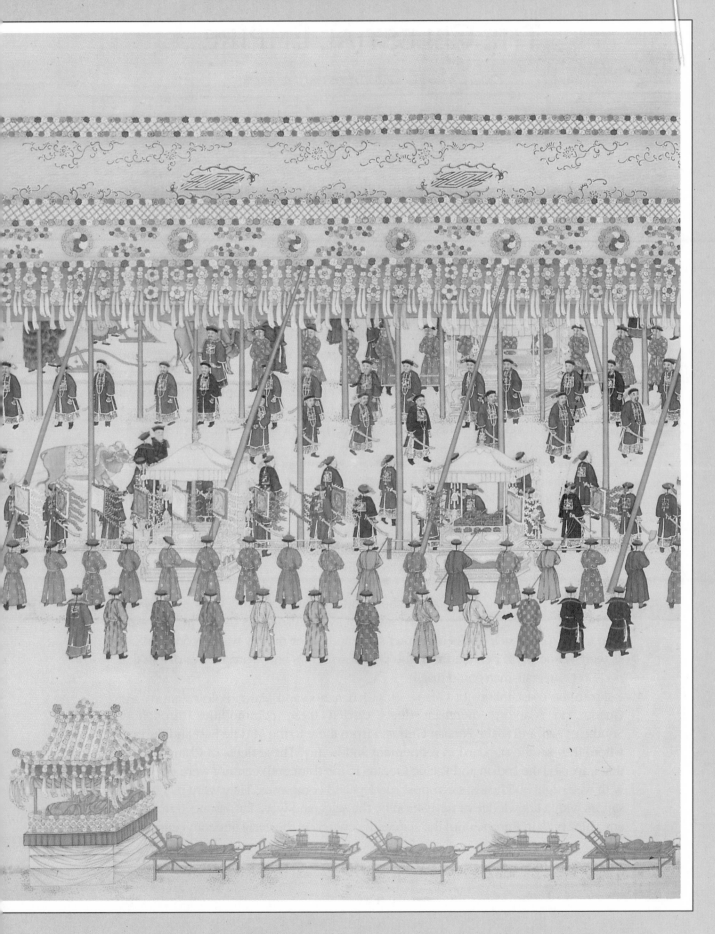

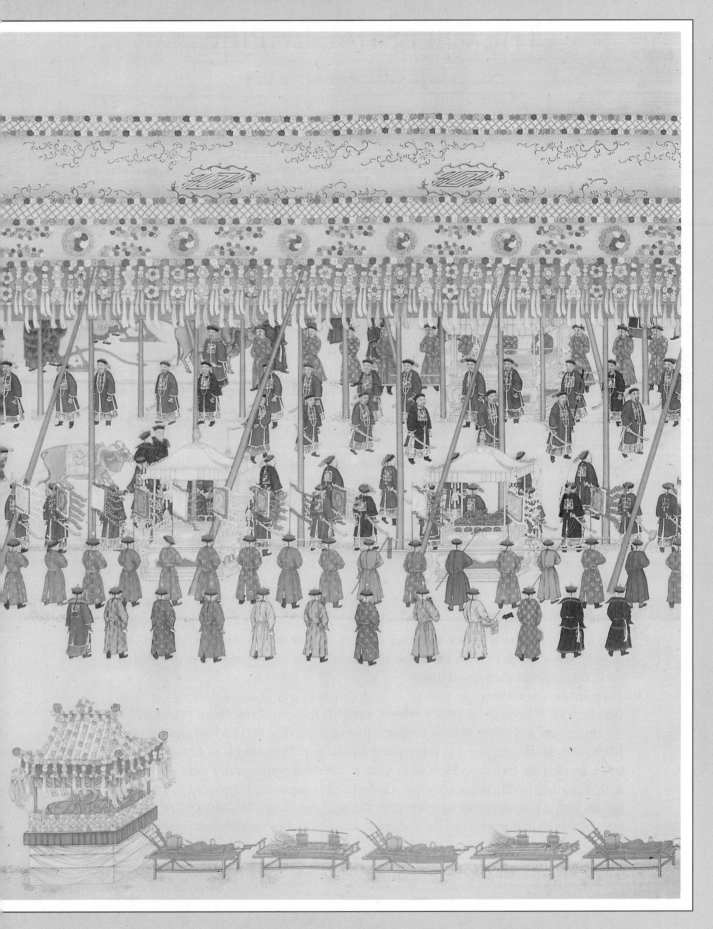

THE CELESTIAL EMPIRE

China is a sea that salts all rivers that flow into it

Marco Polo, 1275

When Marco Polo arrived in China in the thirteenth century he was astounded by what he saw. China under the Yuan (Mongol) dynasty consisted of a vast empire that extended from the Yellow Sea to the Mediterranean, from the Steppes of Siberia to northern India. China was the jewel in this empire. Not only were the Chinese producing salt on an industrial scale — 30,000 tons a year in Sichuan (Sze-ch'uan) alone — but their internal economy dwarfed that of Europe. Iron production was in the vicinity of 125,000 tons a year, a level not reached in Europe until the eighteenth century. Metal-casting techniques and mass production could deliver standardized military and agricultural equipment anywhere in the empire. A canal-based transportation system linked cities and markets in a vast commercial network in which paper money and credit facilities within the merchant community were highly developed. As an employee of the Great Khan, Marco Polo passed through cities in the rich Yangtze valley with populations of more than a million inhabitants, which astounded even a sophisticated Venetian:

> At the end of three days you reach the noble and magnificent city of Kin-sai [Hangzhou], a name that signifies "the Celestial City" and which it merits from its pre-eminence to all others in the world, in point of grandeur and beauty, as well as from its abundant delights, which might lead an inhabitant to imagine himself in paradise . . . According to common estimation, this city is an hundred miles in circuit. Its streets and canals are extensive, and there are squares, or market places, [these] being necessarily proportioned in size to the prodigious concourse of people.

Not only Hangzhou, but also Suzhou and Nanjing (Nanking), dwarfed Marco Polo's native Venice, then the most powerful city in Europe. In China, people were able to buy paperback books in market stalls and paper money was in common use as were tissues. The rich ate from fine porcelain bowls and wore fabrics of silk that no European craftsman could match.

From the coastal cities of Quanzhou (Ch'uanzhou and Marco Polo's Zaitun) and Guangzhou (Canton) merchant fleets carried these commodities throughout Southeast Asia and to the Persian Gulf and from there to the Middle East and Europe, where they set the standard in refinement and luxury. These fleets of Chinese junks that traversed the Indian and Pacific Oceans in the thirteenth century were equipped with watertight bulkheads, stern-post rudders and compasses. They were manned by sailors with a knowledge of navigation by the stars, and were far advanced in size to any ships built in Europe until the sixteenth century. In the early fifteenth century the

The Mansell Collection Ltd, London

The fabled Silk Road through Central Asia is depicted in this fourteenth century manuscript. Along this route passed not only the riches of the east, but Arab and European merchant-adventurers. In the late thirteenth century most of Central Asia was under the control of the Mongol empire and, with a "passport" in the form of a seal issued by the great Kublai Khan, Marco Polo and his uncle were free to travel unhindered from the Mediterranean to the Yellow Sea.

Ming emperor was able to send a fleet of 60 ships or more carrying 40,000 troops to the east coast of Africa and India to wave the flag. Between 1405 and 1433 the Great Three Jeweled Eunuch, Admiral Zheng He (Cheng Ho), settled a succession dispute in Sumatra and also brought back the King of Ceylon to Beijing (Peking) as a disciplinary measure for his failure to show due respect to the representatives of the Son of Heaven. In short, China at this time was the most cosmopolitan, technologically advanced and economically powerful civilization in the world.

To understand why China failed to maintain this technological lead over the west and why the priorities of the Chinese emperors were so different from those of the European monarchs, it is necessary to go back to the beginning of the Celestial Empire and the source of China's wealth — the land.

* * *

15

The Emperor Kublai Khan and his entourage on a hunting trip. Kublai Khan completed the conquest of China begun by his grandfather, the remarkable Mongol leader, Genghis Khan. The Mongols were prepared to employ foreigners, such as Marco Polo, since they were initially unsure of the loyalty of the traditional Chinese scholar-officials.

If you fly across the great plains of China, you can still clearly see the economic foundations of its ancient civilization. The great rivers wind down from the mountains in the far west and meander through the huge alluvial plains that make up the country's heart. Running off from these can be seen a network of canals interlinked like the fine veins on the surface of the human skin. These carry the life-giving energy, the rich silt and water that still allow this land to support an extraordinary density of people. China, after all, has the largest population in the world, more than one billion people, around 80 per cent of whom still live in villages in the countryside. These villages can also best be seen from the air. They radiate like a web that covers the landscape. Within what appears to be reasonable walking distance, there is a larger market town that dominates a region. If you take a wide-angled view, you will see that these towns also cluster in a web around a major city. But the essential and most basic element in this economic system remains the village with its surrounding agricultural land. It has formed, over the millennia, the basic social unit of traditional China.

From ancient times these villages were more or less self-governing production units, which were taxed in the form of grain and corvée labor. This labor was demanded each year to support public works, such as the maintenance of the canal system and the building of roads or even walls to defend the provincial capital. What is most striking is the extent to which this is a human-made landscape. The structure of this remarkable economic enterprise was built up over thousands of years by generations of peasants and government officials — a structure that for more than two thousand of those years supported the most stable empire the world has ever known, one that existed, with minor breakdowns, from 221 B.C. to A.D. 1911.

China's agriculture was able to support such a vast population because geography and Chinese culture came together to transform the land into an extraordinarily

It was on a Chinese junk like this that Marco Polo, after ten years in the service of the Great Khan, traveled on his return journey to Europe. Such vessels regularly made their way from China to the ports of Southeast Asia, India and the Middle East. These boats featured a number of important nautical innovations such as the stern-post rudder and watertight bulkheads, which were later to be taken up by Arab and European shipbuilders.

productive agricultural system. One of the key elements was the control of water.

China is dominated by two great river systems, the Yangtze and the Yellow rivers. Known as "China's Sorrows," they and their numerous tributaries originated in the foothills of the Himalayas and the Kunlun Mountains in the far west. The Yellow River, (Huang He in Chinese), gets its name from the rich loess silt that, since the last ice age, was blown from the plateaux of central Asia and now covers much of northern China.

The perennial flooding of these great rivers renewed the productivity of the land but the destructive power of these rivers was such that they would not only inundate fields but would also wipe out all trace of human habitation. The Yellow River, over its 2,700 miles from the western mountains, has changed course on a number of occasions, devastating vast areas of agricultural land. The coastal plains are essentially flat and any significant rise in water levels can flood hundreds of thousands of acres. Because the Yellow River carries and deposits so much fine silt, it therefore frequently silts up and breaks its banks. Today, the Yellow River flows within dykes high above the surrounding land. Over the centuries these dykes have been built up to control flooding while also providing access to river water for irrigation.

Efforts to control China's great rivers date back to before the founding of the Empire in 221 B.C. From these very early times, the independent kingdoms that made up "China" were of necessity concerned with the control of water, not just to prevent flooding, but also to increase agricultural productivity and thereby the surplus wealth that could be taxed by the kingdoms. Growth in output allowed small kingdoms to support larger and larger armies with which they could subdue their neighbors and thus increase their territory, power, wealth and prestige. It is a familiar story.

Waterways also provided a means of transport, not only for troops in their efforts to command wide regions, but also for merchants and their wares. The canal networks encouraged commerce, and thus increased the size and complexity of the market and led to craft specializations in specific regions. The division of labor required a large market system with good communications linking villages to towns, which in turn were linked to provincial capitals.

An interesting example of water control is to be found in the great water conservancy system at Dujiangyan, which still serves the Chengdu plains and the capital of Sichuan, Chengdu itself. This remarkable system of canals and dams was started about 250 B.C. by the Governor of Sichuan, Li Bing. The system still irrigates an area of around two million acres, supporting about five million people.

Li Bing had the Minjiang River divided into two channels. This was done at Dujiangyan because of a natural island and sandbar in the center of the river. The outer channel carried the fast-flowing flood water downstream to join the Yangtze; the inner channel carried water into the irrigation canals. In ancient times, it was found that by building up the sandbar in the center of the river (called the "fish's snout") it was possible to keep a fairly constant level of water flowing into two canals. These canals carry silt-rich water through a network of smaller and smaller canals that intersect on the Chengdu plains and finally join the Yangtze River further downstream. During periods of drought it was possible to block off the outer

Above: The building and maintenance of the dykes that held "China's Sorrows" — the great Yangtze and Yellow rivers — on their course was a major responsibility of the imperial state. This section of a seventeenth century scroll depicts the massive earthworks carried out by corvée labor on the dykes that had to be maintained to stop the Yellow River from breaking its banks.

Left: This nineteenth century representation of water conservancy shows how dykes were built up using the silt and sand deposited on the bed of the rivers. Without such dredging, river courses would shift with devastating consequences.

channel (with barriers made up of long baskets of stones), forcing more water to flow through the canals; in times of flood the main stream was opened up and a shallow bar or spillway would allow the bulk of the water to be channeled down river.

At Dujiangyan today there is still a temple dedicated to Li Bing and his sons, one of whom was supposed to have been killed during the construction of the project. It is a beauty spot for tourists but local people still come to make offerings to this great public benefactor as they have done for the past two thousand years. It is quite understandable for contemporary Chinese to pay such respect, not just to Li Bing the good public official whose modern plaster image still gazes heroically over the river, but to the water control system that he established; one that continues to provide them with the water essential for intensive farming. Intensive irrigation systems like that at Dujiangyan have allowed the population of China to grow to its present size. From Li Bing's time onwards, the maintenance of the water control systems was one of the central responsibilities of the state. If the canal systems were not maintained, the people starved.

The engineering significance of Dujiangyan is matched by other equally remarkable hydraulic works carried out at the same time. The Zheng Gou Canal was begun in 221 B.C., the first year of the reign of Qin Shi Huangdi (Ch'in Shih Huang-ti), who was the first emperor of China. It was designed by a hydraulic engineer, Zheng Gou, after whom the canal is named. This canal, 93 miles long, directs the water of the Jingshui River across the Guanzhong plain, irrigating around 350,000 acres. This system was designed not just for irrigation but for fertilization as well. The canal runs off the river at a point where maximum silt can be drawn, allowing the alkaline soils of central Shaanxi (Shensi) to become fertile.

When the Minjiang River flooded, a weir on the inner channel at Dujiangyan allowed excess water to be spilled back into the main stream, keeping the water in the canals at a constant level.

In terms of sheer audacity, the Dragon Head Canal in Shanxi (Shansi) province is perhaps the most remarkable. This canal, which passes three and a half miles under the Shangyan Mountains, was built on the orders of the Emperor Wu Di of the Han dynasty (206 B.C.– A.D. 220) that followed the short-lived Qin dynasty. Because of the scale of the imperial state, Wu Di was able to marshal the labor of 10,000 soldiers to redirect water to irrigate the dry Zhongquan region of Shanxi province.

These are just a few early examples of a tradition that became a major responsibility of the Chinese imperial state for the next two thousand years. Men such as Li Bing and Zheng Gou are significant in Chinese history because they represent the ideal public official or bureaucrat. One of the distinguishing characteristics of traditional Chinese culture was the importance of what we would call public servants. This is true of most civilizations dependent on large-scale water control systems. In Persia and Egypt, at different times, they produced equally complex administrative systems. Like them, China's culture developed in response to the economic realities of maintaining an increasingly large and centralized kingdom. Between 230 and 221 B.C. the kingdoms of Han, Zhao, Wei, Chu, Yan, and Qi fell in rapid succession to the king of Qin, Shi Huangdi, who became the first emperor of China.

The unification of the empire was of profound significance. It made peace possible after centuries of warfare, but it also permitted a unique form of bureaucratic feudalism to replace the feudal kingdoms of the earlier period. The creation of a class of administrative and bureaucratic officials, operating throughout the length and breadth of China on behalf of the emperor, meant that technological innovations developed in one part of the country could be spread easily to all parts of the empire. In addition, a unified empire allowed for a high level of technological specialization, for example, iron and steel production rose to meet the demands of the empire for standardized products. Shi Huangdi introduced a system of common coinage, weights and measures. He even standardized the width of the axles on carts and chariots to prevent damage to the empire's highways. Military technology was also standardized, allowing for large-scale mass production of cast-iron weapons.

Although the empire brought peace within its borders, there remained the constant threat from nomadic tribes to the northwest. This threat necessitated large standing armies, which had to be supported by the state. By the time of the western Han dynasty, government monopolies in key commodities such as salt and iron, along with the traditional resources from agriculture, provided the revenue with which to support this large military and the imperial administration. As early as 119 B.C. there were at least 46 state-run iron-casting centers throughout China. In Henan (Honan), the scale of cast-iron production was massive by any standards. The core or salamander left from one of the damaged crucibles used in smelting was found to weigh 20–25 tons, a capacity not reached in Europe until well into the eighteenth century. In A.D. 806 China was producing 13,500 tons of iron a year but by 1078, during the Song (Sung) dynasty, this had risen to 125,000 tons. This period also marked a high point in Chinese industrial development, which could be described as an industrial revolution of sorts.

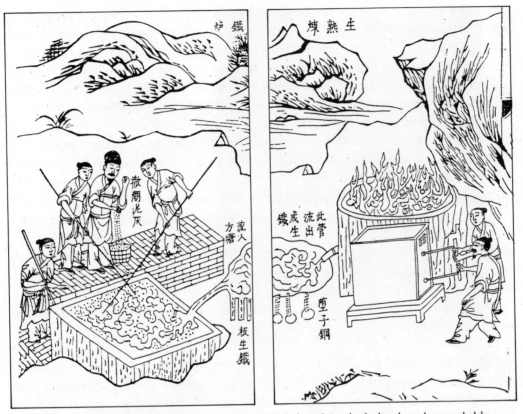

Chinese iron masters working in state-owned foundries had developed remarkably sophisticated techniques for iron and steel production. They had even discovered the principle of blowing air through molten iron as a means of gaining the increased heat necessary to produce fine steel — the same principle that was used in the blast furnace developed by Henry Bessemer in the nineteenth century.

Making state monopolies of essential commodities such as salt and iron, like the contemporary practice of "nationalizing" strategic industries, occurred early in Chinese history. It allowed for the standardization of products needed, for example, by the army and also provided a source of revenue. In 1083 the production of iron farm implements was turned into a state monopoly. This meant that hoes, plows, mold boards and scythes were produced on an enormous scale. The demand for cast-iron implements and the scale of the Chinese market rewarded specialization and technological innovation. At two government arsenals at this time 32,000 suits of armor in three standardized sizes were produced each year. Iron and steel were also being used for the construction of bridges and even for the building of a cast-iron pagoda, 70 feet high.

In Han dynasty the widespread use of the iron-tipped plow and the mold board, which turned the earth, allowed for deep plowing, which significantly increased the productivity of the land. In the northern provinces where the crops were mainly wheat and millet, the mechanical seed drill, which may have come from India, was in use allowing farmers to sow in even rows. This was of enormous importance since it permitted weeding between the rows as well as easier irrigation.

Courtesy Film Australia

A contemporary statue of Li Bing who, as Governor of Sichuan in 250 B.C., had the water control system built at Dujiangyan. A temple dedicated to him still over-looks his project and, even to this day, people come to light joss sticks in his honor. As a dedicated government official, Li Bing embodied the Confucian ideals of selfless service to the welfare of others and was the subject of a recent feature film in socialist China.

Prior to this the technique had been to broadcast grain by hand, which was both wasteful and inefficient. (This seed drill, or at least the concept, may well have come into Europe from China in the eighteenth century when it was introduced into common use by the famous British agricultural innovator, Jethro Tull.)

The most significant revolution in Chinese agriculture came with the population shift from the north to the rich rice-growing areas south of the Yangtze delta from the ninth century onwards. By 1380 the south had two and a half times the population of the north: 38 million in the south compared with 15 million in the north, according to official statistics. This profound demographic change involved not only the migration of people but also a change in diet from wheat and millet to rice.

Wet-rice agriculture was given an enormous stimulus in China with the introduction of a new variety known as "Champa rice" from Vietnam in about 1012. This rice ripened faster than local varieties, allowing for the production of two and even three crops a year. Like other innovations this one was sponsored by imperial officials and, in turn, encouraged investment in more widespread land reclamation and water control systems. Because of the obvious benefits to the state of this eleventh century "green revolution," officials promoted the use of these new farming techniques through tax relief, credit facilities and through the establishment of a system of model farms. Books were also published to inform government officials of the benefits. For the new variety to be fully productive it required paddy-field cultivation and new water control techniques. Water loaded with fine silt provided the essential nutrients for an enormous increase in the yield per acre, but it also allowed more people to be supported on far less land than in Europe, as the French economic historian, Fernand Braudel, has argued:

SALT OF THE EARTH

Approaching the city of Zigong in western Sichuan province, as Marco Polo may well have done on his tour of inspection as an imperial bureaucrat in the service of the Great Kublai Khan, Emperor of China, you immediately notice the towering derricks, which still stand out against the skyline as they did in the thirteenth century. For this is one of the oldest salt-producing areas in the world.

Salt was essential for the preservation of food, and in China, as in all other ancient civilizations, people starved in winter unless they could store sufficient salt meat, fish and vegetables. Starving people also threatened the stability of the empire and it was therefore not surprising that salt should become a state monopoly and was not left to the vagaries and greed of merchants. This monopoly by the state meant that production techniques developed in one area were rapidly spread by imperial officials throughout the country.

One of the most impressive things about this ancient technology was not so much its size but the ingenious use of local materials.

The traditional derricks were timber structures, some as high as 200 feet and made up of three upright poles like a tripod. From a massive capstan, turned by bullocks, a rope lifted and dropped a ten-foot long iron bit. This form of percussion drilling was used to sink the well. The rope used was made of twisted strips of bamboo and had a tensile strength equal to that of steel wire. This rope would manipulate the iron bit 2,000 feet below the surface. The wells were also fitted with bamboo linings. From the wellhead, bamboo pipes joined together by tarred cloth carried off the brine and natural gas to the processing room. The brine was drawn off into a tank and the natural gas used to boil off the water in large woks (vats) leaving behind the high-quality salt. This was the world's first industrial use of natural gas and also of drilling wells.

Methane gas struck at levels of 2,000 feet was dangerous unless mixed with the right amount of oxygen. The Chinese solved this problem by covering the wellhead with a large wooden barrel into which air was drawn to achieve the right balance, as in the carburettor of an automobile. From one wellhead it was possible to heat 600 – 700 reducing vats; one well was reported to have run as many as 5,000 vats. This

was salt production on an industrial scale not seen in Europe until the eighteenth century.

Sealed bamboo pipes and leather bags were also used by travelers to carry the gas around the countryside (as we use gas cylinders when camping) to provide light and heat. There is even an account of gas being used to provide street lighting.

As early as the sixteenth century at Leshan, not far from Zigong, these same techniques were also used to drill for oil, which came into common use in that region as a form of fuel. The lack of the chemical knowledge to refine the oil meant that its discovery in China did not have the revolutionary economic impact it was to have in the west in the late nineteenth century. In the 1850s it was, however, these Chinese techniques of drilling that were used to open up the Pennsylvania oil fields.

The rice-field is thus a factory. In Lavoisier's time [the eighteenth century] one hectare of land under wheat in France produced an average of five quintals [1 quintal = 220.46 pounds]; one hectare of rice-field often bears thirty quintals of rice in the husk. After milling this means twenty-one quintals of edible rice at 3500 calories per kilogram, or the colossal total of 7,350,000 calories per hectare, as compared with 1,500,000 for wheat and only 340,000 animal calories if that hectare were devoted to stock-raising and produced 150 kilograms of meat.

Unlike the agricultural revolution that was to occur in Britain in the seventeenth and eighteenth centuries, that of Song dynasty China did not lead to the same loss of people to the cities. Wet-rice agriculture by its nature is labor intensive. What the new varieties and greater sophistication of production meant was that more people could be employed on the same area of land and still produce a surplus. Rural villages were able to absorb more and more people as double cropping spread throughout the rich river delta of the Yangtze.

Wet-rice agriculture also required a high degree of social discipline and co-operation. In both China and Japan, the five-month turnover of rice crops required enormous amounts of labor at key times such as harvests in June and November, and

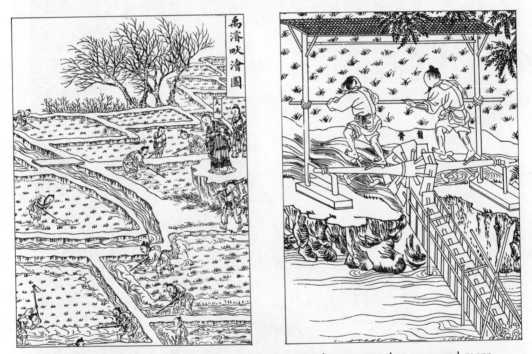

Left. The extraordinary productivity of wet-rice agriculture meant that more and more land was turned over to this form of cultivation. It required sophisticated hydraulic engineering and considerable social organization, as this late Qing woodblock illustrates.

Right. Encyclopedias on agriculture were widely circulated among the scholar-bureaucrats to promote the use of new technology. The square-mallet chain pump, more commonly known as the "dragon's backbone pump," was introduced to lift water from one paddy field to another, and a more modern version is still widely used throughout the countryside.

Until the eighteenth century European agriculture was rarely as productive or as labor-intensive as that of wet-rice cultivation in China. The system of broadcasting grain by hand, shown here, was both inefficient and wasteful with birds often taking a good deal of the seed before it could even germinate.

27

planting in January and July. Failure to get one crop in could mean starvation for a family. Social organization at the village level was also needed to see that the water was available to each paddy field when needed. The coercive power of the village community over the individual was enormous. It was at the level of the village, which was often an extended family with most people in some way related, that the Confucian hierarchy of relationships served to maintain order and discipline. It should also be appreciated that under the legal practices that existed in China throughout the imperial period, any family member was liable to be punished for the wrongdoing of any other member of the family, if the perpetrator could not be found. This too had a powerful effect on encouraging social conformity.

Ironically, the very success of Chinese agriculture was in a sense a trap. While productivity per acre went up enormously with the widespread adoption of wet-rice cultivation, making it the most productive agriculture in the world, there was a price to be paid. Wet-rice cultivation was extremely vulnerable to natural disasters. Any breakdown in the flow of water because of drought, flood or simple neglect could lead to widespread famine and a consequent breakdown in social order and, thus, the harmony of the state. This meant that the government was locked into the development and maintenance of complex water control systems and was forced to stockpile grain to quell potential uprisings of starving peasants.

With so many people engaged in paddy-field cultivation and living in the warmer regions of the south, new parasitic diseases became widespread throughout the population. Schistosomiasis, a disease carried by tiny snails that lived on the edge of slow-flowing water courses, and malaria both became endemic. These parasitic diseases do not lead to immediate death but sap energy and shorten life expectancy. The productivity of the individual may well be significantly reduced by these diseases, as was the case in southern Europe when malaria was endemic. It therefore meant that more people were required to achieve the same levels of output.

Interestingly, the pressure to bring more and more land under paddy-field cultivation also meant that there were fewer grazing and draft animals than before. Fortunately for Europe, the large number of draft animals required for farming the larger acreages needed to support an average family not only freed peasants from back-breaking labor but also provided an additional source of protein and an alternative source of blood for the malarial mosquito — a source of blood in which the malarial parasite cannot live. Thus the spread of such diseases was kept in check by the different ecology of northern Europe and the draining of fen and swamp lands for use as dry-land farming greatly reduced the breeding grounds of mosquitoes.

The increasing dependence on rice and the complex, interlocked water control system needed to maintain China's dense, rural population meant that the needs of agriculture became the imperial administration's central and constant concern. With productivity so high there was little room or reason for change. In China, therefore, it made sense to be conservative. In Europe, with an agricultural system much less dependent on one type of crop and the control of water, and with far fewer people to be supported per acre, there was scope for change and development through the application of labor-saving technology.

SCHOLARS AND BUREAUCRATS

To enrich your family, no need to buy good land:
Books hold a thousand measures of grain.
For an easy life, no need to build a mansion:
In books are found houses of gold.
Going out, be not vexed at absence of followers:
In books, carriages and horses form a crowd.
Marrying, be not vexed by the lack of a good go-between:
In books there are girls with faces of jade.
A boy who wants to become a somebody
Devotes himself to the classics, faces the window, and reads.

Song Emperor, Renzong (Jen Tsung)

The system of imperial government that developed in China was different from that of Europe or Japan. It was not based on the power of feudal clans but was organized around a centralized bureaucratic structure. In fact, the Chinese could be said to have invented the idea of a meritocratic civil service. From the Song dynasty power and status were based on scholastic merit, as determined by results in the world's oldest written examination. The empire was actually run by a relatively small number of scholar-bureaucrats, not by a hereditary, warring caste bound by ties of blood and clan loyalty, as was the case in both Europe and Japan.

The use of public examination as a means of deciding who should occupy the top positions in the imperial administration had its beginnings in the sixth century. Although the formation of new dynasties was basically dependent upon military power, the Chinese emperors soon realised that, once having gained imperial power, they needed more than military strength to maintain the vast empire. Military men too close to the center of power might also threaten the stability of the empire. From the time of Shi Huangdi, the first emperor, there was a systematic effort to destroy the roots of feudal and aristocratic power in the previous existing kingdoms, now under the control of the rulers of the state of Qin. Throughout the following centuries, and with a good deal of bloodshed, aristocratic feudalism disappeared in China and the tradition of rule by an administrative bureaucracy was established. The military was given low status and kept, as much as possible, under the control of the scholars — on tap but not on top.

Each year up to 30,000 students would gather at the local provincial capital. Here they would spend an average of five days locked in tiny cells. They would enter the examination compound at about 5 A.M. each morning and after being verified by a known teacher or local official (to prevent substitution) they would be given a number and a cell. The examination paper, like those used internationally today,

Above: The Song Emperor Renzong, whose poem extolling the benefits of study was criticized by later generations as giving a false impression of the real objectives of scholarship.

29

A Song dynasty painting of a group of scholars. Those who successfully graduated in the imperial examination system ran the empire. By gaining even an elementary degree one was exempt from doing corvée labor or receiving corporal punishment, and was given a small state pension.

would have on it only the student's number. Even the written work completed by each student would be copied out by a scribe so that favored students could not be identified by their calligraphy.

The students' future careers, social status and even the prosperity of their family depended on the results of this examination. The pressure was enormous. Even to be able to sit for the first of three levels of examinations, the student would have had to spend at least six years studying the Confucian classics and memorizing long texts, which he would be expected to quote accurately. It is little wonder that, despite great security precautions, some students reverted to the time-honored tradition of cheating. Silk crib sheets containing key passages of text and model essays were hidden in food, in clothing or anywhere else the wit of man could devise. One ingenious student had a silk inner lining made for his jacket, which he had covered with a vast amount of text. There were even cases where an official was bribed and a student used a code to identify himself, but the consequences of being caught were extremely serious, with some corrupt officials losing their heads.

If you were able to pass this first, county-level exam *(xian)* you had a foot on the first rung of the ladder to a career as an imperial official. This qualified you to sit for the prefectural examination *(fu)*. If you passed this exam you would be given the lowest level qualification, a licentiate or bachelor degree known as *juren* or "flowering talent." You were now part of the "literati," which meant you were exempt from doing corvée labor, could not be given corporal punishment and were entitled to a small state pension. Above this were two more levels. At the highest level, an examination was held in the Forbidden City (during Ming and Qing dynasties) and supervised by the emperor himself. By passing this exam you became a *jinshi* or "presented scholar." From this group would be chosen the officials who administered the provincial and central organs of government. These men were expected to be as adept in law as they were in art, poetry, mathematics or engineering. These scholar-officials were generalists, men of integrity and sound judgment that made them good civil servants. They were also extremely conservative, regarding themselves as guardians of the Confucian ideals of harmonious government.

In the late eighteenth century this Chinese system of examination, described in glowing terms by Jesuit missionaries working in China, was introduced in France and, later, in Britain, as a means of selecting public servants. The education in classics offered by the universities of Oxford and Cambridge, which became the primary intellectual training for nineteenth century civil servants, aimed at producing the same sort of all-rounders who, as judges and administrators in the far-flung regions of the British empire, performed the same role as the Chinese scholar-bureaucrats.

One of the consequences of the Chinese examination system was that it encouraged a conservative and often narrow intellectual orthodoxy, particularly as access to the top positions of power in the bureaucracy was dependent on years of study for examinations set by bureaucrats who were themselves the products of the system.

Courtesy Film Australia

This is a reproduction of the tiny cells used by students sitting for the imperial examinations. Over a number of weeks students would come to such cells to sit for their exams. As many as 30,000 students would put themselves through the grueling county exams in the hope of becoming officials. Through the doorway of these cells lay the only legitimate path to power and status throughout the empire.

Courtesy Film Australia

Above: As early as the twelfth century printed books made on woodblocks like these were being sold in market places throughout the empire.

Left: In imperial workshops, using movable type, encyclopedias of useful knowledge on agriculture, medicine, engineering and military affairs were produced and circulated among scholar-officials.

Another interesting aspect of this written examination was that it was made possible because of the development of paper in China in the second century. The early development of printing also allowed the basic texts used in the examinations to be widely available, even though the time needed by students to study them was dependent upon their families having the means to support them for many years; a simple economic fact that excluded a large number of people from gaining access to power, despite the system's avowed intention of being open to all.

* * *

To support and legitimate the imperial government there also evolved a cosmology and ideology that drew on a wide range of philosophical schools, which blossomed in the period just prior to the unification of the empire. During the Han dynasty (206 B.C.–A.D. 220) something of a synthesis of ideas occurred. Although always evolving and changing with new influences such as Buddhism (which came to China in the second century) there were nonetheless a number of basic principles that remained remarkably intact right up until 1911, when the Chinese imperial system was finally abandoned. These ideas, embodied in the Confucian "four books and five classics" shaped the intellectual, scientific, aesthetic and political perspective of generations of Chinese. They also formed the all-important basis of the imperial examination that

A Song dynasty painting entitled "The Return of Lady Wen." The family lay at the heart of all Confucian values — filial piety and respect for seniority in the large extended family provided the basis for all relationships. Those in seniority, including the emperor, were expected to devote themselves to the well-being of their dependents.

selected those who, in the final analysis, would rule the country.

The two dominant schools of thought, which came together in the Han, were Confucianism and Taoism. Confucius (Kong Fuzi in modern transliteration), or Master Kong, is often described as the patron saint of Chinese bureaucracy. Confucius (551–479 B.C.) lived in a time known as the Spring and Autumn period, when kingdoms were battling for control of territory, each trying to absorb its weaker neighbors. For Confucius, the violence and destructiveness of this form of military adventurism proved that it was no way to run a civilized society. If one wanted to categorize his approach to government and to morality, Confucius could be described as a radical traditionalist. He believed that China had gone downhill since the relatively peaceful dominance of the kingdom of Zhou came to an end in 771 B.C. He therefore endeavored to change society and government according to the values that he believed had existed in the past. He did this in his role as a government official in the kingdom of Lu and as a teacher within his own school.

For Confucius the primary model of social harmony was the family, but a family in which the status and role of each individual was clearly defined and formalized. He argued that if each individual was brought up to show the correct respect and deference within the family then respect and deference for the greater order of society at large would be possible. He believed that society should not be governed by military power or legalistic rules but by officials, men of learning like himself, who had been inculcated with the five essential virtues — benevolence (*ren*), righteousness (*yi*) propriety (*li*), wisdom (*zhi*) and trustworthiness (*xin*). He did not believe that such virtues were innately part of any aristocratic, religious or military caste but believed that human nature was capable of being molded. It was the duty of the state to inculcate these principles into its citizens. For this reason, he placed great emphasis on education since he believed that all men were equally capable of becoming sages given the right training and example. The place where this was to be done was within the family.

This humanistic philosophy bears some resemblance to that developed in Greece at a similar time (fifth century B.C.) by Socrates and Plato who promoted the idea that society should be governed by a group of benign intellectuals, or "philosopher kings." In Greece and even in Italy during the Renaissance, when such ideas had great appeal, they were rarely to become embodied in social institutions. In Europe aristocratic or military elites were to remain dominant well into the eighteenth and

Courtesy Film Australia

A Taoist monk from the White Cloud Temple in Beijing.

early nineteenth centuries. In China, on the other hand, these humanistic ideas, embodied in the examination system, were to be the dominant social and political values of generations of scholar-officials who ran the empire for most of its 2,000 years of existence. But these highly rational and ethical concerns were to be tempered by another powerful influence in Chinese intellectual and cultural life — Taoism.

Taoism developed in China as something of an antithesis to the purely social and ethical concerns of the Confucian school. Taoism, like Confucianism, had its roots in the ideas of a particular teacher or sage, Laozi (Lao Tzu). He was a somewhat anarchistic figure who believed that social harmony was not to be found through the rational ordering of society but through the achievement of inner harmony on the part of the individual — a harmony and balance that parallelled that which governed cosmic forces and underpinned the ecological balance of the natural world.

Taoist philosophy formed a rich intellectual tradition that played with philosophical paradoxes as a means of pointing to the limitations of purely rational systems of thought. Taoist religion on the other hand was infused with ideas that date back to the animistic and pantheistic world of ancient Chinese culture. So while the Confucians had little interest in investigating natural phenomena, the Taoists were concerned with understanding the *dao* (*tao*) or "way" of nature through contemplating its myriad manifestations and cycles. It would be wrong to make too much of the separation of these two schools since, in practical terms, they complemented each other, as can be seen in the classics. This corpus of learning included both Confucian texts and books like the *Yijing* (*I ching*), which embodies Taoist ideas. Therefore the scholar-bureaucrats who espoused Confucian ideas in their capacity as public officials could well, on returning home, take up esoteric contemplative practices that were clearly Taoist.

This eclecticism, common throughout much of Asia, is due in part to the fact that China was spared the dogmatic obsessions of the credal religions of the Middle East and Europe — Judaism, Christianity and Islam. By postulating a supreme and single creator-god whose "will" or plan for the world and humanity was revealed only to a select few, these religions could claim that they not only had a monopoly on the truth but also a mission to convert all of humanity to the truth of their revelation. This has led throughout the history of Europe and the Middle East to a high degree of religious intolerance and persecution. Either you are on the side of the truth or you are against it, so "off with your head." In Chinese culture, a wide range of religious and philosophical beliefs have been tolerated at different times, including Buddhism, Christianity, Judaism and Islam. Muslim communities in the southern and western provinces were, by the time of Marco Polo's arrival, large and prosperous.

Confucianism is not a religion in the western sense. It is primarily a system of ethics. The respect for ancestors or ancestor worship, often associated with Confucianism, was no more than an extension of respect for the achievements of the elders in the family. Given the reliance of all Chinese on the vast water control systems and other public works on which civilized life depended, it made sense to show reverence for men like Li Bing and other, similar, social benefactors.

THE MANDATE OF HEAVEN

The first month [February in Gregorian calendar]

Biological phenomena: hibernating insects wake up; wild geese fly north; pheasants drum and call; fish rise beneath the ice; leeks appear in the garden; field rodents emerge; otters seek for fish as food; hawks become turtle doves [turtle doves, which came in spring, were mistaken for hawks]; catkins burst forth on the willow; the plum, apricot and mountain peach blossom; the cypress flowers; hens begin to lay.

Meteorological phenomena: in this season sweep gentle breezes; though chilly still, they melt the frozen soil.

Celestial phenomena: Ju star is seen; at dusk Shen [Orion] culminates; Doubling [the "handle" of the seven stars of the Great Bear] hangs downwards.

Farm tasks: [Farmers maintain their] implements for tilling; the farming inspector proceeds to mark off the fields; yellow rape is picked as sacrificial flowers for the ancestors.

From the *Xia xiao zheng* (Xia dynasty calendar).

The Chinese imperial system of government evolved over a long period and it would be misleading to write about its institutions as if they were somehow static and immutable. Nevertheless, there were some basic assumptions embodied in the Confucian classics, which, because of the examination system, shaped the outlook of those who governed and therefore the course of Chinese history.

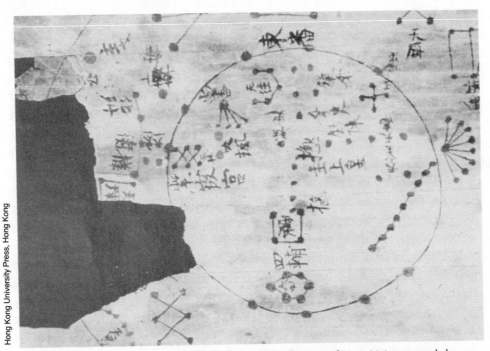

This eighth century star map depicts the constellations of Ursa Major around the North Pole. The stars representing the emperor, his army, the imperial household, and even the imperial kittens are contained within the area circled. A number of stars have represented the emperor over the long history of Chinese imperial astrology, but he has most consistently been associated with the pole star.

While the imperial system was built around maintaining and taxing the surplus of the world's most productive agriculture, there were strict limitations imposed on those who wielded imperial power. The Chinese emperor did not rule by "divine right" like many European monarchs. The right to rule or the "mandate of heaven" was conditional upon the emperor fulfilling the functions laid down by tradition: a tradition established by the Confucian scholars and bureaucrats who gradually came to dominate the management of the empire. The right to rule was dependent on maintaining social, economic and cosmological harmony. The Son of Heaven (the emperor) was the mediator between the people and the forces of nature. He was responsible for seeing that the water conservancy system was kept in order, that relief was provided in times of famine or when natural disasters struck (as they often did with devastating effect) and, more importantly, that the population was adequately forewarned of these disasters (a drought, flood or famine occurred in one of China's provinces every year). He was also expected to predict eclipses and other unusual astronomical events, for it was believed that events in the sky were directly related to events on earth. For this reason, one of the major institutions of government was the department of astronomy and mathematics.

From earliest times Chinese astronomers documented the events of the night sky in their constant search for these portents or warnings. However, while their initial concerns were primarily astrological, they developed in the process a very advanced understanding of astronomy, sufficient to predict eclipses and to apply mathematical techniques to the analysis of the movement of the planets.

There was another important reason why accuracy of observation was important and this was the requirement for the emperor to publish a calendar each year. This calendar specified the day on which the winter and summer solstices would occur, enabling imperial bureaucrats around the country to co-ordinate essential agricultural events such as the release of water for irrigation, the celebration of public festivals or the arrangement for corvée labor to be set to work on major public projects, such as the building of the Great Wall or a new water conservancy system. Corvée labor required all men, apart from scholars and Buddhist monks, to give a percentage of their time every year to carrying out public works — a system similar to the requirement in feudal Europe for peasants to work their lord's lands in exchange for military protection. The calendar also provided a precise astronomical catalogue of the most auspicious days and times for carrying out all sorts of functions, from getting married to fixing and painting the house.

The institution of this imperial calendar dates back to the beginning of the empire itself. It served to affirm the emperor's role as the intermediary between his subjects and the cosmos. By understanding, and thereby predicting the ways of heaven, apparently inauspicious events such as eclipses or the arrival of comets could eventually be accommodated into a cosmological status quo and thereby lose some of their doom-laden character.

Each evening, on the city walls of Beijing or earlier centers of imperial government, astronomers would record with meticulous detail the events in the night sky. With these records, kept within the department of astronomy, they were

Above: An armillary sphere used to calculate the position and predict the movement of stars. This instrument, which still stands on the old city wall in Beijing, was built with the help of Jesuit missionaries in the seventeenth century.

Left: Chinese scholar – bureaucrats contemplating an armillary sphere, similar to that used in the Su Song astronomical clock of 1088.

able to recognize and predict the periodic arrival of at least 40 comets before A.D. 1500, among them Halley's comet, first identified in Europe in the seventeenth century. These records have also provided contemporary astronomers with an invaluable resource, allowing them to confirm the dates of past astronomical events such as the birth of new stars or supernovae.

What is astounding is the detailed empirical approach taken by these Chinese astronomers. Though not "scientific" in the modern sense, they possessed a sophisticated understanding of the causes of astronomical phenomena. For example, as early as the end of the first century the astronomer Zhang Heng, in his book *The Spiritual Constitution of the Universe,* was able to explain accurately the cause of lunar eclipses ". . . since the moon reflects the sunshine, it will be eclipsed when it travels into the shadow cast by the earth."

Star maps of considerable accuracy were being produced and recorded on stone tablets by the eleventh century. One of the most famous of these is the Suzhou planisphere of 1247, which records a total of 1,434 stars. At this time mathematicians such as Guo Shoujing who built the famous gnomon near Kaifeng (the capital of the Northern Song dynasty) were measuring the length of the year as 365.2425 days. The gnomon measured the length of the shortest and longest day in the year, relating this date to the position of stars.

The Chinese gained this understanding of astronomical processes, not from any belief in the intrinsic value of scientific knowledge but because it fulfilled important functions for the imperial state by improving the accuracy of the calendar and allowing the emperor to fulfill his cosmological responsibilities. The cosmology itself was clearly pre-scientific, as its major use was not astronomical but astrological. Everything on earth was believed to have its counterpart in heaven and this included the emperor, the imperial palace and the various government ministries. A cluster of stars at the head of Scorpio were believed to represent the emperor, the imperial palace and a number of senior government ministries. In A.D. 340, the minister of justice, who also held the post of attorney general, was a man by the name of He. It was reported that the planet Mars was approaching the star that represented his ministry. On hearing the news he immediately petitioned the emperor to allow him to resign and take a lower government job, that of keeper of the imperial seal, in order to avert what might well be a disaster for him or his department. His request was granted by the emperor and disaster averted.

It is interesting to note that the reporting of unlucky portents in the vicinity of the stars representing the emperor and the imperial household increased dramatically during unpopular dynasties. In other words, the department of astronomy was in a politically strategic position to make veiled or, at times, quite pointed criticism of the behavior of the emperor. After all, his "mandate of heaven" was dependent on support from the bureaucracy and there were always many contenders for the position waiting in the wings. Events that had not been predicted were interpreted as heaven's warning. For this reason, many emperors treated the findings of this department as a state secret. Leaks, which might get into the hands of opponents and were regarded with as much concern as official secrets are by contemporary governments. Given the importance of the department of astronomy, it is no wonder that the Chinese should have calculated the precise orbit of at least 40 comets.

A late Qing illustration showing the use of a small gnomon. With this instrument, which measured the length of the shadow cast by a perpendicular rod, it was possible to measure the shortest and longest days of the year — the summer and winter solstices — with great accuracy. This knowledge was essential for maintaining the accuracy of the imperial calendar.

CELESTIAL CLOCKWORK

Perhaps the most remarkable achievement of the scholar-officials, and the imperial workshops they maintained, was the invention of clockwork.

Understanding both the motions of the planets and the cyclic nature of the position of the fixed stars led Zhang Heng in the second century to apply water power to drive astronomical instruments. This description of Zhang's water-driven armillary sphere was given in an official history of A.D. 132:

"Zhang Heng made his bronze armillary sphere and set it up in a closed chamber, where it rotated by the force of flowing water. The order having been given for the doors to be shut, the observer in charge of it would call out to the watcher on the observatory platform, saying the sphere showed that such and such a star was just rising, or another star just culminating, to yet another star just setting. Everything was found to correspond with the phenomena like the two halves of a tally."

The device was further developed by the Buddhist mathematician and astronomer Yi Xing in the eighth century, who added a clock to it. The best known model of this astronomical clock was the one produced by Han Gonglian at Kaifeng (the Northern Song capital) under the direction of Su Song, Minister of Personnel, in 1088. Though knowledge of this form of clock disappeared at the end of the Northern Song dynasty, Su Song's directions for its construction remained in a book, *Xin yi xiang fa yao* (New Design for an Armillary Clock). From the description contained in this book, Professor Yang of the Beijing Historical Museum was able, in the 1950s, to construct a model of this remarkable clock — remarkable because it included the first use of the escapement mechanism, "the soul" of all mechanical clocks.

The Su Song clock was housed in a wooden tower 39 feet high. On the top was a platform with an armillary sphere similar to that developed by Zhang Heng, which was covered by a movable roof, like that of a modern observatory. This sphere, when aligned through a sighting tube, kept time with the motion of the planets. It was connected by gears to the driving mechanism of the clock, which was worked by water filling wooden buckets. When one bucket was full, the weight would lift a lever allowing the next bucket to move forward; with a constant flow of water the motion produced would be precise and regular.

Courtesy Film Australia

Constructed in the 1950s by Professor Yang, this model of Su Song's clock is housed in the Beijing Historical Museum.

The first floor housed a celestial globe also geared to move time with the natural cycles of the heavens. On the ground floor was the clock mechanism and a series of windows at which 24 puppet figures announced the *shichen* by ringing a bell. The *shichen* or *shi* was a measure of time equivalent to two European hours. At another window a figure beat a drum at each *ke* (equivalent to approximately 15 minutes). Additional to the 12 *shi* in each Chinese day, there were 100 *ke* — the first beginning at midnight and the fiftieth at noon. Another series of puppets would emerge to play stringed instruments for each *geng* and *chou*. A *geng* was one-fifth of the length of the night and a *chou* was one-fifth of the length of a *geng*. The length of the night, varying with each season, meant that these measurements were constantly being adjusted.

One of the most important functions of this astronomical clock for the imperial household was the setting up of imperial horoscopes. In China these were calculated from the moment of conception not from the moment of birth, as is the case in European tradition. Where the destiny of a future Son of Heaven was concerned, the moments of imperial ecstasy with empress or concubine had to be recorded and correlated with the rising and setting of the planets, whether the sky was visible or not.

The intriguing thing is that such an important discovery — the regulation of motion through the use of precise clockwork mechanisms — should have been discovered in China and then allowed to disappear from use altogether, two centuries before it was developed independently in Europe. When the Song emperor was driven out of Kaifeng by the invading Jin Tartars in 1127 the clock was allowed to fall to pieces. For the scholar-officials who governed the empire such technology was not relevant to the needs of ordinary people. The celestial clock at Kaifeng provided information appropriate only to the needs of the emperor and his court. Being made largely of wood, the mechanism must have been notoriously inaccurate, which made it more of a novelty than genuinely useful for it was never rebuilt.

Mechanical clocks, so fundamental to the later technological and industrial development of the west, did not reappear in China until the arrival of Jesuit missionaries in the sixteenth century.

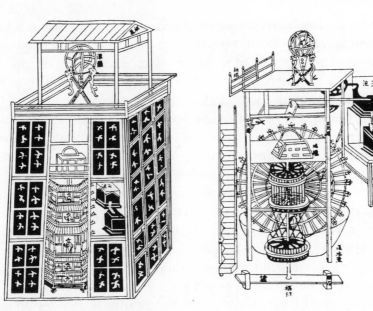

These illustrations were taken from Su Song's original plans for the great astronomical clock he set up for the Emperor in 1088.

SELF-CULTIVATION AND THE COSMOS

By studying the organic patterns of heaven and earth a fool can become a sage. So by watching the times and seasons of natural phenomena we can become true philosophers.

Li Chuan, *Yin fu jing,* A.D. 735

The sage can rival the skill of the shaping forces;
Raising his hand, he plucks the sun and moon from the sky
To put in his pot.

A Chinese alchemic verse

The power of the imperial bureaucrats was considerable, for it was through them that the emperor ruled and was himself ruled. For he too was educated in the Confucian cultural values that they espoused. Any propensity to autocratic power and radical action was checked by traditional precedents and limited by bureaucratic inertia.

Scholar-officials were posted from the imperial capital, on passing their final exams, to junior positions in a provincial bureaucracy. From here, by dutiful service, they would begin to climb, as officials do today, to the top of the greasy pole becoming, if they possessed the "right stuff," ministers and eventually close advisers to the emperor himself. As scholars they would be expected to conform to the behavior expected of a Confucian gentleman, which, like the nineteenth century European ideal of the gentleman, embodied many patronizing assumptions of superiority.

At its best, however, this bureaucratic tradition encouraged the spread of knowledge and learning throughout the empire. These imperial civil servants were not allowed to govern in the province in which they were brought up or had close family ties and they were transferred regularly to prevent the forming of corrupt relationships with the powerful local landowners or gentry, who held local administrative posts. Corruption did, of course, occur and a blind eye was often turned to the profiteering carried out by members of the civil service. By tax farming and squeezing local merchants' profits bureaucrats were able to make a comfortable livelihood, well above that allowed by their modest imperial salary.

To regard all officials as corrupt would, however, be wrong. Many were genuinely imbued with Confucian ideals and were dedicated to improving the lot of the people they served. Together with the local gentry, officials established medical temples such as the Yao Wang Mountain Medical Temple in Shaanxi province. Here there are sculptures celebrating the great medical figures of the past, particularly Su Simao, a physician of the Sui and Tang dynasties, to whom one section of the temple was dedicated during the Ming dynasty. Throughout the courtyards they set up steles (granite slabs) on which were carved medical texts containing recipes and methods of treatment for a wide range of common ailments. These were carved in the form of

Courtesy Film Australia

Courtesy Film Australia

Above: The Yao Wang Mountain Medical Temple in Shaanxi; for a thousand years people have come here to obtain medical advice and the ingredients to make up prescriptions.

Left: Sun Simo, a physician of the Tang dynasty, is still venerated at the Yao Wang Mountain Medical Temple for his pioneering work in cataloging the medicinal properties of plants. Though a brilliant scholar, he is reported to have consistently declined the offer of an official position in the imperial bureaucracy on the grounds that it would interrupt his medical research. He must have got something right for he lived to be over 100 years old.

pages and, by taking rubbings on rice paper, could be cut to form books.

The local community could come to this temple and not only get the necessary ingredients for the medicines — the herbs that were collected and stored in the temple — but also take rubbings from the steles. These were the libraries and photocopiers of the ancient world.

In the famous forest of tablets at the Confucian temple in Xi'an (Hsian) there is a vast hall of such granite slabs that provided students and the general public with access to the Confucian classics needed to pass the imperial examination. These were, in effect, public printing presses, which allowed useful knowledge to be dispersed. However, one had to be able to read and basic literacy was not available to everyone in China, any more than it was in Europe until the twentieth century. Literacy was confined, for the most part, to public officials and the landowning gentry, from which class most students came.

One of the important functions of these officials posted to the far reaches of the empire, was the collection of information and knowledge that might be useful in other regions of China. With governors and officials moving regularly from one area to another this meant that any knowledge of medical, agricultural and industrial techniques invented in one province was soon dispersed elsewhere. This dissemination was augmented by the official publication and distribution among these bureaucrats of technical encyclopedias. These covered useful knowledge from agriculture and irrigation to medicine and military defense.

In 1057 the Song emperor Renzong (Jen Tsung) instructed Su Song (who had the

The forest of tablets at the Confucian temple in Xi'an on which are carved the Confucian classics. These tablets were the public libraries and photocopiers of ancient China.

famous astronomical clock built) and the naturalist Zhang Dong (Chang Tung) to gather together all knowledge about medicinal plants within the empire. In 1082 this was published under the title *Bencao tujing* (Pharmaceutical Natural History). This encyclopedia was then circulated throughout China and significantly expanded the common knowledge of a wide range of medicinal plants and their uses.

To standardize medical practice within the imperial household a college of medicine was established in the Tang dynasty from which students graduated after a proper training and examination. This, however, was not a prerequisite for medical practice outside the court. A book on forensic medicine, the first in the world, was published by a Chinese judge, Song Ci (Sung Tz'u) in 1247 and circulated among magistrates throughout the empire.

Public health was a matter of prime concern. By the thirteenth century China had many large cities of more than a million people, far larger than any cities in Europe. In the Southern Song capital of Hangzhou the population density was extremely high. The outbreak and spread of epidemics was a constant problem causing appalling death tolls. One of the reasons why Chinese medicine was so highly developed at this time was that the imperial scholar-officials had to cope with the epidemics and other health problems that came with crowded urban living, long before this became a problem in the west.

One remarkable Chinese discovery in the tenth century was the technique known as "variolation," a form of inoculation used against smallpox. Doctors took swabs from smallpox pustules, dissolved them in water and kept them at body temperature

Above: Ginseng, found in the mountains of the north and west, was used widely as a medicinal plant throughout China and was made an imperial monopoly.

Left: These statues of medical heroes at the Yao Wang Mountain Medical Temple were made in the Ming dynasty. Chinese scholars and physicians such as these developed the world's first method of inoculation and started forensic medicine.

for a few weeks to allow for detoxification. The inoculum was then placed on cottonwool balls in the nose of a healthy person. The patient would get a mild dose of the disease allowing the body to develop immunity. This technique later spread to Russia and Turkey where, in the eighteenth century, it was used by Lady Mary Wortley Montagu, the wife of the British ambassador to Turkey, to provide her family with immunity during an outbreak of smallpox, which occurred in Constantinople in 1718. Details on the use of the technique had already been published in the *Philosophical Transactions of the Royal Society* in London in 1714. In all probability Jenner, who developed his method of vaccination in the second half of the eighteenth century, was aware of this Chinese technique.

Medical knowledge and discovery were not necessarily the exclusive prerogatives of the scholar-officials. For the most part medicine was in the hands of medical practitioners independent of the official examination system. In fact, medicine was one of the fields that a Confucian scholar could enter. It was considered a respectable profession because it served the people and was in the public interest. In this respect, the Confucian tradition succeeded in establishing an intellectual orthodoxy, endowing some professions with respectability while others were deemed to be heterodox and inappropriate for a scholar or gentleman.

Alchemy was one of these heterodox fields, which, nonetheless, was to have a considerable influence on medicine, metallurgy and the military. There were in fact two traditions or schools of alchemy, which were dominated, for the most part, by Taoist ideas. There was an outer or *wai tan* school that was concerned with studying chemical processes and an inner or spiritual school called *nei tan*. The alchemists of the *wai tan* school aimed at understanding the cosmological processes by studying the transformation of metals and chemicals when heated. By contemplating the changes from one state or phase to another they believed they would not only understand the cycles that govern all change but could even produce elixirs of immortality.

These ideas were also associated with a commonly held view that all natural phenomena were divided into two polarities of *yin* and *yang*. *Yin* represented elements such as water, dark, cold, the feminine and the yielding, while *yang* represented the sun, heat, the masculine, dominance and so on. The elements of *yin* and *yang* were believed to be present in all phenomena. The energy that drove the universe and animated biological life was called *qi* (*ch'i*). This could take either a *yin* or *yang* form.

The Chinese also recognized that all things were in a stage of flux or transformation from one state to another. Both the animate and inanimate worlds were seen to be in one of five phases that moved in cycles. For example, the phases known as wood and fire were associated with spring and summer and were *yang* parts of the year; the phases of metal and water, autumn and winter were the *yin* phases representing increasing slowness and receptivity. Apart from these four, there was earth representing the balancing of these opposites and the completion of the cycle. This passage from *Inner Writings of the Jade Purity* gives some sense to this view of the world:

Taoist sages contemplate the symbol of *yin* and *yang*. The unity of *yin* and *yang* is expressed by a light *yang* dot inside the dark *yin* half of the circle and vice versa.

In the great *tao* of heaven and earth, what endured of the myriad phenomena is their primal and harmonious *qi*. Of the things that exist in perpetuity, none surpass the sun, moon and stars. *Yin* and *yang,* the five phases [elements], day and night, come into being out of earth, and in the end return to earth. They alter in accord with the seasons, but that there should be a limit to them is also the *tao* of nature. For instance when pine resin imbibes the *qi* of mature *yang* for a thousand years it is transformed into fungus. After another thousand years of irradiation it becomes spirit; in another thousand it becomes amber and in another thousand years crystal quartz. These are the seminal essences formed through irradiation by the floriated *qi* of sun and moon.

The alchemists believed that they could produce these cycles of change artificially. One by-product of this tradition was the conviction among some alchemists (who seemed to mix their metaphors as often as their chemicals) that, by heating and reheating a mixture of mercury and sulfur (to produce cinnabar), they could make immortality pills from the compound. However, the mercury they contained, taken over a long period of time, led to the poisoning of numerous emperors, princes and high officials, particularly during the six dynasties. The reddish gold color of cinnabar was associated with gold, and since gold was a stable substance immune from decay, it was clearly a metaphor for permanence or immortality.

This poetic analogy to gold became lost over time and, when these alchemic ideas spread to Europe, the object of the exercise was thought to be the production of gold from base metals. However, despite the abuse of this early form of chemistry, by the tenth century the Chinese were using a wide range of metals as part of compound

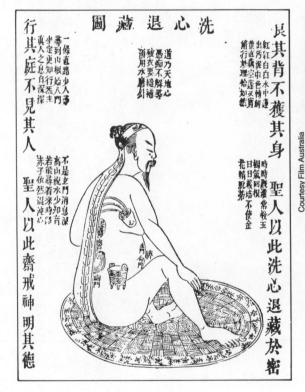

Above: A small burner used by alchemists during their experiments.

Left: This illustration from a *nei tan* alchemic text (1615) shows the *qi* flowing up the spinal column and feeding through to the heart. The cauldron in the abdomen is where the energy is transformed and immortality formed.

medicines. Chinese physicians eventually understood that mercury, used in very small quantities, could be used to kill bacteria. And as early as the Tang dynasty (618–906) the Chinese were using silver-tin amalgams for filling holes in teeth. It was not until the time of Paracelsus in the sixteenth century that the idea that the function of alchemy was to make better medicine gained currency in Europe.

It is ironic that out of the efforts of Chinese alchemists to understand the harmony with the cosmos came the discovery of the most destructive compound known — the mixture of sulfur, saltpeter and charcoal to produce gunpowder. Interestingly, even gunpowder was first used as a medicine to treat skin diseases and as a fumigant to kill insects long before it was taken up by the military in the eleventh century.

The second school of alchemy, *nei tan,* was concerned with the internal transformation of the individual, the final goal being the achievement of spiritual immortality by the refinement and transformation of the body's basic energy. As in the *wai tan* school this involved heat as the transforming agent. This heat was produced by the breathing exercises involved in meditation, which fanned the fires of sexual energy at the base of the spine and lifted them to the higher mental centers. In some writings this process gave birth to a "homunculus" or new embryonic but immortal being within the body. The meditative practices and ideas associated with this *nei tan* school have a great deal in common with Tantric Buddhism and the esoteric yogic practices of India, and there may well have been shared origins. In India the idea was that the awakening of the forces of Kundalini (the twin serpents dormant at the base of the spine) and their movement up the spinal column would bring higher and higher levels of spiritual awareness, detachment and ecstasy.

Among Chinese scholars and physicians, these esoteric practices were often taken up as a means of achieving a psychic and physical balance between *yin* and *yang.* Illness was the result of an imbalance in these basic forces within the body and psyche. The role of the doctor was to restore this balance and create harmony. In acupuncture, needles were used to stimulate the circulation of the *qi* or life energy into areas that would increase the *yin* or *yang* elements. There was also the common belief that, in the act of sex, *yin* passed from the female to the male and vice versa. Sex was, therefore, regarded as a means of restoring psychic and physical balance — an idea perhaps drawn originally from Tantric Buddhism.

Sex in China was not associated with the sort of puritanical obsessiveness found in the west, where the separation of spirit and body was a fundamental assumption of Christian dogma: the escape from the corruption of the body requiring its denial as a means of elevating the spirit. In China there was no such split. The idea of another world or creator-god outside this one pulling the strings like a grand puppeteer never took hold. Although Buddhism had a considerable influence in China during the Sui and Tang dynasties, its other-worldly concerns meant that it was, for the most part, the religion of the poor and disadvantaged.

Despite the influence of some of these religious ideas, the dominant values that shaped Chinese culture were the rational and humanistic values of Confucianism. As Master Kung himself wrote: "It is man that can make the *tao* great, not the *tao* that can make the man great."

BOMBARDS AND CATHAYAN FIRE ARROWS

The properties of saltpeter (potassium nitrate) were known and used by Chinese alchemists from the second century to dissolve metals. It was often known as "solve stone." In the west, the first record of its use is to be found under the name of "Chinese Snow" in *The Book of the Assembly of Medical Samples* by Ibn al-Baitar published in 1240.

Arab traders had been operating out of the southern Chinese cities of Guangzhou (Canton) and Quanzhou since the Tang dynasty (618–907). In both these cities there were large Islamic communities who were engaged in international trade and who acted as the conduit for ideas and technologies transmitted between the two cultures. Through the Arab world Chinese alchemic ideas and technology reached Europe.

By A.D. 300 the alchemist Ko Hung (Ge Hong) was mixing sulfur, saltpeter, mica hematite and clay, and heating them to produce a purple powder, which was supposed to turn mercury into silver when heated. Sulfur was the common ingredient in all recipes for elixirs. Its poisonous properties were well known and a technique of "subduing the toxicity and volatility of sulfur by fire" was adopted by alchemists and could well have led to the development of gunpowder itself.

Courtesy Film Australia

Cathayan fire arrows, as they were known in the west, represented the first use of rocket propulsion in warfare. By the eleventh century these arrows were often fired from rocket launchers loaded on wheelbarrows. Many had explosive warheads, which, although not of great destructive power, could cause mayhem among cavalry.

Alchemists would mix sulfur and saltpeter then ignite it until there was no longer any flame. This was the subduing process. One of the earliest alchemic texts (which dates from around 850) referring to the inflammable properties of sulfur and saltpeter was the *Classified Essentials of the Mysterious Tao of the True Origin of Things*:

> Some have heated together sulfur, realgar [arsenic disulfide] and saltpeter with honey; smoke and flames result, so that their hands and faces have been burned, and even the whole house where they were working burned down. Evidently this only brings Taoism into discredit and Taoist alchemists are thus warned clearly not to do it.

However, despite all the warnings, knowledge of the incendiary properties of gunpowder were to move out of the domain of alchemists and into the hands of the military. The significance of its use in the military field was clear by 1067, when the emperor banned the sale of sulfur and saltpeter to foreigners and turned their production and use into a state monopoly. Twenty-three years earlier, in 1044, Zeng Gongliang (Tseng Kong-liang) compiled his *Collection of the Most Important Military Techniques* in which he described many kinds of gunpowder weapons and gave a number of instructions for making them. One such instruction provides the first

As Chinese military strategy was primarily defensive these new gunpowder weapons were to play a significant role as the Song dynasty came under siege from northern invaders throughout the eleventh and twelfth centuries. Here, fragmentation bombs are seen doing their all too familiar work among the invaders.

account of a bomb producing poisonous gas. To produce a *du you yan qiu* the following ingredients were mixed:

30 liang of saltpeter	Arsenic
15 liang of sulfur	Roots of langdu
5 liang of charcoal	Bamboo and hemp fibers
Croton seeds	Wood oil and tar

[1 liang = 1.75 ounces]

Within a period of less than two hundred years the Chinese were to field a vast number of gunpowder-based weapons, including cannons or bombards, bombs that were lobbed on invading troops, two-stage rockets and fire arrows, land mines and even submarine mines. The reason for this proliferation of new weapons was not just the knowledge of the explosive properties of gunpowder, but the fact that the Song emperors were constantly under siege from invading armies of the Jin Tartar from the northwest. The production of gunpowder weapons was to be taken over by a special government bureau, which established 11 large workshops employing more than 40,000 workers. In *Xinsi qi qi lu* (Tearful Records of the Battle of Qizhou) Zhao Yurong wrote of the output of these imperial factories in 1221:

This late Qing illustration shows imperial officials surveying one of the imperial workshops where a variety of weapons were made.

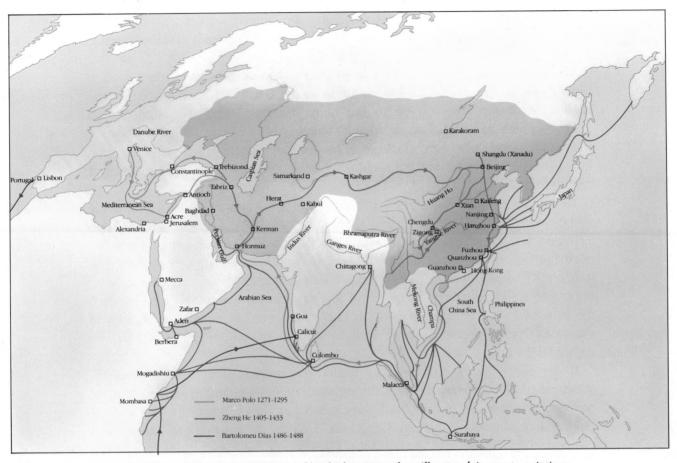

This map traces the complex routes by which gunpowder, silk, porcelain, paper, printing and the compass were transferred from China, through Central Asia, to Europe where they were to play a crucial part in the breakdown of feudalism. A technological arms race was set in motion, which would not only transform and refine gunpowder weapons, but would return them to the gates of the Celestial Empire with quite devastating consequences.

On the same day there were produced 7,000 gunpowder crossbow arrows, 10,000 gunpowder longbow arrows, 3,000 barbed gunpowder bombs and 20,000 ordinary gunpowder bombs.

By this time the Chinese were producing fragmentation bombs (*zhentian lei*) that could devastate an area the size of a house. A graphic description of its destructive power is found in *Jin shi* (History of the Jin Dynasty) 1126:

When it went off it made a report like sky-rending thunder. An area of more than half a mu [one-twelfth of an acre] was scorched on which men, horses and leather armor were shattered. Even iron coats of mail were riddled.

The scale of the Chinese army was enormous by European standards. By 1040 the regular army comprised about 1.25 million men. The cost of maintaining such an army was also enormous. Quite apart from the production of gunpowder weapons, the traditional bow and crossbow departments were producing 16.5 million arrowheads a year. By 1160, the yearly output of the imperial armaments office came to 3.24 million weapons. Iron production during the eleventh century reached 125,000 tons a year.

The troops were stationed primarily on the northwestern borders. They lived in fortress towns, which extended in an arc from the Great Wall in the north to the Kunlun Mountains that run up to the high Tibetan plateau. The strategy was defensive, with the armies acting as self-sufficient frontier communities, growing their own food wherever possible. The military strategy was to create an impenetrable barrier against the highly mobile armies of the nomadic peoples of central Asia.

Despite enormous efforts to limit the spread of their advanced military technology to the enemy beyond China's borders, there was a constant dispersion of knowledge as traders and captured soldiers provided the Khitan and Jin Tartar kingdoms, to the northeast, access to crossbows, methods of making armor plating and, finally, to gunpowder weapons. So that, despite China's technological superiority and enormous resources, the Jin Tartars were able to occupy the north of China and take the Northern Song capital of Kaifeng in 1127. The spread of military technology to the west was to be greatly increased with the Mongol invasion in 1279, which in turn displaced the Jin.

Under the Emperor Kublai Khan, China was reunited and a loose imperial structure of kingdoms established throughout central Asia that extended Mongol power and influence from the Pacific to the Mediterranean. It was this vast Mongol empire that allowed European merchants such as Marco Polo to travel, with passports bearing the seal of the Great Khan, along the famous silk route from Constantinople to Xanadu, the emperor's summer residence. Along this highway camel trains carried the exquisite industrial products of China — porcelain, silk and even silkworms smuggled in bamboo poles, which were used to found the silk industry in Europe. Accounts, like those of Marco Polo, of the fabulous wealth and power of China were to fire imagination and greed.

By this same route that brought gunpowder weapons to the west, came the "black death" (the bubonic plague) the other great scourge that was to devastate Europe in the fourteenth century. These two imports from the east were to play a significant part in breaking down the feudal social and economic structures of medieval Europe.

MERCHANTS, ARTISANS AND BUREAUCRATS

I assure you that this river runs for such a distance and through so many regions and there are so many cities on its banks that, truth to tell, in the amount of shipping it carries and the total volume and value of its traffic, it exceeds all the rivers of the Christians put together and their seas into the bargain. I give you my word that I have seen in this city fully five thousand ships at once, all afloat on this river. Then you may reflect, since this city, which is not very big, has so many ships, how many there must be in the others. For I assure you that the river flows through more than sixteen provinces, and there are on its banks more than two hundred cities, all having more ships than this.

Marco Polo, on passing through the city of I-ching on the Yangtze
in the thirteenth century.

To maintain the vast Song and Mongol armies, the imperial workshops as well as the state monopolies in iron and salt required economic organization and technology of considerable sophistication. By the Song dynasty (960–1279) merchant guilds were involved in large-scale internal and international trading

Despite the low social status of merchants, government revenue generated from trade became increasingly important. Along the waterways of the rich rice-growing regions of the Yangtze delta, depicted in this Song dynasty scene, prosperous cities such as Suzhou, Hangzhou and Nanjing grew up. Here, rich merchant families were employed to manage the trade in government monopolies, such as salt, tea, iron, porcelain and even silk.

operations. As Marco Polo observed, the volume of trade through the waterways of the Yangtze delta was clearly greater than that of Europe. Craft specialization and increasingly wide markets for industrial products allowed for a division of labor that was not achieved in Europe until the eve of the Industrial Revolution in the late eighteenth century. Paper money was being used, in part, to alleviate the growing demand for metal currency, which was always in short supply. In fact, China at the time that Marco Polo was employed by the Great Khan seems to have been on the threshold of a mercantile and even an industrial revolution.

The Industrial Revolution in Britain in the eighteenth century was essentially built around the factory system of production, particularly in the spinning industry where water power was combined with the mechanical skills of instrument makers who were able to automate the spinning of thread. Economic historians have pointed to the silk and cotton spinning factories established by John Lombe and by Richard Arkwright as forming the "leading edge" of technological and industrial innovation, which was to spread to other industries such as the potteries of Staffordshire and the iron foundries of Derby. Yet, as early as 1313, the scholar Wang Chen in his *Treatise on Agriculture* described the mechanical spinning of hemp, which was used widely throughout northern China. Wang was so delighted by this example of industrial innovation that he wrote the following poem in praise of mechanical spinning:

> There is one driving belt for wheels both great and small.
> When one wheel turns, the others all turn with it.
> The rovings are transmitted evenly from the bobbin rollers.
> The threads wind by themselves on to the reeling frame.

But this technology was not to have the same impact on China as it was to have on Europe.

In ceramics, Chinese porcelain was not only one of the most sought after commodities for trade but was actually produced on commission for Arab merchants or their agents living in the ports of Guangzhou and Quanzhou. The skill of the craftsmen and the quality of the glazes were not matched in Europe until the late eighteenth century. Large quantities of Chinese porcelain were shipped throughout Southeast Asia and the Middle East, and the scale of production was enormous. Silk and cotton weaving, despite being essentially "cottage" industries, used complex two-man draw looms, which allowed for the weaving of rich and magnificent patterns sought after throughout the world.

Despite this large-scale trade, the status of merchants in China up until the Song dynasty was low. They were at the bottom of the social hierarchy, as they were in the same period in Europe. In cultures relying primarily on agriculture for their wealth, the trader was often regarded as a parasite who failed to contribute to the productive well-being of the state. Until the advent of money as the dominant mode of economic exchange, taxes were collected in the form of grain, cloth or other domestic produce but with traders constantly on the move, taxing them on the basis of a percentage of productive output was, to say the least, difficult. Even when taxes

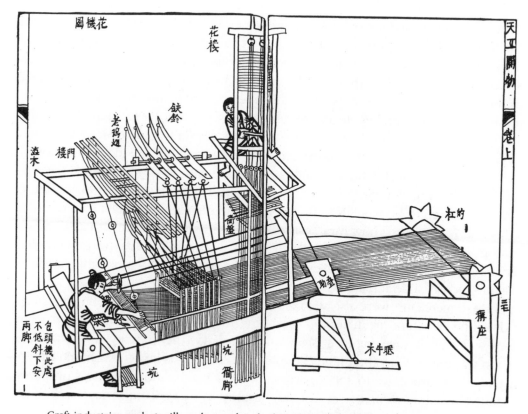

Craft industries such as silk and porcelain had reached remarkable levels of technological sophistication. The two-man draw loom allowed for the weaving of intricate patterns, which made Chinese silk a prized luxury throughout the ancient world.

could be extracted, the actual extent of a merchant's wealth was never easy to verify. In China, from the time of the Han dynasty, laws had been enacted restricting the commercial activities and the power of merchants.

In *Five Evils,* Han Fei had this to say on the issue of merchants and artisans:

> An enlightened administrator causes the number of merchants, artisans and vagrants to be few and places them in a humble post in order to make them desire to engage in the basic occupation [agriculture] and to reduce the numbers engaged in the subsidiary occupation [commerce].

As late as the Yuan (Mongol) dynasty (1279–1368), Wang Chen in his book *Nong shu* extolled the activities of the farmer and criticized the inability of the wandering merchant to fulfil his moral obligation as seen from the Confucian perspective:

> In his public relations he [the farmer] pays his tax and does his corvée service; at home he feeds his parents and rears his wife and children. In addition he concludes marriage relationships and has social contact with his neighbors. In the field of social customs nobody is better than the farmer. Craftsmen on the other hand rely on their skill and merchants manipulate surpluses. They move around and are without a definite place to live. They cannot be perfect in the fulfillment of their duties of caring for their parents and their feelings of friendship.

Such moralizing about the virtues of the farmer and the turpitude of the merchant and artisan did not prevent some Chinese merchants from becoming both rich and influential. However, traditional Confucian attitudes clearly affected the merchants' official status. For example, the sons of merchants were, at times, banned from sitting for the imperial examinations. For a wealthy merchant to gain social status he had to give up trade, buy a rural estate and become one of the gentry. He might thereby be able to get his children into the imperial civil service and through them achieve high social standing. Only scholars and Buddhist monks were free from the humiliation of corporal punishment and the obligations of corvée labor. (A similar attitude towards trade continued in Europe well into the nineteenth century. Trade or manufacture were considered to be of sufficiently low status, particularly in Britain to cause rich industrialists to retire, buy rural estates and send their children to Oxford or Cambridge, so allowing them to join the elite who manned the British imperial service as governors of Bengal, New South Wales or Canada — a possible factor in Britain's industrial decline in the late nineteenth century.)

Chinese merchants were also seen to be making immoral profits by buying cheap and selling dear, and from usury — lending money and obtaining wealth from interest. Given human nature's propensity for envy, the capacity to accumulate wealth was regarded by the Chinese Confucian scholars (as it was by Church fathers in Europe) as disruptive to social harmony — a social harmony that was primarily designed to allow *them* to control the surplus from agriculture and with it to maintain their own power and privileges.

Until the Tang Dynasty (618–907) the major challenge to the power and

Merchants were, for the most part, treated as necessary parasites by the Confucian scholars who ran the empire. In the Confucian social hierachy scholars were at the top followed by farmers, while merchants and artisans were at the very bottom.

The Art Institute of Chicago

prerogatives of the Confucian scholar-bureaucrats had been the threat from military and aristocratic families intent on establishing a feudal structure similar to that which existed in Europe and Japan. But by the Song dynasty the meritocratic imperial examination had become accepted as the normal route to political power by the dominant rural gentry. It also provided an avenue, however indirect, by which merchants with talent could gain social mobility. Merchant wealth, or an alliance with such wealth, could also provide the means by which poor officials and gentry could support a son through the arduous examination system, which took a minimum of six years even to be ready to sit for the qualifying examination.

A change in both the status and power of merchants in Europe and China occurred as rulers came to rely increasingly on money, despite the fact that laws aimed at keeping merchants separate from the rest of the community remained in the statute books. Sumptuary laws controlling all aspects of consumption were common in both cultures with the same intention of preventing merchants from using their wealth to achieve social status and, in some cases, were designed to make them look ridiculous. In China, in the Tang dynasty, no merchant was permitted to ride on a horse or wear rich clothes. (One of the factors creating a demand for luxuries in Europe was the relaxing of these laws there in the fourteenth century. With social mobility new craft industries grew up to cater for the demands of socially mobile merchants and artisans.) In China, by the twelfth century, merchants were nonetheless being employed to manage many of the great state monopolies, as well as to control the supplies that kept the border armies functioning.

In Song China the transition to a money economy was to happen much earlier

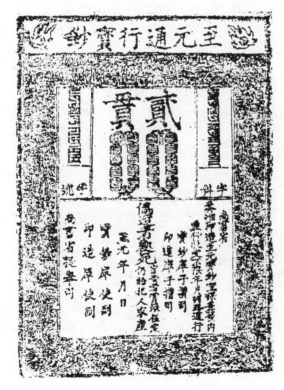

The world's first paper money; the rings towards the top of the note represent the number of strings of "cash" (100 copper coins) it represented. Throughout the eleventh and twelfth centuries trade grew at such a rate that a cash economy began to emerge. To cope with the demand for currency the Song emperors printed paper money, and suffered the inevitable consequences of rampant inflation.

than in Europe. For example, in 749 less than 4 percent of taxes and revenue were collected in money but by 1065 this had risen to over 50 percent. There were, however, a number of crucial changes during the Song dynasty that led to a marked increase in commerce and, particularly, in international trade. The financial and military plight of the Song empire was to change, briefly, the status of merchants and to shake the Chinese Confucian bureaucrats out of their traditional conservatism.

The empire was saddled, not only with an army four times the size of that required in the earlier Tang dynasty (because of the significantly greater military threat on the northern borders), but also with an equally large increase in the number of bureaucrats needed to serve it. To meet the consequent need for extra revenue the Song took measures to stimulate foreign trade. They established a maritime trade commission to supervise and tax merchant ships. In 987 four separate missions or trade delegations were sent to other Southeast Asian countries carrying a selection of Chinese goods, including silk and porcelain. These delegations offered special licenses to foreign merchants and also issued them to Chinese merchants going abroad. During the Tang dynasty there was only one port — Guangzhou — that was allowed to trade with foreigners. The maritime trade commission opened up seven more points along the Guangdong (Kwantung) and Fujian coasts, as well as a dozen naval bases from which armed vessels patrolled the coast protecting merchant fleets from Japanese and other pirates.

With the splitting of the empire after the successful invasion of northern China by the Jin Tartars, the Song emperor was forced to turn his attention to building a navy to hold the invaders at the Yangtze River.

The strategy seems to have worked. In 1098 foreign trade represented 0.82 percent of the gross cash income of the Song government; 13 years later, in 1111, it had doubled to 1.7 percent. However, the pressure to raise more and more revenue to support almost constant warfare with the Jin Tartars on the northern borders forced the Song into the classic response of printing more money. By 1107 the value of paper currency in China had dropped to 1 percent of its face value, perhaps one of the first examples in history of inflation caused by too much money circulating in the economy. Prices soared and the necessary financial stringency, coupled with the famines and internal disarray led to the Jin Tartars overrunning northern China in 1127 and driving the Song south of the Yangtze River. Here they could hold their own against the northern armies of the Jin whose strength lay in the mobility and skill of their cavalry. Among the waterways of the rich rice-growing areas of southern China they were no match for the Song navy.

The need to rely on naval power led to a new emphasis on boatbuilding and the creation of a vast array of vessels. Innovation was rewarded by the administration. The world's first paddle boat was designed, and used to move troops through the shallow waterways and canals that intersect the countryside south of the Yangtze. Huge boats designed like fortresses were sent into battle, equipped with cannon, rockets and bombs of all descriptions. Explosive rockets, which would shoot across the surface of the water, were developed along with submarine mines. But perhaps the greatest long-term impact of this new emphasis on naval defense was its effect on overseas trade.

With the agricultural land upon which the southern Song could draw for revenue reduced enormously, the income from trade in state monopolies and excise duties on trade made up 50 percent of total government revenue. By 1131 overseas trade alone had grown to 20 percent of the total cash revenue. With this change in the basic balance of the Chinese imperial economy there was a subsequent shift in the attitude of the bureaucracy towards merchants. The two merchants who were largely responsible for the increase in overseas trade in 1131, Cai Jingfang (Ts'ai Ching-fang) and a Muslim, Pu Luoxin (Abu al-Hassan) were both given honorary official rank in 1136. The Song court also announced that any merchants whose overseas trade figures for the year amounted to more than 50,000 strings of cash would be given official rank, and that any government official in charge of commercial affairs who supervised more than one million strings of cash would be promoted one grade. (Chinese paper currency represented so many strings of copper cash. The Chinese copper coin had a hole in the middle allowing a thousand of them to be threaded on to one piece of string to represent a single unit.)

It is significant that the second of these two merchants should be a Muslim. In both Guangzhou and, later, Quanzhou large Muslim communities had established themselves during the Song, for, as the overland silk routes that linked the Middle East with China became impassable because of constant warfare on the Chinese borders, the sea routes to the Red Sea became correspondingly more important. By this route silk, porcelain, tea and spices reached the Arab world and from there the growing markets of Europe.

The scale of this trade was considerable: nearly 10,000 pieces of broken Chinese porcelain have recently been found at Fustat near Cairo, one of the factory bases used in this trade since the Tang dynasty. Similar sites have been discovered in Oman and other centers of trade in the Red Sea.

Not only trade goods reached the west via this route; the transfer of Chinese technology was to be equally or more important than the luxuries that found their way into the hands of kings, feudal lords and the great monasteries. Of greater long-term significance were Chinese navigational techniques. The compass and Chinese boat designs were taken up by Arab traders and transferred from there to Europe. The south-pointing compass was adapted for navigation at sea during the Song dynasty. The compass had been used in China for centuries by geomancers for the laying out of buildings so that they would conform to *fengshui,* the earth's vital energy, which the Chinese believed flowed through the surface of the earth like blood through the veins of the human body. Often referred to as the forces of "wind

The descendants of the Arab traders who established themselves at Guangzhou
during the Song dynasty still gather at their ancient mosque.

and water," they governed the correct positioning of buildings in relation to landscape, which was considered crucial for the harmony of humanity and the environment. The compass was also soon to be taken up by the military and by miners who used it to find direction underground. Its arrival in Europe came at a crucial time and was essential for navigation out of sight of land. Before this sailors hugged the shore, a dangerous practice but the only means they had of knowing where they were going.

Another important Chinese device to be taken up by European boatbuilders was the stern-post rudder. Hitherto, European ships had depended upon the use of an oar extending from the back of galleys. The stern-post rudder allowed for the construction of much larger boats whose direction could be controlled by a wheel. The addition of more than one mast and the use of lateen sails, derived from the Arab dhow, allowed European sailors to extend radically the scale and scope of maritime trade. The adoption of this new fore-and-aft rig enabled mariners to tack effectively into the wind. It removed the need to have oarsmen, a basic feature of the medieval galley. This had two results: it lightened the boats, providing more room for cargo, and it also allowed boats to sail at any time of the year, not just when the winds were blowing in the required direction. Ships from the eastern Mediterranean could now travel in all seasons to northern Europe and the Baltic States.

* * *

The European Crusades to retake the Holy Lands from the Islamic infidels from the eleventh century onwards also exposed many northern Europeans to the luxuries and sophistication of Islamic culture, art and technology. With the improvement in shipping, new commodities once only accessible to aristocrats began to turn up in the market places of Bruges, Antwerp, London and Hamburg. Apart from the pepper,

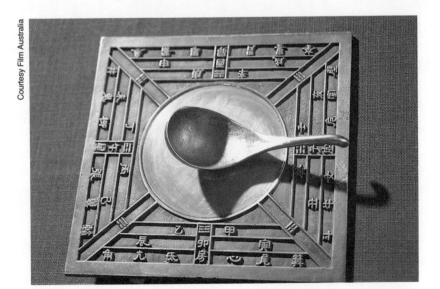

Courtesy Film Australia

An early form of the Chinese south-pointing compass, which was brought to the west by Arab traders in the thirteenth century.

cinnamon, cloves and nutmeg that were increasingly in demand to disguise the flavor and taste of bad food, there were new commodities and, with them, new words entered the languages of Europe. Cotton from the Arab *cotone,* damask from Damascus, baldachin from Bagdad, muslin from Mosul, gauze from Gaza, along with divan, bazaar, artichoke, spinach, tarragon, tariff, orange, alcove, arsenal, jar, magazine, syrup, taffeta, tea and porcelain.

The new all-weather ships, first developed in the Italian city-states between 1280 and 1330, linked Europe in a coherent commercial web as never before, despite the almost constant political and military conflicts. Salt, for example, from southern Europe could be shipped to the Baltic where it was used to preserve fish and cabbage, and markedly improved the diet and the capacity of people to sustain themselves through the harsh northern winters. In return, timber, metals, cloth and wool were shipped back. The trade in these commodities led to a closer commercial interaction in a Europe-wide market.

Credit facilities, bills of exchange and the greater circulation of money began to lubricate the wheels of trade. The access to wider markets allowed, as it had so much earlier in China, for greater specialization on the part of artisans based in towns and in traditional rural industries. It also precipitated a shift in the centers of wealth and power from feudal aristocratic estates into the hands of the merchant princes of the Italian city-states.

POWER, PROFITS AND THE ARMS RACE

At the end of five days' journey, you arrive at the noble and handsome city of Zaitun [Quanzhou], which has a port on the sea coast celebrated for the resort of shipping, loaded with merchandise, that is afterwards distributed through every part of the province of Manji [Fujian]. The quantity of pepper imported there is so considerable, that what is carried to Alexandria, to supply the demand of the western parts of the world, is trifling in comparison, perhaps not more than the hundredth part. It is indeed impossible to convey an idea of the number of merchants and the accumulation of goods in this place, which is held to be one of the largest ports in the world. The Great Khan derives a vast revenue from this place, as every merchant is obliged to pay ten per cent. upon the amount of his investment. The ships are freighted by them at the rate of thirty per cent. for fine goods, forty-four for pepper, and for sandalwood and other drugs, as well as articles of trade in general, forty per cent. It is computed by the merchants, that their charges, including customs and freight, amount to half the value of the cargo; and yet upon the half that remains to them their profit is so considerable, that they are always disposed to return to the same market with a further stock of merchandise.

The Travels of Marco Polo, Book II

In 1271 China was overwhelmed by the Mongol armies of the Great Khan. The northern capital of Beijing was established and Kublai Khan ruled the greatest empire the world has ever known. The Yuan dynasty, which he founded, extended the policies of maritime expansion adopted by the Song. The European end of the trade with China was controlled largely by Venice and Genoa. These city-states were a new and unique phenomenon. They contributed to the rise of Europe as an economic and military power and were eventually to challenge the might of imperial China. However, at the end of the thirteenth century when Marco Polo had returned to his native city of Venice, the Venetians and the Genoese were at war over the control of the trade in Asian luxuries flowing into the ports of Egypt and the Middle East. In fact Marco Polo was to write his account of his journey to the east in a Genoese jail after being captured at the famous Battle of Curzola in September 1298.

The Venetian fleets were funded and maintained by powerful merchant families. The power and influence of the merchants in these cities was in marked contrast to those of Song China. Venice and Genoa were city-states whose major source of revenue and wealth was maritime trade conducted by merchants whose economic fortunes had grown with the power of these city-states. They shipped Asian spices and luxuries such as porcelain and silk to the market places of northern Europe and, in return, they brought salt fish, grain and woolen textiles from the north to the market places of southern Italy. In the republican structure, which underpinned the rule of the doge (the head of the Venetian state and maritime empire), the influence of these merchants had grown to challenge the traditional patrician and aristocratic power.

Venetian merchants trading bolts of cloth, usually woolen, in exchange for pepper and spices from Java or silk and porcelain from China.

Throughout feudal Europe aristocratic lords were concerned with the control of agricultural surplus and the Church itself was one of the great landowners and supporters of this feudal system. The towns of medieval Europe grew up outside this enclosed rural economy. They were the domain of craftsmen and merchants and were the market centers that offered a new freedom. Here, merchants challenged the laws of the Church by using Jews as bankers to escape the prohibition on usury. Here too, new ideas, fashions and tastes were evident; in marked contrast to the Chinese towns, which, however rich, remained administrative centers governed by imperial bureaucrats.

There was another important difference in the position of merchants operating out of the city-states. Florence, Genoa, Milan and Venice were all constantly in competition with one another, each trying to absorb part of the territory of the other. In these predominantly money economies taxes on merchant wealth provided the means for defense and paid for mercenary armies or condotieri (contractors), which were in common use by the thirteenth century. The technological arms race, which

A fourteenth century siege of a stronghold showing the use of primitive cannons and crossbows introduced from China.

this competition spawned, provided new careers for artisans and craftsmen in Europe.

First, crossbows entered the arsenals of Europe from China and then gunpowder and cannons. Between Milan and Genoa there was a race to see which one would produce stronger armor to withstand arrows from increasingly powerful crossbows. The bows were originally made of wood and then of laminated metal, making previous armor redundant. The crossbow also helped to shift the balance of power away from the arbitrary power of those masters of the "feudal blitzkreig," the knights in armor. The longbow took a strong man and ten years of training to shoot accurately. The crossbow, on the other hand, could be fired, like the gun, by almost anyone who could point a stick straight. It therefore provided townspeople with an easily mastered means of defending themselves. The Catalan Company, using crossbows in Sicily in 1282, for example, destroyed an army of French knights. It is little wonder that at the Second Lateran Council (1139) the pope should decree this weapon too lethal to be used by Christians against one another.

There was another import from Asia that was to have an equally profound impact on the fabric of feudal Europe — the black death. In 1346 when the bubonic plague first began its appalling sweep through Europe, it killed about a third of the population within one generation. The source of peasant labor to work the feudal lords' lands was in many areas completely wiped out. There was an acute labor shortage, which provided those peasants who survived with a new mobility. Before the plague they were neither permitted to leave their lord's domain or "hundred" nor to sell their labor. Now there was such an acute shortage of labor that even to plant and bring in the harvest it was necessary to poach labor from neighboring regions and to pay cash wages as an inducement. The corvée labor system of many areas of medieval Europe was broken down. Money wages in the hands of the rural peasantry linked them more closely than ever before to the market place of the town and the mercantile values it embodied.

* * *

It is interesting to speculate on what would have happened in Europe had the efforts of Pope Innocent III (1198 –1216) and Boniface VIII (1295–1303) to create a Holy Roman Empire (like that of China) embracing all of Europe been successful. Within the Catholic church there existed many parallel institutions to those that provided the Chinese empire with its great stability and continuity. First, there was the

Bibliothèque Nationale, Paris

The taking of Rouen by Henry V, 1418 –19. Cannons were becoming increasingly more powerful and were employed to attack the once invulnerable bastion of feudal power — the castle. By the end of the Hundred Years War between England and France, the King of France's artillery train was knocking down English castles in Normandy at the rate of one a month.

68

cosmology provided by the Bible; second, there was the clergy, linked by a common language, Latin, and an administrative hierarchy based, in part at least, on education. There is little reason to believe that the bureaucracy surrounding the thirteenth century popes could not have been extended effectively to the management of an imperial structure, had the geographical, cultural and economic circumstances of Europe been different. However, the marriage of ecclesiastical and temporal authority, embodied in the emperor of China, eluded popes and princes alike, and Europe was to remain fragmented in competing city- and nation-states, with all the consequent violence and rivalry.

For example, when the Hundred Years War between France and England began in 1337, it was little more than a squabble between two families over succession and inheritance. By the time it ended it was a full-scale war between nation-states. In the Battle of Crécy in 1346 it was the English longbow men who brought the flower of French chivalry to their knees and gave Normandy to the English, despite the fact that the French had 24 cannons at their disposal. But in 1453 it was the artillery train of Louis XI that was able to take back this same territory by blowing down the walls of the English castles in Normandy at the rate of one a month. The constant pressure of warfare and the demand for new and better cannons was soon to sweep away the security and political power that was once embodied in the feudal castle and the knight on horseback.

With remarkable speed, new variations on the cannon emerged. Primitive devices made on the same principle as wooden barrels (laying strips of iron side by side and binding them together with metal bands) were soon to be replaced by fully cast bombards of considerable size.

At the other extreme, handguns, known as Hakenbüchse, were being produced in the fourteenth century in Germany. These initially required two men to operate: one aiming and the other lighting the fuse. By the mid-fifteenth century these had evolved into the matchlock, with a trigger allowing one man to aim and fire. At the Venetian-controlled armaments factory at Brescia, matchlock guns — arquebuses or harquebuses — were being produced for the arsenals of monarchs throughout Europe. It was from here that Henry VIII ordered his handguns. The demand required founding and metalwork skills of a high order. The production of the trigger mechanism, in particular, demanded the precision engineering of clock-makers, combined with the steel-making capacities of the finest swordsmith. To cast the massive cannons also demanded metallurgical skills of an extremely high order.

In Venice, the arenali or arsenal (from the Arab word for workshop) was established, which provided a virtual production line in boatbuilding and fitting out. At its peak 16,000 craftsmen and workers were employed. As boats moved down the canal, workshops producing guns, rigging, sails and provisions fitted them out. With these warships the Venetian state protected its maritime empire. A significant element in the struggle for economic power was the control of the lucrative trade in Asian goods and between them the Venetians and Genoese had cornered the market. However, the trade was severely threatened by the collapse of the Mongol empire, and the rise of the Ottoman Turks. The capture of Constantinople by the Turks in

LEONARDO'S LETTER

In the highly competitive environment of fifteenth century Europe the demand for skilled artisans and engineers grew as monarchs competed to attract them to their courts, especially those whose inventive powers might give the monarch a military or economic advantage. Many of these skilled engineers were educated men familiar with the Greek sciences that flourished during the Renaissance. New careers and social status came as they hawked their talents around the courts of Europe. Leonardo da Vinci wrote the following letter to Duke Ludovico Sforza (Duke of Milan) in 1482 selling his services, not as a painter, but as a military engineer:

"Having seen, most Illustrious Lord, and considered to my own satisfaction the specimens of all those who proclaim themselves skilled contrivers of instruments of war, and observing that the invention and operation of such instruments are no different from those in common use, I shall endeavour, meaning no insult to anyone else, to make myself known to your Excellency, revealing my secrets, and offering them as it may please you and at an opportune time, and to put into operation all those things which are briefly described below:

Item 1. I have a method of constructing bridges, both strong and extremely light, so as to be easily carried, whereby you may pursue and at other times fly from the enemy; and others, safe and indestructible by fire or battle, easy and convenient to lift and place in position. Also methods of burning and destroying those of the enemy.

Item 2. I know a way, during the conduct of a siege, to take water out of the trenches, and to make an infinite variety of bridges, corridors and ladders, and other machines pertaining to such expeditions.

Item 3. Furthermore, if, by reason of the height of the defences, or by the strength of the building and its situation, it is impossible to take by bombardment, I have a method of destroying any rock fortress or other stronghold, even if it be founded in solid stone.

Item 4. I also have a method of constructing a kind of cannon, most convenient and easy to carry, that may hurl a small storm of missiles; and the smoke will greatly frighten the enemy to his great harm and confusion.

Item 5. And should the fight be at sea, I have many kinds of instruments for both attacking

and defending ships, which will resist the greatest bombardment, and powder, and smoke.

Item 6. I have a means whereby, by the use of secret and winding passages and paths, and without making any sound, you may reach whatever place you choose, even if it is necessary to pass under a trench or river.

Item 7. I will make covered chariots, safe and impregnable, which may enter among the enemy and his artillery, and so defeat any body of men, however great, and behind them may come infantry without risking hurt or setback.

Item 8. If there should be need, I will make cannon, mortars and lighter ordnance of a fine and useful kind, and quite unlike those in common use.

Item 9. If bombardment should fail, I will contrive catapults, mangonels, *trabocchi* and other machines of marvellous efficacy and uncommonness. And in short, according to the circumstances, I can contrive varied and infinite means of offence and defence.

Item 10. Also, in time of peace, I believe I can satisfy very well, and as much as any other, in architecture, in the composition of buildings both public and private, and in bringing water from one place to another.

Further, I can execute sculpture in marble, in bronze or in clay, and likewise painting, in which I will do whatever is wanted and as well as any other.

And I would be able to fashion the bronze horse, which will be to the immortal glory and the eternal honour of the happy memory of the Lord, your father, and of the great house of Sforza.

And if it should seem to any man that the things described herein are not possible, I offer most freely and openly to make trial of them in your park, or in whatever place it may please your Excellency, to whom, with the utmost humility, I commend myself."

Photo: Scala

This detail from Carpaccio's "Return of the Ambassadors" depicts the new merchant class who, in Venice and other Italian city states, had not only gained enormous wealth but had won political control of the state itself. This would have been unthinkable in Confucian China despite the prosperity of its own merchants.

1453 cut European access to the overland trade routes to the east. Though Chinese and other Asian commodities continued to arrive, taxes and commissions demanded by the Turks, Egyptians and other intermediaries forced up prices.

Other European monarchs had looked on with envy at the profits being made by the Venetians and Genoese in this eastern trade, and the possibility of finding a direct route to its source, thereby eliminating the Arab and Turkish intermediaries, inspired some heroic efforts. In 1291 the Vivaldi brothers from Genoa attempted to find a sea route around Africa but were never heard of again. Mythical stories of the mighty kingdom of Prester John, a knight who went to the Crusades but continued east, kept alive a vision of Christian kingdoms in the east of unbelievable luxury and wealth.

While much of Europe was torn by internecine warfare throughout the fourteenth century, Portugal was a united kingdom and largely untouched by civil disturbance. In 1385 King John I (known as John the Great or John the Bastard depending on one's view of history) seized the Portuguese throne and founded the Aviz dynasty. He was able to defeat the King of Castile, primarily with the aid of English archers. To cement his ties with the English throne, and to help secure his country's independence from Spain, he married Phillippa of Lancaster, the daughter of John of

Gaunt. She bore him six sons, the third of whom was to become known as Henry the Navigator. Henry was to make possible the global expansion of European maritime power and trade.

Like other European princes, Henry and his brothers were expected to prove their manhood by participating in the Crusades and "washing their hands in the blood of the infidel." Henry's father assigned him the task of building an armada at Oporto to invade the Muslim stronghold of Ceuta, opposite Gibraltar on the north African side of the Mediterranean. In 1415 the armada took Ceuta and, apart from the satisfaction of massacring infidels, the loot, consisting of pepper, cloves and other spices from the Far East along with other Asian riches, obviously impressed Henry. He returned to Portugal and established at Sagres, Portugal's most southerly promontory, a court devoted to maritime exploration. At the nearby port of Lagos, Henry began to experiment in shipbuilding. He adopted the design of the Arab dhows that plied the Mediterranean and Indian Oceans and whose lateen sails gave them superb maneuverability. The name of these boats was *caravos* in Arabic and they became known as caravels. They were about 70 feet long, 25 feet in the beam and displaced about 50 tons. These small boats, with crews of around 20 sailors, were equipped with Arab charts and the Chinese compass. Henry was to establish one of the most extensive libraries of charts and maps in Europe. His brother, on a tour to Venice, even acquired charts and an account of Marco Polo's travels for Henry. With as much knowledge as was possessed by Europeans at this time, he sent his tiny fleets on missions to explore the southern African coast and perhaps even to discover the source of oriental trade and riches. When Vasco Da Gama finally succeeded in reaching India in 1498 he provided the Portuguese with direct access to the markets of the east. As a consequence, the Portuguese forced down the taxes levied by the Egyptian, Turks and Italian middlemen to one eightieth of their former level.

Biblioteca Nacional, Lisbon

Henry the Navigator, son of the King of Portugal who, in the early fifteenth century, financed a revolution in boat design incorporating Arab and Chinese techniques, which ultimately enabled the European merchants to find a direct sea route to the east.

ZHENG HE AND THE LAST OF THE TREASURE SHIPS

The ships, which sail the southern seas and south of it, are like houses. When their sails are spread they are like great clouds in the sky. Their rudders are several tens of feet long. A single ship carries several hundred men and has in the stores a year's supply of grain. Pigs are fed and grain fermented on board. There is no account of dead or living, no going back to the mainland when once the people have set forth upon the caerulean sea.

Zhou Chufei, 1178

Among the inhabitants of China there are those who own numerous ships, on which they send their agents to foreign places. For nowhere in the world are there to be found people richer than the Chinese.

Ibn Batuta, 1347

Had Vasco da Gama arrived in the Indian Ocean just 70 years earlier he might well have met the vast Chinese fleet of the Three Jeweled Eunuch, Admiral Zheng He, whose huge treasure ships were five times the size of the Portuguese caravels. Between 1405 and 1430 this great admiral led seven armadas each consisting of as many as 62 ships and carrying around 40,000 soldiers. His journeys of discovery and diplomacy had taken him along the east coast of Africa, to Mecca (he was, in fact, a Muslim) and to the ports of India, Ceylon and Sumatra. He may well have explored the coast of Australia, but most of the accounts of his voyages and his charts were lost or destroyed.

The Ming emperor who approved his journeys was continuing the policy of maritime expansion begun by the Song dynasty and continued by the Yuan (Mongol) dynasty. The Mongol emperors had engaged in an extensive policy of shipbuilding in preparation for the invasion of Japan and Southeast Asia. For his abortive invasion of Japan in 1281 the Great Khan had 4,400 junks constructed. Equally impressive fleets were used in the invasion of Tonking and Champa (Vietnam) in 1283–88 and of Java in 1293. When the Mongol dynasty fell, to be replaced by the Ming, there was an initial continuation of the policy of supporting maritime exploration.

There were two significant aspects of Zheng He's voyages for the Ming government: they were to represent the emperor of the Middle Kingdom to the tributary states of Southeast Asia in order to bring previously unknown kingdoms into the appropriate relationship to the source of all civilization and they were to collect tributes of pepper, sapanwood, and exotic plants and animals in exchange for gifts of silk and porcelain. Zheng He even brought back a giraffe from Africa, as well as several disrespectful monarchs, notably the King of Ceylon.

Then, suddenly, in 1433 the Ming emperor banned Chinese merchants from going abroad. The great treasure ships of Zheng He's fleet, the largest seagoing vessels in

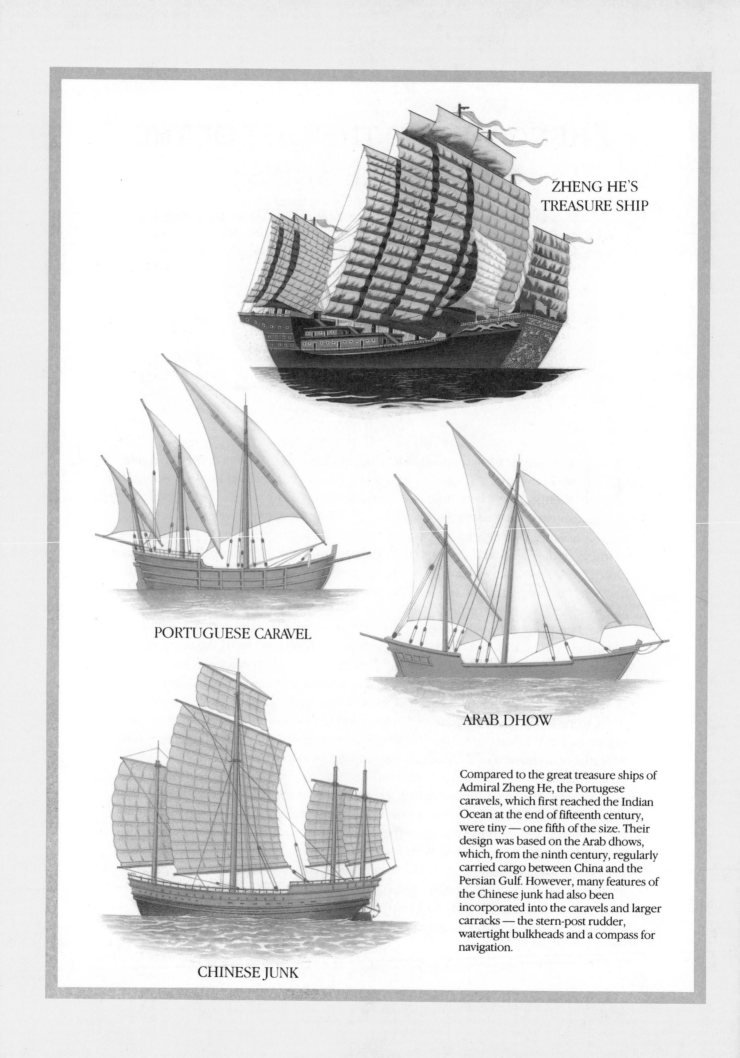

ZHENG HE'S
TREASURE SHIP

PORTUGUESE CARAVEL

ARAB DHOW

CHINESE JUNK

Compared to the great treasure ships of
Admiral Zheng He, the Portugese
caravels, which first reached the Indian
Ocean at the end of fifteenth century,
were tiny — one fifth of the size. Their
design was based on the Arab dhows,
which, from the ninth century, regularly
carried cargo between China and the
Persian Gulf. However, many features of
the Chinese junk had also been
incorporated into the caravels and larger
carracks — the stern-post rudder,
watertight bulkheads and a compass for
navigation.

the world at that time, were simply put out of commission. By 1550 a Ming scholar commented that knowledge of how to build these boats had been completely lost. The Ming navy shrunk into insignificance and China withdrew from the world. It is extraordinary that this should happen at the very time when on the other side of the Eurasian continent, Europeans were just beginning a period of massive overseas expansion and colonization that was to change the world fundamentally. There were in fact good economic reasons for the Ming withdrawal from foreign trade.

As a result of the earlier Song policy of encouraging shipbuilding and overseas trade, Chinese merchant fleets had, by the eleventh century, begun to displace the Arabs in the shipping of goods between Southeast Asia, the Middle East and China. Chinese merchant colonies had also grown up throughout Southeast Asia in the wake of this trade. However, the pepper and sapanwood brought back by Zheng He were an imperial monopoly and no one but the Chinese government could trade in them. Because of its traditionally high value, Ming emperors from 1407 began to use pepper and sapanwood to pay their troops and civil servants. Their monetary value was artificially held 10 times above the actual market value and was considered a better means of payment than paper money, which suffered the constant problem of hyperinflation. By 1424 there were such massive stores of pepper and sapanwood in the imperial warehouses that when the Emperor Renzong ascended the throne, residents and low-ranking officials were given them as part of the celebrations:

> To each banner bearer, horse keeper, soldier and guardsman one catty [1.33 pounds] of pepper and two catties of sapanwood; to each first-degree literary graduate and licentiate, district police chief, prison warder, astronomer and physician, one catty of pepper and two catties of sapanwood; to each resident of the city and the environs of Beijing, each Buddhist priest or Taoist priest, artisan, musician, professional cook, yamen [government ministry] runner and yamen cook, one catty of pepper and one catty of sapanwood.

However, despite the use to which these trade commodities were to be put in the early stages of the Ming dynasty, the economic realities were that revenue from foreign trade as a proportion of total government income had dropped from 20 per cent during the Southern Song to 0.77 per cent in the Ming, due simply to the fact that the area of land now controlled by the Ming was, with reunification, vastly increased. The cost–benefit of maintaining a large navy was losing its economic rationale. The need to protect the grain shipments from the south to the northern capital of Beijing and the armies on the northwestern frontier meant that the early Ming emperors had to maintain the strong navy, which in the 1400s consisted of a fleet of about 6,450 vessels. Of these, 2,300 ships were used as a coastal defense fleet to protect this transport and other merchant shipping from Japanese pirates; the largest of these ships could carry 500 men, cannon and other arms. It was without doubt the most powerful navy in the world. However, with the reopening and expansion of the Grand Canal in 1411 and the abolition of the use of sea transport to ship essential supplies to the north in 1415, the need for this extensive navy was far less obvious.

There was also the fact that the real threats to China were, as they had always been, from the north and west. It was the need to strengthen the armies on these borders and to maintain the security of the empire that obsessed the Ming government. No force, at that time at least, could conceivably have threatened China from the sea. The only threat would come from the Steppes of central Asia and Manchuria. With the Ming, relative peace and harmony were to return to the empire. There was even a movement of population back to areas in the north and west.

The Ming emperors were also of a very different temper and type from the cosmopolitan and highly cultured rulers of the Song dynasty. The first Ming emperor had been a peasant turned bandit who had been able to gather enough support to seize control of the empire. The Ming were from the heartlands of rural China and, after almost two centuries of foreign Mongol rule, a mood of xenophobia seemed to overcome both the court and the scholars who served it.

Obviously the reduced economic importance of foreign trade did not justify

A giraffe from Africa, one of the gifts for the Ming emperor brought back to China by the Three Jeweled Eunuch, Admiral Zheng He, from one of his great voyages of discovery and diplomacy.

continued state support. The Ming Emperor Gaozong summed up the issue in the following terms: "China's territory produces all goods in abundance, so why should we buy useless trifles from abroad?"

In 1433, and again in 1449 and 1452, imperial edicts banning overseas trade and travel, with savage penalties, were issued. Any merchant caught attempting to engage in foreign trade was defined as a pirate and executed. For a time even learning a foreign language was prohibited as was the teaching of Chinese to foreigners.

On the one hand, this policy was designed to eliminate piracy, which had increased along the southern Chinese coast, but it was also designed to control and tax merchant trade more effectively. Sea transport was regarded by many officials as a means of avoiding levies. A Ming account of the process of taxation gives some idea of the constraints on merchants who often complained that the taxes they were forced to pay were greater than the value of the goods themselves, for each province and each market town levied its own duties:

> All goods, whether personal or professional, whether traded or used, were always taxed . . . in a few square miles there will be at least three official posts, which will levy duties on all merchandise. All along the canals the goods will be taxed every time a boundary is passed, that is, every few dozen miles or even few miles and when one reaches the market itself the official flag will immediately be hoisted and duties levied for opening the hold, for boarding the ship and for bringing up the cargo. If goods are transported overland the duties are just as bad.

Transport by sea avoided all these levies, and costs were therefore around 70–80 percent lower than land or canal transport. The effect of the Ming ban on overseas trade was devastating for merchants and the prosperous cities along the southern coastal provinces. It is little wonder that so many turned to piracy to survive. Compared with the situation in Europe where piracy was an equally serious problem a century later the Ming emperors seemed quite uncompromising. It should not be forgotten that between 1573 and 1580, Francis Drake captured treasure from Portuguese and Spanish vessels worth £1.5 million. Elizabeth I, instead of prosecuting Drake, attended a banquet on his ship, knighted him and took a share of his booty, which was used to pay off foreign debt. The rest was invested and formed the capital with which the East India Company was eventually formed. In Europe, piracy came to be regarded as a legitimate state enterprise. In China, even when European pirates joined the Japanese in the seventeenth century, the Ming and later dynasties did little to protect their merchants even after earlier prohibitions on overseas trade were lifted. In order to deny Ming loyalists and pirates supplies and support along the Chinese coast, Qing dynasty officials in the seventeenth century actually cleared a strip of land — 700 miles long and up to 30 miles wide — along the southern coast by moving the population and burning villages.

So completely had the Ming turned from the sea that not only the art of building the massive treasure ships was completely lost but even the constant motif of the sea disappeared from Ming porcelain as if by imperial decree. The oceans and all they meant were to be excluded from Chinese consciousness. What was lost with it was

Courtesy Film Australia

A Song dynasty lighthouse, which guided the great twelfth century Chinese and Arab trading fleets into the port of Quanzhou on the coast of Fujian. Past this lighthouse came Marco Polo, and Zheng He on one of his many voyages. It stands as a legacy to the course China might have taken had the Ming emperors not turned from the sea, repressed the merchants and abandoned the policy of maritime expansion being pursued by European nation states.

the essential stimulus that comes from trade and contact with the rest of the world: the stimulus of new ideas and discoveries, which were to play such an important role in the later development of Europe. Had China become fragmented into small kingdoms, as seemed possible during the Southern Song, then the subsequent history of east Asia may well have been more like that of capitalist Europe. However, the enormous size of the Ming and later Qing empires and the primacy of maintaining social control meant that the traditional Confucian values were never seriously challenged. Merchants and artisans wielded too little economic power compared with the traditional rural gentry, whose priority was, as it had always been, the maintenance of traditional agricultural practices, which, after all, remained the most productive in the world well into the twentieth century. Without economic and political change, there was little opportunity for the promotion of new social institutions to take advantage of Chinese inventive genius.

There had been significant technological inventions and industrial innovations, for example, the mechanical spinning of hemp, the Su Song clock, and the discovery and use of natural gas and oil, but there was no great advantage in displacing the cheap rural labor that already adequately supplied local demand. In manufacturing, labor-saving machines would only have made sense if there was a sudden and massive expansion of markets to justify the introduction of new systems of production. Without the option of wide-scale international trade providing such a demand, the stimulus for social and economic change in Ming China was limited.

This is not to suggest that the social harmony, stability and peace maintained by the Ming government were not desirable or wise choices. However, in the conservatism of Ming policies lay a vulnerability, a potential Malthusian trap of an ever-increasing rural population struggling to live on a finite area of land whose productivity was almost as high as it could be without modern scientific and technological input. This weakness was to become acutely apparent as western maritime fleets and colonial empires shrank the world and confronted China in the nineteenth century with the terrible irony of seeing military technology they had first developed centuries earlier returning to haunt them with gunpowder-based weapons, transformed and refined in the aggressive and highly competitve environment of the European nation states.

Although most European monarchs would have loved to have the level of social control possessed by the Ming emperors, they had no choice but to risk the social disorder caused by the rising power of merchants for the sake of the wealth that it generated. This wealth was essential for the viability of the nation-state. In Europe there was no alternative but to make merchants respectable by allowing them entry into the establishment. In so doing, money and the values of the market place were allowed to change the nations' economic, cultural and intellectual institutions. The price the European monarch had to pay for this was increased social mobility, greater individual freedom and the loss of social control. But for the Ming dynasty the price of harmony was the absence of this new social dynamic. Foreign contact, the only stimulus that might have provided change had been cut off and China's economic and cultural institutions were to remain, refined and perfected but, ultimately, out of step with what was taking place on the other side of the globe. For, as China closed its gate on the world, European nations began to build a new and very different road to Xanadu.

In the late sixteenth century, Jesuit missionaries on board Portuguese merchant fleets arrived in Japan.
The merchants went for profits; the Jesuits wanted souls.

THE INVENTION OF PROGRESS

THE TRANSMISSION OF KNOWLEDGE

Those who labor with their mind rule while those who labor with their physical strength are ruled by others.

Mengzi (Mencius)

We should note the force, effect and consequences of inventions which are nowhere more conspicuous than in those which were unknown to the ancients, namely, printing, gunpowder and the compass. For these three have changed the appearance and state of the whole world.

Francis Bacon, *Novum Organum,* Aphorism 129, 1620

Many of the ancient universities of Europe bear a remarkable similarity to the Islamic Madrassas or schools of the Middle East. In the ancient centers of Islamic civilization — Bagdad, Damascus, Cairo and Istanbul — beside each mosque there is a large rectangular building with an open courtyard in the center, which has broad walkways of arched columns providing shelter from the intense heat. In the tenth century one would have found, in various positions around the courtyard, teachers who specialized in different fields of study gathered with their students in small groups. Some would be teaching Greek logic, others geometry, astronomy, physics, metaphysics, grammar, law and of course the Koran. The teaching method these students were being exposed to was that of the seminar or *halqa,* where ideas were discussed and debated.

In the late Middle Ages the Madrassas were the crucial junction points in the transmission of knowledge from the ancient world of Greece and China to the west. Here the works of classical Greek mathematicians, physicians and scholars were studied. Books saved from the famous library of Alexandria, which was destroyed with the collapse of the Roman empire, included Euclid's geometry, Pythagoras' mathematics, Galen's medical theories and, perhaps most important of all, Aristotelian logic. Here too, Chinese ideas on medicine, alchemy and astronomy mingled with the cosmology and poetry of the Islamic mystics Attar, Rumi and Al Ghazali.

In the Dark Ages, which overwhelmed Western Europe with the fall of Rome in the fifth century, the cultivation of learning and inquiry became centered in the Madrassas and the libraries of the Arab world. When Pope Urban II ordered the first Crusade to the Holy Land in 1095 he could not have known that, in the retaking of Jerusalem in 1099, his pure Christian knights would be contaminated with ideas and tastes that, in the long term, were to help undermine the power and credibility of the Catholic church, the very institution he was concerned to strengthen and preserve. New tastes for refined food, clothing, and the music and ideas of the east were brought back to Europe with the completion of each campaign. The Holy Roman

This painting by Gentile Bellini shows the official reception for the Venetian ambassador to Cairo in 1512. The Arab world was not only the conduit for exotic commodities and technology from the east, it was also a source of classicial Greek learning, which until the fifteenth century was inaccessible to all but a handful of European scholars.

Emperor Frederick II, for example, returned with an entire band of Arab musicians, who not only changed the character of western music, but introduced new instruments such as the lute (from the Arabic *l'oud*) as well as a whole family of reed and stringed instruments.

These are perhaps trivial examples, but they reflect a characteristic of European culture as it began to emerge from the Dark Ages. By the end of the fourteenth century almost all the classical Greek and Arab books on science and medicine had been translated into Latin. There was an enormous appetite for novelty and a willingness to adopt the technology and cultural institutions from the east that could qualitatively improve the basic conditions of life. Of the latter, perhaps one of the most significant was the transformation of cathedral schools into universities along the lines of the Islamic Madrassa. In this the Italian city-states, those "republics of merchants," were to lead the way.

The Madrassa, which formed the model for the University, was not an isolated community like a Christian monastery, but aimed to provide a broad religious education to the community at large. It was usually funded through a property trust or *wakf* set up by wealthy merchants, very much like the system of endowments that continues to support the ancient English universities such as Oxford and Cambridge.

The style of education carried out in the Madrassa, also adopted in European universities, gave primary emphasis to argument and debate. In contrast to China at this time, printed books were not available in the west, and those made of vellum were costly and were locked away in monastic and university libraries. Written examinations such as those common in China were technically impossible until the advent of papermaking in the thirteenth century.

Perhaps the greatest influence on European intellectual life, which came with the establishment of universities, was the discovery of Greek philosophy and science, particularly that of Aristotle and Plato. The impact of these new ideas was as much a revelation to the scholars of medieval Europe, as was the impact of western science on China and Japan in the eighteenth and nineteenth centuries. At first the Church

The Ambassadors (1533) by Hans Holbein the Younger. These Renaissance men are surrounded by the mathematical instruments that gave them not only new insights into nature but also the navigational skills and military power to expand the known world far beyond Europe to the Americas and to the Celestial Empire.

attempted to repress this influence. In 1210 the ecclesiastical authorities in Paris condemned Aristotle's ideas and particularly his scientific works. To teach them either publicly or privately would lead to excommunication. However, the ban was lifted in 1234 and Dominican scholars, such as Albertus Magnus, began to write outlines of Aristotle's essential ideas, spelling out where they contradicted Church dogma. This provided an added stimulus to debate and to a concern with the refinement of the tools of argument, logic and investigation. So keen were medieval universities on the principles of dialectical thinking that students were often divided into positive and negative groups to discuss specific topics. Students were also expected to pass an oral exam that required them to put forward propositions and to argue for and against them.

These European universities were not just teaching institutions. By the early years of the Renaissance they had become the new centers of intellectual life. At the University of Paris, in the fourteenth century, it was commonplace for such heretical notions as that the earth turned on its own axis to be debated with senior scholars taking opposing views. This encouraged a tradition of critical thought and helped to reinforce the tradition of debate as a means of reaching the truth, which was to be introduced later into other European political and legal institutions.

At its worst, this emphasis on argument ended in a shallow scholasticism with debates about how many angels could fit on the head of a pin. However, an appeal to the real world, to nature and natural law soon began to emerge as the ultimate arbiter of truth. Even Christian theology was to be drawn out of the sanctity and mystery of the Church and monastery, and submitted to the rigors of Aristotelian logic.

It was St Thomas Aquinas, a fellow Dominican and student of Albertus Magnus, who first championed this cause, though perhaps not its consequences. Aquinas, like other intellectuals within the Church, was concerned to reconcile the writings of Aristotle with that of Christian dogma, which was based on faith rather than reason. He argued that Christian teachings should be subject to logical reasoning. This in reality opened a theological "can of worms." The more traditional Church fathers, nurtured in the Augustinian tradition of faith and revelation, were horrified. However, the new passion for logic and "the light of reason" was to be applied not only to theological issues, but to the analysis of the underlying principles governing God's creation — in many cases simply to try to justify the Bible and disprove Aristotle's scientific and social theories.

As Christian scholars increasingly accepted Greek mathematics and logic as a road to ultimate truth, revelation and faith, the traditional foundations of their religion came to play a secondary role. As a consequence, metaphysics, the spiritual dimension of Christianity, was kept securely within the confines of the monastery and the Church, while philosophers were now concerned, not with trying to find God's "hidden hand" in biblical texts, but in his creation and in laws governing the natural world. In this search for an understanding of God in the mathematical principles that governed the universe lay the seeds of the scientific revolution of the seventeenth century.

In China, by contrast, education consisted primarily of learning by rote a vast body of classical literature. This became standardized in the seventh century with the establishment of the imperial examination system, which fostered the establishment of a class of scholar-officials who were important for the collection and dissemination of knowledge. Primarily this examination system encouraged an intellectual tradition in which memorization and documentation rather than disputation and debate were encouraged. After all, the object of the system was the creation of bureaucratic generalists familiar with an accepted ethical outlook and body of knowledge, not with the growth of knowledge or with academic specialization. As the Japanese historian Shigeru Nakayama notes:

> The explicit purpose of the system lay neither in education nor in the promotion of learning but in choosing a limited number of men for official posts from among a large pool of candidates seeking to improve their lot in the world by rising through the ranks of public service . . .
>
> . . . The founding of schools and the creation of an education system does not necessarily lead to the growth of learning. As an institution, the school incorporates and maintains knowledge that has been developed from a given paradigm. A vessel that shields the lamps of learning from the winds of external pressure, it also serves to check and control explosive internal developments.

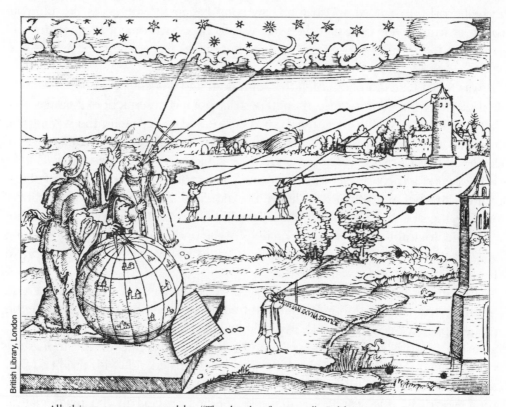

British Library, London

All things were measurable. "The book of nature," Galileo wrote, "cannot be understood unless one first learns to comprehend the language and read the letters in which it is composed. It is written in the language of mathematics."

In China it was assumed that "those who worked with their heads rule, those with their hands serve." The Confucian scholar who dominated intellectual life in China had little involvement in experiment or practical investigations. Because so much emphasis was placed on memory and documentation there was significantly less attention given to logical reasoning than in the west. Take, for example, the common use of circular arguments exemplified by this passage from *Great Learning,* one of the principle works to be studied and memorized:

> The ancients who wished to be illustriously virtuous throughout the kingdom, first ordered well their own states. Wishing to order well their states, they first regulated their families. Wishing to regulate their families, they first cultivated their persons. Wishing to cultivate their persons, they first sought to rectify their hearts. Wishing to rectify their hearts, they first sought to be sincere in their thoughts. Wishing to be sincere in their thoughts, they first extended to the utmost their knowledge. Such extension of knowledge lay in the investigation of things.
>
> Things being investigated, knowledge became complete. Their knowledge being complete, their thoughts were sincere. Their thoughts being sincere, their hearts were then rectified. Their hearts being rectified, their persons were cultivated. Their persons being cultivated, their families were regulated. Their families being regulated, their states were rightly governed. Their states being rightly governed, the whole kingdom was made tranquil and happy. From the Son of Heaven down to the mass of the people, all must consider the cultivation of the person the root of everything besides.

TIME

Two developments in particular — the clock and perspective drawing — embodied the new emphasis on rationality and quantification, which began in Europe with the Renaissance of classical learning in the fourteenth century.

The first mechanical clocks in Europe were a response to the concern of monastic religious orders to regulate the time of prayer both day and night. The Christian monastic communities of the Middle Ages lived in the expectation of the second coming of Christ, which in principle could occur at any time, day or night. Their responsibility was to be spiritually prepared for this event.

There were no fixed times for prayer in the early Christian Church, as there were in both Judaism and Islam. Only with the establishment of the monasteries were strict times for religious observances established. In these communities they took seriously the gospel parable of the bridegroom coming at midnight (Matt. 25:6) and the admonition "Watch therefore: for ye know not what hour your Lord doth come" (Matt. 24:42). After all, with the second coming, as predicted in the Bible, the world would end and only those spiritually prepared would be among the elect. The rest of benighted humanity would be condemned to damnation. Time was of the essence. One's spiritual duty was to rise above the demands of one's body and to feed one's immortal soul through prayer and meditation. The body was of this world — the world of death, corruption and destruction. The soul was nurtured by God's grace, in return for unflinching devotion and preparation for his Son's final coming.

Time in the Christian world was, therefore, unquestionably linear, moving from the creation to the second coming. As the millennium (the year 1000) approached, time was seen to be running out for mankind. Attention to the things of this world was a false and mistaken investment of one's time. In the ninth century the Cluny and Benedictine monasteries adopted a relay of almost continual prayer, while monks engaged in many extraordinary forms of ascetic behavior to induce grace and hallucinations.

This, of course, was in marked contrast to time as experienced by the peasantry, who made up the bulk of the population. Most of them, although nominally Christian, had a way of life that was governed by the cycles of nature and the more animistic religious values of pre-Christian times. They were, for the most part, outside the world of monastic religious communities and did not share their sense of cosmological urgency. Like their Chinese counterparts, the peasants' primary concerns were with survival and this meant working closely with the cycles of nature. Work and leisure were governed by the demands of the land, not religion. They could not afford the luxury of such unworldly asceticism.

The mechanical clock, when it was first developed, offered to the monks the security of being able to keep up their grueling observance throughout the night. It was also to provide a new concept of time — time that was abstract, broken up into mathematically precise units and independent of nature. This was God's time.

Bibliotheque Nationale, Paris

Solomon and a Clock from a fifteenth century Flemish manuscript. The time measured by the first mechanical clocks set up in the churches and monasteries of late medieval Europe was God's time; for, like the deity, its mathematical precision transcended the crude cycles of nature.

COSMOLOGY AND THE CLOCK

Prior to the advent of the clock, time was measured by reference to the familiar cycles of nature and the patterns of work required throughout the agricultural year. Time was approximate and relative — the cycles of the planets and the seasons provided the only manifestation of regularity. Estimates of how long something would take were measured in terms of events familiar to everyone; so there were "paternostra whiles" (the time it took for the paternostra to be recited in church) as well as the more prosaic "pissing whiles." However, with the advent of the clock, time became a mathematically precise entity. For astronomers, using the new geometry of Euclid and the mechanical clock, it was possible to measure both time and space with new precision. It was also possible to understand the actual motion of the planets, which Copernicus, by the fifteenth century, was forced to conclude did not behave in the way that Ptolemy, Aristotle or the Church authorities claimed. The earth went around the sun, and it could be proven by observation, logic and mathematics.

The first European clocks were either sundials or water clocks like those of the Chinese. However, as the metalworking and mechanical skills of European craftsmen developed in the early fourteenth century, the first mechanical clocks began to appear in monasteries and on church spires, to control the ringing of bells. The mechanical clock in Europe may have been invented, Joseph Needham argues, as a result of hearing accounts of the famous Su Song clock in China, but the early devices produced in Europe bore little relation to the Chinese clocks. The escapement mechanism, often described as the "soul" of the clock, was developed in the west quite independently.

The first clocks, situated in belfries, simply rang bells on the hour. Later, a clock face was added. Within a remarkably short time other mechanical devices were included showing astronomical phenomena such as the cycles of the moon and the planets. The clock then passed from the monastery to the towns, and its use grew rapidly with the expansion of trade in the fourteenth and fifteenth centuries. Among the Protestants of northern Europe, who had adopted many of the religious values of the monasteries and brought them into the everyday life of the towns, the clock was used to reinforce the virtues of work and time discipline.

The skilled clock and instrument makers were to form a new class of craftsmen. They combined engineering and metallurgical skills with the mathematical precision promoted by the new sciences.

The millennium came and went without the apocalypse or Christ's reappearance. Living conditions in the world outside the monastery walls began to improve. With increasing political stability populations grew, and increased production from agriculture was encouraged by new farming techniques developed in and disseminated through Cistercian monasteries. However, it was in the growing towns and, particularly, the centers of textile manufacture that mechanical clocks took on their now familiar role. As the workforce in the towns was employed for wages, the length of hours worked, the starting times and finishing times needed to be set by something more reliable than natural light, which varied according to season. No longer were the masters' claims taken on face value. Soon clocks began to appear, not only on cathedral spires, but in specially constructed clocktowers on large public buildings, such as town halls.

The Protestant Reformation of the sixteenth century, which in England led to the dissolution of the monasteries, resulted not in a decline in religious discipline but in its extension into the wider community. The humanistic ideas fostered during the Italian Renaissance shifted the cultural emphasis from a concern with the end of the world to the possibility of improving this one, if only to make it more acceptable for a second coming. This required discipline and the clock was necessary to regulate not only prayer, but also work. Among the merchants and independent artisan-manufacturers of the new towns — the bourgs from which the word bourgeoisie is derived — time mattered. In a money economy the familiar nexus between cost and time determined profit or loss. For the Calvinists, God's grace was manifested by his providence. To the honest, hardworking and pious would come wealth and

With perspective, not only could an accurate representation of an object be made, but by using the technique of chiaroscuro or shadowing it was also possible to represent a three-dimensional image.

A wire grid allowed artists to represent an object in space from the perspective of the viewer. It also allowed the object to be represented in precise mathematical detail.

prosperity. Among the new middle class of the towns, wealth was not to be disposed of in the form of conspicuous consumption but to be husbanded, saved and invested. Like God's time it could be saved, wasted or lost. Time like money was also always "running out." Time *was* money and both were now essential elements in the growth of international trade.

SPACE

Perspective drawing was pioneered by the Italian artist Brunelleschi in 1425. An attempt to explain its use was put forward by Leone Battista Alberti in his book *Della Pittura* in 1435. In the spirit of Aquinas, Alberti stated the principle that the most basic requirement for the painter was an understanding of geometry. Like other humanist scholars of the Renaissance, Alberti believed that nature could best be understood through mathematics; behind all phenomena there were structures with precise mathematical dimensions. Just as Aristotelian logic became the tool for exploring and expressing philosophical and theological ideas, so too was mathematics the tool by which the natural world could be understood. Given that these were aspects of the human mind, God must have created them for a reason: to know him and his creation better. Man, made in God's image, was the point from which the world was to be viewed and measured. The cosmological and mystical perspective that underpinned earlier art gave way eventually to the centrality of the individual viewer.

In the introduction to the *Trattato della Pittura,* Leonardo da Vinci writes "let no one who is not a mathematician read my works." For him painting was a science, a means of exploring the nature of the world:

> . . . for no human inquiry can be called science unless it pursues its path through mathematical exposition and demonstration. . . . The man who discredits the supreme certainty of mathematics is feeding on confusion, and can never silence the contradictions of sophistical sciences, which lead to eternal quackery.

What perspective offered was not only the capacity to see objects in relation to the field of vision of the artist himself, but it also allowed objects to be represented in precise mathematical detail.

We are probably most familiar with the revolution of perspective drawing in terms of its impact on the arts where, along with the rationalistic spirit initiated by Aquinas, it led to a tradition of didactic painting and illustration. However, the attempt to reproduce on paper the precise proportions of an object in three-dimensional form was to become equally important in the growth of technological drawing and the spread of technical books, for example, Vesalius's *Fabric of the Human Body* which for the first time showed the actual structure of the organs of the human body in realistic and accurate proportions. The use of woodblock and copperplate engravings printed on paper was to have a profound effect on education, especially after the development of movable-type printing by Gutenberg (c.1437) made books cheaper and available outside the confines of the monastery and university libraries:

A man born in 1453, the year of the fall of Constantinople, could look back from his fiftieth year on a lifetime in which about eight million books had been printed, more perhaps than all the scribes of Europe had produced since Constantine founded his city in 330.

As can be seen from the technical drawings of Leonardo da Vinci, the representation of objects and technological processes, from the anatomy of the

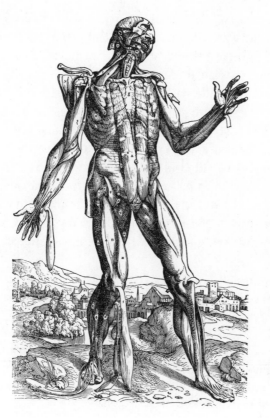

An illustration from Vesalius's *Fabric of the Human Body* published in 1543. This illustrated book was to apply the new perspective-drawing techniques to provide precise images of the "architecture" of the human body. It was to form the model for educational books, which applied these same techniques to mechanical drawing.

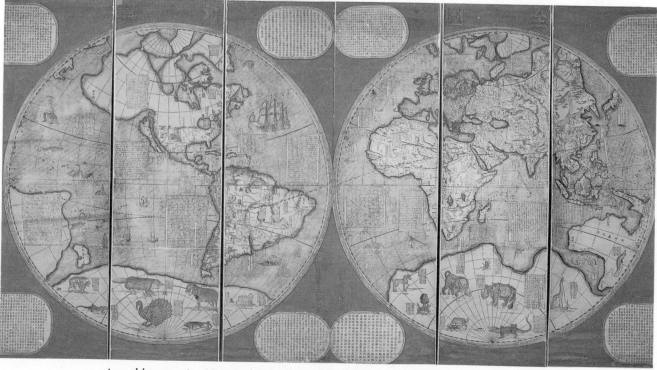

A world map, using Mercator's projection, drawn for the Chinese by the Jesuit missionary
Ferdinand Verbiest in 1674.

human body to the trajectory of a cannon ball could be analyzed and understood in precise geometrical terms. This facility applied not only to the small and domestic but to the depiction of the globe and earth's place in the cosmos. For the perspective screen held before the nude by Dürer is, in its function, little different to the latitude and longitude screen that cartographers began to hold over the image of the earth itself. Gerardus Mercator (1512–94), a Flemish cartographer, was the first to devise a map of the globe that took into account the problem of its spherical shape and came up with Mercator's projection, a technique for dividing the earth into precise measures of time and space without distorting the perspective by reducing it to a two-dimensional image. For the powerful merchant-adventurers of Portugal, Spain and Holland whose livelihood depended on such navigational aids, this was the perspective that really counted.

In the Ming court, on the other side of Eurasia, the image of the world was still governed by a geopolitical fantasy that placed the Middle Kingdom in the center of a flat earth with peripheral states decreasing in importance and levels of cultural development as they radiated out from the imperial capital, the epicenter of the universe and of human civilization.

THE JESUITS AND THE EMPEROR

Coming into contact with barbarian peoples you have nothing more to fear than touching the left horn of a snail. The only things one should be anxious about are the means of mastery of the waves of the sea and, worst of all dangers, the minds of those avid for profit and greedy for gain.

From a Qing dynasty treatise on navigation

It was a star that long ago led the Three Kings to adore the true God. In the same way the science of the stars will lead the rulers of the Orient, little by little, to know and to adore their Lord.

Jesuit Missionary Ferdinand Verbiest, Beijing, 1674

The response of the Church to the great voyages of discovery initiated by Henry the Navigator of Portugal, was to send forth missionaries to convert the poor benighted heathens discovered in the "new worlds" of the Americas and the east to Christianity. While merchant-adventurers attempted to capture the economic resources of east Asia on behalf of mammon, new religious orders such as the Society of Jesus, founded by St Ignatius of Loyola in 1540, took it upon themselves to capture souls for Christ and the Catholic church: "to garner into the granaries of the Catholic Church a rich harvest from this sowing of the gospel seed."

In 1488 the Portuguese Bartolomeu Dias had found the route to the Indian Ocean around the Cape of Good Hope. Four years later in 1492 the Spanish, trying to beat the Portuguese to the source of eastern wealth, sponsored Christopher Columbus to find a western route. The competition between Portugal and Spain had grown so intense that, by the end of the fifteenth century, Pope Alexander VI was forced to intervene with his famous Papal Bull of 1493. This remarkable document divided the world between Portugal and Spain, with Portugal taking Brazil and most of the east, and Spain taking most of the Americas and the Pacific, including the Philippines. The assumption that the world could be carved up in such a fashion reflected a Eurocentric arrogance, which was to reach its height later in the nineteenth century, when European nations did carve up the world.

With papal support, Vasco da Gama arrived in India in 1498, and set the scene for the first European maritime empire in Asia. In 1510 Alfonso de Albuquerque captured the Indian city of Goa, and a year later Malacca, thus giving Portugal control of the rich spice trade with Europe. In 1517 the king of Portugal had sent a mission with eight ships, and Tome Pires as ambassador, to China. After being joined by the mayor of Goa, Fernao de Andrade, the mission arrived at Guangzhou in September. From the start the Portuguese made a poor impression. The letting off of a thunderous salute of guns terrified the Chinese who were not accustomed to their tributary missions behaving with such a fundamental lack of decorum. However, the governor-general received them and allowed them to stay while Pires made his long journey to Beijing. Unfortunately, a year later Simao de Andrade, Fernao's brother, arrived and forcibly occupied the island of Tamao where he built a fort without the permission of the Chinese governor. Their behavior was so highhanded that the Chinese came to regard Europeans as little better than Japanese pirates, and proposed to expel them all. Pires was thrown into prison where he died, while the Portuguese fort of Tamao was besieged and taken by Chinese troops. Despite these unfortunate beginnings, the Chinese permitted the Portuguese merchants to establish a trading base at Macao, which, over time, was treated as a colonial territory by the Portuguese but in reality was leased in return for annual custom dues.

In 1564 while the Portuguese were establishing their trading base near Guangzhou, the Spanish from their base in Acapulco on the west coast of Mexico took the island of Luzon in the name of Philip II; it became known as the Philippines. From here they began to trade with Fujian. From the ports of Quanzhou (Zaitun), Fuzhou and Xiamen (Amoy), Spanish trade routes to the west opened up via the Philippines and Mexico, and began to challenge the dominance of Portugal.

*   *   *

In the wake of all this overseas expansion, the Church was not idle. The Jesuit order sent Francis Xavier to the east in 1541 to begin the great task of converting Asia to Christianity. He established his base at the Portuguese fort in Macao, and from here Xavier began his first assault on Japan. He met a young Japanese, Yajiro, who had killed a man and escaped on a Portuguese merchant ship that was moored in the

Francis Xavier as portrayed by Jesuit missionaries in Japan.

southern port of Kagoshima. The captain of the ship introduced him to Xavier in Malacca, and it was this meeting that persuaded the Jesuit to begin his mission in Japan. On 15 August 1549 Xavier arrived in Kagoshima with Yajiro as an interpreter.

He was impressed by what he found as he recorded in a letter back to the missionaries in Goa:

> The people whom we have met so far, are the best who have yet been discovered, and it seems to me that we shall never find amongst heathens another race to equal the Japanese. They are a people of very good manners, good in general and not malicious … There are many who can read and write, which is a great help to their learning quickly prayers and religious matters.

However, his fellow missionaries as they came to understand Japanese culture were to confront a society far stranger and more challenging than the one for which Xavier had prepared them. Alessandro Valignano, an Italian Jesuit, wrote in 1583:

> They also have rites and ceremonies so different from those of all the other nations that it seems they deliberately try to be unlike any other people. The things which they do in this respect are beyond imagining and it may be truly said that Japan is a world the reverse of Europe …

A Spanish Jesuit, Luis Frois, writing two years later in 1585 was equally perplexed by the cultural differences of these otherwise highly civilized people:

> Most people in Europe grow tall and have good figures; the Japanese are mostly smaller than we in body and stature.
> The women in Europe do not go out of the house without their husbands' permission; Japanese women are free to go wherever they please without the husband knowing about it.
> With us it is not very common that women can write; the noble ladies of Japan consider it a humiliation not to be able to write.
> In Europe the men are the tailors and in Japan the women.
> Our children first learn to read and then to write; Japanese children first begin to write and thereafter to read.
> We believe in future glory and punishment and in the immortality of the soul; the Zen bonzes deny all that and avow that there is nothing more than birth and death.

This first experience of the Far East for the Jesuits, transmitted through their letters to Europe, stimulated a growing sense of cultural relativity, an awareness of cultural differences that provided a new perspective from which to view their own social institutions — an awareness that was to reach its peak in the eighteenth century and form the basis of what were to become the social sciences.

Xavier, although entranced by the manners and cultivation of the Japanese, soon became aware that their cultural roots were to be found in China, and came to the conclusion that if he was to convert Asia to Christianity, then he would have to confront the Celestial Empire itself. He therefore left the Japanese mission in the hands of others and set out for China.

A Japanese view of the European missionaries and merchants who began to arrive at southern ports such as Kagoshima and Nagasaki in the mid-sixteenth century.

St Francis Xavier died before he could establish his mission in China. The task was to fall to a remarkable Italian Jesuit and scholar Matteo Ricci (1552–1610). Ricci, like most of the Jesuits in the Asian mission, was well educated in mathematics and the new sciences that were so much the focus of the humanistic movement then dominant in Europe. After spending four years studying and teaching at the Jesuit mission in Goa, Ricci was transferred in 1582 to the mission headquarters at Macao to take up the task left incomplete by Xavier. Along with a fellow Jesuit, Michele Ruggieri, he established a mission house in the town of Zhaoqing (Chao-ch'ing) west of Guangzhou. Here he spent seven years learning about Chinese culture and its language, with which he became thoroughly conversant. However, he was able to make little headway in his primary objective of wide-scale conversion. The townspeople were extremely suspicious and stoned the mission, believing that Ricci's presence would bring Portuguese pirates to sack the town. He made just as little headway with the local literati who regarded the religion of the Jesuits, in their long and simple monks' robes, as little better than Buddhism, a religion practiced by the poor and underprivileged and hence of extremely low status.

97

Bayerische Verwaltung der Staatlichen Schlösser, Gärten und Seen, Munich

This eighteenth century tapestry shows the Jesuits teaching the Chinese about western astronomy and science.

Staatsbibliothek Preussischer Kulturbesitz, Berlin (West)

Matteo Ricci, Adam Schall, and Ferdinand Verbiest, the three Jesuits who penetrated the Chinese imperial bureaucracy and attempted to convert the emperor to Christianity.

With these seven frustrating years behind him Ricci came to the conclusion that the only way to convert China was to start from the top, and that he would have to approach his task, not through the conversion of the "blessed poor and humble," but through the powerful scholar-official class whose power and influence spread out from the emperor in Beijing. In a masterly stroke Ricci abandoned his humble monk's robe, adopted the guise of a scholar and set off for Beijing for what he hoped would be an audience with the emperor. On approaching the imperial capital, in 1601, he and his companions were arrested and his possessions seized. They carried with them the marvels of European culture: clocks, maps and religious paintings using European perspective and illustrated books on mathematics and science — objects which in Guangzhou had impressed some officials with whom he had made contact. After six months in jail Ricci was released and his gifts delivered to Emperor Wanli. The emperor was so delighted by one of Ricci's remarkable chiming clocks, which "struck all Chinese dumb with astonishment," that officials were persuaded to allow Ricci the almost unprecedented favor (for a foreigner) of being allowed to remain in Beijing.

With his fluent Chinese and remarkable knowledge of the Confucian classics he made a considerable impact among some of the high-ranking scholars in the capital. But his object was to reach the emperor himself. This was no easy task. The emperors of China, by tradition, lived aloof from the world within the Forbidden City, surrounded by the imperial household of wives, concubines and eunuchs who, essentially, managed the imperial household. Audiences with the emperor were for ministers of government, high-ranking scholars and the heads of visiting tributary delegations. The prospects of this solitary Jesuit priest making his way through the labyrinthine hierarchy that surrounded the Son of Heaven, were slim. What finally got him to his goal were his clocks. When one of them stopped chiming, the emperor was so upset that he demanded that Ricci be called to the Forbidden City to repair it and to train four of his mathematicians to repair and maintain the clocks.

This was the first foot in the door, which was to lead to the Jesuits establishing a church and working their way into the structure of the imperial bureaucracy. Not since the time of Marco Polo, three centuries earlier, had any European come so close to the center of imperial power. What made this possible was Ricci's subtle intellect and his familiarity with mathematics and astronomy. For it was these skills that impressed the Chinese, not any interest in what they regarded as his somewhat absurd religious beliefs. As Ricci himself noted:

> These globes, clocks, spheres, astrolabes and so forth, which I have made and the use of which I teach, have gained for me the reputation of being the greatest mathematician in the world. I do not have a single book on astrology [astronomy], but with only the help of certain ephemerides and Portuguese almanacs I sometimes predict eclipses more accurately than they do.

Ricci was familiar enough with the imperial structure to know that what the emperor needed from him were more accurate systems, both for predicting astronomical events such as eclipses and for setting the imperial calendar. It was for this reason that he insisted that the missionaries sent to him from Rome should be well versed in astronomy, mathematics and the sciences. He was playing a difficult cat-and-mouse game. His object was clearly to win converts to Christianity, but he could not afford to alienate himself from the Confucian officials in the powerful ministries who could easily have him expelled if he was seen as a threat. As Ricci noted in his journals: "In order that the appearance of a new religion might not arouse suspicion amongst Chinese people, the Fathers did not speak openly about religious matters when they began to appear in public."

Instead, they attempted to impress upon the Chinese the superiority of European science and of the intellectual world view the Jesuits professed. Like the bait in a carefully constructed intellectual trap they hoped to capture Chinese souls with the very sciences that, ironically, back in Europe were beginning to threaten the very foundations of traditional Church dogma. It was a dangerous game, as Ricci recalled in his journals:

We must mention here another discovery which helped to win the good will of the Chinese. To them the heavens are round but the earth is flat and square, and they firmly believe that their empire is right in the middle of it. They do not like the idea of our geographers pushing their China into one corner of the Orient. They could not comprehend the demonstrations proving that the earth is a globe, made up of land and water, and that a globe of its nature has neither beginning nor end. The geographer was

PERE, Adam Schaal.

Adam Schall in the robes of a Chinese scholar-official. The insignia on the front of his gown indicates his status in the imperial bureaucracy. As director of the bureau of astronomy, he hoped to have more direct influence over the Confucian scholars who surrounded and advised the emperor.

State Library of New South Wales

100

therefore obliged to change his design and, by omitting the first meridian of the Fortunate Islands, he left a margin on either side of the map, making the kingdom of China to appear right in the center. This was more in keeping with their ideas and it gave them a great deal of pleasure and satisfaction. Really, at that time and in the particular circumstances, one could not have hit upon a discovery more appropriate for disposing this people for the reception of the faith. . . .

Because of their ignorance of the size of the earth and the exaggerated opinion they have of themselves, the Chinese are of the opinion that only China among the nations is deserving of admiration. Relative to the grandeur of empire, of public administration and of reputation for learning, they look upon all other people not only as barbarous but as unreasoning animals. To them there is no other place on earth that can boast of a king, of a dynasty, or of culture. The more their pride is inflated by this ignorance, the more humiliated they become when the truth is revealed.

The Jesuits in China were always on thin ice. Hostility towards them from officials in the department of astronomy led to many efforts to have them ousted. Six years after Ricci's death in 1610, Jesuit priests were arrested and their churches closed. Those that did not leave the country went into hiding. This did not, however, stop Johann Adam Schall von Bell.

Adam Schall was a young German Jesuit who, in 1611, met Father Nicholas Trigault who had worked with Ricci in Beijing. Trigault brought to Rome Ricci's journals, which were widely circulated and read. He was so impressed by Schall's enthusiasm and intelligence that in 1618, after finishing his studies, Schall was allowed to join the mission in Macao. It was Schall who was to fulfill one of Ricci's long-term objectives — to penetrate the bureaucratic hierarchy and thus gain direct access to the emperor. Schall was a capable mathematician and astronomer, familiar with the revolutionary astronomical ideas and methods of Kepler and Galileo. Accompanying Schall was a Swiss Jesuit, Father Johann Schreck, who had studied astronomy and mathematics under Galileo at the University of Padua and held a medical degree. The two Jesuits were not able to go to Beijing until 1623 when the ban on Jesuits was lifted. In the meantime they studied Chinese at the mission headquarters in Macao. Here the Jesuit fathers applied their practical knowledge to the casting of cannon, and even participated in the defense of Macao when it was invaded by the Dutch in 1622. The accuracy of the cannons fired from the Jesuit fort of St Paul, which hit the powder from a keg in the Dutch army ranks, turned the invasion into a rout. Three hundred Dutch soldiers were beheaded in honor of St John the Baptist. These were not the retiring ascetics of the ancient monastic tradition, these were men of Renaissance polymaths in every sense.

When Schall and Schreck finally arrived in Beijing they were to attack the Chinese bureaucracy at its weakest point: Chinese pride in the accuracy of their calendars, which Ricci had already observed. In 1623, and again in 1625, Schall was able to accurately predict the occurrence of an eclipse. In 1629 the first real breakthrough came when Xu Guangqi (Hsü Kuang-ch'i), one of Ricci's Christian converts, became vice-president of the board of rites, one of the top positions in the imperial bureaucracy. He was commissioned to head a new calendrical department and to staff it with men of his own choice. He chose, among others, two Jesuits Schreck and Longobardi and initiated western techniques. Schreck attempted to elicit the help of his old professor Galileo but in 1616 the Inquisition in Rome had forced Galileo to recant his belief in the heliocentric astronomy of Copernicus. He was therefore not inclined to provide his services to the Church's missionaries, much to the disappointment of the Jesuits in Beijing. Kepler, the other great astronomer of the time, however, provided help in the reform of the Chinese calendar.

In 1630 Schreck died suddenly, and Schall was called upon to take his place. This was the first step on a ladder that was to lead the Jesuits to the very heart of Chinese power. The Church could now claim several thousand converts, many from the imperial household itself. In April 1644 the Ming dynasty fell before the invading Manchus from the north. The last Ming emperor committed suicide in his palace. Realising that the new Manchu dynasty would have to be governed along the lines established by tradition, Schall petitioned the emperor concerning an eclipse expected the following September: "Your subject humbly begs from Your Highness a decree to the Board of Rites to test publicly the accuracy of the prediction of the solar eclipse at a proper time." The request was granted and Schall had the opportunity to prove, publicly, the superiority of western astronomy over what he knew to be the less precise techniques of the Chinese or Muslim astronomers who had previously dominated the bureau of astronomy. On the appointed day Schall's gamble paid off. He was right and the Chinese wrong. For his success Schall was now offered the directorship of the bureau and was thereby promoted to the fifth grade in the ninth

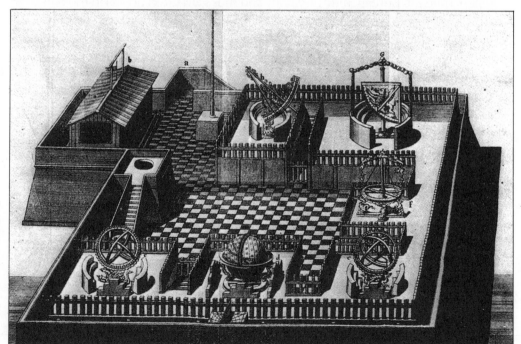

The observatory on the city wall in Beijing has been preserved as a museum with the instruments that were designed and cast by Verbiest for Emperor Kangxi.

tier of the upper echelons of the Chinese bureaucracy. Jesuit patience, persistence and scientific knowledge had, eventually, paid off.

Now in a powerful position within the bureaucracy, one might have expected the influence of the Jesuits to spread more widely throughout the Chinese governing class. In fact, the Jesuits were to remain confined within this specific domain. While they saw science as their means to gain access to power and influence for the sake of their primary objective — the conversion of the imperial court — the emperors of China were far more astute. The Jesuits were useful for their knowledge, which was all that interested the emperors. The knowledge that Schall and his successor in the bureau, Ferdinand Verbiest, brought to the Chinese court was useful as long as it conformed to the central objective of maintaining the Chinese imperial state. The Chinese only took what was useful — the clocks, the mathematical techniques and, especially, the techniques for casting better cannon. Verbiest cast 132 heavy cannon and 320 light cannon at the imperial workshops as well as a range of western astronomical instruments. As for Christianity, there was no real use for it. Even though Verbiest was, in the late seventeenth century, to achieve Ricci's goal in becoming both tutor to the brilliant young Emperor Kangxi (K'ang-hsi) and vice-president of the board of works, the clocks, astrolabes, telescopes, mathematics and other scientific techniques he introduced were of interest and useful but had little real impact on the Middle Kingdom.

In his journals Kangxi (1662–1722), the emperor most influenced by and interested in western science and technology, made the following observations:

Courtesy Film Australia

With instruments like these, modeled on the latest designs developed by the great Flemish astronomer, Tycho Brahe, the Jesuits were able to guarantee the emperor more accurate predictions for the imperial calendar.

I realized, too, that western mathematics has its uses. I first grew interested in this subject shortly after I came to the throne, during the confrontations between the Jesuit Adam Schall and his Chinese critic, Yang Guanxian, when the two men argued the merits of their respective techniques. ... Schall died in prison but, after I learned something about astronomy, I pardoned his friend Verbiest in 1669 and gave him an official position, promoting him in 1682. ... For even though some of the western methods are different from our own, and may even be an improvement, there is little about them that is new. The principles of mathematics all derive from the *Book of Changes,* and the western methods are Chinese in origin: this word algebra — a-erh-chu-pa-erh — springs from an eastern word. And though it was indeed the westerners who showed us something our ancient calendar experts did not know — namely how to calculate the angles of the northern pole — this but shows the truth of what Zhu Xi arrived at through his investigation of things: the earth is like the yoke within an egg. ... I did praise their work, saying "the 'new methods' of calculating make basic errors impossible" and "the general principles of western calendrical science are without error." But I added that they still could not prevent small errors from occurring, and that over the decades these small errors mount up. After all, they know only a fraction of what I know.

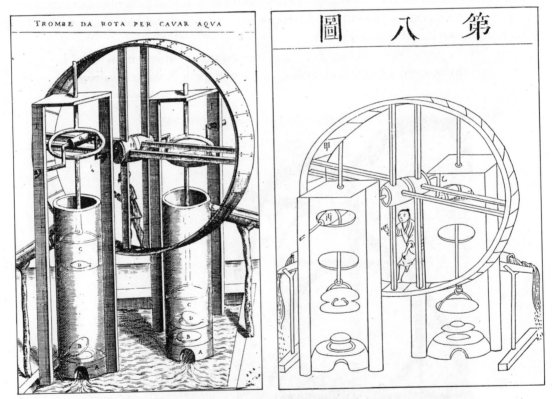

The Jesuits' library in Beijing offered Chinese scholars access to western scientific books illustrated with the new perspective drawings of technical detail. However, it was difficult to translate this illustrative technique into the Chinese style. The crucial mechanical detail is almost completely unintelligible in the Chinese copy of seventeenth century mechanisms for lifting water. Traditional Chinese encyclopedias were designed by and for the use of scholar-officials not craftsmen or artisans.

Even with an enlightened emperor such as Kangxi there remained a tendency, which was to become a habitual response of Chinese scholars for the next two hundred years, to regard western learning as no more than a refinement of what was already present in the traditional Chinese classics. A century after Kangxi, in the 1782 edition of the *Siku quanshu tiyao* (The Index to the Grand Library) there was this entry regarding the uses of western learning:

> In regard to the learning of the west, the art of surveying the land is most important, followed by the art of making strange machines. Among these strange machines, those pertaining to irrigation are most useful to the common people. All the other machines are simply intricate oddities, designed for the pleasure of the senses. They fulfill no basic needs.

Within the priorities of Chinese culture, from the perspective of an eighteenth century scholar-bureaucrat, these sentiments were probably right. It would be equally arrogant of us to dismiss the Chinese literati for showing little interest in western science and technology, given the values in which they were educated and the stability and harmony of the imperial culture they maintained. After all, in Europe too the scientific revolution was greeted by the Church and its aristocratic patrons with little enthusiasm. The treatment of Galileo is but one example of numerous efforts at repression. The appeal of the new sciences came from the advantages they provided in the highly competitive battles for economic and military power, which dominated the relationships between the expanding nation states of Europe: they appealed to necessity and greed.

The Jesuit mission proved, eventually, to be a failure. Kangxi was, understandably, to lose his patience with the Jesuits who, though accepting official positions in the Chinese imperial service, were in the final analysis accountable to the pope in Rome. Torn apart by the famous "rites controversy," where competing Catholic orders criticized the Jesuit policy (begun by Ricci) of bending Christian dogma to conform to the Confucian view of the world, the Jesuit order was disbanded by papal decree in 1773 and the emperor formally restricted the activity of Christian missionaries throughout the country.

TIME'S CHARIOT — NEW HORSES
AND NEW COURSES

The skill originated in the west
But by learning, we can achieve the artifice:
Wheels move and time turns round,
Hands show the minutes as they change.
Red-capped watchmen, there is no need to announce the dawn's coming.
My golden clock has warned me of the time.
By first light I am hard at work,
And keep on asking, "Why are the memorials late?"

"Lines in praise of a self-chiming clock," Emperor Kangxi, c. 1705

Kangxi was clearly enthusiastic about his clocks. He is reported to have had over two thousand in the imperial palace alone, including clockwork globes and elaborate mechanical toys of great ingenuity given as tributary gifts by European states, usually in the hope of gaining more favorable conditions of trade. They were regarded largely as curiosities in the same way that we might regard a Chinese gnomon or armillary sphere today, ingenious but largely irrelevant. In Chinese culture and economy there was no great need for them except as collectors' items among the imperial bureaucrats and gentry.

This was due to the fact that the contemporary generation of scholars' interest in technology was extremely limited, compared with that of earlier dynasties such as the Song. From the time of the Ming dynasty's withdrawal from the world in the fifteenth century, the intellectual horizons of many scholars had become similarly introverted, concerned essentially with maintaining traditional Confucian values and the agricultural economy on which it was built.

Meanwhile, in Europe there was to be little or no stability. By the early seventeenth century Holland and Britain had supplanted Portugal and Spain, largely through their dominance of international maritime trade. It was a time of almost constant warfare between the Protestant north, centered on the northern Dutch provinces and the Catholic south dominated by Spain and France. The repression of Protestants and particularly the Huguenots in France benefited the Dutch and the English. Many of the most entrepreneurial merchants and artisans were driven out, bringing with them their skills and capital. They included skilled weavers and potters, clockmakers and educated merchants. The Protestant movement was a focus, not only for religious reformers but also for those rebelling against the repressive remnants of the old feudal order. The Protestant emphasis on the freedom of individual conscience, frugality and on popular literacy (ostensibly so that all would be able to read the Bible in their own language) provided this new and increasingly powerful class with a religion that expressed their values. Wealth was nothing to be ashamed of, it was an expression of God's providence and individual diligence. With

Amsterdam Historical Museum

Return from the Second Voyage to the East-Indies by H.C. Vroom (1566 – 1640). The Dutch East India Company, which dominated sixteenth century trade with Asia, became the model for other European powers who were to enter the China trade.

wealth one was better able to benefit society as a whole and demonstrate one's Christian charity by endowing orphanages, hospitals and schools.

With the growth in wealth that came from an expansion in international and local commerce, new economic and scientific institutions were created, which, in turn, stimulated both economic growth and technological innovation.

Holland, that great "republic of merchants," had by the end of the sixteenth century eclipsed Genoa and Venice as the financial capital of Europe. This was partly because of its proximity to Antwerp, the clearing house in Europe both for Asian goods and for gold and silver coming in from the Spanish colonies in South America. Antwerp, unlike the earlier tightly controlled trading centers in the Italian city-states, was perhaps the first city in Europe to match the cosmopolitan character of Quanzhou in the twelfth and thirteenth centuries. From here Italian and Jewish bankers, and English and French merchant guilds established their trading networks that covered northern Europe. Here vast loans were negotiated on behalf of monarchs like Henry VIII of England.

An example of the importance of the new freedoms that the Netherlands offered can be seen in the decline of Antwerp after 1558 when the Spanish occupied the city together with much of southern Holland and Flanders. The repression of Calvinists and other Protestants led to a mass exodus north to the city of Amsterdam, which as a consequence took over Antwerp's role as the center of international trade throughout the early seventeenth century.

Amsterdam and other cities of the United Provinces offered merchants unprecidented political and economic freedom. Here they were to establish three new commercial institutions essential to the growth of capitalism. The Amsterdam deposit bank which stabilised the currency and made commercial transactions more secure. The stock exchange or Bourse which provided a new source of capital and where shares in the great trading companies could be bought and sold on an open market. Linked to both the Bourse and the bank was the joint stock company now independent of the state and beholden primarily to its investors. The difference with these new joint-stock companies was that their profits could not simply be drawn off by the state or the monarch to be used for conspicuous consumption or for waging war. The profits could be used as capital for further investment by the directors of the company, who acted on behalf of the investors.

As Adam Smith argued in *Wealth of Nations*, this new financial institution became the foundation stone of western capitalism. It had the advantage of avoiding "the agency risk" common in all bureaucratic organizations, where those in power within the hierarchy use the organization to serve their own private interests, at the expense of its ostensible purpose; financial corruption being the perennial problem especially where accountability was in the hands of those easily bought off. In both

This painting by Job Berckheyde shows the courtyard of the Amsterdam exchange in 1668. The Dutch pioneered the most essential institutions of European capitalism — the joint-stock company and the bourse or stock exchange where shares could be traded. This provided the capital that allowed Dutch merchants to build the great fleets, which enabled them to dominate trade with the east.

State Library of New South Wales, Sydney

Dutch naval architecture in the sixteenth and seventeenth centuries was the most developed in the world . . . and it needed to be. It took anything up to three grueling years to complete the round trip to China, and few ships survived more than two or three trips.

China and Europe the "squeezing" of large surplus profits from merchants and their enterprises was a quick method for governments to gain much-needed revenue or for officials to gain personal wealth.

The capacity to buy and sell shares in an enterprise allowed investors to put their money into other companies if their interests were not being served. This form of financial accountability became centered on the bourse in Amsterdam, the clearing house for such investment and the prototype of the modern stock exchange. The operation of this financial market system was to have profound consequences. Perhaps the greatest of these new companies was the Dutch East India Company or VOC (Verenigde Costindische Compagnie), which controlled and managed Dutch interests in the east. Its power was enormous. It has been described as a "state within a state" and was rather like the modern multinational corporation. As merchant fleets were armed with cannon and marines to protect themselves from piracy, they tended to run their trading settlements like states, with the cost of garrisons being included in the overall cost of trade. In Java, their main base in the East, they established plantations and enslaved native people, repressing the traditional economy and culture. These companies, which were to be duplicated in Britain, France and elsewhere in northern Europe, had the virtual capacity to make war or peace anywhere in the world, supported by their government. As many of these merchant-adventurers were raised in the tradition of European piracy, best exemplified by the exploits of Sir Francis Drake a century earlier, they now pursued their more legitimate commercial interests with equal ruthlessness.

FROM GUNPOWDER TO THE STEAM ENGINE

At the Académie des Sciences in Paris the great Dutch scientist Christiaan Huygens, one of its founding members, had encouraged the experiments of Denis Papin, a French mathematician and physicist. Huygens had been fascinated by Leonardo da Vinci's idea that if gunpowder could drive a cannon ball down a shaft why could it not be used to drive an engine. Papin had been experimenting with gunpowder testers, which were needed by the military in order to test the most appropriate mixtures of saltpeter, charcoal and sulfur for the great array of new weapons being developed — from massive cannon to small handguns. The tester worked by placing a specific amount of gunpowder in a small cylinder; on the top of the cylinder was placed a cap attached to a ratchet or spring; the gunpowder was ignited forcing up the cap and the explosive force then measured on a calibrated gauge.

Papin took this idea a step further. If the amount of gunpowder and the explosive power within the cylinder could be controlled, then the movement up and down of the cap within the cylinder could be used as the driving force for an engine. He made several designs and even attempted to produce such a machine. However, gunpowder was impractical and he turned to steam. He was never actually to develop a working machine himself but he did

James Watt and one of his steam powered beam engines.

lay down the principle that was later to be taken up by Thomas Newcomen, an ironmonger from Dartmouth in Devon. Papin did, however, produce the world's first "digester" or pressure cooker, which incorporated the most essential device later used in the steam engine — a valve that could control the pressure within a vacuum or cylinder.

Newcomen, aware that one of the major problems in mining was flooding, designed what he called an "atmospheric engine" to pump water out of the mines. This was first used at a colliery near Dudley in Staffordshire in 1712. In 1763 a working model of this engine was given to an instrument maker at Glasgow University, James Watt, for repair. The consequences of Watt's repairs and his further development of this machine would help turn Great Britain into the industrial powerhouse of Europe.

Dionysius Papin M. D., Anno (1689)

POWER IN NUMBERS

The merchant empires established by the East India companies in far-flung parts of the east (the Dutch in Batavia, the British in India, the Portuguese in Macao, the Spanish in the Philippines) provided a stimulus to the intellectual ferment that was occurring in Europe. As the world of the Europeans expanded, so did the boundaries of knowledge. Prior to the sixteenth century and reinforced by the Italian Renaissance, the intellectual world view of scholars was confined to rediscovering what was known to the ancients, the Greek philosophers and mathematicians. This, along with the Bible, provided all that was needed. However, it was soon discovered, as reports of strange animals, plants, people and places circulated through the libraries and universities, that this knowledge was not complete.

The Dutch merchant-adventurers were to establish great collections of these animals and plants. In their libraries there were journals and accounts of the societies with which they came into contact. It was becoming obvious that knowledge was not static but, like wealth, was capable of growing. Societies too were changing as new customs, from the smoking of tobacco to the drinking of tea and coffee, and eating off china plates, were taken up with extraordinary enthusiasm. But more significant were the possible sources of wealth that might exist in remote and unexplored parts of the world. Thus, the scientific interest in the exotic and the accumulation of new knowledge were clearly tied up with a concern for profit.

This link was not lost on the monarchs of Europe. They were soon to become the patrons of new scientific institutions whose broad interest in the growth of knowledge were predicated on the benefits of providing solutions to economic and military problems. In 1662 the Royal Society of London was founded to advance scientific knowledge with King Charles II as its patron. In 1666 the Académie des Sciences was established in Paris under the patronage of Louis XIV. In order to solve the problems of longitude that made accurate navigation impossible, the Royal Greenwich Observatory was set up in 1675, under royal patronage.

Isaac Newton, as President of the Royal Society, was as acutely aware of the importance of this issue as anyone else. In his *Principia Mathematica* and other publications in which he was to explore his theory of gravity and the mechanics of planetary motion, there is the underlying assumption that the universe works like some giant clockwork device, which, having been set in motion by God, follows its own inexorable course. This course was none other than that determined by the laws of mechanics, which, in turn, could be understood with an increasingly high level of mathematical certainty. The predictive power of Newton's mathematical methods was to be passed on to the other experimental sciences emerging under the umbrella of the Royal Society. If God had made a universe that worked on the basis of mathematically precise mechanisms and could be understood in terms of laws, which operated like clockwork, could not the rest of nature be understood in the same terms? It was in the investigation of natural phenomena not in sacred texts that the "hidden hand" of God would be revealed.

But the problem for devout Christians such as Newton was that if the universe ran

The impact of Asia and the exploration of the New World undertaken by the seventeenth century Dutch merchant fleets were to expand intellectual horizons. The Dutch began making vast collections of zoological and botanical curiosities, which, in turn, stimulated scientific interest in species and their origins.

112

like a giant clockwork machine, how was it possible that God could intervene in his creation as the Bible stated? Such metaphysical issues, however, are beyond the scope of this book and, possibly, beyond most of the natural philosophers who took up Newton's question.

With new institutions that could sponsor scientific research, new careers began to emerge. The demand for scientific instruments, to investigate the inner workings of nature and the universe, meant that the natural philosophers had to leave their libraries in order to work closely with craftsmen. Clockmakers like John Harrison were to turn their precision-engineering skills to the design of new instruments; instruments that were to be as important for navigation as they were for astronomy. As finer microscopes and telescopes, electrical gauges, orreries and sextants were required, mathematicians and instrument makers worked closely together. Of the instrument maker George Graham, the Astronomer Royal James Bradley had this to say in 1747:

> I am sensible, that if my own Endeavours have, in any respect, been effectual to the Advancement of Astronomy; it has principally been owing to the Advice and Assistance given me by our worthy member Mr George Graham; whose great skill and judgment in mechanicks, join'd with a complete and practical knowledge of the use of Astronomical Instruments, enable him to contrive and execute them in the most perfect manner.

An engraving from Thomas Sprat's *The History of the Royal Society of London for Improving Natural Knowledge* published in 1667, five years after the founding of the Society. The bust is of Charles II the Society's founder; on his right is Francis Bacon whose writings promoting science led to its foundation, and on the left is the Society's first president.

TIME, SPACE AND THE LONGITUDE PROBLEM

The problem of establishing longitude had occupied the best minds of Europe for more than a century. As early as 1567 Philip II of Spain had offered a prize of 9,000 ducats to anyone who could come up with a solution; the States General of Holland offered 30,000 florins and the Venetians and Portuguese also offered prizes.

Even Galileo set his mind to the problem. Having first applied the telescope to the observation of the moons of Venus, he proposed that the regular rotation of these moons could be used as a celestial clock. In 1616 he submitted his proposal to the Spanish with tables listing the times of eclipses. However, the Spanish were not impressed, first because it required a telescope and good weather to take a reading at sea, and also, they argued, the eclipse occurred too slowly to allow for the precision needed to measure longitude. Galileo presented his idea to the Dutch but without any success. He did, however, come up with the·idea that the regular oscillations of a pendulum could be used to drive a clock, without the cumbersome system of the traditional weights. This he developed into a mechanism in 1642, the last year of his life.

The Dutch scientist Christiaan Huygens knew of Galileo's work and, in 1657, he tried to produce a pendulum clock that would work at sea. Experiments and trials were made but the movement of the boat produced such huge errors that the project was abandoned. The Académie des Sciences in Paris pursued the problem as did other scientific institutions throughout Europe. In 1668 Louis XIV offered a prize of 60,000 livres to a German inventor who came up with an ingenious form of nautical odometer, which he hoped would record precise distances at sea, but this too was a failure.

The Royal Observatory at Greenwich was established in 1675 primarily to resolve the problem of longitude. It was here that many of the major advances in observational astronomy were to be made over the next two centuries. Here too, using a clock with a four-metre long pendulum, designed on the principles developed by Galileo and Huygens, John Flamsteed the first British Astronomer Royal was able to determine the precise time it took for the earth to complete one rotation, the first step for fixing longitude.

This did not stop other astronomers from coming up with novel ways of using the regular motions of planets, including the moon, as a celestial clock capable of being read from anywhere on the globe, and especially at sea.

In 1714 the British parliament received the following petition from a group of London merchants calling for a prize to be established for anyone who could solve the problem of longitude. It was subsequently published in the *House of Commons Journal*:
"A Petition of Several Captains of Her Majesty's Ships, Merchants of London, and commanders of merchantmen, on behalf of themselves, and all others concerned in the Navigation of Great Britain, was presented to the House, and read; setting forth, That the Discovery of the Longitude is of such consequence to Great Britain, for Safety of the Navy, and Merchant

The famous Octagon Room at the Greenwich Observatory designed by Sir Christopher Wren. The clock faces at the end of the room were controlled by a giant pendulum designed by the instrument maker Thomas Tompion for the Astronomer Royal, John Flamsteed.

The Royal Greenwich Observatory was established in 1675 with the basic purpose of improving astronomical knowledge for the purposes of navigation.

Ships, as well as Improvement of Trade, that, for want thereof, many ships have been retarded in their voyages, and many lost; but if due Encouragement were proposed by the Publick, for such as shall discover the same, some Persons would offer themselves to prove the same, before the most proper judges, in order to their satisfaction, for the Safety of men's Lives, her Majesty's navy, the increase of trade, and the Shipping of these Islands, and the lasting honour of the British Nation."

In response to this request a Committee was formed and the proposal passed on to Isaac Newton who discounted the possibility of using either the "eclipses of Jupiter's satellites" or the "place of the Moon" and argued that what was needed was a "watch regulated by a spring, and rectified every visible sunrise and sunset." Parliament accepted Newton's recommendations and the House of Commons passed a Bill on 17 June 1714 "Providing a Publick Reward for such Person or Persons as shall Discover the Longitude at Sea." The commission set up to manage the prize money — £20,000, more than $1 million in today's terms — was the Board of Longitude.

The man who was to win most of this prize money was typical of the craftsmen and instrument makers who were to play a significant role in the early stages of the Industrial Revolution. John Harrison (1693 – 1776) was the son of a country carpenter from Yorkshire. He and his brother, although originally carpenters, turned to clockmaking when the family moved to Lincolnshire. Harrison showed early talent and, in 1730, was able to gain the support of Edmond Halley, the Astronomer Royal, and George Graham, one of the most influential clock and scientific instrument makers in London. They, in turn, approached the East India Company for funds to allow Harrison to devote his time exclusively to the problems of developing a spring-controlled maritime clock. Over the next thirty years, with the support of the Board of Longitude and the British Navy, Harrison perfected his famous marine clock, an early version of which Captain Cook was to take with him on his voyages to Australia and the Pacific in 1770. For his efforts he received most of the Board of Longitude prize money and the Copley Medal from the Royal Society. For a craftsman and artisan this financial reward and public recognition from the highest institutions in the land, and the social mobility they entailed, was unprecedented.

Until the sea routes to the east were established in the sixteenth century, Chinese porcelain had the rarity value of precious treasure. Nowhere in Europe could anyone produce anything to match it. The word "porcelain" in Italian means "shell-like," which indeed some of the best pieces were — fine translucent bowls and cups, richly decorated with glazes in subtle colors that did not easily chip or break like traditional European clay-based pottery. This Chinese porcelain clearly belonged to a culture of great refinement — an impression that was supported by the writings of the Jesuit missionaries. This impression was reinforced by many other products from the east, especially silk fabrics, which were also far superior to anything being produced in Europe. To Marco Polo the porcelain he came across throughout his journeys was not only of exquisite beauty but extremely cheap by European standards.

This was not lost on either Portuguese or Dutch merchants. By the early seventeenth century the Dutch had established trading bases at Batavia in Java and at Nagasaki in Japan, and huge boatloads of Chinese porcelain began to arrive in the port of Amsterdam. From here it was either distributed to local markets or transhipped to ports throughout northern Europe. The trade was enormous as was the demand. However, in 1644, when the Ming government fell to the invading armies of the Manchus, production in and export from China ground to a standstill for nearly 30 years.

The town of Delft, situated in the center of Holland, about 60 kilometres from Amsterdam, is connected by canal to the port of Rotterdam. In the early part of the seventeeth century Delft was a major center for brewing beer, having achieved something of a monopoly in the surrounding region. This monopoly was challenged by other brewers and, by the middle of the seventeenth century, Delft's major industry was in decline, with many breweries closing down.

The response of the brewers was to convert their breweries into pottery works. They could see there was a demand for Chinese porcelain so they moved their capital to where potential profits were to be found. They began to make imitation porcelain out of clay, taking advantage of the high prices and limited supply of the original. The famous blue and white pottery, for which Delft has for centuries been famous, is in

fact no more than a copy of Chinese blue and white porcelain.

By 1660 there were at least 32 pottery works employing around one quarter of Delft's population of 24,000. What is remarkable is that it was possible to mobilize capital, and import and train skilled craftsmen in so short a time. The availability of capital was an advantage the Dutch had over many other European countries at the time; money was available from Dutch banks at interest rates of 3–6 per cent, half the interest rate of other European countries.

However, the quality of delftware in the early years could not possibly compare with that of Chinese porcelain. Some firms even went so far as to put imitation Chinese characters on the bottom of their pieces to make them appear like the genuine article. In the twentieth century, European consumers have often scoffed at the poor imitations of well-known European brand names manufactured by the Japanese and Chinese as if such imitation was an admission of cultural inferiority. It should not be forgotten, however, that Europe in the seventeeth and eighteenth centuries pioneered this course of action, with flagrant efforts to produce cheap imitations not only of Chinese and Japanese porcelain but also of Asian silk and cotton fabrics.

Princeton University Press, New Jersey

Spectators gathered in 1783 to catch a glimpse of the Montgolfier brothers' demonstration of their hot-air balloon.

The expansion of public education among the sons of craftsmen and merchants allowed the revolution in quantification and precise measurement to be applied broadly to a wide range of craft industries. The competitive demands for new technology and the rewards being offered for innovation created a climate in which experimentation could flourish.

The application of mathematical principles to the design of new technology and instruments was to become widespread as the new scientific and economic institutions mediated fashion, status and wealth. The use of precision instruments in drawing plans and the ability to analyze structural possibilities on paper was a stimulus to the creativity of engineers. The work of the seventeenth century French hydraulic engineer, De Beladoir, provides a good example of this.

From Jesuit descriptions and drawings, the idea of the "dragon's backbone pump" was introduced to Europe. A small portable example may well have been brought back on a merchant ship. The pump was a simple wooden chain pump, which was used to lift water from one paddy field into another. There was a long rectangular box, like a gutter, along which a chain of pallets moved lifting the water. The whole device was pedal-driven, the source of energy being strong leg muscles. It was an extraordinarily efficient and practical machine. In China there were, however, only two sizes and the dimensions remained essentially the same for a thousand years. In

Popular science was promoted throughout the eighteenth century by lectures and demonstrations of scientific principles. Creating a vacuum in a glass jar, and rendering a bird momentarily unconscious, provided a graphic, and fairly sensational, demonstration of the importance of oxygen.

Europe, when the machine finally arrived, it was deemed to be ideal for lifting water to help firefighting in Strasburg. De Beladoir, however, was not satisfied with the models he had received from China. Applying the methods of differential calculus devised by Newton and the other great European mathematician and philosopher, Gottfried Leibnitz, he began to design a whole array of different sizes and systems to cope with different scales of lift, some involving large numbers of people all pedalling at the same time. This method of lifting water was superseded by the suction pump and the "dragon's backbone" had only a brief period of glory. Its passing reflected the widening gap between the technologies of China and Europe.

This was also the case with hot-air ballooning, first developed in eighteenth century France by the Montgolfier brothers. The Chinese already used the principle in their floating paper lamps. These were simply paper globes in which a candle was placed, the hot air causing the lantern to float in the air. These were used in festivals throughout China and yet the principle behind the phenomenon was never investigated nor was its potential as a means of flight ever seriously considered.

It is interesting to note that the Montgolfier brothers were from a family of papermakers from Annonay near Lyon. Both were well educated in the new sciences and were aware of the debates about the nature of air and the effect of heat upon gases. A common experiment in the eighteenth century involved putting a bird and candle in a sealed jar to show that when an animal is denied oxygen it becomes unconscious and will eventually die. Experiments to discover the constituents of air engaged some of the best scientific minds in eighteenth century Europe — Priestley in England, and Charles and Lavoisier in France.

The issue here is not so much why the Chinese did not go in for ballooning, after all why should they, but why the Europeans did. What was the impetus for experimentation and invention that seems to have been such a dominant feature of European culture in the seventeenth and eighteenth centuries? Money is one part of the answer but there was also a recognition that progress through technological and social change was a "good" thing and that society as a whole was moving towards some ideal end. This was to be found in earlier visions of the future put forward in popular literature such as Thomas More's *Utopia* (1516) and Francis Bacon's *The New Atlantis* (1620). Bacon was the first European thinker to put forward seriously the notion of a society led by a high priesthood of scholars and engineers — a vision, paradoxically, not unlike the Chinese Confucian ideals. However, rather than being concerned with ethical and philosophical issues, Bacon's bureaucrats were practical men imbued with the ethos and methods of science, and committed to the goal of material rather than moral progress.

What perspective drawing and the new mathematical techniques offered was the ability to play on paper with three-dimensional models and extend the possibilities of the known world. It was a perspective, in a sense, that saw people not only as the center of the world, in the humanistic sense, but also as creators. As God's chosen agents they were here to fulfill his will. Thus the new scientific prophet would lead humanity to the promised land. It was this faith in social and intellectual progress that was one of the driving forces of the remarkable technological and scientific creativity of seventeenth and eighteenth century Europe.

CHINOISERIE AND THE CHINESE MIRROR

Interestingly enough while all this was going on there was, among the aristocracy and the wealthy, a fashion for all things eastern. It was not just the flood of Chinese and Japanese porcelain and textiles, which were obviously important, but a recognition that China had perfected a form of benign autocracy; an imperial system whose stability and longevity was the envy of European monarchs and aristocrats. The Jesuits were largely responsible for the generation of this image. The journals, letters, and translations of Ricci, Schall and Verbiest were widely read and translated. They painted a picture of Chinese culture as seen from the imperial perspective — a somewhat idealized view.

For this reason it could be said that the Jesuit mission probably had more long-term impact on Europe than it did on China, although this was certainly not the Jesuits' intention. In a sense China provided eighteenth century Europe with a mirror with which to view their own social institutions. As early as 1621, in Robert Burton's *The Anatomy of Melancholy* there are passages that compare the example of China's meritocratic system of government to the traditions of aristocratic privilege still common in Britain:

This painting by Cu Liu Peng shows a traditional group of scholars gathered in a rock garden.

Out of their philosophers and Doctors they [the Chinese] choose Magistrates; their politick Nobles are taken from such as be *moraliter nobiles,* virtuous noble, as in Israel of old, and their office was to defend and govern their country, not to hawk, hunt, eat, drink, game alone, as too many do. Their Mandarins, Litterates, Licentiaters, and such as have raised themselves by their worth, are their noble man, only thought fit to govern the state.

China was held up as the mirror against which the institutional inadequacies of Europe could be paraded in the hope of encouraging reform. Du Halde's *Description de la Chine,* published in Paris in 1735, was widely circulated and translated into numerous languages. From Jesuit sources and with illustrations taken from drawings done by artists attached to the Jesuit mission, China was presented to Europe as a model of civilization.

For social critics such as Voltaire and Montesquieu in France, China was a society with no Christian Church and no aristocracy, run by a class of bureaucratic officials who owed their position in the vast imperial hierarchy to their scholastic achievement, to merit, and not to birth. This for Voltaire was a revelation and was used to good effect in his polemics against the privileges and corruption of both the Church and the aristocracy.

The human mind certainly cannot imagine a government better than this one where everything is to be decided by the large tribunals, subordinated to each other, of which the members are received only after several severe examinations. Everything in China regulates itself by these tribunals.

Courtesy Film Australia

A passion for chinoiserie swept through eighteenth century Europe, with architects and designers attempting to incorporate Chinese motifs into their work. This wallpaper in the Chinese room at Woburn Abbey, came with additional flowers and birds, which could be attached to the wallpaper if a more ornate effect was desired.

121

Courtesy Film Australia

At Woburn Abbey the Duke of Bedford had this dairy built in the Chinese style to keep up with the eighteenth century fashion for chinoiserie.

These sentiments were to be echoed by enlightened intellectuals, from the encyclopedist Diderot to the economist Quesnay. By the end of the eighteenth century, even before the French Revolution in 1789, Talleyrand had adopted the Chinese system of a written examination for civil servants, a practice which was later taken up elsewhere in Europe.

In many respects, China's distance from Europe made it a suitable mirror in which reformers could project their hopes and ideals. The fact that many of these were half-truths did not detract from their potency. This was complemented by a corresponding taste for Chinese decor and even clothes. Rooms were decorated in the Chinese style. Furniture such as that produced by Chippendale reflected this new vogue for things Chinese. Wallpaper from China was introduced into Europe for the first time. At Woburn Abbey the fourth Duke of Bedford, who had financial interests in the China trade through the East India Company, had a whole room hung with wallpaper specially ordered from China. The notion of "hanging" wallpaper dates from this time when the paper panels of an original painting were far too expensive to stick to the wall and so were hung. (Only much later when printed wallpaper was being produced in Europe in large quantities was it stuck to rather than hung on the wall.)

The vogue for chinoiserie extended further: at Woburn a Chinese dairy was built; pagodas were put up in Royal Kew Gardens and, at Brighton, an extraordinarily lavish and vulgar mixture of Asian designs was put together in the Brighton Pavilion. On the continent, the vogue was the same, with magnificent rooms being created in the Louvre and the Potsdam Palace.

The English habit of taking tea in the afternoon is attributed to the Duchess of Bedford who made it fashionable in the late eighteenth century. With a family stake in the East India Company, whose major import from China at this time was tea, it made good sense, although tea drinking was not greeted with universal enthusiasm. Some like Jonas Hanway in his "Essay of Tea" railed against this pernicious habit:

> We have abundance of milk; beer of many kinds; lime which we import from countries in Europe near at hand; infusions of many salutary and well-tasted herbs; preparations of barley and oats; and above all, in most places, exceedingly good water. . . . Tea when it is genuine it hurts many, when adulterated or dyed, it has been found poisonous. . . . The young and old, the healthy and infirm, the superlatively rich, down to vagabonds and beggars, drink this enchanting beverage, when they are thirsty and when they are not thirsty.

In respect of water, Hanway was not altogether correct. The quality of drinking water in many of the crowded cities, especially London, was downright dangerous,

The Duchess of Bedford, who was said to be responsible for initiating the English habit of taking tea in the afternoon.

This late Qing painting shows the emperor granting an audience in the imperial gardens. China was portrayed in idealized form, with the emperor presented as the embodiment of a philosopher king or benign autocrat — positions of power to which European aristocrats aspired though rarely achieved.

with open drains, carrying sewage, polluting wells and spreading diseases like cholera. The boiling of water for tea, although few were aware of it at the time, prevented the spread of disease. It was also an alternative to drinking beer and other alcoholic beverages. Among the sober merchants and gentry tea provided a social habit appropriate to clear thinking and hard work. With this new habit came new demands for "China" cups, teapots and plates.

China, because of its inaccessibility and exotic character, was to represent all things to all people. For the radicals and reformers it was to be used as a lever for change whereas, for the aristocrat, its benign and stable despotism offered a model and a future, in a political climate that was growing increasingly democratic and republican. It is amusing to find Louis XVI of France and Frederick the Great of Prussia both imitating the Chinese emperors' ritual of plowing the first furrow to open the spring plowing season. Such affectations, however, were not to hold back the floodgates of political and social reform.

DESPERATION AND SKULDUGGERY IN THE CHINA SHOP

The power of this new spirit of inquiry is perhaps best seen in the manner in which the Europeans went about trying to "reverse-engineer" or copy the Chinese method of making porcelain. Nowhere, except perhaps in the Japanese postwar takeover of the international automobile industry from the Americans, has there been such a systematic effort made at industrial imitation, eventually leading to innovation.

The raw materials for European ceramics were natural clays covered with a heavy white glaze. Despite their achievements, the Dutch could not match the translucence and hardness of the Chinese originals. As supplies of Chinese porcelain came on to the European market, the local industries were pushed to the limits of their technological ability in trying to produce ceramics that could compete with the Chinese originals. The Chinese kept the production process a carefully guarded industrial secret.

It was a German alchemist by the name of Johann Friedrich Böttger (1682–1719) who was to make the first breakthrough, but in a most surprising manner. European alchemists were believed to be able to produce gold by chemical transformations. Eastern European monarchs, concerned with maintaining revenue, were in the habit of imprisoning or putting under house arrest anyone claiming to be an alchemist. These unfortunate souls were kept by the state for ten years and, if they did not produce gold in that time, they were executed.

Böttger was one such character who was imprisoned by the Elector of Saxony, Augustus the Strong, who had just become King of Poland and badly needed revenue to pay his armies. Böttger was no fool and, while desperately trying to come up with the gold the Elector wanted, he had to think of some way of saving his neck. For heating metal, he required crucibles that could withstand extremely high temperatures. In experimenting with materials that could be used for this purpose he noticed that, in applying high temperatures to a mixture containing crushed kaolin and quartz he came up with crucibles that markedly resembled Chinese porcelain. The penny dropped and Böttger abandoned the futile task of trying to produce gold by chemical processes. With the help of an eminent scholar, Ehrenfried Walter von Tschirnhaus, he turned to the problem of making "hard-paste" porcelain. In 1711 he was able to announce to the Elector that he had been able to produce, not gold, but a very good source of it. As a result he was released and given the title of Baron. At the chateau of Albrechtburg at Meissen the Elector of Saxony established the first porcelain workshop in Europe and began to produce fine porcelain bowls and "objets d'art" of extraordinary beauty that were the equal of anything produced in China.

However, while the Elector of Saxony was establishing his works at Meissen, in Paris the French were busily engaged in industrial espionage to achieve the same ends. Orrey, a senior government official, who was eventually to become minister of finance, had interests in a ceramics works established at Vincennes in Paris. He contrived through a relative, who was head of the Jesuit order in Paris, to have Father

D'Entrecolles, a French Jesuit missionary in Beijing, visit the famous porcelain center of Jingdezhen. The purpose of his visit was to try to discover the Chinese method of making porcelain and, if possible, to smuggle back samples of the materials used. D'Entrecolles did his father superior's bidding and visited Jingdezhen, an industrial city unparalleled in the world until the Industrial Revolution in the north of England. Here the imperial workshops produced porcelain for export and for the imperial palace. The fire from the kilns was said to light the night sky, and the general atmosphere was one of great industry. In 1712 there were around 18,000 families associated with porcelain production in the city. D'Entrecolles reported that there were 3,000 kilns in operation (300 of them in the imperial factory) and that 80 per cent of all export porcelain was manufactured there.

D'Entrecolles achieved his task of getting samples without getting caught and, with accompanying descriptions of all he had observed, sent the lot back to Paris. There was one problem, however. He got the labels confused and no one could make sense of his descriptions. The Académie des Sciences was brought in to help with chemical analysis, one of the first examples of their direct involvement in the application of science to industrial research. Even eminent savants of the Académie could make no sense of the letters from D'Entrecolles. With a round trip from Paris to Beijing, without any mishaps, taking about three years, the frustration must have been enormous. However, one researcher, Réamur, who had carefully studied the letters and misunderstood their meaning, accidentally invented an entirely new form of "soft-paste" porcelain, which could be molded like clay. In this way the French porcelain industry was established. It became a royal monopoly and the workshop was moved to Sèvres on the outskirts of Paris.

Courtesy Film Australia

Left: The figure of Emperor Qianlong reproduced at Sevres from the original eighteenth century molds. This figure made of "soft-paste" porcelain was sent to the Emperor as a gift to encourage him to take an interest in French manufacture.

Right: Porcelain production in China was depicted in eighteenth century illustrated volumes as a romantic, pastoral process when, in reality, the major center of production at Jingdezhen was far more like the crowded industrial cities that were just beginning to emerge in Europe. Many of the labor-intensive stages in Chinese porcelain production have changed little since that time . . . and the west still comes to buy.

126

127

In 1768 Henri Bertin, a trade minister in the French government, commissioned a statue of the Emperor Qianlong (Ch'ien Lung), taken from a drawing by the Jesuit missionary Panzi, to be made out of this porcelain. The gift was sent back to China with two young Chinese Jesuits who had been studying in Paris. The statue was part of a package of goods, including silk tapestries, clocks and other automata sent in the hope of encouraging trade. To the Chinese it must have seemed the height of impudence.

Important though this achievement was in dispelling some of the mystique attached to Chinese industrial technology, the development of a porcelain industry also encouraged original designs and techniques, which made European porcelain increasingly different from that of China. By the end of the eighteenth century European porcelain was preferred to the Chinese original. However, porcelain was always a luxury in Europe. It was to remain the "china" of the aristocrat and the rich. It was to be in England that the real revolution in the production of crockery for everyday use was to occur.

Josiah Wedgwood was representative of a wholly new craft tradition. He was an industrialist and entrepreneur with close ties to the scientific community and, more important perhaps, equally close ties with the growing middle class who were demanding access to luxury goods hitherto only accessible to the aristocracy. Like

This illustration, from de Milly's *L'Art de la Porcelaine,* of 1771, shows techniques of production that are still used to make this most refined of luxuries. Genuine porcelain remains extremely expensive and labor intensive.

Thomas Edison in the nineteenth century, Wedgwood was both an inventor and businessman, with an acute awareness of what the market needed and he set his considerable talents to meeting it.

Wedgwood was born into a Staffordshire family, which for four generations had worked in the pottery trade. He began school at the age of six but when he was nine years old his father died and he had to take up an apprenticeship as a potter. However, poor health kept him from work, allowing him time to study, particularly the sciences. With connections in the trade and with an obvious entrepreneurial flair Wedgwood opened up a small pottery works of his own in 1754 in partnership with a successful manufacturer Thomas Whieldon.

In England, by the mid-eighteenth century, there was not only a significant growth in population (due in part to improved public health) but also a significant rise in wealth from improvements in agriculture and growing trade. The habit of drinking tea, for example, had become widespread among the new middle class, and there was a great demand for good quality crockery at modest prices.

Wedgwood was fully aware of this as he noted in his experiment book: "I saw the field was spacious, and the soil so good as to promise ample recompense to any who should labor diligently in its cultivation." Wedgwood applied his efforts to developing a form of earthenware pottery that would have all the characteristics of

Josiah Wedgwood & Sons Limited, Barlaston, Stoke-on-Trent, England

Josiah Wedgwood and his family as portrayed by George Stubbs in 1780. Wedgwood was typical of the new northern English industrialists, most of whom began as humble craftsmen but were to achieve a status and influence unthinkable for craftsmen in China.

porcelain but would be cheap. The ingredients for porcelain were expensive, and the time and labor involved too great to be able to manufacture it cheaply enough for ordinary people. So in a laboratory in the basement of his house Wedgwood set about systematically experimenting with different mixtures of clays and glazes, all faithfully recorded in his experiment book. He was to apply the methodology of the new sciences and seek the advice of many of the leading figures of his day. He was a member of the Luna Society, a group of like-minded experimentalists who met every full moon to discuss scientific matters. Joseph Priestley, one of the most famous chemists of his day, and Erasmus Darwin, grandfather of Charles, were both members of this group.

In 1763 Wedgwood described what was to be one of his major achievements:

[A] species of earthenware for the table, quite new in appearance, covered with a rich and brilliant glaze, bearing sudden alterations of heat and cold, manufactured with ease and expedition, and consequently cheap, having every requisite for the purpose intended.

This cream-colored earthenware made from a mixture of Cornish China clay, China stone, ground flint and Devon ball clay covered with a tough lead glaze, was to become known as queen's ware — an order was placed by Queen Charlotte and Wedgwood was astute enough as a businessman to realize the commercial advantage of that. What he had produced was the stuff of the commonplace: "china" to be used

The Staffordshire potteries where Josiah Wedgwood established his factory. Here he experimented with clays and glazes, which were to lead to the mass production of basic crockery for everyday use.

Mary Evans Picture Library, London

in daily life. Because of its low price and the demand created by large-scale marketing, Wedgwood was able to establish a factory at Etruria on a truly industrial scale. This factory was on a canal linking the Trent and Mersey Rivers, allowing the clays and flints needed by the Staffordshire potteries to be brought in by barge and the chinaware to be shipped out to the markets of London. Here Wedgwood opened his own shop and engaged agents to handle his overseas exports. One shipment from his Etruria works to continental Europe was worth £20,000. He was a leading figure in the local chamber of manufacturers, and was the model of the new wealthy industrialist. He was to continue, for the rest of his life, to pursue practical scientific experiments to improve methods and techniques used in his works: improvements that were later adopted by the many other pottery works established in Staffordshire. He even met some Chinese potters in London in 1775 through a friend, John Blake, a member of the East India Company. He recorded in detail their conversation and methods used for firing and kiln construction.

Perhaps his most important scientific achievement was the development of the pyrometer — an instrument for determining the precise heat of a kiln. In his "commonplace book" there is the following entry:

> In the long course of experiments for the improvement of the manufacture I am engaged in, some of the greatest difficulties and perplexities have arisen from not being able to ascertain the heat to which the experiment pieces had been exposed.

Wedgwood was probably the first manufacturer in Europe to engage in scientific research and development. He operated a laboratory in the basement of his house and was a leading member of the Luna Society, which was concerned with promoting scientic methods in industry. Shown here is just one of the 3,000 trials he carried out and documented in trying to perfect his jasper ware.

He set his mind to the problem and came up with a simple but ingenious method of measurement. Like any potter, he realized that clay shrinks at a fairly uniform rate according to the heat of the kiln. However, existing methods using thermometers could only handle temperatures to a maximum of 300 degrees Celsius. Wedgwood needed to know the precise temperature of kilns to 1,000 degrees or more. He therefore constructed a calibrated brass gauge (narrower towards one end) in which a square groove had been cut. A cylinder of clay was placed on one end and would gradually move down the gauge as it shrank in the heat of the kiln. With the pyrometer it was possible to get a precise temperature measurement. This was not only important for his experiments but was to be adopted widely within the industry, not only to achieve more uniform products, but also to minimise loss. For the invention of this simple but useful device, Wedgwood was made a member of the Royal Society in 1783.

The differences between the English and the Chinese ceramics industries were interesting. In China, the knowledge of how to fire a kiln and measure its temperature was a carefully guarded secret kept within the families of craftsmen and taught only to apprentices who were taken into the business. It was considered and remained a trade secret. In China a tradition of observational methods using subtle changes of color and atmosphere in the kilns had evolved over the centuries. These methods had allowed the Chinese to produce some of the finest porcelain in the world. As with the great violins of Italy, few craftsmen even to this day can match the quality of some of the finest pieces. This secrecy prevailed in all the craft guilds in China. There was no tradition of recording techniques or producing technical manuals, except by scholar-officials who did it as part of the amassing of technological information for the great imperial encyclopedias. However, these books were never meant to be read by craftsmen and were usually circulated only among scholars and bureaucrats. Although they contained woodblock illustrations showing the processes, these were never plan drawings. The end result was that this knowledge was never disseminated.

European craft industries in the Middle Ages were also governed by secretive guilds like China's but, by the seventeenth and eighteenth centuries, it had become widely recognized that the growth of scientific and technological knowledge was a public asset. This had been acknowledged as early as the reign of Elizabeth I, when the first British royal patent was given to a stained-glass maker on condition that the knowledge of his techniques be made readily available to other glass makers. The patent system was to be very important in this regard, for it rewarded invention and innovation by giving an individual a limited monopoly while, at the same time, allowing technological knowledge to be widely disseminated. In the highly competitive European climate this obviously made sense. For this dissemination the capacity to make geometrically precise three-dimensional drawings was to play an important role. In China no such development occurred, in part, because there was neither the competitive environment nor the rapid change in taste and demand that there was in Europe. After all, many of the craft industries were imperial monopolies and produced in bureaucratically managed state factories, with little competition.

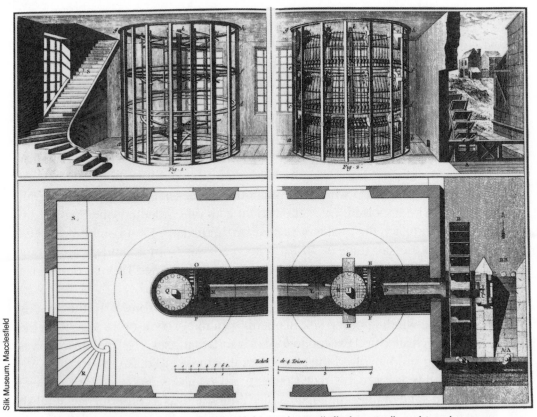

Silk Museum, Macclesfield

This engraving shows the operation of the Piedmont "silk-throwing" machine, the secret of which John Lombe, an early industrial spy, was to bring back to England.

Craft traditions were established and knowledge of techniques kept a carefully guarded secret, an attitude that was commonplace in China until very recently. The danger of this was that important technological knowledge could be completely lost, for example, the methods of construction of the great treasure ships used by Zheng He and the methods of building water-powered spinning wheels or mechanical clocks. It would be fair to say that institutional innovations were as important as the more obvious technological innovations to the growing industrial power of Europe. This is nowhere more evident than in the silk and textile industries where, for centuries, the Chinese led the world.

SILK STOCKINGS AND COTTON SOCKS

From the thirteenth century, when silkworms were supposedly smuggled in bamboo poles from China to Europe, Piedmont in northern Italy was the center of the silk weaving and spinning industry. The region kept a monopoly on the industry by maintaining draconian laws governing the practice of the trade. This was especially true of the spinning of the powerful warp threads used in the weaving of silk fabric. The Italians had developed what was called a "silk-throwing" machine to spin these threads, for which they held a virtual European monopoly. The industry was centered around the city of Lucca and the technology was a carefully guarded secret. In 1308 there was even a guild statute that stated that any man practicing the craft outside the city would be hanged and any woman burned. By 1589 the Piedmontese were so concerned about losing control of this industry that they were even prepared to offer a 50 ducat reward to anyone who killed an artisan practicing their method of silk throwing outside the province.

In 1714 a young Englishman, John Lombe, left London for Piedmont with the sole purpose of stealing the secret of the Lucca "throwing machine." The reason was simple, there was a growing demand in England for silk fabric but a major factor affecting the cost of production was the Piedmont monopoly on the production of the essential warp thread, which, throughout the seventeenth and eighteenth centuries, had to be imported. Try as they might with other methods the English did not seem able to match the quality achieved by the Italians. John Lombe had been apprenticed into the silk trade at an early age and was from a family with a long association with silk and wool weaving. At the age of 20 he joined Thomas Cotchett, a retired solicitor who had established a silk-spinning mill in Derby.

There were four processes involved in the making of the strong warp thread. The first involved the winding of the silk filament from the cocoon on to a bobbin; the thread was then cleaned and twisted to form a standard thread. The final process was called "doubling" and involved the twisting of this thread to make the strong warp thread. It was this last process that Cotchett and Lombe were unable to achieve satisfactorily, in spite of importing Dutch machinery, and, as a consequence, English silk made from local thread was inferior to that made from the expensive Italian warp thread.

Lombe, in an act of extraordinary bravado, decided to become an industrial spy. For this task he learned Italian, draftsmanship and mathematics, and left for Italy with the support of his half-brother, Thomas, who ran the Lombe family business. Lombe was able to enlist the help of a Jesuit priest who, so the story goes, on the payment of an "oblazione" or bribe secured him a position in a Lucca mill as a machine winder. He would wait behind in the evenings and make detailed plan drawings of the throwing machine and its various parts. He smuggled the drawings back to his brother, hidden inside bales of silk thread. However, he was discovered and had to flee Piedmont. If he had been caught he would have been hung by one leg from the gallows "until dead," a gruesome end. Fortunately, he was able to get to the coast and on to a British merchant ship that was leaving for London. On finding out he had escaped in this manner, gunboats were sent in hot pursuit but the British ship succeeded in escaping them.

On his return to London in 1716, John Lombe immediately took out a patent on the machine and, with money from his half-brother Thomas, set up England's first water-powered textile factory in Derby. This was to be the prototype of the modern textile factory whose widespread adoption throughout northern England was to form the foundation for the Industrial Revolution. It was powered by a single undershot water wheel, which, by means of gearing, drove a whole battery of throwing machines tended by 300 factory workers. This was mechanization on an unprecedented scale.

Derbyshire County Council

Above: Lombe's water-powered silk spinning factory, built in Derby in 1720, was the prototype for the factory system of production. The factory system was to provide England with the industrial wealth and power that would shake the foundations of the Celestial Empire in the east.

Right: A scale model of Lombe's "silk-throwing" machine built for the Silk Museum in Derby. The original was three times the size, and was driven by water power.

Courtesy Film Australia

NUMERICAL CONTROL — FROM LOOMS TO COMPUTERS

In the early eighteenth century at Lyon, the center of the French silk industry, weavers were confronted with increased competition both from Chinese imports and from other centers within Europe. The master weavers of the town began to look for technological solutions to the problems of quality and cost. Basil Bouchon, one of these master weavers, was impressed by the engineering skills of craftsmen making the ingenious clockwork dolls or automata, which were then in vogue. These automata, which played the harpsichord or performed complex acrobatic movements, were controlled by sophisticated clockwork gearing driven by a cylindrical drum with jacks, the same method as used in musical boxes that played melodies. The jacks on the cylinder were arranged to trigger different movements, in sequence, as the cylinder turned.

It struck Bouchon that the same principle could be applied to the weaving of the complex new designs required for silk fabric (given the increased competition in the silk industry it was necessary to be able to change patterns to suit changing tastes). With traditional techniques, changing the pattern was difficult and very laborious. The traditional loom used in silk production required two men, one doing the actual weaving and the other, the drawboy, controlling the pattern by holding up various combinations of the warp threads. This technique, originally developed in China, was satisfactory if a standardized product was required and if labor costs were low. However, unless the drawboy was very skilled, inaccuracies in design were inevitable.

Bouchon decided to encode the design on to a roll of paper (the same principle still used in the pianola or player piano), which would control the movement of the warp threads. Bouchon never got the idea to work effectively and it was another Lyon silk weaver, Jean-

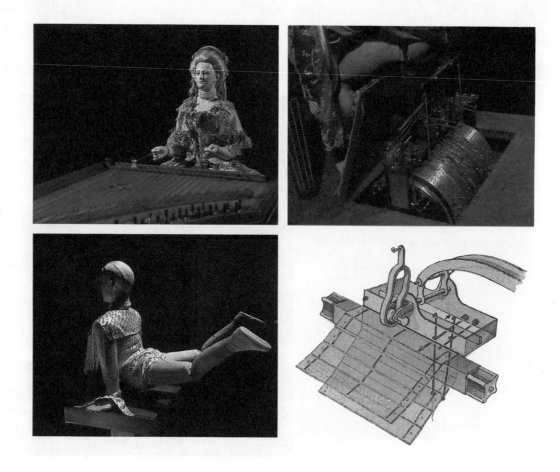

Marie Jacquard, who was to perfect the system. Jacquard exchanged the continuous roll of paper for a chain of cards, each card representing one movement of the shuttle. As many as 30,000 of these cards could be used in the production of one piece of silk fabric. Jacquard's loom caused a sensation when he finally perfected it in the early 1800s. In 1806 he was awarded the Chevalier de la Legion d'Honneur by Napoleon and given a state pension of 3,000 francs for his efforts.

Not all the reactions to his invention were as appreciative. In 1810 drawboys went on the rampage through the streets of Lyon, smashing Jacquard's looms; Jacquard himself was lucky to escape with his life. However, the economic advantages of his machine were obvious to every silk weaver. Even those who may not have wished to change to the new methods had to, or be forced out of business. Drawboys were but one of a number of craft skills that were to

disappear overnight in the momentum of technological change. By 1812 there were 11,000 Jacquard looms operating in France alone.

This method of encoding information or sequences of instructions on to punched cards, developed by Jacquard and the other weavers of Lyon, was to have profound consequences far beyond the silk industry. These same Jacquard cards were to be used in the early development of computers, first by Babbage in Britain and later by Hollerith in the United States. The cards were eventually used to encode data in the first electronic computer, the ENIAC, developed at the end of World War II and used by John von Neumann to perform the mathematical calculations necessary to make the first atomic bomb. In the 1950s IBM would turn these same cards into an international symbol of efficiency and innovation.

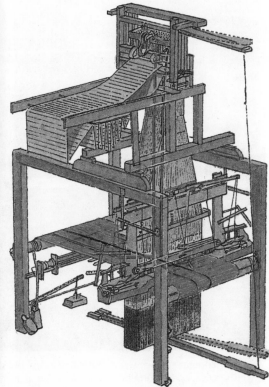

The story has a dark ending. In 1722 John Lombe died suddenly at the age of 29, only six years after his return to England. A mysterious Italian woman who arrived in Derby soon after the establishment of his factory was employed there and it was later believed by many that she had been sent by the Piedmontese to seek revenge, presumably by slowly poisoning him; she disappeared soon after his death. The factory was not a huge success but it was to become the model for the use of water-powered gearing to drive spinning machines and was soon taken up in the cotton industry.

If there was a growing demand for silk in England in the second half of the eighteenth century, the demand for cotton cloth was even greater. The industry had grown out of the demand stimulated by the East India Company's import of cotton cloth from India and China. The center of the local cotton industry was on the damp side of the Pennines around the city of Manchester. The major problem was the supply of yarn. Traditional hand-spinning techniques could not meet the demand. Supplies of cotton were readily available from North America and the West Indies, and flax from Ireland. In 1733 John Kay had invented the flying shuttle, which meant that the weavers were able to work at much greater speed, with the shuttle being thrown by springs from one side of the loom to the other. This increased the speed of weaving and therefore the demand for thread.

In 1761 the Society for the Encouragement of Arts, Commerce and Manufactures offered a reward of £50 to anyone who could invent a spinning machine. James

Popular science was promoted throughout the eighteenth century by a new class of instrument makers and scientists who gave popular lectures and demonstrations of scientific principles. Here, a lecture is being given on pneumatics.

Richard Arkwright's cotton spinning mill, established at Cromford in 1771. In this remote valley he built a massive factory complex and established an entire industrial community. Many of these communities, which grew up around the factories of Lancashire, were run with a benign paternalism; the conditions in others were appalling.

Hargreaves came up with the spinning Jenny, a machine that would allow eight cotton spindles to work at the same time, but it was difficult to operate. It was the youngest son of an impecunious barber and wigmaker, Richard Arkwright, who solved the problem. In conjunction with a clockmaker, John Kay (not to be confused with the inventor of the flying shuttle), Arkwright developed a spinning machine known as the water frame, which he patented in 1769. Arkwright continued to experiment with the water frame and debated whether to market it for domestic use. However, he had seen what the Lombe brothers had been able to achieve in their factory at Derby. By applying water power, geared by engineers familiar with clockwork mechanisms, it was possible to drive a whole army of machines. He therefore decided to set up a factory but had the difficult task of finding the capital.

While continuing in the family's profession of wigmaking, he traveled the countryside collecting hair. In Nottingham he made contact with a hosier (stocking maker) Jedediah Strutt who was impressed with the strength and fineness of the yarn produced on Arkwright's water frame, which was ideally suited for the hosiery industry. In 1770 Arkwright, Strutt and another man, Samuel Need, set up in partnership.

In 1771 Arkwright and his partners, with investment from bankers in Nottingham, set up a mill at Cromford, then a small village near Matlock north of Derby. The virtue of this site was its good supply of water to drive the water wheels, and it was also sufficiently far from the center of the textile industry where riots had begun to break out as machinery began to displace labor. In the *Derby Mercury* of 13 December 1771 this advertisement appeared:

> Wanted immediately, two Journeymen Clock-makers, or others that understands Tooth and Pinion well: Also a Smith that can forge and file — Likewise two wood turners that has been accustomed to Wheelmaking, Spoleturning etc. Weavers residing at the Mill may have good work. There is Employment at the above Place for Women, Children, etc. and good Wages.

In order to set up an entire industrial community, Arkwright built not only a large factory, but also houses for weavers, a school, a church and other essential amenities. Here, we begin to see the formation of the industrial community, and the breakdown of the production process like the cogs in a giant machine. Skills were no longer embodied in people but in machines; machines that could be owned by those with the capital to invest in their invention and the establishment of a factory. Thus the independence of small craftsmen, who had been engaged, usually with their entire families, in the production of cloth, was eroded. The benefits went to the new industrialists and to consumers who now had access to better and cheaper cloth. The cost was borne by the displaced artisans who now had little alternative but to give up their cherished independence and become wage-earning workers in the new factories. It is little wonder that some ran amok breaking looms and industrial machinery.

So successful was Arkwright's first mill and so large the demand that a second mill, 125 feet long and seven-stories high, was put up at Cromford in 1776. As Arkwright's original patent expired, other mills were opened up on the basis of his success at Cromford. Throughout the Midlands the factory system with its use of water power, geared to drive increasingly sophisticated machinery, led to the mechanization of all aspects of textile manufacture. This was made possible by the application of engineering skills first developed by the earlier clock and instrument makers — skills that had been evident in the great astronomical clock of Su Song and in the elaborate robotic devices such as musical boxes, which had so entertained the Chinese court and the European aristocracy.

GOD AND THE NEW FACTORY

Religion must necessarily produce both industry and frugality, and these cannot but produce riches. But as riches increase, so will pride, anger, and love of the world . . . How then is it possible that Methodism, that is, a religion of the heart, though it flourishes now as a green bay tree, should continue in this state. . . . So, although the form of religion remains, the spirit is swiftly vanishing away.

John Wesley, founder of Methodism

The new factory system was built on the driving force of water (and later steam power) and on machines that could break down the production process into rational units or tasks. But these technological developments were not enough in themselves to account for the phenomenal growth of output, which was to be such a feature of the British Industrial Revolution. After all, the Chinese 500 years earlier had had water-powered spinning. The difference in eighteenth century Europe was that new economic institutions supported by international trading networks had vastly increased the size of the market that was available; a market far larger than was possible within the Chinese empire, which was vast by any national standards.

The new emphasis on free trade, which was being demanded by merchants frustrated by state monopolies, led to the articulation of economic theories that provided a philosophical rationale for free-market capitalism. Adam Smith in his

Styal Mill at Quarry Bank, near Manchester, was established by the Greg family in 1790, after Richard Arkwright's original patent on the water frame expired. The clocktower and the chimney were the two potent symbols of the new discipline demanded by the factory system. With the application of machinery for spinning and weaving, the cost of producing simple cotton cloth was to fall to levels that would make Manchester synonymous with cotton fabric throughout the world.

Courtesy Film Australia

141

Wealth of Nations provided a completely new concept of national wealth, based, not on the control of trade (the traditional mercantilist theory), but on production. Smith saw in the rational division of labor the economic advantage of producing better and cheaper goods. His famous example was the pin factory. If one man was to make a whole pin by himself he would produce fewer pins than if the process was broken up into discrete tasks with one worker specializing in each. He also believed that, if manufacturers were left to compete freely with each other in the market, the price of goods would be regulated, and the cheapest and most efficient production techniques automatically encouraged. For the British utilitarian philosophers such as Bentham and Mill this freedom was seen to "provide the greatest happiness for the greatest number." In this market mechanism Smith saw what he, along with new industrialists such as Arkwright and Wedgwood, believed to be "the hidden hand of Progress." The new market system would find the correct balance between the factors of production — labor, capital and land.

What was not taken into account in this unbridled enthusiasm for the free market was the position of those who sold their labor and who were to become its unquestioned victims. No one could deny the benefits of increased productivity or that the freedom of the individual to pursue his or her "enlightened self-interest" was an advancement, but at what cost. The legacy of Aquinas and the Calvinists was to be restated for the new working class by the fire-and-brimstone preachers of the

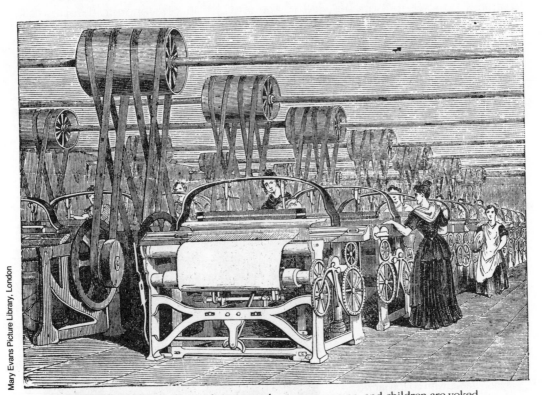

Mary Evans Picture Library, London

"While the engine runs people must work — men, women, and children are yoked together with iron and steam," commented Dr J.P. Kay in 1832 on the work discipline demanded in the cotton mills of the north of England.

Methodist Church. The almost monastic discipline of the Protestant middle class had centered on the virtue and urgency of work and its rewards of grace and providence. This was now to be extended to the new factory workers, the displaced weavers, spinners and potters forced to abandon their independent semi-rural existence to become wage laborers in the rapidly growing cities of northern England. For as the price of the cotton cloth produced in the new factories halved and halved again in a matter of years, the small weaver was put out of business.

The rigorous discipline demanded by the factory owners was alien to many of their employees' traditional way of life. Much of the early factory labor was supplied by women and children who were pliable and more able to withstand the monotony of 12–14 hour days tending machines. Traditionally, the weaver worked at his craft between periods of agricultural labor, work followed the pattern common to rural life of following the cycles of nature, with its seasonal demands and numerous holidays. The weavers had been, above all else, moderately independent as they owned and controlled the means of production — their looms and spinning wheels.

The factory system demanded that they be cogs in a giant machine, whose interdependent parts operated like clockwork. Dr Andrew Ure in *The Philosophy of Manufactures* (1835) described it in the following words:

> [The factory]... involves the idea of a vast automation, composed of various mechanical and intellectual organs, acting in uninterrupted concert for the production of a common object, all of them subordinated to a self-regulated moving force....
>
> To devise and administer a successful code of factory discipline, suited to the necessities of factory diligence, was the Herculean enterprise, the noble achievement of Arkwright. Even at the present day, when the system is perfectly organized, and its labor lightened to the utmost, it is found nearly impossible to convert persons past the age of puberty, whether drawn from rural or from handicraft occupations, into useful factory hands. After struggling for a while to conquer their listless or restive habits, they either renounce the employment spontaneously, or are dismissed by the overlookers on account of inattention.

Apart from rationalizing the use of child labor in factories, Ure was probably accurate in his observations about the difficulties with which rural workers came to terms with the conditions of employment in the new factory system, which had its beginnings in the cotton mills of Lancashire and, by the early nineteenth century, had spread to other industries throughout England. Ure realised that an inner change had to take place in individual workers, and the most powerful weapon to use to inculcate this internal work and time discipline was fear. The chapels and Sunday schools constructed by the millowners were a source of conditioning, as important as the clocks and bells that governed the working day and towered above the factory roofs like the spires of the ancient monasteries. The fire-and-brimstone preaching of the early Methodist chapel, along with the puritanical sexual repression it demanded, gave to the rural workforce the sense of urgency that the factory system demanded. For Ure this was part of what he described as the "moral economy of the factory system":

It is, therefore, excessively the interest of every millowner to organize his moral machinery on equally sound principles with his mechanical, for otherwise he will never command the steady hands, watchful eye, and prompt cooperation, essential to excellence of product.... There is, in fact, no case to which the Gospel truth, "Godliness is great gain", is more applicable than to the administration of an extensive factory.

The fear of losing work or money was not sufficient to inculcate the virtues that Ure envisaged. These virtues had to come from a sense of almost revolutionary zeal; a self-discipline that would make individuals abandon their traditional values for those of the industrial system in which they now worked.

However, the missionary zeal with which the Methodists approached the inculcation of work discipline among the recalcitrant working class of England was nothing to the efforts that were to be expended on behalf of the heathens in the rest of the world. It was with very different eyes that Protestant missionaries regarded Asia and the culture of imperial China. Compared with the Jesuits two centuries earlier, the Protestant merchants and missionaries of the early nineteenth century who arrived at the ports of Guangzhou and Nagasaki regarded the culture they saw as decadent, corrupt and lacking the dynamic character embodied in the European drive for progress. Having mastered and even surpassed the Chinese in many of the industrial arts and technology that had for centuries inspired awe, respect and emulation, the European merchants now came to promote their own versions of the porcelain, cotton textiles and guns in the very market places where they had first appeared a thousand years earlier.

THE CHINA TRADE, TRIBUTES AND THE OPIUM WAR

It may be perhaps supposed that the sight of the masterpieces of art, which the Chinese receive annually from Europe, will open their eyes and convince them that industry is here carried further than amongst themselves and that our genius surpasses theirs; but their vanity finds remedy for this. All those wonders are included in the class of superfluities and by placing them behind their wants they place them at the same time beneath their regard.

Van Braan, leader of a Dutch mission to the court of Emperor Qianlong, 1792

On 26 September 1792 the "Ambassador Extraordinary and Plenipotentiary from the King of Great Britain to the Emperor of China," Lord Macartney, left England. The primary objective was to win from the aging Emperor Qianlong trading concessions and the lifting of the severe restrictions on foreigners, who were forced to operate only through the port of Guangzhou where all overseas trade was conducted. Above all, Lord Macartney was to promote British manufac-

James Gillray's prophetic caricature of Lord Macartney's reception in China was published a week before Macartney left London for the east.

tured goods, which could be traded in exchange for tea and other Chinese products. At that time 90 per cent of Chinese imports to Europe had to be paid for in bullion, which was apparently all the Chinese would accept.

Trade had expanded greatly throughout the latter part of the eighteenth century. In 1751, 19 foreign ships arrived at Guangzhou; by 1797 this had increased to 81. In the first quarter of the eighteenth century the East India Company was importing, on average, 400,000 pounds of tea; by the end of the century this had grown to 23.4 million pounds, such was the demand not only in Britain but also in her American colonies. American merchants were not allowed to trade directly with Guangzhou for Chinese commodities but had to deal through the East India Company in London. This meant that the price of tea in the American colonies was significantly higher than it would have been if they had traded directly. Dutch merchants were constantly smuggling tea to the New England coast, much to the chagrin of the British colonial government.

The Boston Tea Party of 1773 — when boxes of tea shipped from London were thrown into Boston harbor by colonists and merchants protesting at the duty on tea and frustrated by their lack of freedom under British rule — was the first incident in what was finally to lead to the War of Independence and the formation of the United States. The arrival of the *Empress of China* from New York in 1784 was the first from a country that was to become a major new player in the China trade.

Conditions in Guangzhou for foreign merchants were severely restricted. The trading season was short, lasting from October to January, and they were required to deal only with officials sanctioned by the Chinese government. This was equally difficult for the Chinese merchants who were forced to ship tea, silk and other products over 800 miles from the production centers in Fujian, Anhui (Anhwei) and Jiangxi (Kiangsi) to Guangzhou in the far south. No foreign merchants were allowed at any other port. The rules of behavior laid down by the Governor-General Li Siyao

In the eighteenth and nineteenth centuries idealized pictures of the production of tea, porcelain and silk were produced for the west. There was great curiosity about these products, and methods of production were obviously of interest to the growing number of consumers of Chinese goods in the west, particularly in the United States.

Hong Kong Museum of Art, Hong Kong

Conditions at the foreign trading bases at Guangzhou were unduly restrictive. The arrival of American merchants resulted in further crowding, and it was, in part, to change these conditions by allowing greater freedom of trade that George III sent his Ambassador Extraordinary, Lord Macartney, to China.

(Li Ssu-yao) in 1759, designed to minimize conflict and contact between Chinese and Europeans, were considered demeaning and insulting by many of the European and American merchants forced to wait for as long as three months for the turn round in their cargoes:

1. No foreign warship may sail inside the Bogue [the entrance where the Pearl River reaches the South China Sea].
2. Neither foreign women nor firearms may be brought into the factories [the name given to the warehouses used by the merchant companies].
3. All pilots and compradores [Chinese middlemen who assisted in negotiations] must register with the Chinese authorities in Macao [the first point of entry]; foreign ships must not enter into direct communication with Chinese people and merchants without the immediate supervision of the compradore.

A Chinese view of the procession of gifts brought by Macartney to China. Included were the traditional objects, which Europeans assumed were of interest to the Chinese emperors — astronomical and scientific instruments, and elaborate clocks. However, what interested the court most were pieces of Wedgwood's jasper ware.

4. Foreign factories shall employ no maids and no more than eight Chinese male servants.

5. Foreigners may not communicate with Chinese officials except through the proper channel of the co-hong [officially recognized association of merchant middlemen].

6. Foreigners are not allowed to row boats freely in the river. They may, however, visit the Flower Gardens (*Hua-ti*) and the temple opposite the river in groups of ten or less, three times a month — on the 8th, 18th and 28th. They shall not visit other places.

7. Foreigners may not sit in sedan-chairs, or use the sanpan boats with flags flying; they may ride only in topless small boats.

8. Foreign trade must be conducted through the hong merchants. Foreigners living in the factories must not move in and out too frequently, although they may walk freely within a hundred yards of their factories. Clandestine transactions between them and traitorous Chinese merchants must be prevented.

9. Foreign traders must not remain in Guangzhou after the trading season; even

The Emperor Qianlong arriving to meet with Lord Macartney at Jehol, his summer residence to the north of Beijing. Here, the Manchu emperors could return to the nomadic traditions of their forefathers. This picture was painted by Alexander who accompanied Macartney on his journey as the recorder of events.

during the trading season when the ship is laden, they should return home or go to Macao.

10. Foreign ships may anchor at Whampoa but nowhere else.
11. Foreigners may neither buy Chinese books, nor learn Chinese.
12. The hong merchants shall not go into debt to foreigners.

With the intention of changing all this, Lord Macartney arrived off Guangzhou on 19 June 1793 and immediately sailed north to Tianjin (Tientsin) for his meeting with Qianlong. As tradition demanded, Macartney's mission was to be treated as any other tributary mission. He had come prepared with presents costing around $30,000 including a planetarium, globes, mathematical instruments, chronometers, a telescope, measuring instruments, chemical and electrical instruments, window and plate glass, carpets, goods from Birmingham, goods from Sheffield, copperware and some of Wedgwood's latest jasper ware. Of all the goods, this new pottery most amazed and delighted the Chinese who had seen nothing like it before.

As the emperor was at his summer retreat north of the great wall at Jehol, Macartney traveled there for his audience on 14 September. He was expected to do the usual kowtow, numerous bowings and prostrations lying flat on the ground, but Macartney refused. He considered it to be beneath his dignity. There was some contention over this break with tradition but, as it was Qianlong's eighty-third birthday and he was said to have been in a good mood, Macartney was allowed to sink to one knee as he would before his own king.

Alexander's portrait of the Emperor Qianlong. Despite Lord Macartney's appeals, Qianlong saw no reason to break with tradition and grant the British, or any other European nation, rights other than those of a tributary state to trade in the customary manner from Guangzhou.

Gifts were exchanged and a letter from King George III was presented to the emperor. The event was seen to have been a great success and Macartney and his mission were treated with great courtesy. But to Qianlong, the ambassador of George III was doing no more than showing the appropriate respect of a tributary state on the occasion of the emperor's birthday. The event so inspired Qianlong that he composed the following poem:

Formerly Portugal presented tribute;
Now England is paying homage.
They have out-traveled Si-hai and Heng-zhang;
My ancestors' merit and virtue must have reached their distant shores.
Though their tribute is commonplace, my heart approves sincerely.
Curios and boasted ingenuity of their devices I prize not.
Though what they bring is meager, yet,
In my kindness to men from afar I make generous return,
Wanting to preserve my good health and power.

Macartney remained with the emperor until 9 October and left with the following edict addressed to George III, rejecting all requests for a relaxation in the conditions at Guangzhou or any extension of the terms of trade, which would allow British goods to be sold in China:

Yesterday your ambassador petitioned my Ministers regarding your trade with China, but his proposal is not consistent with our dynastic usage and cannot be entertained. Hitherto, all European nations including your own country's barbarian merchants, have carried on their trade with our Celestial Empire at Guangzhou. Such has been the procedure for many years although our Celestial Empire possesses all things in prolific abundance and lacks no product without our borders. There was therefore no need to import manufactured goods of the outside barbarians in exchange for our own products. But as the tea, silk and porcelain which the Celestial Empire produced are absolute necessities to European nations and to yourselves, we permitted, as a mark of favor, that foreign business houses should be established at Guangzhou. . . . It behoves you, O King, to respect my sentiments and to display even greater devotion and loyalty in future so that, by perpetual submission to our Throne, you may secure peace and prosperity for your country thereafter.

The mission was a complete failure. Macartney was, as one wit in the East India Company observed, "received with the utmost politeness, treated with the utmost hospitality, watched with the utmost vigilance and dismissed with the utmost civility." The whole exercise had cost the British government more than $150,000. Although in 1816 they were to send another mission, led by Lord Amherst, in the hope of persuading Qianlong's son the Jiaqing (Chia-ch'ing) emperor to open the country to greater trade, nothing was achieved.

Despite this, the China trade through the port of Guangzhou was to grow enormously, particularly as New England merchants began to play an increasingly important role during the Napoleonic Wars when much of European shipping was tied up. By the 1830s in many of the coastal ports of New England such as Salem, Boston and Mystic as much as 20 per cent of domestic furnishings were being imported from China. Chinese merchants acted as commission agents for porcelain, crockery, furniture, silverware, wallpaper, cotton and silk fabrics as well as tea. Hauqua, one of the Chinese compradores who handled these commissions and controlled much of the tea trade out of Guangzhou, was reputed to be the richest man in the world. In 1834 he was reported to have a fortune of $47 million. When traditional designs fell out of favor, Chinese artisans proved adept at copying western products and producing them to order. In 1833, for example, imports from China to the United States were worth about $7.5 million. In the same year, customs duties made up $29 million of the $34 million total treasury receipts. The expansion of international trade was clearly a significant issue for the United States government.

In Britain, the East India Company had grown so powerful that it virtually ruled India on behalf of the British government. The shift in interests from purely trade concerns to economic power was to be seen in the ruthless destruction of the traditional cotton spinning and weaving industry in Bengal in order to provide a market for cotton cloth manufactured in Manchester. The Company was soon exporting raw cotton from India and importing cotton cloth from factories in Britain. It is little wonder that Mahatma Gandhi should use the spinning of cotton as a symbol of defiance to British rule during the independence movement of the 1920s and 1930s.

For both the East India Company and the British government the situation in

Jardine Matheson & Co. Ltd, Hong Kong

Hauqua, a compradore merchant in Guangzhou, was considered to be the richest man in the world in the early nineteenth century, with a personal fortune of $47 million. His money came from acting as a middleman between foreign merchants and Chinese producers.

China was intolerable. From 90 to 98 per cent of all trade was conducted with gold or silver; no other import being considered acceptable. But by the mid 1820s this was to change and the agent of change was opium. The East India Company had, in 1770, gained a monopoly on opium production in Bengal. The Chinese had banned its use and sale from as early as 1729 when the Portuguese had begun to import the drug. But as contraband it had become, by the 1830s, the major item of trade, with deals being arranged with Chinese merchants at the foreign factories in Guangzhou, and delivery taking place at sea, outside Chinese waters. The illicit trade was large, with American ships transporting the drug from Turkey and the Levant, and the British from India. Private trading companies such as Jardine Matheson and Sassoons from Britain, Robert Forbes from Boston and Wilcocks & Latimer from Philadelphia were involved in the trade. Although the East India Company tried to distance itself from the trade in China, it was the major supplier of the drug through its factories in India.

It was not just with China that opium was traded. The drug was also being imported into Britain and Europe where it was mixed with alcohol and sold under the name of laudanum. There, the consequences of addiction were not as severe as they were in China although many writers, such as De Quincy and Coleridge, became addicts. It is ironic that Coleridge should write his famous poem "Kubla Khan" after taking the drug. For the romantic poets contemplating the turmoil of industrial England, the oriental vision of order and harmony had almost as much appeal as the euphoric effects of opium. But Coleridge ends his poem with an oblique warning:

And all should cry,
Beware! Beware!

. . .

For he on honey-dew hath fed,
And drunk the milk of Paradise.

In the land of Xanadu itself the economic consequences of the opium trade were disastrous. The addiction to the drug was widespread and affected all classes. The human cost was great with an estimated two million people using opium, many of them becoming addicts. Around 20 per cent of government officials used the drug. The economic consequences were to be equally harmful. While, between 1800 and 1810, large amounts of silver flowed into China as a result of foreign trade; between 1828 and 1833 the British alone shipped out $29.6 million in hard currency. For the East India Company the situation was ideal. In 1836, for example, they sold opium in China, worth $18 million, which was traded for tea and silk worth $17 million. The parliamentary debates, which failed to ban its sale in Britain, were prepared to condone the trade, regarding the social consequences as a Chinese problem. The more important issue, it was argued, was the right of free trade. In 1834 parliament repealed the monopoly held by the East India Company on British trade with China and a bill was passed allowing all merchants the right to trade wherever they wished. The system of trade in Guangzhou was therefore challenged by a new and far less respectful body of merchants buoyed up by the unquestioned moral virtues of free trade and Britain's obvious international naval and military supremacy.

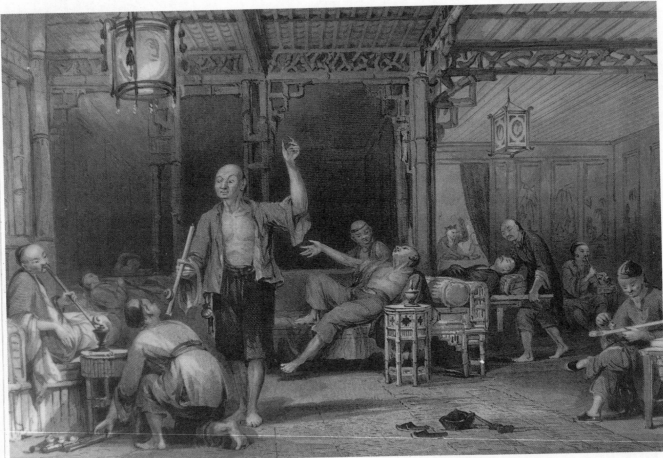

Although opium was officially banned in China, access to cheap opium led to widespread addiction, with scholars as well as laborers falling prey to the habit. Because of a high level of corruption the trade was able to flourish under the very noses of officials.

This confrontation with recalcitrant foreign merchants was unprecedented for the Chinese. Because of the lack of interest in international trade shown by the imperial government, the institutions to deal with the situation had not evolved as they had in Europe. The Chinese navy was ineffectual and there was no customs system to control illegal imports. Smuggling along the southern coast had gone on for centuries under the very noses of government officials who were usually the beneficiaries.

The Chinese government was, however, determined to do something about this insidious trade in opium. After a long debate, the emperor decided to send an experienced and incorruptible scholar-official Commissioner Lin Zexu (Lin Tse-hsü) to Guangzhou to stamp out the trade. Lin's approach was, initially, to avoid confrontation and to research the problem carefully, even consulting western books on international law to develop a case to be put to Queen Victoria to stop the trade:

I have heard that smoking opium is strictly forbidden in your country. Why do you let it be passed on to the harm of other countries? Suppose there were people from another

154

country who carried opium for sale to Britain and seduced your people into buying and smoking it; certainly your honorable ruler would deeply hate it and be bitterly aroused. . . . Naturally you would not wish to give others what you yourself do not want. . . . May you, O Queen, check your wicked and sift your vicious people before they come to China, in order to guarantee the peace of your nation, to show further the sincerity of your politeness and submissiveness.

The climate in Britain was not responsive to such moral reasoning. First, the letters probably did not even reach the Queen herself and, second, the idea that moral arguments of this sort should be allowed to undermine the mechanism of the free market and of free trade — the principle of laissez-faire to which the dominant political groups within the British government were now committed — was perhaps too much to expect. British wealth and prosperity depended on free trade and the idea of the government acting as an international moral censor as the Chinese demanded was not possible.

Lin received no response to his appeals. On 18 March 1839, like the head of a modern drug-enforcement agency, he got tough. He demanded that all opium should be surrendered and that merchants should sign a pledge forgoing such trade in the future under threat of death. He confined 350 foreign merchants to their factory compounds, stopped all trade out of Guangzhou and withdrew the services supplied to the foreign factories, leaving them without any resources until the merchants complied. The Superintendent of Trade, Captain Charles Elliot, took on the negotiations on behalf of the British government, which shifted the incident to a new political level. On 18 May he delivered 21,306 chests of opium to Lin. Three large trenches were dug, 150 feet long, 75 feet wide and 7 feet deep; the opium balls were crushed with lime and salt and, when dissolved, were flushed into a nearby creek.

The situation escalated, with demands for reprisals coming from powerful merchant groups in London, Manchester and Liverpool. Lord Palmerston sent an expeditionary force to blockade the port of Guangzhou. On 3 November Admiral Guan (Kuan) leading 29 Chinese war junks engaged the British fleet and the first Opium War began.

The British then began to blockade all Chinese ports in the hope that a show of strength would lead to the Chinese backing down. Over a period of almost two years negotiations were attempted, with the British making demands for territorial rights to Hong Kong Island and trading rights throughout China as well as compensation for their opium, all of which were completely unacceptable to the Qing court. Finally, in the spring of 1842, with 25 warships carrying 668 guns, 14 steamships carrying 56 guns and 10,000 men, Sir Henry Pottinger led the British forces up the Yangtze taking strategic cities: Wusong on 16 June, Shanghai on 19 June, and Jinjiang (Chinkiang) on 21 July. Jinjiang was a major port on the Grand Canal, which carried grain supplies to the imperial capital of Beijing. The threat of a blockade on essential food supplies moving north and the threatened destruction of Nanjing forced the Chinese to concede to all the British demands.

The Chinese confronted the reality of European industrial power for the first time.

National Library of Australia, Canberra

The Opium War, which followed the confinement of foreign merchants and the destruction of opium stocks by Commissioner Lin, confronted the Chinese with a military machine refined by centuries of conflict in Europe and the colonial territories. The relative peace and social harmony that the Chinese had been able to maintain within their borders had not prepared them for the firepower of British gunboats.

The fall of their forts, which were helpless against the superior fire power of the British gunboats, was to bring home a vulnerability for which there was no precedent. In the past no power could seriously have threatened China from the sea. The fort of Wusong had fallen in a matter of hours. Of the three hundred cannons captured by the British most were made of bamboo, and many of the Chinese soldiers were still using crossbows as they had done at the time of Marco Polo. The Chinese governor of Shanghai described the siege as the city's defenses fell:

> . . . cannon balls innumerable, flying in awful confusion through the expanse of heaven, fell before, behind and on either side . . . while in the distance [I] saw the ships of the rebels, standing erect, lofty as the mountains. The fierce daring of the rebels was inconceivable. Officers and men fell at their posts. Every effort to resist and check the coast was in vain and a retreat became inevitable.

The emperor had no alternative but to sue for peace on any terms. On 29 August 1842, Chinese officials were taken from the city of Nanjing to the gunboat *Cornwallis.* Here the Treaty of Nanjing was formally signed, ending the first Opium

War. The Chinese agreed to pay the British $21 million in reparations, including the cost of the opium destroyed; to open up five ports for international trade; to lease the island of Hong Kong to the British as a base and, above all, to accept that communications between the British and the Chinese would be carried out under conditions of equality as befitted sovereign states. This last point was an interesting one for, in the view of John Quincy Adams, United States Secretary of State at the time, the war with China was not over the importation of opium any more than the American War of Independence was over the throwing of tea into Boston harbor:

> The cause of the war is the Kowtow — the arrogant and insupportable pretensions of the Chinese, that she will hold commercial intercourse with mankind not upon terms of equal reciprocity, but upon the insulting and degrading forms of relations between lord and vassal.

The idea that the Chinese might have a right not to engage in international trade or relations with the outside world was not regarded as a serious proposition. On the other hand, the concept that China was merely a nation state on an equal footing with others was contrary to the traditional Chinese world view, and one that was to prove extremely hard to change.

In the calculations of the British government, the moral issue of the opium trade was clearly to take second place to the higher principle of free trade and international commerce. Like the steam engines that now powered the cotton looms of Lancashire and drove the new gunboats on the Yangtze, the market was seen as a self-regulating mechanism. Driven by the forces of supply and demand, it would serve everyone's interests as long as the government allowed the individual consumers and producers maximum freedom to do what they liked, even, some would argue, to consume opium. This was regarded as enlightened self-interest. In this concept of a market running as a self-regulating mechanism, like Newton's clockwork universe, the political economists of the day believed that they had discovered the hidden hand of progress, the secret of unlimited wealth and power.

For the Chinese the British justification for the war, in terms of the sanctity of free trade, was only to reaffirm the widely held opinion in the imperial capital that the western barbarians were morally bankrupt, and that their traditional policy of keeping them out of the Celestial Empire had been entirely justified. But, however reassuring this sense of moral superiority might have been, it provided little consolation as the Chinese reviewed their battered forts and hopelessly inadequate means of defending themselves against the obvious technological superiority of the British gunboats.

Contemptuous though many Confucian officials were about the European preoccupation with "mere ingenious technology," they, like the Japanese and other Asian nations, now had no alternative but to try to come to terms with the alien values and economic institutions, which allowed these Europeans their remarkable industrial wealth and overwhelming military power.

The Prosperity of an English Trading Firm in Yokohama in 1871 by Ochiai Yoshiiku. Having for centuries looked to China as the centre of civilization the Japanese in the late nineteenth century turned to the west, avidly adopting not just European military and industrial technology but their cultural and economic institutions.

DREAMS OF WEALTH AND POWER

ON THE WINGS OF CHANGE

Win the War
And Japan will be denounced as a yellow peril
Lose it,
And she will be branded as a barbaric land.

Mori Ogai, on the Russo-Japanese War, 1905

The great questions of the day will not be settled by
resolutions and majority votes but by iron and blood.

Otto von Bismarck

The Opium War of 1839–42 sent shock waves, not just through China, but through all of Asia. The vast Chinese empire had been brought to its knees by the power of the European gunboats, which meant, in effect, that the traditional tributary relationship offered by China to the smaller countries in the region had been fundamentally devalued. China, for the first time in two thousand years, was no longer the dominant military power in east Asia.

This reality was not lost on the Japanese. For centuries they had operated uneasily within the Chinese sphere of influence; uneasily, despite the fact that from the eighth century their written language, art, music and technology were offshoots of Chinese culture. During the Tokugawa shogunate (1603–1868) there was even a self-conscious effort to introduce Confucianism as a means of gaining stability and peace after centuries of clan warfare.

Both Japan and China were now confronted with an external threat to their sovereignty more serious than any internal rebellion. Their different responses to this threat from the west illustrate some of the important economic and political differences that separate them despite their shared cultural heritage. It is also an intriguing story; one that is essential for an understanding of the extraordinary re-emergence of east Asia as a center of industrial innovation and economic power over the past two decades.

When Commodore Perry turned up in Edo (Tokyo) harbor in 1853, his iron ships bristling with cannon, his mission for the United States government was to open Japan to international trade in the same way that the Opium War had opened China — by sheer might of arms.

The gifts brought by Perry to convince the Tokugawa shogun of the advantages of trade were of more than symbolic significance. They were not just the products of the Industrial Revolution, but lay at the heart of the United States' growing wealth and power — guns, pistols, a telegraph and a miniature steam locomotive along with tender and passenger cars. There were even some crates of champagne to jolly the proceedings along.

The Japanese, for their part, offered the traditional luxury goods that had formed the basis of their trade with the west — silk, porcelain and lacquer ware — cultural

One of the "black ships" of Commodore Perry as seen by a Japanese artist. These ships
were not just a military threat, they also confronted the Japanese with the industrial and
technological power of the west in the mid-nineteenth century.

products still sought after but no longer the sole monopoly of east Asia as they were
when the Portuguese first arrived in the sixteenth century.

For the Japanese the objects on Perry's ships were a source of endless fascination.
Artists were employed, not only to depict the gifts they brought, but also every
product, weapon, utensil, machine and item of clothing on the ships. Their attention
to detail was extraordinary.

The American account of the Japanese response to the model train, telegraph and
armaments has all the smug self-satisfaction of the trader bringing beads and axes to
a primitive tribe. The image of Japanese samurai going round and round on model
trains, like children at a fairground, must have reinforced this impression.

When Commander John Rodgers, in 1855, visited the island of Tanega-shima 20
miles off the coast of the main southern island of Kyushu, he was amazed to find the
Japanese almost completely ignorant about the use of firearms:

It strikes an American, who from his childhood has seen children shoot, that ignorance
of arms is an anomaly indicative of primitive innocence and Arcadian simplicity. We
were unwilling to disturb it.

Rodgers' romantic ignorance of Asian history, though understandable, was
common among nineteenth century Europeans and Americans, who were inclined

to regard civilization as synonymous with technological power. In reality the people of Tanega-shima had known about guns well before European colonies were established in the Americas. In 1543 Portuguese merchants, en route to China, were blown off course by a typhoon and drifted ashore on the island. The merchants were Antonio da Mota, Francisco Zeimoto and Antonio Peixoto — the first westerners to be encountered by the Japanese.

The feudal ruler, or daimyo, of Tanega-shima was Tokitaka who, when confronted with the matchlock muskets brought ashore by the Portuguese, immediately bought two of them for 2,000 ryo; a very high price equivalent to about $1 million in today's terms. He then gave them to his swordsmith to reproduce, or reverse-engineer. There is an apocryphal story associated with the craftsman, Kimbei, who was given the task of producing a Japanese version of the musket. He was able to reproduce all the parts except for the spiral grooves cut on the inside of the barrel and the safety cap at the end. With his lord and master having invested a large amount of money in this new technology, Kimbei was confronted with a real dilemma. It was resolved, however, when another Portuguese vessel arrived at Tanega-shima and Kimbei was able to find someone who knew how to make these crucial parts. The condition on which the Portuguese merchant would impart this knowledge was that Kimbei should give him his only daughter, Wakasa, as a wife — an appalling notion for a Japanese father. Kimbei was confronted with a dreadful choice, which he resolved in classical Japanese fashion by sacrificing his daughter to the foreign barbarian in the interests of serving his feudal lord Tokitaka.

Tokyo Communications Museum

The telegraph brought from the United States as a gift for the Tokugawa Shogun — a sophisticated device for its time, operating as it did on an early form of ticker tape.

Saga Prefectual Museum

The miniature train, which was included among the gifts designed to lure the Japanese out of their self-imposed isolation, actually worked and was to be the source of endless amazement and fascination.

This story, though mythical, is important in two respects. It shows something of the loyalty that the Japanese feudal lord commanded and the power that the daimyo had over his domain — a level of power and independence that no provincial governor in China would ever have been permitted. With regard to the Tanega-shima gun, Tokitaka was soon able to manufacture matchlock muskets, which he then began to sell all over Japan. There was a huge demand, for Japan was in a state of almost continual clan warfare, and these guns, along with Portuguese military advisers, were to become of ever-increasing importance.

By the late sixteenth century the quality of matchlock muskets was equal to anything that was being produced in Europe at the same time. The Japanese capacity for the reverse-engineering of foreign technology had been a long-established tradition. The Japanese had, after all, derived much of their basic technology from Korea and China and so imitating what the west had to offer had a precedent.

With the aid of these superior firearms, the Tokugawa clan by 1603 was able to achieve dominance over the entire country and to take on the role of shogun, or military dictator, governing a loose confederation of clans, many of whom were fiercely independent, particularly those in the south.

Having gained control of the country, the Tokugawa then systematically set about getting rid of guns. First, they centralized gun production at Nagahama in 1609, requiring that gunsmiths produce weapons only for the state. They then gradually reduced orders to the point where, by 1673, only 53 matchlocks and 334 small guns were produced in one year. With over half a million samurai, or knights, to be armed

163

the gun ceased to be an important military weapon, and the gunsmiths of Tanega-shima, most of whom had previously been swordsmiths, returned to making swords.

There was also a good cultural reason for the Tokugawa shogun's actions. The gun, like the crossbow in Europe five hundred years earlier (which had been banned by the Catholic church for similar reasons), threatened the traditional feudal order. It did so by democratizing military power. A peasant could easily be taught to draw a crossbow or fire a gun; it did not take years of training and both were lethal against sword-wielding samurai or knights no matter how well they might be protected by armor. The codes of behavior of the dominant military castes in such a culture would also be undermined. Single combat with a sword was the acceptable mode of doing battle. The gun clearly challenged this crucial element of traditional Japanese culture and was not to be encouraged in times of peace. It was hard enough for the Tokugawa to control the activities of half a million samurai armed with swords, let alone the threat posed by the wide-scale adoption of such undignified weapons as guns. It was to prevent such subversion that the Tokugawa also banned contact with foreigners and ordered the Portuguese advisers, merchants and missionaries out of the country. Foreign contact was restricted to the small island of Deshima in Nagasaki harbor, which was a base for Dutch merchants, who dominated trade with Japan for the next two hundred years. Such then was the power and social control possessed by the shogun.

Tokugawa Art Museum, Nagoya

One of the decisive battles that allowed the Tokugawa clan to unify Japan and take over the role of shogun in the early seventeenth century. The Tokugawa relied, not only on their own capable gunsmiths, but also employed European weapons and military advisers.

THE TAIPING REBELLION

In China the impact of the Opium War was extremely destabilising to the Qing (Manchu) government. Having to give way to European military pressure and trading demands was regarded as a sign of weakness, and of dynastic decline.

In 1852 the Huang He (Yellow River) also broke its banks, shifting its route to the north of the Shandong (Shantung) peninsula. This was to have disastrous economic consequences for millions of people and blame was laid at the feet of the Manchu government. In traditional terms, to maintain the dykes, dredge the great rivers and keep the canals operating was one of the primary imperial responsibilities. The fact that the Yellow River broke its banks was taken as another clear sign of dynastic decline.

As a consequence, rebellions broke out throughout the empire. These were often led by secret societies such as the Triads, The Heaven and Earth Society and the Hung League, which had come into existence as a focus for opposition to Manchu rule during the seventeenth century. Between 1850 and 1878 there was some form of rebellion going on continuously.

The most disastrous of these uprisings was the Taiping rebellion, which between 1850 and 1864 raged through 16 provinces and tied up much of southern China. It was led (as were many such rebellions in Chinese history) by a failed and disillusioned scholar by the name of Hong Xiuquan (Hung Hsiu-ch'üan). Hong came from Guangzhou and had therefore been exposed, not only to the traditional values and expectations of the scholar, but also to those of Protestant missionaries. Through an early convert, Liang Afa (Liang Ah-fa), Protestant religious tracts were widely circulated in Guangzhou. Hong came into contact with these in 1836. Perhaps as a consequence of the arduous nature of the traditional exams and the disappointment of his constant failures, Hong went through a period of severe psychological stress. He saw visions and entered a delirious state. He claimed to have seen God and to be the younger brother of Jesus Christ. He ended up with an odd mixture of Christian fundamentalism and Confucianism. The former gave him an acute concern for social justice with a consequent need to reform Chinese society; the latter gave him a traditional form into which to channel his revolutionary zeal.

In 1840 he organized himself and his followers into the "God Worshippers' Society" and was soon attracting members from the old Triad societies, the poor and the landless, as well as other disaffected opportunists such as pirates. By 1851 his army of misfits and idealists captured the city of Yongan (Yung-an) in Guangxi (Kuang-hsi) province, which gave him sufficient strength to challenge the imperial government under the title *Taiping tianguo* (*Tai-ping t'ien-kuo*) — the Heavenly Kingdom of Great Peace. In 1853 his power and following had grown to the point where he was able to capture and hold the southern capital of Nanjing. From here he was to dominate much of southern China and to represent the most serious challenge yet to the beleaguered Qing dynasty.

Hong's challenge was consistent with Chinese tradition. Many of his ideas for reform were drawn from the Confucian classics but they were coupled with Christian ideas. He offered communal ownership of land and equality of the sexes. The

THE TOKUGAWA AND RANGAKU

*Dutch letters
running sideways
like a row of wild geese
flying in the sky.*

Eighteenth century Japanese
description of European writing

Until the nineteenth century and the arrival of western gunboats, the center of civilization for the Japanese was China. From the sixth century, when the country was unified, students were sent to the Celestial Empire to learn the arts of civilization. From that time on, a self-conscious effort was made to introduce Chinese social and economic institutions — Buddhism and Confucianism, the written language, craft industries like silk and porcelain, as well as Chinese art and music.

Though deriving much of its early culture and technology from China, Japanese society, nonetheless, had much in common with that of medieval Europe. Unlike China, with its vast imperial bureaucracy, Japanese society was organized around powerful feuding clans who controlled their domains from fortified castles. These clans were dominated by a military caste of samurai who served their feudal lord or daimyo like European knights.

In the sixteenth century, when contact was first made with Europeans, the Tokugawa clan were keen to use western military technology and advisers to help them win control of the country. However, to manage the

Yokohama Archives of History

peace, they turned, as Japanese rulers had always done, to the model of Confucian China.

To control his feudal lords and to prevent revolt the shogun forced his daimyo to house their wives and families at Edo, the center of Tokugawa power. Ming Neo-Confucianism was introduced in the hope of turning the sword-wielding samurai to more civilized pursuits. Schools were established where children were taught the Confucian classics, and the five virtues of benevolence, wisdom, propriety, righteousness and trustworthiness. As in Ming China, these Confucian ideas were used to reinforce a strict social hierarchy with shogun, daimyo and samurai on the top, farmers next, and merchants and artisans at the bottom.

The samurai class, freed from the preoccupation with constant warfare, was now concerned with managing agriculture and craft industries in the domains, in order to maintain the daimyo (and their considerable households) at the capital of Edo. This resulted in greatly

Yokohama Archives of History

increased commerce and improved communications. In order to ship supplies from the domains to Edo, roads were improved and large commercial networks established, particularly at Osaka. Here, many of the great merchant families, such as the Mitsui, established their trading houses. Urban life grew rapidly and the Japanese were bound in a unified culture as never before.

In 1639, over two hundred years after the Ming emperor had cut China off from the rest of the world, the Tokugawa shogun adopted a similar policy of isolation. The large Japanese merchant fleets, which had been found in ports throughout Southeast Asia between 1600 and 1639, suddenly disappeared from the scene — this at a time when Japan was producing a third of the world's silver.

Not only were Japanese merchants restricted but foreigners as well. In 1634 the Tokugawa Shogun decided to restrict all movement of foreign merchants to Deshima, a small artificial island he had built in Nagasaki harbor, connected to the mainland by a narrow bridge. Initially, both Portuguese and Dutch merchants were forced to take up residence on this tiny island, 180 metres by 60 metres. However, in 1637, after a rebellion involving Catholics broke out at Shimabara, the Portuguese were expelled from the country and the Dutch gained a virtual monopoly of trade with Japan.

The German physician Engelbert Kaenpfer, who was employed at Deshima at the end of the seventeenth century had this to say about the place:

"So great was the covetousness of the Dutch, and so strong the alluring power of Japanese gold that, rather than quit the prospect of a trade (indeed most advantageous), they willingly underwent an almost perpetual imprisonment — for such, in fact, is our residence in Deshima."

Despite extreme restrictions, the Dutch settlement was to have a considerable influence, not only on the economy of southern Japan, but as a conduit by which western science, astronomy, medicine and industrial technology found their way into Japan.

As the restrictions on contact between the Dutch merchants and Japanese scholars lessened, a school of Dutch learning, Rangaku,

arose. Its impact, however, was limited to a relatively small group of enthusiastic scholars. Honda Toshiaka, a leading eighteenth century Rangaku scholar observed:

"In recent years European astronomy has been introduced into Japan. People have been astonished by the theory that the earth is actually whirling about, and no one is ready to believe it. In Japan even great scholars are so amazed by this notion that they assert, 'If the earth were in fact spinning about, my rice bowl and water bottle would turn over and my house and storehouse would be broken to bits. How can such a theory be true?' "

Apart from useful technology such as the musket, the telescope, the mechanical clock and the camera obscura, which helped to introduce perspective into Japanese art, European influence on Japan was limited, and certainly secondary to the influence of China, which for most Japanese remained the center of civilization. It was not until China's power in the region declined in the face of European expansion in the nineteenth century, that it occurred to the Japanese leaders that they would have to take seriously the culture and technology of the "hairy barbarians of the west."

crippling custom of binding women's feet, first begun under the Song, was banned, as was opium smoking, slavery, alcohol and tobacco. Economic activity was carried out by groups of 25 families who formed a unit with a church and a treasury, which distributed wealth equally.

Their religious devotions included the worship of God, Jesus and Hong. What the Taiping offered was some hope to the landless and poor, at a time when China's traditional economic and political institutions seemed incapable of stemming the rising tide of rural poverty. Economic decline was a result of an extremely rapid increase in population without an equivalent increase in productivity. The population rose from 143 million in 1741 to 430 million in 1840. This was a gain of around 200 per cent while the amount of arable land grew by only 35 per cent. In other words there were 3.86 *mu* (one *mu* = one-sixth of an acre) per person in the 1750s and only 1.86 *mu* in the 1850s. Of this arable land 50–60 per cent was in the hands of rich gentry, another 10 per cent in the hands of government officials and the remaining 30 per cent was divided among the 400 million who made up the rest of the population; 60 per cent of these had no land at all. The Opium War had resulted in the drug being sold in China without government controls. The foreign and Chinese merchants had, by 1850, almost doubled the amount being brought into the country and, as a consequence, there was a massive outflow of silver currency, matched by a decline in the demand for Chinese exports of silk, porcelain and tea. There were, therefore, purely internal economic reasons why China was in serious difficulties, quite independent of the imperialist pressures on the coast. The Europeans were, however, now to play a significant role in determining how Chinese reformers were to go about trying to solve the difficulties.

* * *

To cope with the Taiping rebellion the Qing government was to bring to the fore some remarkable, traditional scholar-officials who were to set China on the first tentative steps towards institutional reform.

The first was Zeng Guofan (Tseng Kuo-fan) (1811–72), a graduate of the highest imperial exam who, in 1852, was sent to Hunan by the Qing government to raise an army to fight the Taiping. Zeng was a committed Confucian who was to apply its basic principles to raising an army with a sense of morals and commitment sufficient to meet the revolutionary forces of Hong. For Zeng this was not a war in which the issue was to be decided by superior technology; this was a challenge to the very credibility of Confucian culture, which had sustained the Chinese empire for two thousand years. With the support of the local gentry, and a commitment to three cardinal principles drawn from the Confucian classics — respect for superiors, concern for the common people and cultivation of good habits — Zeng's Hunan army was to be a formidable force. In 1853 they were able to retake Wuhan (Wuchang). In the rest of the country there was neither the same success nor the same commitment.

The second scholar-official to emerge was Li Hongzhang (Li Hung-chang) (1823–1901) who also came from a long tradition of scholars. His father had been a

Wan-go Weng

This painting depicts imperial troops in battle against the Taiping rebels. For almost fifteen years China was engulfed in an enervating civil war in which it is estimated that around forty million people lost their lives.

student with Zeng Guofan in Beijing. On graduating, Li went to the imperial capital to continue his studies under the direction of Zeng who became his patron and friend. When Zeng was sent to Hunan to combat the challenge of the Taiping, Li and his father returned to their native province of Anhui where, on Zeng's recommendation, the governor employed Li to organize recruits and to lead them against the rebels. (Li was to become a close ally of Zeng and was eventually made governor of Jiangsu province.)

In the meantime, European attitudes towards the Taiping vacillated. Because they were at least a quasi-Christian movement concerned with social reform, they appealed to Protestant missionaries and foreign diplomats who saw advantages in supporting what might become a new dynasty, for, in the 1850s, there was considerable doubt as to whether the Qing government could withstand this challenge. However, when the Taiping moved against the treaty port of Shanghai, sympathy began to swing behind the government. A brigade mounted with funds raised by European and Chinese merchants, and led by an American, Frederick Townsend Ward, successfully pushed the Taiping back up the Yangtze. This force was to be given honors and the title of the "Ever Victorious Army" by the emperor.

However, in September 1862 Ward was killed trying to take the town of Tseki.

His position was eventually taken by a British army officer, Charles ("Chinese") Gordon who, with Zeng's and Li's armies, eventually took back the territories controlled by the Taiping and, finally, their capital at Nanjing in July 1864.

This rebellion (civil war would be a more apt description) dwarfed the American Civil War and any European war in its destructiveness and dislocation. At least 20 million people lost their lives and the imperial government was further impoverished by the lack of revenue with which to build up its defenses and to withstand further foreign undermining of its sovereignty.

NARIAKIRA'S DREAM

While the impact of the Opium War on China was to stimulate a challenge to dynastic power, in Japan the arrival of Commodore Perry's "black ships" was to have equally shattering consequences for the power and status of the Tokugawa shogun.

The authority of the shogun had, by the 1850s, been eroded to the point where the southern daimyo were openly disobeying almost all of the traditional rules about isolation from foreigners and trade. After all, these were not imperial civil servants like the governors of Chinese provinces. The Japanese daimyo was similar to a medieval European feudal lord in the sense that he was the head of an independent clan whose primary loyalty was to him and not to the shogun or the emperor. He also owned the lands of his domain and was directly responsible for their development and exploitation. A prime example was the Satsuma clan whose domains covered the eastern side of the southern island of Kyushu. The Satsuma had a long tradition of foreign trading through their port of Kagoshima with the Ryukyu Islands (Okinawa), with the Chinese and with the Portuguese. As the European presence in the region increased throughout the early nineteenth century these southern daimyo became interested in the superior European technology. Initially, this interest was confined to military and naval matters but soon extended to making more thorough investigations of European industrial methods and institutions.

It was to fall on the head of the twenty-fifth lord of Satsuma, Nariakira Shimayu, to try to come to terms with all of this. Nariakira took over the position of daimyo in 1857 at the age of 42. He had, by dint of his own enthusiasm for western learning, become well versed in some of the achievements of the European Industrial Revolution. To gain greater access to western science and technology, Nariakira secretly sent some young members of the clan to study in London, despite the shogun's prohibition. These students also acted as agents, buying cotton-spinning machinery from Platt Brothers of Oldham, the leading textile-machinery producer in Europe.

In 1856 on a portion of his estate on the outskirts of Kagoshima, he had constructed a reverberatory furnace in order to produce iron for cannons. The design was taken from a Dutch textbook he had studied for six years. He was able to produce about fifty 200-pound cannons, which he placed in batteries around Kagoshima Bay. Not satisfied with this he built a stone British-style factory and began to manufacture farm implements and glass. Across the harbor on the shores of the

Courtesy Film Australia

This is the European-style stone factory Nariakira Shimayu had built overlooking Kagoshima Bay.

volcanic island (which lit up during its occasional bursts of volcanic activity) he established Japan's first modern shipyards. By 1857 the factory and shipyards were employing some 1,200 people producing telegraphic equipment, gas lamps, ceramics and swords.

The shipbuilding began at Kagoshima with the arrival of John Franjiro in 1851. Franjiro had, some years earlier, been picked up while drifting at sea by an American whaler. He was taken back to the United States where he worked in a large shipbuilding yard. Nariakira soon had him on his payroll and, four years later, he produced Japan's first steam-driven boat. In the same year construction began on a western-style warship, which, when it sailed into Tokyo harbor, was to cause almost as much amazement as Perry's ships had a few years earlier. Flying from the mast was a flag Nariakira had designed: the red sun of Japan's rising power against a white background of purity and integrity. A flag that less than a century later was to be flying all over Southeast Asia and the Pacific.

Nariakira was well known for his fascination with pyrotechnics. At his villa he would arrange demonstrations of torpedoes and land mines, detonating them out in

171

THE TREATY PORTS

The Treaty of Nanjing in 1842, which ended the Opium War with Britain, forced China to abandon her traditional policy of restricting international trade to the southernmost port of Guangzhou. Four new ports — Shanghai, Xiamen (Amoy), Fuzhou and Ningbo — were opened. In these ports an entirely new system was introduced giving the British unprecedented freedom and rights within China. The three crucial elements of this Treaty were a fixed tariff of 5 per cent on all goods, extraterritoriality and most-favored nation status. Perhaps the most significant of these three clauses for the sovereignty of China was that of extraterritoriality. This meant that, although living in China, British subjects would be governed by their own laws, and responsibility for their behavior rested with the British government representative. Foreigners were also able to acquire land on which to establish their own businesses, factories and residences. At the time, it made some sense to the Chinese for it meant that the onus of managing the foreigners lay with the British government. However, as soon as the Treaty became public knowledge, the other western powers demanded to have similar rights and, in 1844, the Americans and French signed similar treaties.

As the foreign settlements grew they had the effect of undermining the Chinese government's control of the economy. These treaty ports, controlled by foreign interests, were to become the dominant economic and industrial centers in the country. As further conflicts erupted, the Chinese were forced to accept even more humiliating backdowns, and more ports and inland cities were opened up to western trade and influence. It was the thin end of the wedge of western imperialism, which ultimately reduced China to semi-colonial status. By 1907 foreign domination of the modern sector of the economy was such that 84 per cent of shipping, 34 per cent of cotton spinning and 100 per cent of iron production were under foreign control. By 1911, 93 per cent of railways (of vital strategic importance) were also in foreign hands.

Japan too was to be subject to these "unequal treaties." Perry's blockade of Edo harbor led to an American demand for conditions similar to those achieved by Britain in China, with two and then six Japanese ports being opened up for trade. Britain, Russia and Holland immediately followed suit, gaining similar unequal rights of fixed tariffs and extraterritoriality. The port of Yokohama near Tokyo, and Kobe, across the bay from Osaka, eventually took on many of the same characteristics as Shanghai and Guangzhou. The second-class status that this conferred on both the Japanese and Chinese was galling.

The quest to regain national sovereignty was to become a central preoccupation for both countries. Japan's size and the simple-minded commitment of the Meiji government to emulating western social and economic institutions, allowed it a level of economic growth sufficient to build its own industrial base. Thus, unlike China, key areas of technological development such as railways, shipping and textile production were in Japanese hands. This made the presence of western imperialist powers far less damaging than it was in China.

Unlike the Chinese, who had always regarded their country as the center of the universe and their traditional Confucian culture as superior to that of any other nation, the Japanese had seen themselves as being on the periphery of China's great civilization from which they had derived most of their early technology, written language and cultural institutions. When the west appeared on the scene and exhibited its far greater wealth and power, it was easier for the Japanese pragmatically to accept a different model and turn to the west as the new center of civilization. There was even a policy developed during the Meiji of "de-Asianization." The sociologist Sugimoto Toshio has argued that much of the hostility and racism exhibited by the Japanese towards their Asian neighbors resulted from an acute feeling of inferiority in relation to Europeans and Americans. For Japan, therefore, the passion to catch up with the west was both an economic and a psychological necessity.

Kagoshima Bay and all round the harbor by pulling an electric switch in a special pavilion he had had constructed for staging such spectacles. These displays astounded visitors and may well have given the twenty-sixth daimyo a false sense of security after Nariakira died at an early age.

In 1862 on the road from Edo to Kyoto an Englishman, Lennox Richardson, was killed by Satsuma guards for failing to show sufficient and customary respect for their lord. As a consequence, the British government demanded that the perpetrator of the act be brought to justice and that £25,000 be paid in compensation. While the shogun was prepared to accede to the demands, the young daimyo and his clan were not. On 11 August 1863 the British declared war on the Satsuma and sent seven warships to Kagoshima harbor. In spite of Nariakira's fortifications and cannon, the superior fire power of the latest British Armstrong guns left the city devastated and the daimyo in no doubt that he must find out the real secret of the Europeans' economic and military power; acquiring their technology was obviously not enough.

The Japanese were, in the 1860s, in a state of profound uncertainty about how to deal with the foreign incursion, with western merchants establishing prosperous businesses operating out of the ports of Yokohama and Nagasaki. These foreign merchants and the embassies that were established to represent European and American interests were governed, not by Japanese law, but by their own — the same conditions that prevailed in the Chinese treaty ports. The unequal nature of these treaties under which Europeans operated galled both the Chinese and the Japanese. In Japan a group of southern reformers who had greater exposure to western influence took command of government when both the shogun and emperor died in quick succession. In 1868 the young Emperor Meiji was established as a European-style constitutional monarch, and a new focus of loyalty and nationalism was created.

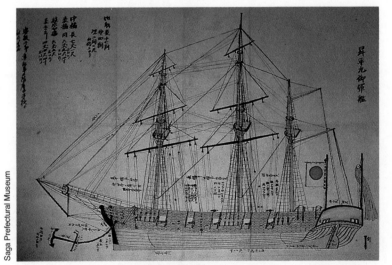

Saga Prefectural Museum

The European-style warship built at Kagoshima in 1855. Flying from its mast is the flag that Nariakira designed, which, when taken up by the Meiji reformers in 1868, was to become the new symbol of Japanese nationalism.

SELF-STRENGTHENING WITH TI AND YONG

In China reformers like Li Hongzhang and Zeng Guofan were confronted with a far more difficult situation. While the reunification of the country in 1865, after the disastrous decade of the Taiping rebellion, was described as the Tongzhi (T'ung Chih) restoration, any comparison to the Japanese Meiji restoration is limited indeed.

While reformers in both countries perceived the need to understand the west and "learn the superior technology of the barbarians in order to control them," the political and economic circumstances of China were profoundly different to those of Japan. For a start, Japan was the size of one Chinese province.

A significant ally of the reformers in China was Prince Kung, the brother of the Xianfeng (Hsien-feng) Emperor. As head of the grand council and the *zongli yamen,* the newly created office concerned with foreign affairs, Kung had considerable power and influence. With his support Zeng and Li set up a number of arsenals and shipyards at Shanghai, Nanjing and Fuzhou. In his diary of June 1862 Zeng notes the following concerning the self-strengthening movement:

Royal Geographical Society, London

Li Hongzhang one of a new generation of Confucian scholar-officials who was to play an important part in the suppression of the Taiping rebellion. He was also to become one of the leaders of the self-strengthening movement, which attempted to adapt western technology to traditional Chinese culture.

If only we could possess all their [the barbarians'] superior techniques, then we would have the means to return their favors when they are obedient, and to avenge our grievances when they are disloyal.

To justify their policy among conservative officials, the reformers put forward the policy of *ti* and *yong* — "Chinese spirit and western means." What China needed to do was simply to graft western technology on to its traditional political and economic institutions.

To this end the Jiangnan arsenal was established at Shanghai in 1865, with machines purchased in the United States. This arsenal had a multiplicity of functions. It was to produce ships and guns, but also to act as a conduit for western science and technology. The arsenal was to set up an entire department devoted to the translation of western books, and for this Zeng Guofan employed a number of Europeans, including John Fryer, a Protestant missionary. By 1868 they had produced their first ship and, by 1872, had produced five additional 400-horsepower gunboats each carrying 26 guns. In seven years they had translated 98 western books; 47 were in the fields of natural sciences and 45 on military tactics and technology. At Fuzhou they had produced 40 ships under the guidance of two French engineers Giguel and d'Aiguebelle.

A number of other Europeans were employed at this time. Perhaps the most influential was the Englishman Robert Hart. Hart was employed by the Chinese government to set up and run the department of maritime customs. He staffed the department with a mixture of Chinese and European officers, and ran it with the utmost firmness and with a genuine commitment to the interests of the Chinese government. Prior to this, the administration of the collection of customs duties was a shambles. In a circular dated 21 June 1864 Hart spelled out a code of behavior for all the foreigners he employed:

> . . . it is to be distinctly and constantly kept in mind that the Inspectorate of Customs is a Chinese and not a Foreign Service, and that, as such, it is the duty of each of its members to conduct himself towards the Chinese, people as well as officials, in such a way as to avoid all cause of offence and ill feeling. . . . It is to be expected from those who take the pay and who are the servants of the Chinese Government, that they, at least, will so act as to neither offend susceptibilities, nor excite jealousies, suspicion, and dislike.

However, this code was not followed by many of the other Europeans who operated out of the treaty ports.

Resources raised by Hart provided the Chinese with an important new source of revenue with which to carry out their policy of modernization. But despite the efforts of Prince Kung and the other reformers there remained a basic mistrust of westerners on the part of conservative officials who were prepared, grudgingly, to accept the need for western military technology but believed that was the extent of what was needed. The basic assumption, which bordered on blind arrogance, was that China could afford to ignore the changes that were taking place in the world around them. The notion that they could continue to retreat into the self-sufficent complacency of Qianlong was not only being challenged by the presence of the imperialists on their doorstep but by the reality of their own internal economic conditions. The reformers were acutely aware of this but, unlike their counterparts in Japan, their ability to unify the country behind genuine reforms was limited. China was an empire not a nation-state. Its vast size meant that, apart from those living on the coast and in direct contact with foreigners, there was little appreciation of the threat that China faced. Li Hongzhang, however, clearly did appreciate the situation:

> Chinese scholars and officials have been indulging in the inveterate habit of remembering stanzas and sentences and practicing fine model calligraphy, while our warriors and fighters are, on the other hand, rough, stupid and careless . . . In peace time they sneer at the sharp weapons of foreign countries as things produced by strange techniques and tricky craft, which they consider it unnecessary to learn. In wartime, then, they are alarmed that the effective weapons of western countries are so strange and marvellous, and regard them as something the Chinese cannot learn about. They do not know that for several hundred years the foreigners have considered the study of firearms as important as their bodies and lives . . .

In response to such arguments the conservatives continually played upon the moral shallowness and untrustworthiness of foreign barbarians to deflect the arguments of the reformers for widespread reform of education and institutional practices. Prince Kung's suggestion that western professors of mathematics and

The Jiangnan arsenal established in 1865 at Shanghai. The arsenal was run with the help of European advisers who not only helped with technical matters but translated western books on science and engineering. From here the Chinese launched their first steam-powered gunboat in 1872.

astronomy be invited to teach in traditional institutions was greeted by the grand secretary Wo-jen with a restating of the traditional Confucian attitude that China had no need to learn from barbarians:

> If we seek trifling arts and respect barbarians as teachers regardless of the possibility that the cunning barbarians may not teach us their essential techniques — even if the teachers sincerely teach and the students faithfully study them — all that can be accomplished is the training of mathematicians. From ancient down to modern times, your servant has never heard of anyone who could use mathematics to raise the nation from a state of decline or to strengthen it in times of weakness. The empire is so great that one should not worry lest there be any lack of abilities therein.

The problem facing the traditional scholar elite of China was that, if they were to accept more than the very minimum from the west, they would begin to invalidate the very basis of China's claim that its culture was the essence of civilized existence. To adopt western cultural institutions would be to admit the inadequacy of their own. This tended to eliminate any inclusion of western social or economic institutions in the process of reform. The old bureaucratic institutions in China were, however, not well suited to take the graft of European systems of technological innovation and industry. Among the Japanese there was no such inhibition, having in the first place adopted many of their institutions from China.

In trying to sow the seeds of industry the efforts of the reformers were considerable for, apart from arsenals, Li established foreign language schools and machine factories. However, the enterprises that were set up by officials were run as government-owned but merchant-managed concerns. This made them vulnerable to the long-established practice of government officials drawing off capital without consideration of the need to provide for expansion or reinvestment. There was also a tendency to have a misplaced faith in foreign experts; these foreigners were often completely inexperienced. Halliday McCartney who ran the Nanjing arsenal was a medical doctor; the two Frenchmen who ran the Fuzhou (Foochow) arsenal and dockyards had never built a ship in their lives.

The first problem was that, while the new arsenals could build adequate boats, there were few locally trained engineers or the industrial infrastructure to allow for much local innovation. Even the scholars who accepted the necessity of military improvement for the sake of defense, had no idea of the scientific and technological training that was needed to support and keep them abreast of the ever-changing international arms race. This meant that even though they had produced warships at Fuzhou and Shanghai, they could not seriously compete with those being produced in the west. To keep abreast the government was forced to invest in buying expensive military technology direct from Europe.

There was a second problem that resulted from the fact that most of the industrial enterprises were set up and owned by the government, either through direct financing or on the basis of investment by wealthy merchants and landowners. As was traditional in China these industries became state monopolies and were to become the victims of nepotism and inefficiency. In other words, the agency cost was too high as the function of the organization was lost in the self-interest of those who controlled its operation and purse strings. The fate of the Chinese Merchants' Steam Navigation Company, which was set up by Li Hongzhang, is but one example of profits that should have been reinvested being channeled out of the company into the hands of government officials. Although initially successful, it could not compete with the lines run out of the treaty ports by foreign firms. There was a long-standing mistrust of merchants and a lack of interest in providing new institutional structures that would foster entrepreneurial activity. A visitor to the busy port of Shanghai in 1870, who might have formed the impression that China was on the brink of leaping into the industrial age, would only have had to go 50 miles inland to find that the impact of European industry was superficial. Much of the resistance came from the powerful and conservative families who dominated local politics at the regional level, and whose support imperial officials required in order to govern.

The conflict between the interests of the gentry and the increasing demands of the Europeans and Americans in the treaty ports came to a head in 1876 when Jardine Matheson built a short railway line from Shanghai to the port of Wusong on the main channel of the Yangtze River.

There had been many proposals put forward by foreign firms and governments to build railway networks and to set up telegraph lines throughout China but these had been firmly resisted. For example, in 1863 Sir MacDonald Stephenson came to China in the hope of persuading the government to let him build an entire network connecting China through to India where railways had already been installed by the British. The Russians also applied considerable pressure but the Chinese government consistently refused. In this, paradoxically, they were supported by Li Hongzhang and other supporters of westernization.

In July 1863 Li Hongzhang, in his position as governor of Jiangsu province, was petitioned by 27 foreign firms working in Shanghai to allow a railway line to be built from Shanghai to Wusong. His reply was to the point: " . . . he would consider it his duty to oppose the attempt on the part of foreigners to gain such an undue degree of influence in the country as the concession sought for would confer upon them." The policy of self-strengthening was to use technology to contain foreign influence not to expand it. Railways in foreign hands would give them direct access to China's rural heartland. In this there was common agreement among reformers and conservatives within the government.

Jardine Matheson attempted to force the issue and eventually went ahead and built the line, claiming at first that they were actually building a road. The road company, set up in 1865, was run by Jardine Matheson with a number of western and Chinese merchants as shareholders; it must be appreciated that Chinese merchants and some compradores (commercial agents) living in the treaty ports were inclined to support the greater freedom and access to resources that railways would have brought. The Wusong line was completed in June 1876 and ran very successfully despite official opposition. However, on 5 August a Chinese was killed on the line, perhaps run over, although the precise details have been lost. The governor of Nanjing was called in to negotiate a settlement, which had the gentry up in arms. They argued that the railway

Royal Geographical Society, London

Through the arsenal in Nanjing Chinese officials and soldiers learned to use the latest
European weaponry, in this case a Gatling gun. Unfortunately the Chinese had to rely on
advisers of very limited experience — Halliday McCartney who ran the Nanjing arsenal
was a medical doctor.

not only extended foreign powers but that it offended *fengshui,* the veins of energy
or *qi* that ran through the natural contours of the landscape. Straight roads or even
telegraph lines, which were also opposed, were believed to cut across the flow of this
energy and could cause natural disasters — floods, famines, droughts and even
earthquakes.

This was a persuasive argument for it was to prevent such calamities that the Son
of Heaven was given his mandate. For officials who had just restored the empire after
the Taiping and other rebellions, there was an obvious need to be responsive to the
local gentry on whose support the whole imperial system of government depended.
It should be pointed out, however, that the appeal to the offended *fengshui* was also
an appeal to traditional economic interests. The gentry and the compradores in the
treaty ports had an obvious interest in maintaining their control over the
countryside. Railways not only cut across the earth's vital lines of energy but across
their own lines of control and financial interests. It also threatened to displace large
numbers of people working in the traditional transport systems, thereby driving
more families into poverty and providing more potential fuel for revolt.

At the Chepo Convention when Li Hongzhang met with Sir Thomas Wade, the

Mary Evans Picture Library, London

One of the problems of establishing either railways or telegraph lines in China was the opposition from the peasantry and rural gentry who were opposed to them on the grounds that cutting straight across the landscape would disturb ancestral graves and upset the fengshui. Unstated, however, was the fact that such development also cut across the well established traditional transport systems and, therefore, conservative rural interests.

British Ambassador, to resolve the issue, Li argued that the railway should be in the hands of the Chinese government and offered to buy it back. The railway was eventually sold to the Chinese government who promptly ripped it up and sent it to Taiwan where it could not cause trouble. This was not an irrational act but a highly logical one under the circumstances.

Seen in the broader perspective this was only one of many setbacks to the modernization of the Chinese economy and a reinforcement of the power of the conservative landed gentry, for at this time railways were helping to create new economic networks throughout the world. They were opening up the vast resources of Russia and the American west. They linked the rich grazing lands of Australia and Argentina to the markets and industrial centers of Europe. With the advent of steam-powered ships, the world was being linked into a vast market network, which, for all China's desire to ignore it, was encroaching increasingly on the vulnerable Celestial Empire.

STRONG ARMY, RICH NATION

King Leopold thus spoke to the Prince [Prince Mimbu], "A nation that uses iron is strong, and a nation that produces iron is wealthy. It is necessary for Japan to become powerful by using iron. This means that Japan should import iron from a foreign country, and I hope that that country will be no other than Belgium." The King presented the case in an interesting manner. But to me who was raised according to the teachings of Confucius and Mencius and in an atmosphere thick with bushido spirit, which scorns material interests, the King's words appeared very strange, and made me question in my mind whether it is kingly for a royal personage to act like a merchant.

Shibusawa Eichi, 1867

In Japan, in the early years of the Meiji government, there was social chaos as the traditional policy of isolation ended. With extraordinary speed the new government demolished Japan's ancient feudal institutions. Many of the samurai were devastated when, in 1871, the government abolished the feudal system of domains and the annual stipends on which they depended. Now, loyalty, once focused on the daimyo and the clan, was to be redirected to the nation, as embodied in the person of the emperor. The Meiji reformers created a new cult of emperor worship in order to build a nation out of the fiercely independent clans. Their task was in many ways similar to Germany's under Bismarck, or Garibaldi's in Italy.

The breakdown of the system of feudal domains also meant that the samurai, who

The Emperor Meiji as a young man in traditional clothing, and in the new uniform of a European-style constitutional monarch. He became the focus of a somewhat contrived cult of emperor worship that was used as a means of shifting loyalty from the old feudal clans to the new nation state for which he became the symbol.

181

This nineteenth century woodblock print *Salesroom in a Foreign Business Establishment* is by Sadahide Hashimoto. Western merchants in Yokohama, like their counterparts in Shanghai, provided access to western manufactured goods and shipped local silk and porcelain to Europe and the United States.

depended on their yearly stipends for survival, were suddenly forced to find new careers. Some profoundly resented the change and with quixotic spirit attacked both foreigners and the Meiji government. In 1877 there was a last-ditch stand by the samurai when 40,000 took on the government's conscript army, whose western guns were to completely outclass the samurai with their swords. (Ironically, this battle took place in Nariakira's old domain of Satsuma, and was led by one of his sons.)

Others, like the self-strengtheners in China, were aware of the need for fundamental change and embraced it with enthusiasm. The difference for the Japanese reformers was that they had behind them a powerful and united government committed to their aims, in spite of much public opposition. The students and missions sent to Europe and the United States had, by the 1870s, returned with accounts, not just of the west's technological achievements, but of the cultural and economic institutions that made them work.

Because the Japanese were less tied to the cultural institutions that had been introduced from China (particularly neo-Confucianism during the Tokugawa era) it was easier to abandon them when they ceased to serve their needs. They were, unlike the Chinese, also used to borrowing pragmatically from others.

* * *

In a small wooded corner of Keio University campus stands one of the few buildings in Tokyo from the Meiji era that withstood the appalling firebombing of World War II. It survived not because it was particularly strong or well built (quite the opposite, it is timber); it was luck that preserved Fukuzawa's "Speaking Hall." Coming across it on a stroll around the campus you might mistake it for some postwar gift from the United States since the building looks like an eighteenth century Quaker meeting hall or New England church. It was built in 1875 by Fukuzawa Yukichi, one of Japan's great educational reformers who established the first private university and school at Keio, and was also one of the most popular writers and newspaper editors of his day.

Fukuzawa was born in 1835 into a low-ranking samurai family, as were many of the early reformers. His father was something of a scholar and encouraged his son in the study of the Confucian classics that made up the educational curriculum of the samurai class. After an early education in Osaka, he left there at the age of 19 to study "Dutch learning" or Rangaku in Nagasaki. This was in 1854, a year after Perry's arrival at Edo, but even at this time the only official place to make contact with foreigners and their ideas was in Nagasaki. With the new foreign threat posed by the United States, Fukuzawa decided in 1858 to learn English. In the following year he was asked to sail with the *Kanrin-Maru,* a Japanese boat purchased from the Dutch, which was to accompany a Japanese delegation to the United States to sign a treaty opening Japan to foreign trade. With limited English, he set out on the journey to San Francisco. The impression the west made on this young 23 year old must have been overwhelming, as he was to write later:

> Foreign countries are not only novel and exotic for us Japanese, everything we see and hear about these cultures is strange and mysterious — a blazing brand has been thrust into ice-cold water, not only are ripples and swells ruffling the surface of men's minds but a massive upheaval is being stirred up at the very depth of their souls.

Fukuzawa Yukichi as a young samurai during a visit to Paris in 1862. He was a translator on various missions sent by the Tokugawa government to the United States and Europe, an experience that had a profound impact on his outlook and development.

Keio University Library, Tokyo

Fukuzawa was to travel on a number of foreign missions as a translator for the Tokugawa government. With the establishment of the Meiji government he reached the conclusion that what the Japanese needed most from the west was education. He therefore set up a small school on the site of what is now Keio University. Here he had the Speaking Hall built, based on designs sent to him from the United States. The Japanese, he believed, needed to learn public speaking. A seemingly insignificant thing though this might appear, to Fukuzawa it was one of the characteristics of western culture that most impressed him. In feudal Japan there was no such tradition of public debate on issues of social concern. Because of the authoritarian character of feudal relationships, those in power had no tradition of rationally justifying their behavior nor were they accountable in any democratic sense.

In the Speaking Hall a new generation of Japanese students were to confront a teacher who encouraged them, not only to absorb new western ideas and concepts, but to express themselves and their ideas publicly. A new domain of national public life was to come into existence to replace the autocratic ways of feudal Japan.

It was not simply as an educationalist, introducing a western-style school system, that Fukuzawa was to have an impact on Japanese intellectual life, but as a liberal and democratic editor and as a popular author. His book *Conditions in the Western World* (1866) was extremely influential, as was *The Encouragement of Learning* (1872) which sold 20,000 copies. In *Conditions in the Western World,* Fukuzawa described, in great detail, every aspect of European life and behavior:

> The bed linens are extremely clean. The sheets are white as snow, and you never find any fleas or lice. The container that you see under the bed . . . is a chamber pot. You always find this thing underneath the bed when you stay in a westerner's house. You should be careful not to mistake this container for something else when you visit a western country as some Japanese actually did.

Some of Fukuzawa's companions, on their first mission to the United States, mistook the chamber pot for pillows since, in Japan, a hard porcelain block was used instead of a soft pillow to support one's head.

In his enthusiasm for western learning Fukuzawa was clearly not alone. Another young reformer who was to join one of the many missions to Europe was Shibusawa Eichi. Shibusawa (1840–1931) had been brought up, like Fukuzawa, on the Chinese Confucian classics, although he was not born of the samurai class but was to be adopted into it. He was, for a time, a member of an anti-foreign terrorist movement whose aim was to rid the country of westerners. However, after being chosen to accompany the Tokugawa mission to the Paris Exhibition in the early 1850s he changed his mind completely. With remarkable pragmatism, he came to the conclusion that if the Japanese were to be successful in these efforts at modernization they would have to adopt, not only the technology of the west, but also the cultural and political institutions that underpinned them. As a gesture of liberation Shibusawa abandoned his samurai garb for the frock coat and tie of a European gentleman.

In the two years Shibusawa was to spend abroad he studied European social and economic institutions. Europe's strength, he believed, was built upon an industrial system that rewarded innovation and individual enterprise but also led to great social inequalities.

On returning to Japan he was employed in the ministry of finance, whose primary task was to support and encourage the establishment of western-style industrial enterprises. The return of students and fact-finding missions sent abroad to study the ways of the west provided the Meiji government with a number of models from which to choose — one of the advantages of being a late developer. Like shoppers in a world supermarket, the reformers went about systematically choosing their new institutions. They adopted a German public health system, a French–American education system, a British navy and financial institutions, and a Prussian army and constitution. Apart from modeling their institutions on the best that the west had to offer, they also brought to Japan large numbers of foreign experts, often referred to as "live machines," who were to act as technical advisers.

While working for the ministry of finance Shibusawa was involved in setting up Japan's first western-style factory. He was to confront many of the same problems as Li Hongzhang in China.

A remarkable historical accident was to benefit the Japanese at this time. In the 1860s a blight hit the French and Italian silk industries, which prevented them from meeting the growing demand for silk thread. This provided an opening for the traditional Chinese and Japanese silk industries. However, the quality of the silk thread produced in the local "cottage industry" was neither sufficiently standardized nor of the quality required by European manufacturers.

It was therefore decided to establish a European-style silk spinning factory at Tomioka in Gumma prefecture, about 100 miles from Tokyo. For the design of the factory the government went to Lyon in France, one of the centers of the European silk industry. They employed Paul Brunot to manage the plant and brought out a

Courtesy Film Australia

The Speaking Hall that Fukuzawa had built at his school (now Keio University) in 1875. Modeled on an American Quaker meeting hall, it was used to encourage public speaking. Fukuzawa believed that if the Japanese were to catch up with the west they needed a western-style education system to inculcate "the spirit of number and reason." In Japan's traditional feudal culture those in power had never had to justify their actions through rational argument, which Fukuzawa saw as one of the great virtues of the western liberal and democratic tradition. At the far end of the Speaking Hall, Professor Eiichi Kiyooka stands beneath a portrait of his grandfather Fukuzawa Yukichi.

whole range of European advisers. The factory was begun in the early 1870s and immediately ran into local opposition for, while the Meiji bureaucrats might have been enthusiastic for all things western, local people brought up on the xenophobic policies of the Tokugawa found the presence of foreign barbarians, and their proposed industry, unacceptable. Even getting the factory built was extremely difficult and frustrating. First, the French architects and engineers designed it as they would in France, to be built of brick, but in Japan such building materials were not used, so they had to set up their own kiln and import cement. Second, there was a basic conflict with the Japanese carpenters employed. Local contractors would not, at first, supply timber for the project, and then the carpenters argued that the European design was unsafe and refused to work on it unless it conformed to the traditional timber structure that had been proven, over centuries, to withstand earthquakes. A compromise was finally reached and what emerged was a traditional Japanese wooden structure faced with brick to make it look like a European factory.

In 1872 the plant was finally ready but again there were serious problems. The French could not get a sufficient number of girls to apply to work in the plant. They were forced to try to bring employees to the factory from other areas. However, there was no tradition of moving to another area to accept work, particularly when this involved living and working with another and alien clan. When the factory finally went into production it was understaffed and the discipline of the workers suffered many of the same problems exhibited by European factory workers in the eighteenth century.

The silk spinning factory at Tomioka was set up by the Meiji government as a model factory in 1872.

Metropolitan Museum of Art, New York

The demand for Japanese silk thread and fabric in the west provided the impetus for small private factories to set up in business. This factory, in Tokyo, shown using silk-reeling technology imported in 1872. Experience gained in the state-run factories like Tomioka provided trained workers for the growing private sector, which was funded through new commercial banks established by the Shibusawa and Mitsui families.

For the government this was to be a model factory, which it was prepared to support. It had set up a somewhat idealized European model of a factory and left the running of it to the French manager. He, of course, took no account of the indigenous culture and ran it as he would have in Lyon. There were eight-hour days and a holiday on Sunday, despite the fact that the notion of the European week was completely alien to the staff, who were housed in dormitories and were even expected to attend church.

Despite such setbacks, the Meiji government plowed ahead with its policy of western-style modernization. The Gregorian calendar was adopted in 1873, along with European dress and social habits, much to the contempt of Chinese visitors. The enthusiasm for all things western was such that in Tokyo there was even a European-style reception hall built where, dressed in the latest European fashion, Japanese officials would hold charity concerts and balls to entertain foreigners. It was known as the Rokumeikan, or Deer Cry Pavilion, and was extremely popular among the new Japanese leaders. One Japanese observer of this new cultural institution, Okura Kihachiro (1837–1928), described a remarkable scene on the floor of the ballroom:

The partners were both men, one with the huge build of a sumo wrestler, the other an especially skinny fellow; the couple was dancing in all seriousness but since their contrast was peculiar it created a commotion among the spectators, who were trying to determine their identity. On closer observation the huge man turned out to be Oyama, Japan's Minister of War, and the skinny man was the then Governor of Tokyo. . . . Now

Metropolitan Museum of Art, New York

At the Deer Cry Pavilion or Rokumeikan, the new Japanese leaders could meet and entertain the growing western community living in Tokyo and nearby Yokohama. Here, the Japanese would learn ballroom dancing and hold charity concerts, in an imitation of upper class groups anywhere in Europe or the United States. In this way the Japanese hoped to be accepted as being civilized, and equal with the west.

on this occasion Oyama was in formal western military attire while his companion was in Japanese kimono and hokama, and they were earnestly engaged in dancing, at which neither was very good.

This activity was brutally satirized by European visitors such as the French cartoonist, George Bigot, which offended and bewildered the Japanese who expected that such an endorsement of Europe as the new center of civilization would have been applauded. (There was even a "civilization ball game" invented in the late 1870s to help educate children in the virtues of western technology: as a child bounced or threw a ball, he or she would name desirable western inventions — gas lamps, steam engines, cameras, telegraphs, lightning conductors, newspapers, schools, post boxes and so on.) Although many government-sponsored model factories were to be financial disasters they did provide an important training ground in industrial management with staff going from Tomioka to other smaller private firms, bringing to them new skills and ideas. The demand for silk was sufficiently great that Japan was able to gain the lion's share of the European market by the late 1870s. However, the real impetus for growth was not to come from government. The industries they established were often run by ex-samurai with little business experience and with wage structures unrelated to profitability.

Shibusawa, aware that such enterprises were doomed to failure, left the ministry of finance and, with the support of the Mitsui family, established Japan's first commercial bank. Through this bank he provided financial support for new firms outside government control — firms modeled on the joint-stock companies, which, he believed, formed the basis of European and American wealth.

In this he was, initially, up against some deep-seated cultural prejudices. The dominant samurai class had absorbed from Confucian China a distrust of and disdain for merchants, who were believed to be concerned only with private gain and were therefore of very low social status. The ideal of a samurai was selflessly to serve the interests of his traditional lord, and in this he was governed by a rigorous code of discipline. While the Meiji government had tried to shift the focus of loyalty to the nation they had failed to find a role for this largely dispossessed and very influential military class. Shibusawa, from his studies of European institutions, realised that what Japan needed was the entrepreneurial spirit that was at large in the west. However, without an indigenous bourgeoisie and an equivalent of Adam Smith to sanctify the market system, he had to find a new way of making commerce acceptable to the samurai educated in and inculcated with a Confucian world view.

Like his contemporary, Fukuzawa, he was to argue that the west offered a model of efficient economic management of the nation's resources. As Japan now faced a crisis affecting its very survival as a sovereign state, the object of industrial enterprises was to build a rich nation. The efficient management of commercial industry was

University of Nagasaki Library

Samurai, the once dominant caste in Japan, lost their guaranteed state stipend and social role in Meiji Japan. They remained powerful but largely ineffectual after the suppression of a Satsuma-led rebellion in 1877 when an army of samurai challenged the Meiji reformers and the direction they were taking towards ever-greater westernization. It was Shibusawa, himself a ex-samurai, who was to present the argument that working to build Japan's new industries was not merely a matter of trade or the pursuit of personal gain but was of service to the state and therefore, consistent with the Samurai code of bushido.

Yokohama Archives of History

Railway companies set up with capital made available through the new banks, began
to take over many areas previously dominated by government. The first railway line
ran from Tokyo to Yokohama and was opened in 1872.

therefore a task consistent with the code of service to the state promoted by the
samurai. The new nationally sponsored industries could be regarded as social
organizations like the old feudal domains. The dedication of the businessman to the
social and economic goals of the new firms was similar to the Confucian concern for
the interests of the clan, rather than that of the selfish merchant concerned simply
with private profit.

Shibusawa believed in the idea of a moral economy: "all sorts of industrial work
and the existence of co-operative systems are conducted on moral reasons and
mutual confidence." So while the Japanese were to adopt both the technology and
institutions of the west, they were to mold them effectively on to their existing social
systems. While in Europe and the United States aggressive merchants and bankers
used their capital to build industrial empires, which were ends in themselves, and
were accountable only to shareholders, the enterprise in Japan as it emerged under
the new ideology of Japanese nationalism was an extension of the government policy
of "strong army, rich nation."

With the money raised by his bank Shibusawa was to invest in a wide range of
activities. First, the Osaka Cotton Spinning Company and then paper, gas, railway and
shipping companies. His firms, like his bank, were to be supported by the old
merchant family, Mitsui. In the same way that the Protestant Reformation was to take
the time discipline of the medieval monasteries and apply it to the demands of the
market place, so too did Shibusawa and other early Meiji industrialists take the values
of the samurai and apply them to the economic goals of building powerful

横濱海岸通之圖

Large European-style buildings were erected to house the new public schools, banks, insurance companies and business houses that flourished on the back of the silk industry centred in Yokohama.

corporations and industrial enterprises. The function of these firms was to manage the essential transfer of western technology and adapt it to the problems of production in Japan.

Linking the commercial interests of private firms with national goals allowed capitalist economic rationalism to be squared with Confucian notions of loyalty and service to the collective good of society. As the new industries were responsible for training the essentially unskilled rural workers who made up the growing industrial labor force, there was a high priority on not losing this investment — a labor market operated to a very limited extent. The firms tended to function like extended families or clan enterprises, and notions of loyalty and commitment, similar to those that existed in the feudal domains, were expected. The idea of private property rights sanctioned by law, which were so basic to western capitalism, did not exist. (The wealth of the feudal domains was regarded as a collective asset with rights based on clan and caste associations.)

After a decade of rapid growth the new private sector was to be further enhanced in 1881. The international demand for silk had provided new wealth in some rural areas, and also provided the capital for the building of better transport systems based on railway networks, which gradually linked the whole country, providing new markets and increased demand. It also led to rampant inflation, forcing the government to intervene in the economy. The finance minister, Matsukata Masa-yoshi, once a leading samurai of the Satsuma clan, began to divest the government of their draining and unprofitable enterprises such as the Tomioka silk mill.

Shipyards at Nagasaki and Hyogo, established by the government as part of its efforts to improve transportation and to support the navy, were sold off to Iwasaki Yataro (the founder of the firm Mitsubishi) and Kawasaki Shoya respectively. (Kawasaki was a supporter of the Meiji who, although not a samurai, had started a small shipping firm.) Not all government-sponsored enterprises were even capable of being sold off. The Kamaishi steel mill set up in 1874 with the aid of British engineers was, by 1882, declared a complete failure due to the poor quality ore and smeltable coke and, equally important, the incompetence (or inexperience) of the workforce. When put on the market in 1882 there were no buyers.

The sale of many strategic industries into private hands was to create a close bond between the government and the large trading and industrial conglomerates or *zaibatsu*, which were formed at this time.

There was another and increasingly important factor in the remarkable speed with which Japan was able to build up its industrial base. This was the connection between government-owned arsenals and the rest of industry. Like those established in China, these arsenals were the earliest centers of industrial training and large-scale production. For example, in the 1880s arsenals and government shipyards employed around 10,000 people, compared with 3,000 employed in private firms. These government arsenals were also to apply the latest iron and steel casting techniques to produce better guns, and, indirectly, better machine tools for private industry. Six of the ten private cotton textile firms, which began operation in the 1880s using spindles imported by the government, relied on steam engines produced at the Yokosuka arsenal. The military were also to play an important role in modernizing private industry, as the suppliers of essential technological components.

The Osaka arsenal provided a large number of machines, such as lathes, planers and grinders operated by steam engines, for private firms. The congruence of interests of government and private institutions was to be a characteristic of Japanese industrial success; as important an element in postwar Japan as it was in the Meiji. It was, however, to be a factor fundamentally lacking in China.

Connections established with the major armament makers of Europe, such as Krupp of Germany and Armstrong of Britain, gave the Japanese an immediate awareness of the arms race and the crucial role of industrial innovation in that process. From the numerous students sent abroad and the advisers brought to Japan, they had become aware of the spread of technological change in Europe and the United States, from which they could not afford to isolate themselves.

Windows on the World

Whatever happens we have got the Maxim gun and they have not.

Hilaire Belloc

The Japanese and Chinese students and missions that went abroad to learn from the west were to confront a culture and industrial system in the process of rapid transformation. The problem was to understand what within that apparent anarchic chaos was the key to its success and the secret of its growing wealth and power. Cheap steel clearly had something to do with it.

In 1851 in a small Kentucky town, William Kelly who cast the reducing vats for sugar production began to experiment with the production of a more economical method of making steel. The basic problem was that the normal methods of burning off the excess carbon from pig iron to produce mild steel required very large amounts of fuel. It was both slow and very expensive; sufficiently economic for the production of knife blades and fine mechanisms but not available on an industrial scale. Kelly was believed to have employed a number of Chinese at his foundry. It is possible that it was they who suggested to him the method of blowing air through molten iron to produce the heat required to transform it into fine steel; the oxygen burning off impurities such as sulfur and carbon. This ingenious method had been used in China for centuries and was now to transform western industry.

Kelly was to spend a great deal of time and effort getting the process to work on an industrial scale. In 1857 he took out a patent on the process but went bankrupt the following year. However, it was not Kelly but an Englishman, Henry Bessemer, who was to build his reputation as the inventor of the blast furnace.

Bessemer was a classic nineteenth century inventor. His first achievement was to produce European gold lacquer that could compete with the Japanese product, which at that time was extremely fashionable in Europe. Bessemer's reputation was such that, in 1854, Louis Napoleon of France offered him unlimited credit for access to his latest invention. Bessemer had come up with a shell that spun on its axis as it left the barrel, giving it greater stability in flight and, ultimately, greater accuracy. The problem was that the traditional iron and bronze cannon could not handle the additional pressure the shell produced and would split. So to make the invention practicable it was necessary to find some stronger material for the cannon. Steel was the obvious choice but at that time was much too expensive. Bessemer, therefore, set about trying to find a means of producing cheap steel.

There is some controversy surrounding the issue of whether he knew of Kelly's earlier work since he came up with the same solution. But, whereas Kelly was unable to gear his process to operate on an industrial scale, Bessemer was to design a blast furnace that could reduce the time taken to transform pig iron into steel from hours to minutes — saving energy, time and money. In 1856 he was to outline this process in a paper, "On the Manufacture of Malleable Iron and Steel without Fuel," which he presented to the British Association for the Advancement of Science.

193

Great exhibitions, the first of which opened in Paris in 1853, promoted the technological inventiveness of European industry. It also presented to bewildered Japanese and Chinese visitors a specter of constantly changing military and industrial technology.

It took a decade to perfect this method of steel production but it was increasingly clear throughout the latter half of the nineteenth century that applied scientific research enabled existing industrial products to be made more cheaply and therefore to be more readily available.

Metallurgists in Germany were soon to take Bessemer's original blast furnace and adapt it to cope with wider ranges and qualities of iron ore. In 1864 the Siemens-Martin open-hearth furnace was being used by Alfred Krupp in the Ruhr valley to produce steel for massive cannon, which were to be used to pound the outskirts of Louis Napoleon's Paris when Germany invaded France in 1870.

In the United States the Bessemer revolution was to see a fall in the cost of steel from around $100 a ton in the 1870s to $12 in the 1890s. Andrew Carnegie in Pittsburg was producing 1,200 tons of iron and steel a week by 1880. Carnegie was one of the first to recognize the benefits of employing scientists in industry. The competitive demands of providing more durable steel railway lines and steel for the growing machine-tools industry led Carnegie to employ a German chemist by the name of Fricke. In a letter, Carnegie made the following comments on the benefits that were to flow from this decision:

We found . . . a learned German, Dr Fricke, and great secrets did the doctor open to us. [Ore] from mines that had a high reputation was now found to contain ten, fifteen, and even twenty per cent less iron than it had been credited with. Mines that hitherto had a poor reputation we found to be now yielding superior ore. The good was bad and the bad was good, and everything was topsy-turvy. Nine-tenths of all the uncertainties of pig iron making were dispelled under the burning sun of chemical knowledge. What fools we had been! But then there was this consolation: we were not as great fools as our competitors [who] years after we had taken chemistry to guide us [the steel industry] said they could not afford to employ a chemist. Had they known the truth then, they would have known they could not afford to be without one.

This realization was to be reinforced frequently as apparently insignificant resources were to become valuable assets overnight through the application of scientific knowledge to the problems of industrial production. This was the case with crude oil. In 1854 Professor Silliman at Yale University discovered that by heating and distilling crude oil it was possible to produce two new and more functional products — kerosene and petroleum. This discovery was to make oil, a resource known by the Chinese for a thousand years, accessible for widespread industrial and domestic use.

Edwin L. Drake, who first discovered oil in Pennsylvania in 1859, used Chinese-style drilling rigs, which were soon popping up all over the United States. Refineries provided the fine oils needed for industry and for the railway locomotives that now linked the United States' vast internal market to that of Europe and the rest of the world. In 1880 Standard Oil was in a position to open three large-scale refineries bringing the price of kerosene down from $1.50 a gallon in 1882 to $0.45 in 1885. The greater efficiency of production that came with applying science to industry was clearly seen by the end of the nineteenth century and had profound economic implications.

The work of German chemists had forced down the price of blue dye from DM 200 in 1870 to DM 6 by 1886. New methods of refining aluminum saw the price fall from Fr 39.8 per pound in 1888 to Fr 1.70 in 1895. This pattern of price reductions made new products possible, which, in turn, fueled a revolution in domestic technology. Singer sewing machines came on the market along with steel-framed bicycles and Remington typewriters. The scale of the market for these new consumer goods was also greatly expanded by mail-order firms, which used the railways and fast international steam ships.

This second industrial revolution, based on scientific discovery, allowed the formation of new institutions and opportunities for ingenuity and invention. In 1876 an inventor like Thomas Edison was able to establish his research laboratory at Menlo Park employing trained scientists and engineers in what he described as an "invention factory." The Edison Company not only invented the electric lamp, or light bulb, but also the entire distribution and delivery system for domestic lighting. The General Electric Company that was to grow out of Edison's original firm had as its basis a tradition of industrial research and development, which increasingly held the key to industrial innovation. This was to be taken up by the new German-style universities, springing up throughout the United States, whose research departments

Within a few years of the illumination of New York in 1882, the Tokyo Electric Company had lit up the Ginza area of Tokyo, to the amazement of all. Through licensing agreements between the Edison Company and firms such as Toshiba, Japanese enterprises gained access to the western technology vital for both industrial and military purposes.

were increasingly linked to the needs of local industrial enterprises.

All this was absorbed by the Japanese and Chinese students sent abroad to study science and engineering. However, when they returned home, the political response to their new knowledge was to be markedly different. Japanese students returned, not just to academic jobs in institutes of learning, but to positions in the new industrial enterprises being funded by people like Shibusawa and his Dai-Ichi Bank. The Japanese students were often sent by their companies to learn specific industrial applications of new technology. Within a few years of New York being illuminated by the Edison Company in 1882, the Tokyo Electric Company (later Toshiba) switched on street lights in Tokyo. Through the international patent system Japanese firms were, by license, able to gain access to the new technology as it emerged in the west. More often than not they reverse-engineered what they could not license and adapted it to their own requirements. This was to be particularly true of textile technology. For example, the heavy metal looms introduced into Japan from Europe presented serious problems. They were extremely expensive and, when broken, parts had to be sent from Britain, France and Germany. Toyoda Sakichi in 1896 took the heavy European power loom and rebuilt as much of it as possible in wood. He also made it small so that it would take the standard width of cloth used in kimonos throughout Japan. These he was able to sell at around ¥93 each as opposed to ¥872 for a German machine or ¥389 for a French machine. At this price the Toyoda loom was accessible to small-scale cottage industries. This simple innovation was to play an important part in the modernization of the Japanese textile industry and was to provide a model for the adapting of western methods to Japanese conditions, which was to occur in a number of technological fields. The adaptation and refinement of this original Toyoda loom was to lead to the Platt Brothers in England, the world's leading supplier of textile machinery, buying the patent to it in 1929 for £25,000.

In the fields of heavy industry, firms like Mitsubishi were able to diversify from shipbuilding into locomotive and armaments manufacture. Government and military contracts under the "strong army, rich nation" policy meant that Japanese industrialists, many trained in universities in Europe and the United States, recognized the importance of research and were prepared to carry the costs of sending capable engineers abroad for training. These overseas-trained students and observers provided access to what was being done in industrial and military fields.

There was, therefore, by the 1880s an industrial context in which innovation could occur, especially as the Meiji government's comprehensive western-style education system in the 1870s now turned out well-trained technicians and engineers able to take on the new roles defined by the growing industrial base. The demand for western-style consumer goods, and the money with which to pay for them, provided the basis for new industries and new careers.

* * *

Chinese students returning from abroad were increasingly frustrated in their efforts to bring about change. With the possible exception of the European-dominated treaty ports of Shanghai and Guangzhou, the basic ambivalence of government officials towards western values and institutions meant that industrial growth and change were slow and often inhibited. Even in Guangzhou, for example, when a Chinese textile mill was burned down, government officials would offer no help or support to the local entrepreneur, arguing that such an industry was basically immoral because it simply made the factory owner rich, and undercut the economic viability of the traditional handicraft industry.

In this they were quite right but the cost of maintaining their traditional rural-based craft industries was unrealistic in the face of overseas competition. British and American textiles sold through the treaty ports undercut this local craft industry and placed increasing strain on an already depressed economy. Even the modern manufacturing and transport systems set up by reformers like Li Hongzhang were constantly in difficulties. The state-owned but merchant-run firms had many of the same failings as the early Meiji enterprises. Without the support of the Chinese government, to protect and nurture these fledgling industries, they had little opportunity to compete with those European-owned enterprises in the treaty ports whose power and influence over the coastal economy continued to grow.

CARVED UP LIKE A RIPE MELON

[Such scientific subjects as] electricity, heat, astronomy, air, light, dynamics, and chemistry are what the English call real knowledge, while they consider the teaching of our Chinese sages as empty and useless talk. Chinese officials who are deceived by their words often agree with them. I argue against these beliefs, saying that their real knowledge consists only of petty, miscellaneous tricks, which can be used to make "a utensil" of but limited capacity . . . They concentrate on such miscellaneous tricks, using boats and vehicles made to bring in profit, and firearms made for killing, trying to produce more and more of such things to become wealthy and strong. How can we call all this useful, real knowledge? Since the beginning of history, China has endured longer than any other civilization, and has produced a hundred and several dozen sages one after another, daily refining and completing their [social and moral] institutions. The depth of our philosophical discussions greatly exceeds those of the west. Foreigners consider material wealth as true wealth; western nations think brute force is strength: China takes deference as strength. This is the real truth. It cannot be explained in a few hurried words.

Liu Xihong, Chinese envoy to London, 1877

Just as good iron is not made into nails, so good men do not become soldiers.

Popular Chinese saying

While traditional Chinese scholar-officials like Liu Xihong, one of the first Chinese ambassadors to London, had confidence in the Confucian moral virtues that had sustained Chinese imperial culture for 2,000 years, others were increasingly concerned for the very survival of China as a sovereign entity. In the late nineteenth century the forces of western economic imperialism were reaching a pitch that even the Celestial Empire could not ignore. The scrabble for colonial territories in Africa and much of Southeast Asia confronted China with the prospect of being next on the agenda. In fact the view expressed in the capitals of Europe was that it was ready to be "carved up like a ripe melon."

The failure of self-strengthening to unite the government and empire in the sorts of change embarked upon by the Meiji government in Japan was understandable. The price of China's commitment to its traditional world view was that it was increasingly out of kilter with what was actually happening around it. The tragic double bind faced by the Chinese governing elite was not merely a consequence of having a group of intransigent and xenophobic mandarins in power: they were genuinely caught between two stools for which their culture and education had not prepared them. They had to affirm the traditional cultural values that legitimized their power and held the empire together. They were also forced to contain the European influence that increasingly threatened to split up the empire as had happened in India, with the British playing one state off against another to divide and rule.

Too much change could destabilize the whole empire, too little made it vulnerable to attack and foreign encroachment. In 1874, for example, the Japanese under a pretext took over Formosa (Taiwan) and five years later annexed the Luich'iu Islands; the British became involved in trying to take over Yunnan in 1875, and the Russians successfully occupied Ili in Xinjiang (Sinkiang) in 1871–81. In 1884–85 the French seized Annam (now Vietnam), which was regarded as a part of China, and the resulting war ended in a humiliating backdown on the part of the Chinese government, and large payments in reparation. Above all else these wars, like the disastrous Taiping rebellion, cost the Chinese government dearly, weakening both the credibility of the Qing dynasty and the government financial reserves.

The financial plight of the empire had never been worse, In the late eighteenth century the government of Qianlong had surplus reserves of around 70 million taels ($7 million). One hundred years later China had an annual budget deficit of 10 million taels.

It was only by taking foreign loans that the Chinese were able to purchase the increasingly sophisticated military technology needed for defense — cannon from Krupp and battleships from Britain — despite the establishment of their own arsenal. The problem was that Chinese military production had little connection with the sources of innovation and, without a modern education system, was unable to keep abreast of scientific and technological advances. This was to be most painfully revealed in 1894 in the humiliating confrontation with the Japanese over Korea.

Korea had, until the 1880s, been one of the most loyal of China's traditional tributary states. Intensely xenophobic it was, however, like many other Asian

China and Japan fish for control of Korea, once a tributary state loyal to China but, by the 1890s, under pressure from reformers to follow the path of social and economic reform taken by Japan; Russia looks on eager to increase its territory and power in the east. The competition between them came to a head in 1894.

On 17 September 1894 the Chinese and Japanese fleets confronted each other off the coast of Korea. Although numerically stronger, the Chinese ships were older and much slower than the Japanese, which gave the Japanese a tactical advantage.

With the fall of their forts to the Japanese army, the Chinese were forced to sue for peace. At Shimonoseki in Japan, the Chinese delegation, led by Li Hongzhang, had no alternative but to concede to terms that gave Japan territorial rights within China, similar to those won by the European imperial powers, as well as a hefty indemnity payment.

cultures, divided into those loyal to the traditional Confucian values of the past and those drawn to the pragmatic modernization of Japan.

Inevitably these political factions called on support from their respective mentors. The conflict over the position of Korea and its independence or lack of it was to lead to a head-on military confrontation between the brashly self-confident Japan and imperial China. This was, in a sense, to be a test of the achievement of the two approaches to self-strengthening. In reality it was Japan's final step in its efforts to join the exclusive club of imperialist powers. The Japanese had clearly learned the principles of western industrial production and, as good students, had learned the other essential lesson of nineteenth century western political economy — controlling colonial territories whose resources could feed the expansion of industrial power.

The extension of the United States westward beyond Mexico and the west coast to Hawaii and the Philippines in the late 1880s provided the model for what the Japanese could only come to perceive as a global game of chess.

In a subtle political move the British were prepared to encourage Japanese expansionism in northeast China as a bulwark against imperial Russia whose expansion into Afghanistan and the Crimea had threatened British interests. The construction of the trans-Siberian railway also gave Russia direct access to the east. So with what seemed to be the tacit support of the British, Japan began to extend its sphere of influence to include Korea. In China this challenged the traditional tributary relationship, which had to be honored, and the die was cast. Li Hongzhang, as governor to the northern provinces was at the heart of the negotiations with the Koreans to try and head off a confrontation with the Japanese. His success with the Taiping, and in numerous other foreign conflicts, made him eminently suitable in the eyes of the imperial government in Beijing.

In August 1894 the Japanese army occupied the capital P'yongyang on the pretext of preserving its independence. They sank a Chinese boat in the harbor and China sent in its navy. China had twice the naval strength of Japan: 65 ships as opposed to 32 ships. But lack of centralized control over this navy meant that two of the three Chinese fleets available remained in harbor in the south, due to the fact that they were under the control of the provincial authorities whose bureaucratic mechanism was not designed for rapid decision making.

On 17 September 1894 a Chinese Peiyang fleet of 25 ships led by Admiral Ting met the Japanese fleet of 21 ships near the Yalu River in Korea Bay. There was one essential difference between the two forces. The Japanese navy was equipped with newer battleships, which could travel at speeds of up to 23 knots, while the Chinese ships were much slower, heavier and older, and could travel at only 15 knots. The consequence was that the Japanese navy could easily outmaneuver the Chinese and, within four hours, the Chinese had lost four ships and about a thousand officers and men. The Japanese lost one ship. The Chinese fleet retreated to Port Arthur where they had established powerful fortifications, only to find that the Japanese had captured the forts from the landward side, and were able to turn the 70 Krupp cannons, which Li had installed there and at Weihaiwei, upon the helpless Chinese navy. Admiral Ting committed suicide and the Japanese captured seven Chinese warships.

The repercussions of these events were enormous. Li Hongzhang was severely criticized and lost the right to wear the yellow jacket, the mark of imperial favor. He was also forced to go to the negotiation table with the Japanese who, like the Europeans before them, were to demand large economic concessions and reparations.

At the city of Shimonoseki, Li confronted the Japanese negotiating team of Ito and Mutu — Li dressed in the gown of an imperial court official, Ito and Mutu in European military uniforms. All three were of a generation concerned with self-strengthening. (Ito had been one of the early students who was smuggled into Europe in the 1860s with the help of Thomas Glover, an English merchant and entrepreneur living in Nagasaki.)

Li was to open the negotiations with an appeal to their shared Confucian heritage and the common threat, which should unite them against European expansion throughout Asia, but his words fell on deaf ears. The Japanese had for centuries suffered from the superiority and condescension of Chinese imperial officials to a tributary state; now the tables were turned.

However, in the middle of these negotiations a Japanese fanatic shot Li, hitting him just below the left eye. Suddenly, public opinion, as expressed in the press and by the negotiators, softened a little out of acute embarrassment over the incident. Sympathy was to be shortlived.

In April 1896 a treaty was drawn up that forced China into accepting Korea's "independence" (under Japanese domination). China was forced to pay an indemnity of 200 million taels ($20 million) to Japan; to secede Taiwan, the Pescadores and the Liaodong Peninsula, and to open the ports of Chongqing (Chungking), Suzhou and Hangzhou to international trade. Finally, and perhaps most importantly, Japanese nationals had the right to open factories within China on the same basis as other imperialist powers. The Chinese had little option but to accede to these demands now or suffer the possibility of having to give up more the next time.

For Japan the benefits of the engagement were encouraging. The reparations from China represented 15 per cent of Japanese gross national product in 1895. The success of the military was to strengthen their hand in government and their call for government-sponsored steel production was now to have some effect. Twenty-five million yen went to the establishment of a new steel mill to supply material, particularly for the navy. German engineers, experienced in the Krupp steelworks, helped to set up the massive Yawata steelworks, later to become Nippon Steel. The foundry ensured that this most fundamental material, the key to nineteenth century military and industrial power, was readily available.

There was, however, to be one major and bitter setback amid all this triumph. Japan was, for the most part, to be blackballed by the imperialist club. This parvenu in their midst had the Germans, French and Russians up in arms, largely because of the territorial concession of the Liaodong Peninsula in southern Manchuria, which Ito and Mutu were able to extract from the Chinese. Under considerable pressure the

Japanese were forced to back down on their claims to the territory only to find that three years later these same European powers made similar territorial claims, with Russia gaining the Liaodong region.

With all this came a torrent of racist invective directed against the Japanese by European states concerned that Japan might be moving in on territories they wished to control themselves. The German Kaiser, Wilhelm II, whose interests in Shandong (Shantung) were threatened by Japan, even invented the term "yellow peril," while the United States and Australia adopted exclusionist policies directed against Asians, in particular, the Japanese. A German political commentator, Baron Von Falkenegg, was to whip up anxiety within Europe:

> The European powers should have realized in good time that the cunning, skilled and valiant Japanese people would soon be uttering the slogan "Asia for the Asians"... [that] is directed at all those Europeans who want to take political and commercial advantages in Asia. But for the Japanese, "Asia for the Asians" has the obvious implications "Japan dominates Asia, and Asia dominates Europe."

In France best selling novels such as the *The Yellow Invasion* by Emil Driant fictionalized the threat of oriental hordes sweeping across central Asia like Gengis Khan and his army. Rene Pinon, a French writer of the time, had this to say about the hysteria of the "yellow peril," which was used in some quarters to draw attention to European decadence:

> Whether one likes it or not, the "yellow peril" has entered already into the imagination of the people ... Japanese and Chinese hordes spread out over all Europe, crushing under their feet the ruins of our capital cities and destroying our civilizations, grown anaemic due to the enjoyment of luxuries and corrupted by vanity of spirit.

Japan's success in taking on the might of imperial China meant that they had finally qualified for membership of the exclusive imperialist club. However, Japan was not admitted; the reaction of the Europeans was to succumb to racist paranoia and to invoke the specter of the "Yellow Peril" rising in the east.

203

The racist assault upon the Japanese at this time cut deep, and brought about an inevitable swing against Europe, and against western values and institutions in general. Although not slowing the pace of modernization, ballroom dancing at the Rokumeikan was to come to an abrupt end. An imperial edict on education promoted the virtues of Confucian values and Japanese traditions. Racism was to be fought with racism.

Ten years later, in 1905, the unthinkable was to happen. The Japanese, smarting from the insults and maneuvers to limit their access to the mainland of China, finally came to a showdown with imperial Russia over the control of Manchuria. Both at sea and on the plains of Manchuria they were to drive the Russians out of the Liaodong Peninsula and gain their rightful status as an imperialist power. They had joined the club despite the "whites only" sign above the door. Some European commentators were more honest about the events taking place in the Orient. The French novelist Anatole France wrote:

> What the Russians are paying for at this very moment in the seas of Japan and in the gorges of Manchuria is not just their avid and brutal policy in the Orient, it is the colonial policy of all the European powers... It would not appear to be the case, however, that the yellow peril terrifying European economists is comparable to the white peril hanging over Asia. The Chinese do not send to Paris, Berlin or St. Petersburg missionaries to teach Christians *feng-shui* and cause general chaos in European affairs . . . Admiral Togo did not come with a dozen battleships to bombard the roadstead of Brest in order to help Japanese commerce in France. . . . The armies of the Asiatic powers have not taken to Tokyo or Peking the paintings of the Louvre or the china of the Élysée.

In an editorial in the influential science journal *Nature* in June 1905, this perceptive comment appeared, drawing the attention of complacent Europeans to the relevance of what the Japanese had achieved in less than fifty years:

> The operations of the present war with Russia have clearly demonstrated the importance of the introduction of the scientific spirit into all the national activities. . . . The lesson, which our educationalists and statesmen have to learn from Japan is that the life of a modern nation requires to be organized on scientific lines in all its departments, and that it must not be directed chiefly to personal ends, the attainment of which may, to a large extent, intensify many of our problems, but that it be consciously used for the promotion of national welfare.

*   *   *

In China the response to the debacle over Korea and the conditions of Shimonoseki was to bring home as never before the empire's critical vulnerability. Clearly the attempt to simply graft military and industrial technology on to existing imperial institutions was not working. In the wake of this a new group of reformers emerged with a far more radical approach, one which was based very much on the Japanese model.

One of the leading intellectual figures, who was to lash out at the failings of earlier reformers such as Li Hongzhang was Yan Fu (Yen Fu). At the time of the war with Japan

Yan Fu had been superintendent of the Peiyang Naval Academy and it was many of his students and colleagues who went with the ill-fated Peiyang fleet to meet the Japanese off Yalu.

Yan Fu was one of the early students sent from China to study naval engineering in Britain. He was a contemporary of Japanese students such as Ito and Togo who were to rise rapidly to positions of power and influence in Meiji Japan, while returned students such as Yan Fu were to have little influence on the conservative Confucian scholars surrounding the Qing court.

Yan Fu (1854–1921) came from a scholar family from Fujian and he was brought up with a thorough grounding in the Confucian classics. He was an extremely capable student and, instead of following the traditional career path into the bureaucracy, Yan Fu was sent at the age of 14 to Li Hongzhang's Fuzhou naval dockyards, to study English, mathematics and science. In 1876 he was sent to study at Greenwich Naval Academy.

Britain in the 1870s was in the midst of the great Darwinian debate on the nature of evolution. The social and cultural implications of Darwin's theories of natural selection were not explored by Darwin himself but by his most ardent disciples, Thomas Huxley and Herbert Spencer, who were to popularize his ideas. The young Yan Fu, like Ito of Japan, was to fall under the spell of this intellectual movement. (Spencer was to become an adviser to the Japanese government after Ito became prime minister.) In essence the crude social Darwinists, as they were known, justified the intense competitiveness of the capitalist market place, as well as the conflict between nation-states on the basis that it conformed with the natural order of "survival of the fittest." This notion of "survival of the fittest" was taken from Darwin's biological examples and elevated to an economic and moral virtue. Why were the Europeans apparently "fitter" than the Chinese? This was what concerned Yan Fu.

It was not only Darwin, but writers such as John Stuart Mill and Adam Smith, who were to provide him with some of the answers to the secret of the west's wealth and power. It also provided him with a position from which to see the limitations and strengths of his own cultural and economic institutions. With the support of renegades in the London embassy, such as Guo Songdao who believed that China must reform its traditional institutions, and quickly, Yan Fu began to translate into classical Chinese the works of Huxley, Smith, Darwin, Spencer and Mill. In these annotated translations Yan Fu was to provide Chinese scholars with their first real understanding of the roots of western economic and political institutions, as well as its cultural values. The failure of Confucian culture to release the creative and dynamic potential of the individual was to be one of the recurring themes that Yan Fu was to derive from Mill and Adam Smith. For while Adam Smith convinced him of the virtues of the free market regulated by individuals pursuing their own "enlightened self-interest," John Stuart Mill provided an extension of this to cultural and intellectual freedom. The growth of knowledge was possible only in a "free market of ideas." This was the key to the growth of Europe's liberal-intellectual tradition. What Yan Fu also emphasized was the need for European-style individualism, as well as the legal and political institutions, to protect enterprising individuals from the arbitrary power of the state — in China's case the imperial bureaucracy. He came to regard the refined, isolated and contemplative Confucian mandarins as effete. His call for educational and democratic reforms was to have a considerable influence on the thinking of a whole generation of scholars, particularly those who were not able to travel abroad and who otherwise had only official prejudices to guide them.

With the military debacle at the hands of the Japanese forcing conservative officials to look for some real solutions, Yan Fu and other returned scholars demanded fundamental reforms; reforms that would strike at the very heart of the Chinese imperial system. Kang Youwei (K'ang Yu-wei) and Liang Qichao (Liang Ch'i-ch'ao) were scholar-officials close to the center of imperial power and both were profoundly influenced by the writings of Yan Fu. With clear examples of what Japan's Meiji reformers had achieved they began to work within the government structure to bring about radical change. After three years of agitating for reform, and with some adroit political maneuvers against conservative government officials, Kang was finally to get the support of the Emperor Guangxu (Kuang Hsü). A famous meeting on 16 June 1898 was recorded by Liang Qichao:

> After the emperor had asked about his [Kang's] age and his qualifications:
>
> KANG: The four barbarians are all invading us and their attempted partition is gradually being carried out: China will soon perish.
>
> EMPEROR: Today it is really imperative that we reform.
>
> KANG: It is not because in recent years we have not talked about reform, but because it was only a slight reform, not a complete one, we change the first thing and do not change the second, and then we have everything so confused as to incur failure, and eventually there will be no success. The prerequisites of reform are that all the laws and the political and social systems be changed and decided anew, before it can be called reform. Now those who talk about reform only change some specific affairs, and do not reform the institutions.

The emperor was impressed and asked Kang to provide a more detailed outline of his proposals. He was appointed secretary of the *zongli yamen* and produced a radical manifesto that, with the emperor's approval, was promulgated as a series of decrees, which over the next hundred days were designed to transform education, administration, political institutions and industry. These institutional reforms were very much along the lines of those adopted not only in Meiji Japan but in Germany and Russia as well:

> In revitalizing the various administrative departments our government adopts western methods and principles. For, in a true sense, there is no difference between China and the west in setting up government for the sake of the people. Since, however, westerners have studied [the science of government] more diligently, their findings can be used to supplement our deficiencies. Scholars and officials of today whose purview does not go beyond China [regard westerners] as practically devoid of precepts or

principles. They do not know that the science of government as it exists in western countries has very rich and varied contents, and that its chief aim is to develop the people's knowledge and intelligence and to make their living commodious. The best part of the science is capable of bringing about improvements in human nature and the prolongation of human life.

This resolution on the part of the emperor to take decisive action to bring about institutional reforms in China could have changed the course of Asian history. However on 21 September, conservative government officials staged a coup. Supported by the aging, though extremely powerful, Empress Dowager Cixi (Tz'u-hsi), they were able to take over the reins of government and, after putting the emperor under house arrest on a small island in the imperial gardens, they began to persecute those who were responsible for the reforms. Kang was able to escape to Shanghai and Liang Qichao to Japan; others were not so successful. Four reformers in the Grand Council along with Kang's brother were executed without trial. Twenty-two senior officials and scholars were jailed or banished for their involvement in the reform movement. All the edicts issued by the emperor were rescinded except, surprisingly, the one establishing an imperial university in Beijing. The Empress Dowager had now become the de facto ruler of China, and any hope of reform had been lost.

Freer Gallery of Art, Smithsonian Institution, Washington

The powerful Empress Dowager Zixi whose support for conservative officials led to the coup that stopped the young Emperor Guangxu's efforts at institutional and economic reforms along the lines taken by Meiji Japan.

With the obvious success of the conservative element in government, a popularist anti-foreign movement, known as the Boxers, gained both confidence and official support. As with the Taiping rebellion it was spurred on by increased economic hardship. Foreign domination of local trade through the treaty ports meant that imported manufactured goods were driving out local craft industries. The Boxers or the "Righteous and Harmonious Fists" got their name from the form of martial arts they practiced. They also held Taoist magical beliefs, which supposedly endowed the practitioners with protection from western bullets after a hundred days of training. In this they were very similar to the Sioux Indian ghost dancers in their last-ditch stand to drive Europeans from their lands in the 1890s.

The Boxers became a focus of anti-foreign feelings. In May 1900 they were able to take over most of the imperial capital and to hold the foreign legations under siege until relief armies, consisting of British, German, American, French and Japanese troops, arrived to suppress the revolt.

The empress and the newly triumphant conservative forces within the Chinese government had tacitly supported the rebellion in the vain hope that they could in fact drive the Europeans out and reassert their traditional cultural values. But, yet again, the Chinese government was humiliated and forced to pay massive reparations to the foreign powers. The possibility of modernizing the old imperial order was a lost cause.

European missionaries and their schools had been one of the main targets of the anti-foreign movement. They were now given even greater access and rights throughout China to offer their corrosive western-style education. Within six years the Empress Dowager was dead, and the ancient imperial examination system, which for 1000 years had provided the ideological gateway to power and wealth within China, was abandoned. In its place a western-style curriculum was introduced. Students were sent abroad in increasing numbers to gain higher education, with over 40 per cent going to Japan. A new ministry of education was set up and missions sent to Japan to study their system, which formed the model. But all this was too late to save the empire. Ten or fifteen years earlier there might have been some hope of holding the Qing empire together, but the constant repression of those idealists and reformers of earlier years had resulted in disillusionment, which now turned to revolution. It was therefore no coincidence that it should be a western-trained doctor, Sun Yat-sen, with the support of political refugees in Japan, who was to bring the empire to an end and found the first Chinese Republic in 1911.

COMPRADORES AND WARLORDS

Mr Science and Mr Democracy, only these two gentlemen can cure the dark maladies in Chinese politics, morality, learning and thought.

Chen Duxiu, 1919

Sun Yat-sen, known in the Chinese-speaking world as Sun Zhongshan, brought to Chinese politics an idealism almost unmatched by any reform movement in the twentieth century. From the point of view of his European and Japanese supporters he had gleaned the best political models from the west. His revolutionary ideas were based on the concept of "three people's principles" — people's national consciousness or nationalism, people's rights or democracy and people's livelihood or socialism (in other words "of the people, by the people, for the people"). These ideals had the broad support of progressive intellectuals, scholars and the new (and increasingly powerful) class of compradore merchants and industrialists in the treaty ports.

The reality was, however, that as the Qing dynasty went into its final years of decline, power fell back into the hands of provincial warlords. Within five years of the declaration of the Republic the warlords were battling among themselves, each trying to gain sufficient support to claim imperial power and perhaps even found a new dynasty as tradition allowed. In this the European powers were to perform a mischievous role, playing one warlord off against the other with offers of support and funds. Even the President of the Republic, Yuan Shikai (Yüan Shih-k'ai), was to use his position to pursue his own imperial aspirations in the north. Without the

Dr Sun Yat-sen in exile in Japan where he was supported in his revolutionary political efforts both by liberal Japanese and by the large number of Chinese students sent there to gain a western-style education in medicine, engineering or science.

imperial structure, it would seem that no amount of idealism could hold China together. This was a lesson not lost on later revolutionaries.

Despite this political chaos, the fragmentation of power did not prevent the introduction of some long overdue institutional reforms. By 1914 China had 17 modern banks, and chambers of commerce were set up to support local entrepreneurs. However, despite the 200,000 members throughout China, and the success of the international treaty port cities of Shanghai, Guangzhou and Nanjing, the modern industrial sector of the economy remained dominated by foreign capital and firms. Little of this capital was to spread to the great bulk of the population who remained in rural villages, increasingly impoverished and only marginally affected in their day-to-day life by the economic activities in the coastal cities. Although ideals of public education and land reform were basic planks in the republican agenda there was neither the political will nor the money to carry them out effectively. The failure of the efforts at modernization to reach the common people was to be a lasting dilemma for liberal reformers trying to introduce into China the sort of democratic institutions that they believed lay at the heart of western culture.

Profound changes were happening among the traditional educated elite. Instead of being put through the imperial examination en route for the bureaucracy, they now went to missionary schools and colleges in the hope of gaining access to an overseas university. As had occurred in Japan, earlier in the Meiji, Chinese students returning from abroad were now able to take influential positions in government and in the new universities.

For example, Cai Yuanpei (Ts'ai Yüan-p'ei), a traditional Confucian scholar who had studied philosophy in Germany and France, returned to become Minister for Education in the Sun Yat-sen government. In 1917 he became Chancellor of Beijing University, which he transformed from a "bureaucrat-ridden school that prepared officials to hold sinecures" into a radical center of learning.

The Dean of Letters was the journalist Chen Duxiu (Ch'en Tu-hsiu) who had also been a student in France and who was a passionate proponent of the ideals of the French Revolution — the ideals of "liberty, equality and fraternity." Like Fukuzawa in the 1870s, Chen founded a radical journal, *New Youth*. This provided a forum and a focus of identity for a whole new generation attempting to throw off the "mind-binding" character of the traditional Neo-Confucian ideas and values that had dominated China since the Ming dynasty. Chen exhorted his students to give up their passivity and concern with self-cultivation; to "be independent not servile, progressive not conservative, dynamic not passive, cosmopolitan not isolationist, scientific not merely imaginative"; to break the traditional notion that it was somehow demeaning for a scholar to be practical and get his hands dirty. Even physical fitness was promoted, perhaps as a consequence of the "healthy minds and bodies" policy of the missionary schools. (It should not be forgotten that one of the first articles written by Mao Zedong (Mao Tse-tung) was on the importance of physical fitness and strength.)

Chen's major ally at Beijing University was another young Confucian scholar Hu Shi. Hu had been sent to study at Cornell University in New York and had come under the influence of the philosopher and educationalist John Dewey. Hu Shi's relationship with him brought Dewey to Beijing for a lecture series, at about the same time that the British philosopher Bertrand Russell was also giving lectures there. While Dewey tried to convince an eager generation of Chinese students of the virtues of individualism and science, Russell was promoting socialism and a healthy distrust of western imperialism. All this was to provide enormous intellectual stimulus.

In an article in *New Youth,* Hu Shi denounced the classical Chinese that had served as the language of scholars and the imperial government for over two thousand years. He regarded it in much the same way that Reformation scholars regarded Latin, as "a dead language, which could not produce a living literature." What he campaigned for was a language capable of expressing the new values that had been discovered in the revolutionary social movements of the west and, above all, the concepts of modern science.

These frustrations were expressed in popular slogans "Down with Confucius and Sons. Long live Mr Science and Mr Democracy." However, while radical social and political reforms were being aired in the new intellectual forum of the universities and colleges, there was still little link between these erudite intellectuals and the large mass of impoverished and largely illiterate peasants and industrial workers. For many this was to change suddenly and quite remarkably on 4 May 1919.

At the Versailles conference following the Allied victory against Germany in 1918, the German concessions in Shandong were to be given to Japan, with the tacit approval of the warlord government in Beijing. (They had been prepared to trade Shandong for the promise of Japanese support against other warlords.) This betrayal on the part of the Allied Powers, which China had supported throughout the War, brought an immediate and unprecedented response.

Three thousand students from 13 institutions in Beijing assembled in Tiananmen Square to demonstrate. This was the first time such a demonstration had been seen in China. The movement was to spread like wildfire to other major cities such as Shanghai and Guangzhou. The students were soon joined by the workers from the newly formed labor unions, the press and even merchants. In Shanghai workers in some thirty factories went on strike. There was a call for a boycott of Japanese goods. The cabinet in Beijing resigned and the Chinese delegation at Versailles refused to sign the treaty. In some senses Chinese nationalism was to emerge from this final injustice. It was also to turn many students away from the seemingly impractical liberal and democratic ideals put forward by Sun Yat-sen, and those calling for gradual reform such as Hu Shi.

The 1917 Bolshevik revolution in Russia provided some hope for radical Chinese students: hope that the socialist ideal first espoused by Sun Yat-sen might be realized by a backward agricultural country like China and that the laws of human economic and political development, put forward by Hegel and Marx, might not be as absolute as was claimed. Lenin had obviously demonstrated that it was not necessary to go through the phase of fully developed capitalism before one could achieve the goal of socialism. Chen Duxiu, disillusioned by the failure of republican reforms to come to terms with the extraordinary inequalities within China or to provide a force that would give the country some unity of purpose, turned to the Russian example. His enthusiasm for the Russian revolution and its achievement was shared by another scholar from Beijing University, Li Dazhao (Li Ta-chao), who devoted an entire edition of *New Youth* to "The Victory of Bolshevism." One of Li Dazhao's assistants working in the library at the University was a young scholar from Hunan, Mao Zedong.

In September 1920 Chen and Li decided to form a Chinese communist party and in Shanghai in June the following year, with the support of the Soviet Union, the First Congress of the Chinese Communist Party was held with representatives from Beijing, Wuhan, Guangzhou and Jinan. Heading the delegation from Changsha was Li's library assistant, Mao Zedong.

For many who were to subsequently join the Party it was to offer an all-inclusive ideology and clear targets to blame for China's prolonged poverty and underdevelopment. The imperialist powers who exploited the venality of warlords, and the compradores who acted as their agents provided a focus for Chinese nationalism. Marxism-Leninism had the appearance of being scientific and progressive in its social values. It also offered perhaps that most basic and important requirement of traditional Chinese policy, an ideology that could provide an ethical system to fill the vacuum left by Confucianism and the empire. But this all-embracing ideology came at a price, that of intellectual freedom of which Hu Shi was to remind his more romantic colleagues:

> There is no liberation *in toto*, or reconstruction *in toto*. Liberation means liberation from this or that institution, from this or that belief, for this or that individual; it is liberation bit by bit, drop by drop.

However, it seems that time was running out for such subtleties. China was not only to be fragmented by foreign concessions and feuding warlords, but was now confronted with an ideological and civil war between the remnants of Sun Yat-sen's republican movement, the Guomindang, and the communists; a battle for the hearts and minds of the Chinese people.

ZAIBATSU AND THE ZERO-SUM GAME

We are no longer ashamed to stand before the world as Japanese.... The name "Japanese," like the names Satsuma and Choshu after the Boshin War, like the name of the returned explorer Stanley and the name of Wellington after Waterloo, now signifies honor, glory, courage, triumph, and victory. Before, we did not know ourselves, and the world did not yet know us. But now that we have tested our strength, we know ourselves and we are known by the world. Moreover, we know we are known by the world.

Tokutomi Soho, 1894

The "May 4" boycott of Japanese goods in China represented a watershed in the souring of relations between the two countries. In commercial terms it represented only a temporary setback. Japan had done well out of World War I. Not only had it gained German concessions in China, but also, while the Europeans had been busily disemboweling each other, Japanese manufacturing firms had gained access to many of the traditional European markets throughout east Asia.

The stimulus to industry that this provided brought fundamental changes to Japanese society. In 1880 Japan was a predominantly agrarian society with small-scale rural industries; by 1920, 50 per cent of the population lived in cities. Many were employed in the small workshops that had sprung up to supply components for the large corporations known as *zaibatsu* or "money cliques." These *zaibatsu* were set up along the lines developed by Shibusawa in the 1880s, with strong connections to government. They were organized around a central bank and trading company. The largest of these are still household names around the world — Mitsui, Mitsubishi, Sumitomo and Nissan.

The power of these massive companies was extensive, not only because of their wealth and the number of people dependent on them, but also because of their ability to influence political life, now centered on the Diet (the German parliamentary system that was introduced with the Prussian constitution in 1889). The capacity of these large firms to buy politicians became a national scandal by the 1920s and was the cause of a good deal of disillusionment with the government on the part of those liberals who believed that the European model of democratic government was the best means of catching up with the west. (Liberty in both China and Japan was never accepted as an end in itself. It was, for the most part, like other political ideas, adopted because of its promise to deliver a rich and powerful state.)

The *zaibatsu*, though large in terms of the diverse industries they controlled, contracted out a great deal of their work to small workshops with 10–100 employees. These small firms could not offer the job security or the conditions of employment enjoyed by the well-educated and highly skilled workers in the head offices. The workshops often provided seasonal work and employment for those unable to gain a living from agriculture. For example, in 1929, there were two million families engaged in silk production. For the large *zaibatsu* one of the great advantages of this system of contracting out work was that it was much easier for firms to expand, contract and readjust as the market demanded. This was to become evident in 1929 when the demand for Japanese goods virtually dried up, with disastrous consequences.

The Great Depression hit Japan more severely than it did any other industrialized country, with the possible exception of Germany. The large market for Japanese silk in the United States and Europe disappeared overnight, throwing as many as 10 million people out of work. The impact was not restricted to rural industries such as silk; the small workshops contracted by the *zaibatsu* had their contracts terminated and large numbers of semi-skilled workers were forced on to the streets.

The consequent resentment and despair led right-wing groups, particularly in the countryside, to direct their aggression against what they saw as a foreign conspiracy working in league with the old *zaibatsu* companies. From the point of view of those thrown out of work, the destruction of their livelihood was yet another example of foreign greed and malevolence. After all, the *zaibatsu* had, in large part, been set up as a means of gaining foreign technology. There had been close collaboration with foreign firms through licensing agreements for electrical firms such as Toshiba (linked to General Electric in the United States) and Nippon Electric (linked with Western Electric); in heavy engineering the pattern was the same.

This relationship with foreign companies led to the old *zaibatsu*, such as Mitsui, coming under political attack from the new ultra-nationalist forces. As in Germany and Italy in the 1930s, it was the disadvantaged rural communities in Japan who formed the political base for national socialist or fascist movements. They were supported by large sections of the military, which was made up of conscripts also from the countryside. They saw the westernized leaders of industry as traitors because they had corrupted the political institutions to support their own financial interests. By the late 1930s the balance of power in the Diet had begun to shift. The power once exerted by the large *zaibatsu* had begun to give way to the ultra-nationalists and the military. Central to this shift was Japan's expansion into Manchuria and its rise as an imperial power. The mass education system established by the Meiji government had now created a literate urban population, who were increasingly well informed about world events and acutely aware of Japan's disadvantaged position and unequal status as an imperial power.

The Japanese delegation to the Versailles peace conference argued for a clause on "racial equality" but this was rejected by the United States, Britain, Australia and Canada. The myth of the "yellow peril," fostered by hysterical journalism in the west, remained strong. So much so that in 1924 the United States Congress passed an Exclusion Act directed specifically at Asian immigrants. The Japanese, in particular, took this insult very much to heart and it helped to boost support for those among the military and the ultra-nationalists seeking to promote the policy of "Asia for the Asians."

In 1930 the London Naval Conference attempted to set artificial limitations on

Japan's construction of heavy cruisers. This so incensed nationalist sentiment that violent protests broke out and a fanatic shot the prime minister. A spate of assassinations followed with the head of Mitsui also being shot.

The sense that Japan was being relegated to second-class status by the western powers was acute. Japanese citizens were denied the right to emigrate to either Australia or the United States, the last regions with open lands. Japanese manufactured goods were also disadvantaged by European colonial control of the markets in Southeast Asia.

Increasingly boxed in, the Japanese military looked to Manchuria as the only avenue for expansion. Their position in the government had always been a powerful one, enshrined in fact in the Prussian-style constitution. They were also increasingly regarded as patriotic in a way that the leaders of industry and business were not.

Japan already held concessions in Manchuria, won from Russia in 1905, but in 1931 Japanese military officers staged a mock sabotage of the south Manchurian railway. On the pretext of defending their interests the Japanese army occupied Manchuria. By January 1932 the army had established the puppet state of Manchuko, with the last (Qing) Manchu Emperor of China, Pu Yi (P'u-i), as its official head.

In 1934 the support for the military in the Japanese government was such that they were able to take control of Manchurian affairs from the ministry of foreign affairs. The greater centralization of power and the deficit financing of military expansion in Manchuria provided an early solution to the Depression, as did Hitler's similar policies in Germany.

The army, however, was not equipped to engage directly in industrial development but they were openly mistrustful of the old *zaibatsu* such as Mitsui and Mitsubishi whom they saw as being dominated by "greedy capitalists," linked to corrupt politicians and committed to internationalism. The success of fascism in Italy and Germany gave them additional support.

To manage the industrial development of Manchuria the army used a number of the large trading companies. Nissan was encouraged to shift its operation to the new colonial territory with the new name of "Japan Industry Company." Like the British and Dutch East India Companies in the eighteenth century these new *zaibatsu* — the Japan Industry Company and the South Manchuria Railway Company — provided the organizational structure for managing the Manchurian economy.

Through these two companies the Japanese government began to build up the industrial infrastructure in Manchuria as a colonial showpiece; building railways, harbors, and opening mines and chemical plants. By 1938 the Japan Industry Company was the second largest corporation in Japan with 18 subsidiary companies specializing in mining, chemicals and electronics. Many of these subsidiaries were also engaged in armaments manufacture.

The economic benefits of Manchuria were to be more psychological and strategic than economic. In fact the Japanese poured more capital into their colonial territory than they ever got out of it. The benefit was essentially the economic stimulus created by the demand for manufactured goods, and military hardware and machinery.

However, Japan was faced with increasing isolation and prejudicial economic exclusion from markets in the rest of the world. This was partially in response to their takeover of Manchuria but also to prevent cheaper Japanese goods (textiles in particular) from competing on equal terms with European manufactured goods. The Depression called forth protective measures in every country and Japan was no different to others in erecting tariff barriers. Yet the destruction of the bonds of economic interdependence and the mutual necessity of international trade played into the hands of the military.

The Smoot-Hawley tariff established in the United States in 1931, and barriers restricting the import of Japanese goods into the Dutch colonial empire (now Indonesia) in 1933, were seen as hostile to Japan. The Ottawa conference of 1932 at which Britain, with the agreement of its colonial governments and dominions, inaugurated a new system of tariffs and imperial preference, was all part of an "economic offensive" to prevent Japanese goods undercutting British goods anywhere in the empire.

From this perspective it is perhaps understandable that the ultra-nationalists in the military should begin to propose not just "Asia for the Asians" but the concept of "the greater east Asian co-prosperity sphere" — in other words, an economic zone covering most of Asia and the Pacific in which Japan would play the dominant industrial role, with the rest of the region benefiting by being freed from European colonial domination. There were many nationalist movements in the smaller countries that saw the Japanese as a potentially liberating force; China, however, was not one of them.

The occupation of Manchuria was of profound concern to China, as was the possibility of further Japanese expansion. On 7 July 1937 fighting broke out between Japanese and Chinese troops near Beijing. Despite years of appeasement the Chinese government in the north was not prepared to accept the Japanese military commander's terms, which as usual were prejudicial to China.

The nationalist armies led by Chiang Kai-shek (Jiang Jieshi in modern transliter-ation), after a decade fighting an ideological and civil war with the communist guerilla forces led by Mao Zedong, were not going to accept further humiliation. On 14 August they bombed Japanese warships in Shanghai. Given the control that the army and navy had over the Japanese government, a decision was made to invade northern China, despite the opposition of the Japanese emperor who, by this stage, was no more than a symbol of patriotic fervor.

By late August the Japanese had occupied most of northern China and the treaty port cities along the southern coast. With appalling savagery and brutality, the southern capital of Nanjing on the Yangtze was taken. It was almost as if the centuries of racism on the part of the European powers had been internalized and turned, with sadistic hatred, against the Chinese. Thousands of men, women and children were senselessly massacred and a long, and ultimately disastrous, war with China had begun.

Despite Japanese hostility towards the west, commercial relations continued. The transfer of technology was as important as ever, especially with the demands of the military. Access to components for aircraft design and construction meant that the links between the major *zaibatsu* firms and those in the United States and Europe were even more crucial, although at times strained by the political climate. In March 1938 an Airplane Manufacturing Industry Law was passed by the Diet. A technical sub-committee with strong representation from the military licensed 15 companies. The two leading firms were Mitsubishi Heavy Industries and Nakajima Airplane Manufacturing Company. Top engineers from these firms had studied at Massachusetts Institute of Technology, Stanford University and California Institute of Technology, the leading engineering schools in the United States. Many production workers had been apprenticed to Douglas, Boeing and Lockheed, with licensing agreements having been established early in the 1930s.

The demands of the navy for an all-purpose fighter aircraft capable of being used from aircraft carriers presented the Mitsubishi engineers in Nagoya with the necessity of coming up with a totally new design. The Zero aircraft, which were to accompany the Japanese bombers to Pearl Harbor in 1941, were perhaps the best fighter aircraft in the sky. In dogfights in the Pacific war they could outmaneuver the best that others could put up against them. As the British discovered in Singapore months later, the assumption of the technological superiority of the west was no longer a foregone conclusion. In less than a hundred years Japan had been transformed from a small, isolated country on the periphery of China into an industrial power to be reckoned with. The extent of this transformation was not to be fully appreciated in the west for another thirty years.

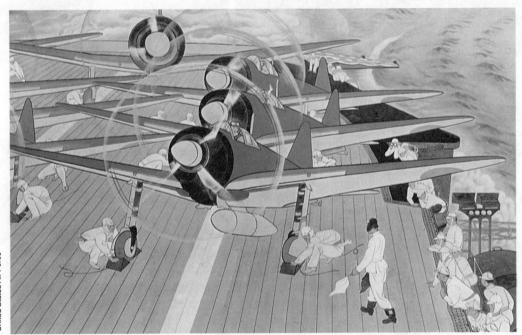

United States Air Force

The artist Shari-arai's impression of Zero fighters on an aircraft carrier during the Pacific War.
This was the first example of Japanese designed technology to have an impact on the west.

217

Today's "Foolish Old Men" Create New Scenes by Cheng Minsheng and Chang Lin, peasant artists from Hunsien country. The scrolls painted in the early 1970s depict the inspiring bounty and cornucopia that would be possible through collective effort.

THE COLOR OF THE CAT

THE DRAGONS AWAKE

Black or white, if cats catch mice they are all right.

Deng Xiaoping, 1962

In the article "Devote every effort to running successfully a socialist research institute of science," "the arch-unrepentant capitalist roader in the party, Deng Xiaoping," should read simply, "Deng Xiaoping."

Notice attached to *Scientia Sinica,* November 1976

During the decade 1966–76 China entered a phase of ideological and political conflict unprecedented in contemporary history. This "Great Proletarian Cultural Revolution" began as an effort to purify the Communist party of what Mao Zedong believed to be the corrupting influence of capitalist ideology.

In the long battle between the leftists, who supported Mao, and the more pragmatic or "scientific Marxists" Deng Xiaoping was to argue that it did not matter what color the cat was as long as it caught mice. In other words, the primary responsibility of social and economic institutions was that they work and the primary responsibility of the Party leadership was to improve the material and social well-being of ordinary people.

Until 1989 history had been kind to this small but resilient survivor of the Long March, and of the equally long and at times tortuous road, which the Chinese Communist party has followed since liberation in 1949. Since the mid-1970s Deng has deftly guided China from an isolation matched only by that of the Ming emperors, back into the international arena. He instituted reforms that produced spectacular levels of economic growth, but in the process was to release forces that were eventually to challenge the very power and authority of the Communist party itself. What has happened in China cannot be understood in isolation. It is increasingly connected to the re-emergence of East Asia, and particularly Japan, as a technological and industrial powerhouse. To fully understand the rise of these "Pan Confucian" economies, it is necessary to go back to 1945 and the end of the Pacific War.

The dropping of the atomic bombs on Hiroshima and Nagasaki, to American minds, brought the war in the Pacific to a close. It was the culmination of a massive conventional bombing campaign on Japanese cities, which, in reality, caused far more destruction than either of the two atomic bombs. The presence of Soviet forces in Manchuria, poised to occupy the northern islands in the Japanese archipelago, was probably as important a factor in Japan's capitulation. The Japanese already knew what had happened in Europe with the partitioning of Germany and saw a similar fate for their own country if the Soviet Union invaded the north and the United States took the south.

In 1945 Japan lay shattered after its defeat in World War II. The Mitsubishi steel works (shown here) was unrecognizable after the dropping of the atomic bomb on Nagasaki.

The occupation of Japan by the Allied Forces was to bring some immediate and obvious changes in the power structure. The objective of the United States State Department was to rebuild Japan as a model democracy. This was undertaken by a remarkable collection of idealists who surrounded General Douglas MacArthur, the United States Viceroy.

Many of these "missionaries for democracy" who surrounded him were brought up with the New Deal idealism of the Roosevelt era. They saw the causes of Japanese militarism as flowing from a conspiracy between big business and the military who, between them, were able to undermine the country's fledgling democratic institutions. To foster democracy they began to rebuild Japan in the image of their own ideals of what the United States should be. The new Japanese constitution was written by these men.

One of their early acts was to break up the *zaibatsu*, which supported Japan's military government. In late 1946 officials, on orders from MacArthur, raided the head offices of Mitsui and Mitsubishi, and confiscated all documents and stocks. The family control of these massive combines was broken up, along the lines of the "trust-busting" that had occurred in the United States in the 1920s and 1930s.

The numerous subsidiaries were separated from the central trading company, becoming independent enterprises with new and younger men brought in to head them. Three hundred *zaibatsu* firms were earmarked but the program proved difficult to implement and was never completed.

The next step in the process of reform was to re-establish trade unions, which had been illegal in Japan since the 1930s. These were set up along western lines and became a powerful force for political resistance to the reintroduction of the traditional power elite. By 1949, 6.5 million workers had joined unions. In the late 1940s and early 1950s Japan was rocked by a series of strikes and occupations of factories. It was in this environment of industrial confrontation that new approaches to management began to be worked out. The behavior of the trade union movement had become so demanding that MacArthur, ironically, had to intervene to break up strikes, which were banned in the public sector. Many "leftists" were also purged as the cold-war politics that dominated the thinking of the State Department led to the great fear that Japan might turn to communism.

Perhaps the most important role that the United States was to take — almost equivalent to the Marshall Plan that helped to rebuild Europe — was to allow the Japanese easy access to American technology on favorable terms. This was not done out of altruism but as a consequence of the victory of the communist forces of Mao Zedong in China against the Nationalists of Chiang Kai-shek backed by the United States. The fear was that, if Japan was not supported, all of Asia might fall to communism. The "yellow peril" had now been replaced by the "red peril." With the intervention of the United States and her allies, Britain and Australia, in Korea in 1950, Japan was soon to become a production base for military equipment and

Courtesy Film Australia

General Douglas MacArthur leaving his office in Tokyo. As head of the allied occupation forces he attempted to reshape Japanese society into a model of capitalist democracy.

supplies. Within a few years of promulgating constitutional rules to prevent Japan from rearming, the Japanese were churning out trucks, jeeps and armaments under license for the United States government. Large amounts of capital in the form of government loans and contracts flowed into the country and were to play a major part in the rebuilding of the Japanese economy. Nonetheless, throughout the 1940s and 1950s, Japan was poor and under profound economic restrictions.

One of the key institutions in the rebuilding and restructuring of Japanese industry at this time was the Ministry of International Trade and Industry (MITI). This was in fact the reconstituted wartime ministry of munitions, which had been responsible for military contracts and for accessing foreign military technology for the army and navy. Its new role was to vet the licensing arrangements between Japanese companies and foreign firms for new technology. MITI could provide or withhold precious foreign exchange and was therefore able to define the industrial priorities of Japan's domestic and export industries. One of MITI's most important functions was to plan the introduction of new industries and, even more importantly, the phasing out of old or uncompetitive ones. This was demonstrated in the way MITI helped to establish the iron and steel industry in the immediate postwar period, then phased it out gradually to replace it with high-value industries such as consumer goods, electronics, and pharmaceuticals. The early recognition that Japan must export to survive meant that restrictive licensing agreements (common elsewhere in the world) were not entered into. The licenses taken up were for technology and products that Japan could realistically produce for the international market. Therefore, very early in the postwar reconstruction, Japanese firms were looking for overseas markets and sales to make their industries viable.

Japan was too poor, too small and had too many people to be able to withdraw into its own economic and cultural boundaries to lick its wounds as China was capable of doing after 1949. However, Japan had one great advantage in the young and well-trained body of engineers and scientists who emerged from World War II with a good understanding of the processes of industrial production and innovation. Between 1955 and 1961 the Japan Productivity Center sent 2,500 business people, engineers and researchers to the United States to investigate advanced technology and its possible application in Japanese industry.

SONY AND THE TRANSISTOR

In 1948 a remarkable breakthrough in electronics was announced by three researchers at Western Electric's Bell Laboratories in New Jersey. Shockley, Bardeen and Brattain had made the first transistor. The potential of this tiny conductor to eliminate the cumbersome valves of the past was obvious to electronics engineers around the world.

In Japan the news was greeted by physicists and electronics engineers with equal enthusiasm, but few believed that they were in any position to profit from this discovery. However, Ibuka Masaru and Morita Akio, two war-time electronics engineers who had formed the company Totsuko — the Tokyo Telecommunications Engineering Corporation — were prepared to act. Ibuka and Morita had already designed and built Japan's first tape recorder, which was, by 1950, being widely used in broadcasting by NHK. They were so impressed by the reports of the American breakthrough that Ibuka flew to the United States in 1952 in an attempt to get a licensing agreement from Western Electric to produce transistors in Japan. To his amazement, senior executives agreed to give Totsuko the Japanese license for $25,000.

Then Ibuka and Morita had to convince the bureaucrats at the Ministry of International Trade and Industry that the transistor was a useful and desirable product on which to spend valuable foreign exchange. At the meeting their proposal was greeted coolly, and it was only after considerable lobbying that they were given access to the foreign exchange needed to enter into the agreement. At the final meeting with Western

Electric's Bell Laboratories in New Jersey. Shockley, Bardeen and Brattain had made the first transistor. The potential of this tiny conductor to hearing aids.

Two years later, under the now international brand name of Sony, Totsuko was to produce Japan's first fully transistorized radio. By 1960 it had manufactured the world's first transistorized television and was fast becoming one of the most innovative electronics companies in the world, with huge sales in the United States and Europe. Sony transistors were to enable other Japanese electronics firms to enter the consumer-electronics field where, by the 1970s, Japan was an international force to be reckoned with.

PERMANENT REVOLUTION

Historical experience has proved that only by first creating revolutionary public opinion and seizing political power, and then changing the relations of production is it possible to greatly develop the productive forces.

Mao Zedong

While the United States was placing its cultural and political stamp on Japan in the late 1940s, the Soviet Union had again occupied much of Manchuria. Here they came across industrial plant and equipment of considerable value, which, as traditional spoils of war, were shipped home to help in the postwar reconstruction of the Soviet Union. Meanwhile they were offering support to the Chinese "red army" in its war against the Nationalists. In an extremely short time, following World War II, the cold-war politics of the superpowers was to draw every country into its bipolar antagonisms.

The victory of Mao Zedong's army in October 1949 and the declaration of the People's Republic of China was to bring about a profound reorientation of Chinese culture and institutions. China's education and industrial structure had been modeled on those of the United States and Europe. Now the new Chinese leadership turned to the Soviet Union not only for aid to rebuild and reform its tortured economy, but as a model of how to build a socialist culture and economy.

In 1946 Soviet troops, once again in control of Manchuria, dismantled Japanese industrial plant and equipment for shipment back to the Soviet Union.

Mao Zedong and the People's Liberation Army entered Beijing in January 1949. In October of that year, Mao announced the formal establishment of the People's Republic of China.

In 1950 Mao Zedong flew to Moscow to meet Stalin. After pledging fraternal loyalty as communist states and after making the appropriate obeisance to Marx and Lenin, they got down to the business of Mao's mission. China needed capital and assistance in its "socialist reconstruction." Capital was not easy to come by, after all the Soviet Union was itself still in the process of rebuilding its war-ravaged economy. Mao succeeded in extracting a loan of $300 million from Stalin but, perhaps more significant, the offer of Soviet personnel — engineers and specialists — who would help construct 50 major projects essential for the building of China's industrial base. Within a year literally thousands of Soviet technicians, scientists and economic planners, with all the enthusiasm of nineteenth century missionaries carrying forward the gospel of Marxism-Leninism, were being shipped off to China. Soviet technicians were to be found working on bridge, dam and factory constructions from Manchuria to Sichuan. By 1952 the number of industrial projects using Soviet technology and technicians had grown from 50 to 141. By 1955 there were around ten thousand Soviet advisers and technicians working in China. They brought with them 63 machine-tool plants, 24 electrical power plants and three large iron and steel plants. By 1957, 50 per cent of all Soviet exports to China was industrial machinery and equipment.

The traffic was not only one way. While Soviet advisers were arriving to help the Chinese to restructure their education system along Soviet lines, 37,000 undergraduates, graduates and technicians were sent to the Soviet Union for education and training. This was one of the largest transfers of technology and personnel ever seen. The educational problems facing the new Chinese government were enormous. In 1949, because of decades of war, 90 per cent of the population was illiterate; by 1956 this had dropped to 78 per cent. Compared with the Japanese, labor skills available to the Chinese were limited. The priority was to raise the educational level as rapidly as possible with the widespread establishment of schools and universities on the Soviet model.

Popperfoto, City

In 1950 Mao Zedong met Soviet leaders, Stalin and Bulganin, to request assistance with China's "socialist reconstruction."

For many of China's leading scholars, scientists and engineers this reorientation of education and academic life was to present real problems. They were confronted with a new, harsh ideological environment. Under Stalin, for example, classical genetics had been categorized as a pseudo-science and was not taught. The reasons for this lay in the deeply held assumption among the ideological commissars in the Kremlin, that human nature and behavior were the product of political and economic circumstances. The idea came from Lenin's response to the Marxist notion that culture was an outcome or by-product of economic structures. Change the economic relationships between people and you would automatically change their world view and behavior. Lenin's "reflection theory" was accepted as the basis of Soviet psychology — the mind was simply a reflection of the objective reality of the political and economic institutions in which the individual was brought up — and the emphasis of the socialist revolution was therefore on changing social relations and creating "new people." According to this argument, society could not be changed simply by changing mental outlook as religious groups and idealists believed.

In the late 1930s an agricultural technician, Lysenko, took these same ideas and applied them to plant breeding. His assumption was that if you changed the plants' physical environment it would be possible to permanently change the characteristics of the plants themselves in one or two generations. Traditional genetics held that such changes were superficial and that effective crossbreeding had to be done over a long period of time.

In the desperate economic circumstances of the war-torn Soviet Union any ideas that promised a rapid increase in agricultural yields were greeted by the leadership with jubilation, especially if they conformed to current ideological thinking. Stalin placed his support behind Lysenko who rose rapidly in the ranks of researchers and was made head of an agricultural research institute. However, his findings were dismissed as nonsense by the great Soviet geneticist Vavilov. The ensuing scientific controversy was resolved with Vavilov being sent off to one of Stalin's labor camps, where he died, and classical genetics being defined as bourgeois and reactionary. Plant breeding and biology in the Soviet Union declined in direct relationship to the rise of Lysenkoism and his "revolutionary" biological ideas.

In the early 1950s the Soviet advisers restructuring Chinese science and education brought this dogma with them and, as a result, affected the work and lives of a number of Chinese academics, among them, the plant physiologist, Professor Cao Zongxun, from Beijing University and the geneticist, Tan Jiazhan, from Fudan University who were both trained in the United States. They had worked with the leading western researchers in what was to be a crucial field for China — the development of new grain and plant varieties that could, potentially, lift the levels of agricultural production. Both scientists were extremely patriotic and, although they could have stayed on in the United States in academic posts, both decided to return to China after 1949 to help rebuild the country. On their return to China they were forced to learn Russian and to teach from Soviet textbooks. As Professor Cao, one of the few women in prewar China to have gained a scientific education, noted:

I had to pretend to accept it. One had to make oneself simple minded and not think about other possibilities. . . . I had to learn how to criticize all the American and European principles. . . . I had to abandon my English for a long time.

A new intellectual strait jacket was to be placed on Chinese scholars, as "mind bending" as the earlier Confucian tradition that Hu Shi's generation had tried to throw off. However, even at the level of the less advantaged — the rural peasantry — a basic problem was to arise that was to set Chinese and Soviet planners and advisers on a collision course.

The basic assumption of the Soviet-style development masterminded by Lenin and Stalin was that highly centralized planning was needed and that the priority had to be the building up of heavy industry — iron and steel works, and electricity grids to cover the whole country — before turning attention to agricultural development. To pay for this, not only had agriculture to be neglected, but revenue from the land had to be used to support the development of city industry. For Mao this represented a basic problem — a betrayal. The Chinese red army had been built on the commitment and blood of peasants, in contrast to the city-based industrial proletariat that had supported the Russian revolution in 1918. Mao himself was the son of a rich peasant. He had not studied abroad, unlike most of the other leading cadres in the Chinese Communist party, such as Zhou Enlai and Deng Xiaoping who had both studied in Paris. Mao's roots lay deep in the Chinese countryside.

By the time Stalin died in 1953 Mao had grown disenchanted with both the policies and ideological leadership provided by Moscow. The attempt to apply Soviet

Courtesy Film Australia

Professor Cao Zongxun, one of China's leading biologists, was one of the few women to gain a scientific education in the 1930s. She studied and taught in the United States during the 1940s, then, like many patriotic Chinese, returned to China in the 1950s to help rebuild her country. During the Cultural Revolution she was sent, like many leading scientists, to the countryside for re-education.

solutions to Chinese problems was perhaps as vain an endeavor as the earlier efforts to introduce European liberalism in China in the 1920s.

Mao was concerned that China should follow a course that would allow development of both sectors at once — what he called "walking on two legs." One "leg" being the commitment to heavy industry and the other pursuing rural development. Perhaps the central importance of agriculture in Chinese culture played a part. The maintenance and improvement of the water control systems could not have been ignored by Mao any more than it could be by the emperors of the past. Stalin could ignore the needs of his peasants; Mao could not. The disproportionate attention given to industry in China's first five-year plan was reflected in the statistics — industrial production grew at a rate of 18 per cent a year compared with 4.5 per cent for agricultural production.

By 1957 the relationship between China and the Soviet Union had passed from the honeymoon to the divorce court, as it were, without there ever having been a marriage. Mao and Kruschev could not get on and in late 1956, when Moscow called on China to repay its loans and the interest bill on the massive amounts of heavy industrial technology, relations rapidly deteriorated. By 1960 many of the engineers and technical advisers sent from Moscow began to leave, taking their blueprints and plans with them. China was left with half-constructed factories, half-trained personnel and partially built bridges, such as the massive structure spanning the Yangtze River at Nanjing, which the Chinese were to complete themselves without plans.

The Sino-Soviet split was also to encourage Mao and the other leaders to return to the spirit of self-reliance they had gained in Yan'an (Yenan) during the long guerilla war with both the Japanese and the Nationalist forces. Mao accepted the Soviet withdrawal as an opportunity to reassert the revolutionary ideals and commitment that had given the Chinese communists their victory — the spirit of the Long March.

In 1957 the "great leap forward" was announced. This was to be a mass movement drawing on the revolutionary achievements of the Chinese people themselves, not on foreign advisers. Its aim was to keep alive at the local level the initiative of the revolution; this was later to be described by Mao as continual revolution. It was also a reaction to the emergence of the bureaucratic structures established under Soviet influence — structures that no doubt seemed to allow the old Confucian scholar-bureaucrats to re-emerge in the guise of party cadres or administrative officials.

The slogan of the "great leap forward" was "industrialize every corner of the country," and the party faithful in each region took the command quite literally. Labor was diverted from agriculture to small open iron and coal mines; backyard or village iron production was undertaken, often using traditional methods that had died out in most of China 50 years earlier.

The enthusiasm took China by storm. Mao's hope of extending to the countryside the benefits of industrial growth seemed to be working. By the end of 1958, 100,000 coal pits were in operation, engaging the labor of some twenty million peasants. According to official figures coal production rose from 7.5 million tons in 1957 to more than 50 million tons in 1958. The only problem to cast a cloud over this remarkable achievement was the report by some officials that the quality of the coal and iron being produced was so low that it was almost completely useless. However, this did not dampen the enthusiasm. The local officials who were now given control of regional planning were able to command labor to achieve public works on a scale not seen in China since the days of Li Bing and the building of his great water control system.

Mao had demonstrated, he believed, that it was possible to motivate people by social ideals and to inspire them to work for the common collective good, once the barriers of the social and economic oppression of the past had been removed. These were the same ideals that had been expressed in Russia in 1919 and by the eighteenth century French revolutionaries. He had seen examples of these ideals at work in the red army during the war with the Nationalists, and afterwards when the revolution was carried into the Chinese countryside.

Using the language of a military campaign Mao exhorted the masses. In some areas extraordinary things were achieved, for example, in the campaign against schistosomiasis, a disease that was endemic in China. It was discovered that tiny snails, which accumulate in the waterways and canals of the southern provinces, were the carriers, and a campaign was then mounted to get rid of the snails. Hundreds of thousands of peasants combed the canal banks and the waterways collecting snails; analogous to the ancient tradition of corvée labor, directed to carry out public works by imperial bureaucrats, which had constructed the basic network of canals in the first place. Now there was something different at work, a form of idealism and participation in the building of a new China — there was nationalism.

In many areas the campaign worked. The snail population virtually disappeared and the disease went with it. Encouraged by such success a new campaign was planned to improve other areas of public health by the same methods. In 1958 the country was mobilized against the "four pests" — sparrows, mice, mosquitos and fleas. These campaigns were systematically organized by party officials at the local level, after receiving directives from the Central Committee. A Soviet scientist, Mikhail Klochko, working in China at the time, described what happened:

> On Sunday, 20 April, I was awakened in the early morning by a woman's bloodcurdling screams. Rushing to my window I saw that a young woman was running to and fro on the roof of the building next door, frantically waving a bamboo pole with a large sheet tied to it. Suddenly, the woman stopped shouting, apparently to catch her breath. . . . I realized that in all the upper stories of the hotel, white-clad females were waving sheets and towels that were supposed to keep the sparrows from alighting on the building. This was the opening of the anti-sparrow campaign.

All over China people took to the streets, banging gongs, firing guns and generally making an enormous racket. The effect was to frighten the sparrows from their nests in buildings and to keep them in the air until they collapsed exhausted on the ground (sparrows can only stay in the air for three or four hours) and were then collected.

The campaign, however, had unforeseen consequences. With the sparrows gone,

Revolutionary idealism and selfless enthusiasm for the Party's campaigns were promoted. Working collectively, some remarkable results were achieved. Commune members rebuilt landscapes, turning previously useless areas into highly productive land. Above all, there was a sense of being freed from the fatalism and powerlessness that had dominated the lives of Chinese peasants for centuries.

Against conservative advice, Mao pushed ahead in 1958 with the full collectivization of agriculture and the creation of 26,000 vast communes responsible for 98 per cent of agricultural production.

insect numbers increased in plague-like proportions and devastated the crops. The Chinese were then forced to revert to insecticides like DDT to control the insects. In turn the insecticides got into the water of canals and rivers and poisoned the fish. Ecological campaigns were clearly not as simple as military ones.

*   *   *

Land reforms introduced by 1950 had redistributed almost 120 million acres of agricultural land among 300 million poor peasants. The old landlord class had either been killed or driven from the land. Agricultural production had begun to rise but there was still rationing of grain in 1957. Mao, against the advice of his former Soviet economic planner, forged ahead with the collectivization of agriculture. By 1957 agricultural production was organized in socialist collectives of around 800,000 co-operative farms. Each farm had around a hundred families or 700 people. Buoyed by the extremely high production levels achieved by these collectives, and by the 600,000 backyard furnaces that had sprung up throughout the countryside, Mao announced the formation of even larger collectives — the people's communes. By November 1958 the co-operative farms had been amalgamated into 26,000 vast

"LET A HUNDRED FLOWERS BLOOM"

In the euphoric period following the Sino-Soviet split, Mao and the Party received continual requests for greater freedom from leading intellectuals and scientists, who felt unduly fettered by the ideological limits that came with the adoption of the Soviet models in education and research. Many, educated in the United States and Europe, argued that only with the free airing of criticism would it be possible for the Party and the country to achieve rapid economic and cultural development. In 1957 Mao declared in a speech that "a hundred flowers should bloom and a hundred schools of thought contend." This was taken by many intellectuals and writers to mean that they were free to criticize the Communist party and its policies. With the tacit encouragement of the Party many came forward.

One of the most important critics was the economist and demographer, Ma Yinchu, from Beijing University. In an attempt to get some long-term perspective on China's economy, Ma had been looking at the relationship between population growth and the possible increase in the yields from agriculture and outputs from industry. At the time, China's population had reached some 700 million people. According to Ma's estimates, China had to take action immediately to curb population growth if it was to achieve its goal of a steadily rising standard of living.

To the alarm of the Party, the criticism of its policies unleashed by Mao's "hundred flowers" speech went, like the production figures, far beyond their expectations. But the criticism cut too close to the bone, challenging many of the basic tenets of Marxism-Leninism. In a sudden reversal of policy the Party bureaucrats organized a savage anti-rightist campaign to counter the assault. Across the country those who had had the temerity to come forward with criticism of the party's policies were declared "rightists" and "anti-revolutionaries." Thousands of intellectuals and workers lost their jobs.

Among them was Ma Yinchu who was savagely attacked as a Malthusian and a reactionary because he did not believe that the new socialist system would be capable of transcending the productive capacities and contradictions of capitalism. Ma was hounded from the University, and China had to wait for another twenty years before the Party would accept the reality of the problem. By then China's population had grown to one billion.

communes of around 25,000 people and representing 98 per cent of farm production.

The commune system was to prove extremely effective in the introduction of new agricultural technology and methods of production. With limited capital resources, the communes provided the means for shared access to tractors, gasoline-driven pumps, electricity and new chemical fertilizers. In economic terms the communes allowed for an enormous increase in productivity and the standard of living of rural communities. The scale of this achievement was incredible — one estimate of the labor-intensive construction carried out on the communes between 1957 and 1960 suggests it was equivalent to the building of 960 Suez Canals.

Party enthusiasm for the ideals and achievements of "the great leap forward" were intoxicating in 1958. There was a sense that anything could be achieved with enough commitment on the part of the Party and by mobilizing the energy and revolutionary zeal of the masses — the liberated energies of previously repressed peasants and workers. Throughout 1958 reports were coming into the Party's Central Committee of record production figures. In July the government announced that miracle targets had been reached and by September it was reported that grain production had doubled and that it was possible to abandon grain rationing. Industrial production had exceeded 1956 figures by 65 per cent. With the conviction that food production was under control, efforts at local industrialization were stepped up. Millions of peasants left the countryside for local towns to participate in the industrial boom. Crops were not being planted in some areas, and in others there was insufficient labor to harvest what had been sown.

By early 1959 alarm bells had begun to ring in Party headquarters in Beijing. It was becoming clear that the figures for grain production on the part of over-enthusiastic Party bureaucrats had been grossly overestimated. Over a quarter of the steel being produced in the local backyard furnaces (3 million of the 11 million tons produced in 1958) was unfit for industrial use. Worst of all, as the harsh winter of 1960 approached, grain stocks were found to be far lower than imagined. Suddenly, with the unusually bad climatic conditions in 1960 – 61, many areas of the country were hit with famine, unseen since well before liberation. It has been estimated that around ten million people died as a consequence. Mao, aware of the chaos brought to the country's economy by his policies, retired to a back seat and left the running of the economy to men of a more pragmatic disposition — Liu Shaoqi, Zhou Enlai and Deng Xiaoping.

MADE IN JAPAN

The nail that sticks up is nailed down.

Japanese proverb

In a Confucian society, each individual must strive to demonstrate his loyalty to the society to which he belongs. The extent of his loyalty is measured in terms of the degree to which he is prepared to sacrifice himself. . . . In this sort of society the freedom of the individual is often regarded as treachery or a challenge to society or to the majority, and anyone who dares to assert his freedom will probably become completely isolated.

Morishima, 1982

As China gradually hauled its economy back on to a more even keel during the early 1960s, Japan was also beginning to step out of the shadow of its wartime ignominy and was beginning to challenge the assumption that "made in Japan" was synonymous with all that was cheap and trashy. This attitude was typified in a scene in the Hollywood movie *The Princess and the Pirate* made in the late 1940s where Bob Hope draws a pistol and tries to shoot at an oncoming troop of pirates. The pistol fails to fire, he tries again and again and then gives up, turns to the camera and with a shrug says, "Made in Japan!" In less than a decade increasingly large numbers of young people around the world were discovering that Nikon cameras, Kawasaki and Honda motor bikes, and Seiko watches were not only cheaper than any of those produced locally but also better. Myths and stereotypes die slowly, not only those held about other cultures but those one holds about oneself. In this the complacency of the west and, in particular, the United States was pervasive and myopic. One of the technological myths in the postwar United States was that "either you did things the American way or it did not work."

Another pervasive myth at this time concerned the relation of government to the economy. While American advisers in Japan in the late 1940s were promoting the abolition of *zaibatsu* and the need to limit the power of big business, back home Eisenhower was railing against the growing power of the military-industrial complex, a nexus of interests similar to that of the old Japanese *zaibatsu*. This conspiracy of interests between the government, big business and politicians arose from World War II when very large contracts to supply military equipment were being tendered. Because of the importance of these defense contracts in providing employment, and in fostering industry and development in whatever region they were placed, politicians lobbied in conjunction with local firms to get the orders. It was encouraged by liberals as a form of Keynesian economics. John Maynard Keynes, in the 1930s, had first put forward the principle of government spending as a means of pulling western economies out of the Depression. Administrations wanting to win support could promise to give contracts to firms who would locate themselves in economically depressed regions.

During wartime this made sense. However, the process did not stop after 1945. In fact it increased with the cold war and the arms race to a degree where, even in the view of conservatives, the tail of military expenditure was beginning to wag the political dog. The demands of the military for a larger and larger slice of government expenditure were supported by the wide range of industries that had grown fat on these lucrative contracts. They, in turn, were capable of putting enormous pressure on politicians to vote for increased military budgets and to bargain for greater expenditure going to their state.

The problem with these political deals was that the normal checks and balances of the market were not able to work. Overpricing, inefficiency and waste were accepted and absorbed by the government. This at a time when the United States was presenting itself to the world as the embodiment of free-market capitalism. With their increasing military involvement throughout the world, in the belief that they were saving it from communism, the United States was falling into the trap that Great Britain and other once-powerful military powers had fallen into. In reality, the

The ENIAC was a useful recruitment device for the United States Army. However, the application of computer-controlled manufacture in the United States was relatively slow except in the machine-tools industry, where it was adopted by larger companies for military production. There was considerable opposition from labor unions who saw increased automation as a threat to the jobs of skilled machinists.

government and bureaucratic mechanisms fostered by ever-growing military expenditure were cutting across the free market as effectively as in many socialist countries. This was to have significant consequences for the United States economy and the industrial competitiveness that had made it the world leader in the 1920s.

Take, for example, the development and use of computer-controlled technology or what is more commonly called robotics, the key industrial technology of the late twentieth century. This technology was developed, as was the first electronic computer — the ENIAC — under military sponsorship. This computer was built during World War II and was used by the mathematician Von Neumann to carry out the calculations essential for the completion of the Manhattan Project, which built the atomic bombs that flattened Hiroshima and Nagasaki. Without this computer, it has been argued, the atomic bombs could not have been dropped before the Japanese capitulation. Ironically, the Japanese were to return the favor by taking this technology and using it to undermine the industrial lead of the United States.

The application of numerical data on punched cards to control the complex movements of machines was first realized by the clock and mechanical doll makers of France in the eighteenth century, and taken up by Jacquard later in the century. The next step in developing the computer to the control of industrial processes was in making the machine tools used in aircraft production. This was carried out by researchers at Massachusetts Institute of Technology in the early 1950s, with support from the Pentagon.

The goal from the military point of view was to get greater standardization and therefore a more reliable product. Once developed, the cost of adopting this new computer-controlled technology was enormous and often uneconomic compared with other alternatives. However, a condition of gaining lucrative military contracts was the use of this technology. The contracts therefore went to larger firms that could afford the massive capital investment and they, in turn, passed the increased cost of production back to the military. Many smaller firms in the machine-tools industry went out of business and, with less competition, prices rose rapidly.

A second factor that affected the spread of this revolutionary technology to other industries in the United States was the nature of industrial relations. Labor unions saw the increased automation of factories as a strategy to wrest control of the factory floor from skilled machinists. In the paranoid atmosphere of the McCarthy era, alleged "communist conspirators" were to be found among the working class. Labor unions, and organizations of industrial workers generally, were regarded as hotbeds of socialism. Class antagonism, which had governed industrial relations in both Europe and the United States since the nineteenth century, with labor treated as just a factor of production, meant that those firms that did invest in the new technology saw the advantages of the automated factory as a means of weakening the power of labor or at least their capacity for industrial disruption. Where military production was concerned this was an important consideration, and was promoted as a benefit of computer-controlled systems.

The attitude of workers in other industries where robotic technology could have been introduced was often hostile and unco-operative. Companies looking at introducing the new technology were confronted with a double bind: first, the cost of the technology was very high because military contracts had inflated its price and, second, industrial relations made their introduction difficult. There was a third factor — things were going very well in the United States and the need for change and innovation was not as obvious as it now appears in hindsight.

In Japan, where class-based industrial relations were not a dominant characteristic, the problem of introducing new technology hardly existed. Because of the commitment of the large firms to their staff — offering them lifetime employment and retraining as opposed to making them redundant when new technology was introduced — there were few industrial problems associated with the introduction of robotics. Instead of being displaced, skilled workers were taught computer-related skills and were expected to participate in the effective introduction of the new technology. These workers were also extremely important in making the new systems more productive since their commitment was to the firm rather than to a specific job or craft skill.

Throughout the 1960s and 1970s the effectiveness of the Japanese production system was to make them more and more competitive with firms in the United States. In 1979 when computer-controlled technology had been available for 20 years, only 2 per cent of American firms had taken it up. At this time Japan was producing 14,000 of these new computer-controlled machining centers a year compared with less than half that number in the United States. Firms like Fujitsu Fanuc in Japan, which had first produced robotic machines under license for General Motors in the United States, were now the world leaders. By 1981 Japan was supplying 40 per cent of the computer-controlled machining centers used by industries in the United States.

The consequence of this for other Japanese industries was to become increasingly obvious. Japanese firms were able to produce basic consumer goods — automobiles, electronic goods and other mass-produced commodities — that were cheaper and better than those produced in the United States and most European countries.

By the late 1960s, as the Japanese began to make inroads into traditional American markets in a whole range of consumer goods the American business and academic elites were still making the same old observation that the Japanese were not creative but were just imitators. This is, ironically, exactly what the Europeans, particularly the British in the late nineteenth century, had said about the Americans as they captured their markets using European technology but applying new methods of production.

In 1977 the number of American patents taken out in Japan made up more than 43 per cent of the total; this had dropped to 41 per cent by 1979. Conversely, in the same period, Japanese patents in the United States rose from 25 per cent to 28 per cent, making Japan the largest foreign source of patents. While OECD countries declined in overall patent rates during the latter part of the 1970s, Japan increased its level of technological innovation to the extent that, between 1977 and 1980, Japanese technological imports increased by only 3 per cent while exports increased by 42 per cent. This increase was particularly marked in fields such as precision instruments,

Survey Japan

A "Motoman" welding robot comes off the production line.

micro-electronics and robotics.

The myopic inability to recognize the importance of continued innovation in industrial processes as well as in the creation of new products left the United States as vulnerable as Great Britain had been fifty years earlier. While the Europeans and Americans would continue to come up with the technological and scientific knowledge from which individual reputations, fame, and Nobel prizes were to be gained, the stress in Japan was on improving the productive efficiency of firms.

For their success the Japanese owed a great deal to an American authority on quality control, Edwards Deming. Deming was a statistician and one of the postwar specialists sent to Japan to help improve the functioning of its census bureau. His major obsession was, however, with quality control. For the Japanese, losing the War had made it necessary to rethink and rebuild. The lack of certainty meant that they were prepared to look for new ways to improve their economic competitiveness and their share of world markets. It was in fact an area where Japan could not only gain immediate benefit but also redeem wounded national pride.

Deming had made a study of quality control and was profoundly disillusioned with what he found at home in the United States. The postwar boom had bred an acceptance of waste and an arrogant disregard for the quality of products, which affronted his common sense and set him at loggerheads with the prevailing assumptions.

Deming's ideas grew out of the work of the physicist, Walter Shewhart, from Bell Laboratories who had pioneered the use of statistical methods to improve quality in industrial products and processes. During World War II his ideas were taken up by the department of defense. But in the postwar boom such concerns seemed less important.

The Japanese, on the other hand, in attempting to rebuild their shattered wartime industries, were looking for the secret of American success; a success that had defeated them both on the battlefield and in the quality of their military technology.

Deming's ideas were basic. Senior engineers had to be on the shop floor and integrally involved with the production process. From the managing director down there had to be a commitment to quality and to the improvement of the production process. In the postwar antagonism between labor and capital in the United States, with automation being seen largely as a means of displacing shop-floor workers, commitment to improving the quality of goods was hard to achieve. When the Americans left Japan in the early 1950s their trade-based union system was replaced with a company-based system — one that was more congenial to the Japanese clannish approach to enterprise.

In this environment, the influence of Deming was to be profound. His first major lecture on the subject of quality control in 1950 was organized by Ichiro Ichikawa who had not only been a professor of engineering but was the head of Keidanren, the most powerful business organization in Japan.

Deming was amazed by the Japanese response; at home he had been largely ignored. In the ruthlessly competitive economic market that the Americans had

Quality control, one of the keys to Japan's industrial success, was promoted by an American, Edward Deming, in the 1950s. The commitment to quality, from the manager of the company down to the manual worker, allowed the Japanese to dispel the notion that Japanese goods were shoddy. At Nissan and NEC, quality-control circles became an essential feature of production throughout the 1960s and 1970s.

Paul Fusco/Magnum/John Hillelson Agency

fostered in postwar Japan, the younger managers were looking for the means to capture the local market and to free Japanese goods from their reputation for being shoddy. Deming provided these means.

Deming's ideas worked; a wire company executive announced a 30 per cent increase in production within months of applying Deming's methods. Other firms reported similar success. Soon an annual Deming Prize was announced for the firm that achieved the greatest improvement in quality control, and Deming was to be turned into something of an industrial guru in Japan where his books were widely studied and applied. In the west, his message largely fell on deaf ears — everything seemed to be going too well so why bother.

The reason for the success of quality control in Japan was that it complemented the Japanese ability to work together in teams. Having a culture that emphasized conformity, as opposed to the individualism of the west, was an unexpected advantage. The family orientation of their Confucian past worked in their favor. Shop-floor workers, like executives, were expected to stay with the company all their working lives and therefore identified with the firm and were committed to its goals. In a Japanese company the heads of sections were not found in their own private offices removed from subordinates. They sat in the middle of a large room surrounded by their workers.

The Japanese sociologist Nakane, when discussing the distinction between Japan and the west, focused on the group orientation of the Japanese as a major feature. She emphasized the very limited significance given to kinship relations in Japan, compared with China, other Asian countries and even Europe. The primary attachment in Japanese society is to "the corporate group based on work, in which the major aspects of social and economic life are involved." This is observed when Japanese are forced to define themselves to an outsider. Rather than identifying themselves by their professional qualifications, for example, "I am a doctor" or "I am an engineer," they will identify themselves by the corporation or institution for which they work — "I am a Sony san [man]" or "I am a University of Tokyo man."

The notion of a labor market where an individual sells his or her labor, or has a purely contractual relationship with a corporation is still alien to the Japanese; professional identity is not based on skill acquisition as it is in the west. Morishima also stressed the all-embracing aspect of the social group or economic enterprise:

> The company is not just a profit-making organization; it is a complete society in itself, and frequently it is so all-embracing that all the activities of the daily lives of the company's employees can take place within the company framework.

In the feudal period prior to the Meiji restoration, clan organizations were concerned with military and economic power in the region but were easily transformed into modern economic organizations. The commercial and mining conglomerate, Sumitomo, is an interesting example of this. The Sumitomo clan built up their resources and organization from the 1850s onwards. The organization still retains the feudal crest as its symbol, and the employees still refer to themselves as

"Sumitomo men" as they would have done during the Tokugawa period.

This sort of loyalty and commitment to the operation of firms has clearly been an important ingredient in the success of Japan as an industrial power, but there are other features of Japanese society that are equally important.

Lifetime employment, until recently, was offered by all major (and some small) companies, and by the government to their employees, including scientists. On graduation, the young person will have the option, depending on which university he or she attended, of applying for a job in a major company or government institution. On gaining entry, they start on an upward path that will provide them with incremental increases in salary and status as their seniority increases. Seniority is determined by length of service and is consistent with Confucian notions of respect for elders. The individual is thereby bound by a complex pattern of vertical relationships, which he or she is expected to honor and reciprocate, for built into the relationship with the group is a very basic dependence and fear of rejection. The psychiatrist Doi Takeo has described this as *amae,* a Japanese word not easily translatable into English, but which means a childlike need to be loved and accepted by others. This dependency, and the guilt associated with it, are inculcated in children from an early age. Devitt described the process:

> . . . the child is taught to be interdependent, rather than individually independent; to be calm, quiet and passive, rather than aggressive and articulate; to be trusting, to fear loneliness; to respond to subtle, implicit methods of discipline, rather than overt definable methods; to respect relative status within the family; to conform to the requirements of the role he is to play within the family group; to have a sense of his own family group versus other family groups and outsiders.

This form of upbringing leads to individuals with relatively weak egos, but with a corresponding sensitivity and responsiveness to the requirements of the social group to which they belong, and a strong fear of rejection. This, Doi argues, has led to a tendency to conformity and compliance, "Just as betrayal of the group creates guilt, so to be ostracized by the group is the greatest shame and dishonor." This has therefore made it difficult for western concepts of individual freedom to gain great currency within Japanese society.

Although such generalizations about national characteristics can be taken too far, nonetheless observations suggest that such qualities as creativity and originality would be held in lower esteem in Japan than in western cultures. A revealing statement was made by Yasuo Kato, assistant general manager of Nippon Electric's Systems Research Laboratories:

> We are not so creative because the creative mind is peculiar, and we Japanese do not like anything peculiar. We believe that everyone should be the same.

* * *

The dream of Shibusawa and the early Meiji reformers was to adapt their country's traditional Confucian value system to the productive powers of western capitalism.

WALKING TRACTORS

In the mid 1960s Japanese industry was not only producing consumer goods for the European and American markets but was manufacturing machinery and equipment to meet local demand. One of these machines was a small tractor designed to work in the tiny paddy fields used for wet-rice cultivation. This tractor, a variation of what was known in the west as a rotary hoe, was extremely popular and was marketed throughout Southeast Asia.

In 1965 at the Sichuan tractor factory at Jianyang, not far from the provincial capital of Chengdu, two young engineers, Zeng Xiuliang and Chen Wanxiong, had begun to look at the possibilities of this small tractor for China. Previously they had been trying to adapt the large Soviet and East European machines to the needs of communes in their region. These tractors, designed for the broad-acre farming of the Russian Steppes, were inappropriate for the needs of the small fields and irrigation systems used in Chinese farming. They also had the great disadvantage of being extremely expensive. A large commune could, perhaps, afford one or

two, and, on top of that, there were the costs of maintenance, which required skilled engineers and mechanics to be on hand.

The government policies of self-reliance and rural mechanization remained firm commitments, despite the excesses of the "great leap forward." Chen and Zeng, who at this stage were part of the large factory-commune, decided to join forces with a similar tractor factory in Shanghai and seek the help of the agricultural machinery research institutes in Shanghai, Luoyang and Sichuan. They began to design what has come to be known as the "walking tractor," the "grasshopper" or the "iron cow." The starting point was the Japanese tractor. They needed to produce a machine that was profoundly versatile — able to maneuver in and out of small fields (unlike the Russian tractors), able to be used as a small truck to get produce to market and with the capacity to drive other machinery and equipment, such as small electrical generators.

By reverse-engineering the Japanese model and making some adaptations, such as increasing the engine's capacity from seven to ten

he would "fry fish on his hand if it worked." With considerable emotion, Chen and Zeng recounted how they took the tractor to the commune, uncertain themselves whether a locally built and designed tractor would match up to the Soviet and East European machines then in use.

The walking tractor was a remarkable success. By early 1966, 10,000 a year were produced. The tractors provided, for the first time, a form of mechanization appropriate to the needs of the majority of Chinese farmers. Now China produces each year more than one million of these small tractors, which are exported throughout Southeast Asia and Latin America to similar peasant communities in need of cheap, simple and small-scale technology.

In China the "walking tractor" is now one of the most common forms of transport in the countryside. Even the canal barges that ply the vast inland waterways of the Yangtze delta are now driven by the same small engines used in the tractors. If this is what Mao Zedong aimed to achieve with his policy of "walking on two legs" he was clearly on the right track.

horsepower and giving the tractor rubber wheels and a detachable chassis, the Sichuan team began to build their prototype. As Chen and Zeng discovered, there was considerable scepticism about whether the odd-looking machine would actually work in practice. The leader of one commune, when confronted with it, claimed that

They were able to retain the sense of collective commitment embodied in the samurai tradition and transfer this loyalty to the large corporations, which by the late 1960s were beginning to spread their operations overseas to become transnational or global institutions. Mitsubishi, Nissan, Toyota, Hitachi, Honda, Sony — these were the new domains. They were not just joint-stock companies in the western sense; they were Japan. Ownership structures as they emerged at this time were markedly different from western corporations. Not only was there a very limited labor market, there was also a limited capital market. Private shareholding remains extremely low; investment in the large companies comes from post-office saving banks, union funds and the giant insurance companies. Perhaps because of the hardships endured after the War, the frugality of the Japanese was in marked contrast to the growing consumerism in the postwar west. In the 1960s the average Japanese would have one year's salary in savings; in the United States, Australia and Europe it would be more common to be one year's salary in debt. This massive pool of savings, held by banks, provided the capital that was invested in the large industrial firms. The heads of major banks were on the boards of these great companies and were concerned with stable long-term investment not short-term return on investment as the capital market in the west demanded. This gave to Japanese firms an ability to engage in long-term planning and to act in conjunction with powerful government departments such as MITI, to take on long-term commercial strategies. It was this that led more paranoid observers in the west to coin the term "Japan Inc." in the 1970s. The success of Japan was not lost on the rest of east Asia, even China.

BETTER RED THAN EXPERT

In May 1966 Mao Zedong launched his "Great Proletarian Cultural Revolution." He was clearly frustrated by the back-seat role to which he had been relegated since the failure of the "great leap forward." He also believed that the Communist party was falling into the hands of technocrats, planners and intellectuals who were quite prepared to be openly critical of his views and who, he believed, were not imbued with the correct revolutionary consciousness. However, in calling upon the youth of China to "bombard the headquarters," in other words to attack the Party and the "capitalist roaders" within it, he had little idea of what he was unleashing on his country.

Revolutionary zeal, fostered by almost twenty years of rhetoric and military-style campaigns against supposed counter-revolutionaries, provided a new channel for personal frustration. Now this energy was to be unleased indiscriminately and often against totally inappropriate targets. Frustration at the lack of personal advancement or achievement allowed disgruntled individuals to seek revenge on those further up the bureaucratic hierachy. However, the cultural revolution went far further than McCarthyism in the United States, although there were some superficial similarities such as the attacks on intellectuals.

Mao and his close supporters — including those who, ten years later, were to become known as the "gang of four" — gave their blessing to the formation of bands of young red guards many of whom were no more than 13 or 14 years old. Because Mao believed that the revolutionary leadership of workers and peasants had been usurped by intellectuals, particularly those who had been educated overseas, he saw his task as preventing the formation of a new technocratic and self-interested bureaucratic elite like the Confucian scholar-class who had dominated Chinese culture for much of its history. He was also smarting from attacks from scholars against the shortcomings of his policies during the "great leap forward." Under the catch phrase "better red than expert," schools, universities and colleges across the country were closed. Campaigns against reactionary and bourgeois teachers were mounted. The *Little Red Book* of Mao Zedong's thoughts was turned into virtual holy writ. One of the major sins to be accused of was that of "separating theory from practice."

The botanist Professor Cao Zongxun was dragged from her laboratory at Beijing University and paraded through the streets of Beijing with a tall dunce's hat on her head because she was found to be experimenting with small cucumbers as part of her research on pollination. Professor Cao now recalls, with some amusement, the grounds given for her being attacked:

> I could not continue my plant physiology research because it was divorced from practice. Cucumbers like mine were too small to be eaten. That is how they criticized me. They said that even kindergarten children knew that cucumbers were grown in fields and I was just crazy to grow them in test tubes.

She and many of her scientific colleagues were sent off to be re-educated in special "May 7" cadre schools in the countryside where they worked with the peasants so that they would come to appreciate the correct revolutionary consciousness. Professor Cao did not fare as badly as many other scholars, teachers and artists who ended up being beaten to death, while others committed suicide rather than endure the continual persecution and torture meted out to them. It is not certain how many people died as a result of this most ambitious of all Mao's campaigns to change irrevocably the consciousness of the Chinese people. Ken Ling, a student at Xiamen No. 8 Middle School, witnessed the violence unleashed against scholars:

> Greatly emboldened by the instigators, the other students also cried, "Beat them!" and jumped on the teachers, swinging their fists and kicking. The stragglers were forced to back them up with loud shouts and clenched fists.
>
> There was nothing strange in this. Young students were ordinarily peaceful and well-behaved but, once the first step was taken, all were bound to follow.
>
> The Principal was the most savagely beaten. He was also forced to kneel on the edge of a vertical drop on the campus. If he had allowed himself to lean slightly forward, the heavy pail around his neck would have toppled him over the edge. He knelt for 15 minutes and was visibly about to collapse. Then he was pulled to his feet and punched in the abdomen; the sound was like that of a basketball bouncing off a wall.
>
> But the heaviest blow to me that day was the killing of my most respected and beloved teacher, Chen Kuteh.
>
> Teacher Chen, over 60 years old and suffering from high blood pressure, was dragged out at 11.30 A.M., exposed to the summer sun for more than two hours, then paraded about with the others, carrying a placard and hitting a gong.
>
> He passed out several times but was brought back to consciousness each time with cold water splashed onto his face. He could hardly move; his feet were cut by glass and thorns. But his spirit was unbroken. He shouted, "Why don't you kill me? Kill me!" This lasted for six hours, until he lost control of his bowels. They tried to force a stick into his rectum. He collapsed for the last time.

One 14-year old red guard, Liang Heng, later described in his book *Son of the Revolution* how he observed musicians and composers at the Beijing Conservatorium of Music being beaten and tortured because they were accused of being more concerned with personal and professional excellence than with working for the socialist revolution. Even highly trained engineers such as Professor Zheng Wei from Beijing's Qinghua University were forced to work as janitors for years while the University was turned over to political consciousness raising by various factions of the red guard.

Lui Shaoqi, the Communist Party Chairman, was killed and members of his family imprisoned. Deng Xiaoping was branded as an "arch-unrepentant capitalist roader" and was forced from office. Mao, "the great helmsman," again took control of the Party. Supporters of the cultural revolution were brought into key positions in all public institutions to see that the Party's new policies were carried out. Any form of material incentive was removed from commune and factory life. Rigorous

People's Fine Arts Publishing House, Beijing

In 1966 Mao Zedong called on the youth of China to attack the "capitalist roaders" in the Communist party and the "great proletarian cultural revolution" was born. China, as it had often done in the past, turned in on itself and away from western cultural influences — western books, classical music and films were banned.

ideological consciousness-raising sessions were held, in which anyone not from a worker or peasant background was expected to engage in endless public confessions of their capitalist tendencies and reactionary thoughts in the hope of gaining political redemption. This sort of activity seemed to replace much formal education on the assumption that real knowledge only came from practice. It was the workers and peasants who "knew," not "reactionary academic authorities," as Mao was inclined to call sceptical intellectuals and scientists. On this basis an illiterate abattoir worker was put in charge of the Shanghai Institute of Biochemistry, which only the previous year had been the first in the world to synthesize insulin. In effect, all serious education and research stopped in China for almost a decade.

As the red guards ran out of more obvious targets to attack they began to fight among themselves. In many major cities, such as Changsha, virtual civil war broke out with rival factions each claiming greater ideological purity as the true heirs of Mao Zedong's revolutionary ideals. The military were increasingly forced to intervene as bands of armed youths held pitched battles throughout the city. China, as it had done on other occasions, withdrew into itself, this time in the confident assumption that once the revolutionary forces of peasants and workers were in command, the Party would prove, once and for all, the superiority of socialism over the degenerate capitalism of the west. With universities closed, large numbers of teachers, graduates and even those just about to enter higher education were shipped off to the countryside in their thousands to work on communes. Some brought with them skills that were of some use to the peasants, others had nothing to offer and were more of a burden to the commune . . . and felt it.

The assumptions that peasants and workers knew best was probably true in many cases but the party concocted phoney models. The "learn from Dazhai movement" was based on a commune in nortwestern China. It was claimed that by sheer determination and collective organization, the members of the commune had rebuilt the landscape, terracing the mountain slopes and redirecting the flood rains into dams for irrigation. In reality, they were financed by the state in the hope of inspiring others; to convince peasants that it was possible to overcome centuries of passive acceptance of their fate and turn the arid and mountainous terrain into a highly productive region. However, while this approach worked in some instances, with examples of remarkable small-scale industrial development, in the wider perspective China was falling behind in the essential development of a nationwide infrastructure — communication systems, energy, power grids to support growing industrial demands, and sources of basic commodities such as iron, coal and oil. In the centrally planned model adopted from the Soviet Union this was the responsibility of state planning, and at this level most of the trained people had been removed from office.

With the Chinese population growing at an unchecked rate, the remarkable increases in production achieved on the communes were offset by more and more people demanding their socialist rights. In many areas this led to serious environmental problems. In order to lift grain production, commune leaders increased the demands on the land, breaking away from the traditional methods used for centuries by the peasants. Without any scientific monitoring, large amounts of pesticides, particularly DDT, were used to control insects and other pests. The unchecked use of such insecticides on a large scale resulted in high levels accumulating in the canals and waterways. Fish died, but DDT also passed through the food chain threatening human health. In many rivers, by the late 1960s, fish populations had been virtually killed off, reducing the availability of one of the most important forms of protein in the Chinese diet.

While "barefoot doctors" with elementary training were able to bring basic health care to those in rural areas who would otherwise have had no access to modern medicines, they could not deal with public health problems of this type. With scientific and technical specialists regarded as "reactionaries" and in no position to warn that short-term gains might have even greater long-term costs, there was little check on the enthusiasm of revolutionary cadres to lift production outputs at all costs. In some areas three crops of rice were planted each year even though total yields were lower, labor costs higher and the environmental balance threatened. Because of the power of the revolutionary cadres whose "redness" clearly outshone their "expertise," the common-sense of the peasants was often overridden.

It was not, however, until the death of Mao in 1976 that any real challenge could be made to the political opportunists who had come to power on the shirt tails of Mao's last drive to keep his vision of China's socialist revolution alive. The cost of his cultural revolution was to be enormous; an entire generation was denied proper education and, without adequate leadership, China's fledgling industrial and economic development fell increasingly behind that of other countries in the region, notably Japan, Taiwan, Korea, Hong Kong and Singapore.

*   *   *

In 1976 devastating earthquakes hit northern China. Many old peasants whose memories were long and whose ancient heritage had not been completely eroded by the cultural revolution saw this event as a portent. In the past such events were seen as heralding the death of emperors or the fall of dynasties. In this case they were right; within weeks Mao Zedong, the great helmsman, was dead. Almost immediately a bitter struggle began in the Party to find a successor, a new chairman. The more important issue, however, was whether the leaders of the cultural revolution could hold power without Mao there to protect them.

In the end the issue was decided by the army, which put its considerable weight behind the pragmatists in the party led by Deng Xiaoping. The notorious "gang of four" — Jiang Qing, Zhang Chunqiao, Wang Hongwen and Yao Wenyuan — were arrested. Maoist policies had achieved an amazing transformation of the country, but at a cost that was becoming increasingly obvious. Basically, it was impossible to maintain a country in a state of permanent revolution. While small-scale industrial development could make an enormous difference locally, without proper economic planning at a national level, erratic supplies of essential commodities made for great inefficiency and, after a certain point, economic stagnation.

The radical swings in policy had left most people either profoundly confused or downright cynical about the ideological leadership offered by the Communist party. The problem for the Party was to find another means of motivating people. Above all else, they had to reinstate some respect for expertise and to overcome the cultural and intellectual narrowness caused by the hothouse experiment of the cultural revolution.

In 1978 Deng reaffirmed the "four modernizations," designed to overcome China's backwardness in agriculture, science and technology, defense and industry. This was the first major step in the restructuring of the Communist party's (and therefore the nation's) priorities. In many respects the direction in which Deng was to take the country in the next decade was to be almost as radical a shift as that first set in motion by Mao Zedong in the early 1950s.

Deng Xiaoping's view of socialism differed from Mao's in one crucial respect — Deng believed that the primary objective of socialism and of the Communist party was to improve the economic well-being of the people. Once the means of production were in the hands of the people, represented by the Communist party, there was nothing wrong with using whatever methods worked. If the use of capitalist economic institutions, such as the markets, could further this goal then it

251

ABC/Warren Duncan

During the Cultural Revolution, communes like that of Dazhai in the northern province of Shansi were held up as models for emulation by mobilizing the enthusiasm and labor of the peasants, local party officials hoped to transform the landscape, turning what had been barren eroded hills into productive agricultural land.

was legitimate, as long as political control remained in the hands of the Party. This was the foundation of Deng's pragmatism and it was with this open-minded approach that he began to rebuild the country's tattered institutions of higher education and the bodies concerned with mapping China's future economic course.

The great fear among the military was that China's technological backwardness would make it increasingly vulnerable. They had become acutely aware that the arms race had left them behind, as it had done so tragically in the nineteenth century.

The opening of diplomatic and economic relations with the capitalist world, particularly with Japan, provided access to much-needed technology for both defense and the civil sector. To build up their industrial and technological capacity the Chinese needed knowledge, communications and energy systems, all of which had gone into decline over the past decade.

In many areas of the country the electricity supply was so primitive that it was impossible to run the local factory when the lights went on at night. What was needed, the Party believed, were modern "turnkey" plants — complete factories or electrical generating systems that could be bought "off the shelf" in the international high-tech market.

The problem with this strategy was that China had very limited supplies of foreign exchange with which to purchase the technology it needed. To pay for the new military and industrial technology China needed to export and, therefore, to turn its attention to the world market. However, much of what the Chinese had to sell was too poorly designed and manufactured to appeal to the sophisticated western consumer market. In an effort to get access to overseas markets and to industrial technology, Deng put forward perhaps one of the most radical suggestions of his stormy career — joint ventures with foreign firms. Within a very short time foreign businesses were flocking to Beijing hoping to make direct sales of technology or to enter into joint ventures producing goods for the Chinese market. The Japanese were in a particularly strong position to take advantage of this change of policy. Although memories of their brutal occupation during the war remained a cause of popular hostility, they were an Asian culture and familiar with many of the Chinese ways of doing business. They were also able to offer deals to the Chinese that seemed attractive. During 1976–78 the Chinese government signed contracts worth over $3 billion for the importation of industrial technology, 88 per cent of which were with Japan.

In 1978 the Chinese government signed an agreement with Nippon Steel for a massive $2 billion steel plant to be constructed at Baoshan outside Shanghai. This ambitious scheme to simply transplant an ultra-modern Japanese steel plant met with considerable setbacks. For a start, the Chinese had not done a proper feasibility study of the site before construction started. When they began to sink the piles to support the blast furnace, they found the site completely unsuitable to take the enormous weight. Not only was it extremely difficult to build, but there was little co-ordination of other elements such as railway lines, electricity and water supplies. It was to be almost a decade before the Baoshan steelworks was running to full capacity. Although problems like those faced in Baoshan dampened enthusiasm for buying in high-technology plants, the determination to catch up with the west and with Japan, Korea and Taiwan had caught hold of popular imagination.

With this came more visible signs of a change in priorities. The universal military-style uniforms ("Mao suits" as they have been called in the west) gave way to more individualistic self-expression — colorful blouses and skirts, and American blue jeans became the height of fashion. China turned suddenly from the dark winter of the puritanical cultural revolution, with its stultifying and mind-numbing ideological strictures, to something approaching tolerance of diversity. Even locally bottled Coca-Cola was being sold in the Peace Hotel in Beijing, and China opened its doors to increasing hordes of tourists eager for some new world to discover.

Tourist dollars, although important, were not going to pay for the foreign technology China needed for modernization. Foreign firms were loath to enter into contracts when there was no consistent code of commercial law in China. To meet this need, and with the intention of reassuring Chinese businesspeople, as well as scientists and other scholars so badly treated during the cultural revolution, a new legal system was developed. In 1980 one of its most important functions was to provide some notion of minimum legal rights for the individual, which until then had not existed. For many survivors of the excesses of the cultural revolution this constitutional right to a fair trial and legal representation gave some hope that the kangaroo courts of the past, which had allowed the brutal political persecution of the 1960s, would never reconvene. By degrees new social institutions were providing unheard-of freedoms, freedoms again challenged by the events of June 1989.

As the bamboo curtain was gradually drawn back, not only did the west begin to gain a more realistic understanding of China, but the Chinese began to gain a more realistic impression of the west.

The restrictions on travel to and from Hong Kong were relaxed and Cantonese eager to make contact with their relatives crossed the borders, and Hong Kong Chinese began to re-establish relations with their families in Guangdong. The consequence was that the ordinary Chinese discovered that relatives in the west or in Hong Kong, Singapore and even Taiwan lived in material conditions far better than their own. Having been told for decades of the superiority of socialism in delivering an ever-increasing standard of living, those of the younger generation who had not known the abject poverty and deprivation of pre-liberation times had little to go on but their own eyes. They were not convinced and wanted what others had — televisions, radios and better consumer goods.

It was this demand that provided the economic planners with one practical means of stimulating the economy — consumerism. By turning their attention to the production of consumer goods, money stored under the bed, out of fear produced by the political instability and the lack of anything much to buy, was circulating once more in the economy.

Regional markets were reopened after decades of state-controlled distribution and production of basic foods. These markets soon stimulated peasants to sell the surplus from their small private plots, allowed within the commune system. Food production increased suddenly, and money began to pulse through the economy with a new energy.

The problem of how to make industry more competitive and economically efficient remained. The state factory-communes were still dominated by Party officials who had been given power during the cultural revolution, on the basis of "better red than expert." The problem with these factories, and what gave them some similarity to Japanese factories, was the fact that labor was not disposable as it was in the west. The factory-commune was a social and political as well as an economic institution. To sack workers was unthinkable.

In the periods of high revolutionary idealism during the "great leap forward" and the cultural revolution when the commune system was set up, the factory-communes were conceived of as being the incubators out of which the new socialist consciousness was to be born. But as Lysenko's adherents were to find out, nature and particularly human nature is less easily transformed. The lazy and corrupt simply exploited the system for what it was worth. These communes came to operate like small fiefdoms, linked to vertically integrated ministries, which, in turn, behaved like

The commune was the center of economic and social life. There was little or no opportunity to leave. As an individual, your destiny was linked to that of the collective.

small states and jealously guarded their resources. This developed to the extent of hoarding valued resources often needed in other industries nearby. If a local factory required steel from the local mill, the manager would have to apply via the appropriate ministry in Beijing — the process could take a long time, and was bureaucratic and cumbersome. Apart from satisfying the state's quotas there was little reason to increase production or improve efficiency through innovation. There was little or no tangible reward for the individual who put in more than the most basic amount of effort; anything more risked an accusation of "bourgeois individualism," or "capitalist roader."

Essential to the new market-orientated reforms introduced by Deng was the idea that industrial enterprises were now allowed to make profits, and to pass the benefits on to their workers. An economic think-tank of scholars brought back from the countryside was established under the auspices of the newly formed Academy of Social Sciences. In 1978 Hu Qiaomu, the president of the Academy, in an address to the State Council argued that productivity had stagnated in China compared with its east Asian neighbors because, for the past 20 years, China had ignored "objective economic laws." Since these objective laws applied in both capitalist and socialist societies, and as capitalist economies had more experience in applying such laws in enterprise management, China should learn from that experience. These so-called "objective laws" were no more than the acceptance that the pursuit of profit by an individual firm was a legitimate aim, and the use of market forces was the best means of determining the price of goods and of controlling supply and demand. If China was to be competitive in the international market then it would have to accept the priority of economic efficiency even at the cost of egalitarianism and social welfare. The driving force of individual greed or enlightened self-interest would have to take precedence over the selfless service to the state that had been the ideal of the revolutionaries. There was still the problem of how to achieve the right balance between capitalist economic mechanisms and the centrally planned elements enshrined in the model China had adopted from the Soviet Union. The agency cost in most of China's highly bureaucratic industries was high. However, to turn these industries around in order to reach the levels of efficiency and productivity being achieved in Japan, Korea and Taiwan was no easy matter.

The economic rationalists in the planning agency began to argue that firms should be allowed to lay off workers and that the "iron rice bowl" (guaranteed employment) should be smashed. For example, a truck factory in Changchun, had 40,000 workers of whom only 12,000 were actually engaged in production; the factory-commune had, however, to support the rest. Underemployment was widespread. But if the factory did lay off their excess workers where would they go,

Society for Anglo-Chinese Understanding, London

Trucks awaiting dispatch at the Changchun No.1 Motor Vehicle Factory in the late 1970s. Despite high production levels the Changchun factory-commune had to support 40,000 people, although only 12,000 were directly engaged in production.

and how could they survive? The commune provided not only work but also food, housing, schooling and hospitals. Planners attempting to make the factory more efficient recommended that 12,000 workers should be laid off.

But there was no market for labor at this stage, and the state and provincial authorities strictly controlled the movement of people from the country to the cities, and from one region to another. The situation was clearly critical. Unchecked population growth had resulted in a 25 per cent rise in population since Mao's rejection of Ma Yinchu's warnings in the 1950s. The children of the communes had to be absorbed into the workforce, fed and housed, and yet productivity was not rising at a rate sufficient to provide any hope of an equal rise in living standards. This was becoming not only an embarrassment but a threat to the viability of the whole system. What was taking place outside China's borders in the rest of Asia could not be ignored indefinitely.

China's economy had, for all the political turmoil of the previous decades, been gradually restructured. This was evident in the shift away from a reliance on agriculture. In 1949–53 agriculture provided 50 per cent of China's gross national product (GNP); by 1983 this had fallen to 27 per cent. Over the same period, the proportion of GNP from industry had risen from 30 per cent to 57 per cent, and the growth in the industrial sector between 1962 and 1980 was twice that of any other country. China's industrial base was now in a far stronger position. However, it was not sufficiently strong to solve the problems facing China's economy.

To chart a course out of this quagmire the Party brought the now disgraced former Party Secretary Zhao Ziyang to Beijing in the post of Premier of the State Council. He had been First Secretary of the Party in Sichuan, Deng Xiaoping's home province. In this role he had transformed the province's industry into a model of economic reform. One of the key policies developed in Sichuan was to allow a high degree of self-management and freedom for industry, particularly the capacity to produce beyond state quotas. For example, at the Chongqing Iron and Steel Works when state demand for steel plate fell below the annual quota and the plant's capacity, the firm was allowed to sell directly on the open market, both within China and also overseas. The profits were then available to be returned to the workers in the form of bonuses. This was an example of the "market socialism" that Hungary and Yugoslavia had pioneered in Eastern Europe. Material incentives were clearly the only thing that was going to work in the climate of increasing disillusionment with the Party and its revolutionary policies; the Party had no alternative but to accept this.

In close collaboration with Deng, Zhao now began to apply these policies across the entire country. The impediments to rapid economic development were not just to be found within the structure of the economy but in the role of the Party itself.

Because of the inflexibility of the system, corruption had become commonplace. The "backdoor" was almost the only way to get around the bottlenecks in the system or to gain any measure of personal freedom or advantage for one's children. *Guanxi* (connections) is the Chinese term for the system of favors and obligations that, by the late 1970s, had become so prevalent that it was almost a medium of economic exchange. In a society where power and privilege is associated with position in the

THE CHINESE COMMUNIST PARTY

The structure of the Chinese Communist party descends in approximately eight levels from the Central Committee at the top, through six regional bureaux, 26 provincial or large city committees, 256 special district committees, 2,200 county committees and some 26,000 communes to more than one million branch committees in villages, factories, the army and other economic/social units. This structure has been the means by which policies developed by the Party's Central Committee could be passed down through the system to be implemented at the commune or factory level. It was also a structure that was intended to allow the feelings of the people to be communicated back up the hierarchy to the planners in the Central Committee. One of the problems with such a system is that information and instructions have to be interpreted as they move down the line. With the rapid shifts in Party policy, which occurred throughout the cultural revolution in particular, middle-level bureaucrats, fearful of the consequences of being identified as "capitalist roaders" or "ultra leftists" simply ceased to implement policies. It was a traditional bureaucratic response, but one that could effectively undermine even the most worthwhile reforms.

ORGANISATION OF THE CHINESE COMMUNIST PARTY

▼ *Elects Central Committee* **NATIONAL PARTY CONGRESS**

▼ *Elects Politburo and its Standing Committee* **CENTRAL COMMITTEE**

POLITICAL BUREAU OF THE CENTRAL COMMITTEE (POLITBURO) ▲ *Convenes plenary sessions of Central Committee*

STANDING COMMITTEE OF THE POLITBURO ▲ *Politburo and Standing Committee fulfill powers of Central Committee when it is not in session.*

MILITARY
CHAIN OF COMMAND

REGIONAL AND LOCAL BUREAUS
Entire Party subordinate to Central Committee under principle of democratic centralism.

MILITARY COMMISSION

26 Provincial and Autonomous Region Party Committees; 3 Municpal Party Committees	Sub-municipal (district) and Commune-level Primary Party Committees and Primary Party Committees at Larger Industrial Enterprises, Major Worksites or Educational Institutions	Party Branches at Medium-Sized Industrial Enterprises and at Other Places of Work, Education, or Residence, and at Brigade Levels in Communes	Party Branches at Small Industrial Enterprises, within Larger Industrial Enterprises, and at Other Places of Work, Education, or Residence, and at Team-levels in Communes	General Political Department of the PLA
Municipal and County-level Party Committees				Party Committees at Military Region Level
				Party Committees at Military District Level
				Party Committees at Regimental Level
				Party Committees at Company Level

bureaucracy and Party hierarchy, this influence can be lucratively farmed.

An interesting play, *Impostor* or *If I were Real,* was written in 1978. It was based on the true story of a young intellectual who had been sent off to the country during the cultural revolution and his attempts to get back to his home in Shanghai. In the play Li Xiaojiang has run away from the commune where he was sent, but to reside in the city he has to be officially transferred back; this he cannot do since he is unable to pull the necessary strings. He has a passionate interest in the theater, but is unable to get in. He waits outside theaters in the hope of being able to buy a ticket, until one night he notices that the theater manager has a bundle of spare tickets. He sees a young girl come up to the ticket office and being given a ticket immediately, even though he has been told that there are none left.

> LI: If these are unused tickets, why can't you sell them?
> ZHAO: (*Theater manager*): Because they're reserved for high-level cadres [party officials].
> LI: What about that girl who just went in? Is she a high-level cadre?
> ZHAO: Her father is. Is yours?

This gives Li an idea. Having heard that Ma, the head of the Propaganda Department, is not going to be able to come to the play, he goes to a public telephone nearby and rings the theater.

> LI: Hello? I want to speak to backstage. I'm from the Propaganda Department of the Municipal Committee, my name is Ma. . . . That's right. . . . I want to speak to the theater manager Zhao. . . . Yes. . . . Yes. . . . It's me. . . . Is that the theater manager Zhao? I'm going on an overseas trip tomorrow, so I won't be able to come to your play tonight. . . . Can I ask you a favor. The son of my only comrade-in-arms in Beijing would like to see your play very much. He just rang me to say he was unable to get a ticket. Could you help him? No problem? Good, he only needs one ticket. His name is Jiang Xiaolin . . . . You'll wait for him at the door? . . . Good. He's in the vicinity of the theater right now. So I'll tell him to come and see you.

The upshot of all this is that Li, having discovered the key to the backdoor, in the guise of the son of a high official, manipulates the system to have himself officially transferred back to the city from the countryside so that he can marry his girlfriend. The play caused an immediate scandal when it was put on in Shanghai and was banned after a week. It was definitely too close to the bone in the late 1970s.

However embarrassing the play might have been to the Party, it presented the system's rigidity all too clearly. Zhao Ziyang now had to cope with the growing number of these displaced and disillusioned citizens, particularly educated young people sent to the country. They had no future on the land, and little in the city of their birth. The State Planning Council set up new enterprise guidelines allowing those people without official work units or communes to form co-operative companies and to operate as independent traders within the growing free markets. They had the right to produce whatever the market would sustain and could keep the profits after paying a tax to the state. To the purists of the cultural revolution, this was as near to heresy as it was possible to get, but it was only the beginning.

THE OPEN DOOR

Closer ties with the outside world broaden people's minds, and this is conducive to overcoming feudal ideas and eliminating backwardness. . . . open wide, help speed the breaking down of the inert elements in the traditional culture, inject new blood into the national culture and achieve cultural modernization.

An Zhiguo, *Beijing Review,* 1978

The train from Hong Kong to the new Chinese city of Shenzhen often looks like a commuter service for businesspeople. In fact, when you cross the border into the People's Republic of China there is little sense of ever having left Hong Kong. Shenzhen is one of the fastest growing cities in the world. In the 1970s it was a tiny village; now it has a population of 250,000 drawn from all over China. Shenzhen, some have argued, is no more than an expensive showpiece; a political stunt to reassure rich Hong Kong merchants that there will be economic life after 1997, when Hong Kong and the New Territories are reabsorbed into China. In reality this city is a window on the world for the new Chinese economic planners; a hothouse in which new technology and methods of production are tried out under conditions that would be politically dangerous in the heartland of China. Shenzhen

Courtesy Film Australia

Shenzhen, one of China's new economic zones, is one of the fastest growing cities in the world. It is also a costly experiment in gaining access to foreign investment and technology

260

has an environment in which western-style consumerism, market forces and profit are the determining characteristics. Subsidiary factories of backward Chinese industries have opened up here. So too have Japanese, Hong Kong, Australian, European and American firms.

In the hope of tapping the technological advances taking place elsewhere in east Asia, the Chinese throughout the early 1980s set up a number of these "new economic zones." These, at first sight, seem to be the recreation of the old nineteenth century treaty-port system, by which the Qing government hoped to contain European influence, while perhaps gaining some benefits from increased trade and access to advanced technology. The crucial difference with the new economic zones is that they serve China and not foreigners. Here the Chinese have allowed legal and business conditions, familiar elsewhere in Asia, to flourish. The object is to attract overseas investment by multinational firms who set up production in Shenzhen and provide access both to new technology and to foreign markets.

When they were first established in the late 1970s, the new economic zones were primarily seen as means of gaining foreign exchange. Contracts specified that the bulk of what was produced must be exported. For foreign firms taking the opportunity to set up their factories in Shenzhen and the other economic zones, the attraction was not merely the cheap labor but the prospect of ultimately gaining access to the vast Chinese market. With the growing costs of production forcing Japanese firms to look for offshore bases, China, despite the bureaucratic irritations, offers some very great attractions.

In 1981 Hitachi set up production in Fuzhou under a fifty-fifty joint venture deal, producing television sets, the bulk of which were sold in China to meet growing consumer demand and dissatisfaction with local products. In 1984 Sanyo Electric set up a similar deal in Shenzhen. The Japanese Otsuka Pharmaceutical Company set up production in Tianjin in 1979 shifting an entire production system and capital worth $7.9 million from Japan. This represents only a fraction of Japan's direct investment in China. The impact of this competition on the Chinese market has meant that state factories are placed under increasing pressure to perform.

For the new generation of engineers and executives freed from many of the Maoist ideological and economic constraints, the new priorities of profitable firms and economic efficiency have forced them to adopt a more pragmatic approach to industrial production. What was desperately needed was some training in management; this the new joint ventures are providing.

The electronics industry is an interesting example of the changes brought about by the opening up of the Chinese economy — changes that are having a profound impact on social values. The Metto factory in Shenzhen was set up in 1986, as a subsidiary of Shanghai No. 3 Radio Factory, to produce transistors and tape recorders for export. The workforce are all on short-term contracts and the majority are young girls aged between 16 and 20. The productivity that is achieved in Shenzhen is about two-thirds higher than that of the parent company in Shanghai. The reasons are obvious to the manager Chen Gaofu. The bonuses he can pay his workers often amount to twice their weekly income. Average wages run at around 38 yuan ($10.20) a week; bonuses range from 50–150 yuan ($13.40–$40.30). The factory is also an interesting institution in itself. Like the factories set up by Arkwright and other textile manufacturers in eighteenth century England, and the Tomioka silk spinning mill in Japan in the nineteenth century, Metto must house and look after the welfare of the young people it employs. This industrial paternalism in Shenzhen is as pragmatic as it was in the early industrialization of England and Japan. The young workers come to the factory from rural communities throughout the region. The turnover is very high: on average 30 per cent leave each year. The onerous work discipline of the production line is alien but compensated for by the high wages offered. There is considerable competition for skilled labor in Shenzhen and to keep the workforce contented the manager of the factory has even taken to providing entertainment, as well as looking after their moral and material welfare.

Once a month Chen Gaofu, a cheerful middle-aged man, can be seen dancing at the latest Shenzhen disco, surrounded by forty or fifty of his young employees. The reason for this paternalism is simple: if he does not provide them with some ancillary benefits they will leave in ever greater numbers and the cost of training and recruitment will be lost to another firm eager to pick up trained factory workers.

Each week Hong Kong businesspeople and their agents arrive with orders for the Metto factory. They bring with them the latest Japanese-designed transistors and tape recorders. They meet with Chen, his engineers and design staff to discuss orders and costs. The models are then sent to the head office in Shanghai to be reverse-engineered, and the production equipment designed and geared up. A year or so later, under a variety of international brand names, they will turn up in supermarkets anywhere from Amsterdam and New York to Rio and Prague. In 1988 the Metto factory began producing three million Walkman radio cassettes for General Electric in the United States.

The scale of industrial development that is going on makes Shenzhen look more like one of the "four dragons" — Singapore, Taiwan, Korea and Hong Kong — than the People's Republic of China. The question that every visitor to the new economic zones inevitably asks is whether China's flirtation with capitalism is just a hothouse experiment to achieve its short-term financial and technological objectives, or whether the freedoms permitted in the new economic zones are to be extended throughout the rest of China. If they are, could China in the twenty-first century begin to do what Korea and Japan have done in the late twentieth century? There is little doubt that the Chinese government's economic planners would like to achieve the economic success seen elsewhere in east Asia, the question is whether the Communist party and the bureaucratic power structure that has been built up around it can be convinced to let go, and risk the social consequences of granting even greater economic and cultural freedoms.

Until 1988 the economic rationalists seemed to be winning. Even in centers not designated as new economic zones, such as Shanghai and Chengdu there is increasing independence for firms, which are expected to operate in a more competitive domestic market. Managers are no longer merely supervisors of a socialist commune in which ideological rectitude is all-important, but executives in a business that is expected to make profits or, in the final analysis, go to the wall. For some years, it has been argued that factories and state enterprises that are not run efficiently should be allowed to go bankrupt and be closed down, although this has happened rarely. Managers are now expected to offer bonuses to workers based on productivity.

At Shanghai No. 20 Radio Factory they make circuit boards for the large Shanghai-based electronics industry. Around the walls of the factory's conference room are framed the awards won for being a model factory. These awards no longer have the currency they once had. The profitability of the factory is a matter of much greater concern, despite the reassurances of the managers that socialist values continue to prevail and that "workers are not just working for themselves but for the collective interests." Given that these are now measured in terms of the profitability of the firm, they seem little different from the type of commitment achieved in Japanese or Korean firms. The factory still looks after the basic welfare of its 1,300 workers. However, those who do not work can be fired, although this has never happened. The commercial success of the factory makes it an attractive place to work. Its capacity to pay high bonuses is linked directly to its profitability, a fact certainly not lost on the employees.

Courtesy Film Australia

The production line at the Metto radio factory in Shenzhen. Here, contract workers, mostly young girls from outlying rural villages, assemble transistor radios and cassette players. Gone is the "iron rice bowl." Wages are pegged to a bonus system based on productivity, along the lines of bonus schemes operating in Japan and the west.

Many of the systems adopted in the last decade have come from Japan; these include the quality-control circle and the use of competing production teams with a prominent notice board showing the relative achievements of the teams. The production line itself was introduced in the late 1970s from Matsushita in Japan. Now this production line operates alongside two other Chinese copies built by the factory's engineers. In May 1988 a large new complex was built within the factory compound to house their latest joint venture with the Australian firm Printronics. The joint venture will allow Shanghai Printronics to sell 80 per cent of its new computer circuit boards internationally, providing them with much sought after foreign exchange.

The big question for innovative firms like Shanghai No. 20 is whether it is to be allowed the independence to pursue its commercial interests like any other international company. At present it has stiff competition from Taiwan and Singapore, which will inevitably provide a test of the extent of the pragmatism that Deng Xiaoping is prepared to allow, especially when this independence cuts across the principles of state planning. Already, small private electronics firms in Shanghai are providing serious competition to the large state-owned enterprises; a phenomenon that is widespread and one that has also had profound consequences in other industries.

Courtesy Film Australia

Shanghai's No. 20 Radio Factory runs its own school, with selected students being given technical training that will allow them to take up more senior positions on the production line or to pursue tertiary studies at the local technical college.

TROUBLE IN STOVE CITY

If we do not carry out reform [political and economic] now, our cause of modernization and socialism will be ruined.

Deng Xiaoping 1978

As economic reform progresses, we deeply feel the necessity for change in the political structure. The absence of such change will hamper the development of productive forces.

Deng Xiaoping 1986

The ancient port city of Quanzhou on the Fujian coast has provided foreign merchants with access to porcelain for a thousand years. The Fujian merchants themselves, despite the Ming suppression of mercantile activity in the fifteenth century, had built up trading networks throughout Southeast Asia, Taiwan, the Philippines and Japan.

Even in the 1930s and 1940s the pottery and porcelain works of the region were major international suppliers of roofing, floor and bathroom tiles; the fine porcelain for which the area was once renowned having given way to more prosaic wares. In the 1950s with the Nationalists in Taiwan just off the coast, and the restructuring of the domestic economy foremost in the minds of the new communist government, this trade went into a steep decline. In some of the towns surrounding Quanzhou small state-run pottery works were maintained to meet the local demand for roofing tiles.

One of these small towns is Jinjiang, known locally as "Stove City" because its skyline consists almost exclusively of smoke stacks — giant chimneys, most made out of forty-four gallon drums welded together. In 1978 there was just one state-run pottery and tile works; now there are 581. This area, set in the denuded hills that look like a permanent quarry, has the atmosphere that Staffordshire in the north of England must have had in the late eighteenth century, when the pottery works of Wedgwood and others were beginning to mass produce common crockery.

What is astounding is the speed with which these changes came about and their effect on the political and social life of the surrounding community. When Deng Xiaoping at the Seventh Party Congress in 1978 announced the economic and political reforms he could have had no idea of the forces he was unleashing. At "Stove City" families who either worked in the ceramics industry or had been associated with it in the past began to set up small backyard furnaces and rented stalls in the town's main street to sell their wares. Many who were only making a subsistence living through agriculture found that this traditional industry could add appreciably to the family income.

These small-scale pottery works had become so successful that, by 1984, the state factory was in serious financial difficulty. The conditions of employment that it was forced to offer its employees made it simply uncompetitive compared with the small private firms. The "iron rice bowl," which guaranteed workers a basic wage whether

FANG LIZHI AND THE ENGINEERS OF THE SOUL

All our workers fighting on the ideological front should serve as "engineers of the soul" . . . they are charged with the heavy responsibility of educating people.

Deng Xiaoping, 1983

Fang Lizhi, an astrophysicist of international standing, has often been described as China's Sakharov. He is perhaps the most outspoken and articulate critic of China's politics and culture, of the Communist party and of his fellow scientists. Until 1986 he was the Vice-Chancellor of China's Science and Technology University, a post he had held since 1984. During December 1986 and January 1987 students demonstrated in Beijing and Shanghai, demanding greater democracy and freedom. This demonstration led to a campaign against so-called "bourgeois liberalism" within the Communist party. Fang Lizhi was sacked from his position at the University, and from the Party. He was not alone; liberal leaders in the Communist party, such as Hu Yaobang, known to be sympathetic to democratic reforms were demoted, and numerous intellectuals and writers were expelled from the Party. Since the brutal repression of student demonstrations in China in June 1989 culminating in the deaths of both civilians and soldiers in Tiananmen Square, Fang Lizhi has been forced to seek political asylum within the compound of the American Embassy in Beijing.

Although there was no direct connection between the student demonstrations and Fang Lizhi, his outspoken criticisms and uncompromising honesty were seen to be partly responsible. In November 1986 Fang gave a series of speeches to students in Shanghai. The following are excerpts, translated by Orville Schell, and published in *The Atlantic,* May 1988:

"Human rights are fundamental privileges that people have from birth, such as the right to think and be educated, to marry and so on. But we Chinese consider these rights dangerous. Although human rights are universal and concrete, we Chinese lump freedom, equality and brotherhood together with capitalism and criticize them all in the same terms. If we are the democratic country we say we are these rights should be stronger here than elsewhere, but at present they are nothing more than an abstract idea."

"I feel that the first step towards democratization should be the recognition of human rights . . . but [in China] democratization has come to mean something performed by superiors on inferiors — a serious misunderstanding of democracy. Our government does not give us democracy simply by loosening our bonds a bit. This gives us only enough freedom to writhe a little. Freedom by decree is not fit to be called democracy because . . . it fails to provide the most basic human rights."

"In a democratic nation democracy flows from the individual, and the government has responsibility towards him . . . We must make our government realize that it is economically dependent on its citizens, because such is the basis of democracy. But feudal traditions are still strong in China; social relations are initiated by superiors and accepted by inferiors."

"People of other societies believe that criminal accusations arising from casual suspicion harm human dignity and privacy. In China, on the other hand, it is not only normal for me to inform on you . . . but considered a positive virtue. I would be praised for my alertness and contribution to class struggle in spite of my disrespect for democracy and human rights."

On the role of the intellectual and the university in China he had this to say:

"To liberate oneself from the slavery of governmental and other non-intellectual authorities, one need only view knowledge as an independent organism. But this is not so in China. Our universities produce tools, not educated men. Our graduates cannot think for themselves. They are quite happy to be the docile instruments of someone else's purposes. China's intelligentsia has still not cleansed itself of this tendency . . . Knowledge should be independent of power. It must never submit, for knowledge loses its value as soon as it bows to power."

At the campus of Shanghai's Tongji University Fang recounted the following story, which was later published in *China Spring* and, no doubt, helped to seal his fate:

"I have often said that a university needs science, democracy, creativity and independence. A reporter later wrote to me saying that this spirit was very good but that I should supplement the transcript of my talk, lest people think that my

Fang Lizhi with his wife Li Shuxian.

opinions are slighting the 'four cardinal principles' [Deng Xiaoping had enunciated these as socialism, the people's democratic dictatorship, the leadership of the Communist party, and Marxism-Leninism and Mao Zedong thought]. Since I had also proposed four principles, he said, people might think this a little dangerous. I wrote back to him and said that I could add a section saying that if science, democracy, creativity, and independence conflicted with the 'four principles' then it was only because the 'four principles' advocate superstition instead of science, dictatorship instead of democracy, conservatism instead of creativity, and dependency instead of independence . . . The editor responded that perhaps the clarification would be unnecessary."

Fang Lizhi should not be mistaken for a promoter of capitalism; he is more in the mold of George Orwell, a socialist attacking the failure of its practitioners. His model of socialism is that of the northern European countries, such as Sweden, where a high level of state ownership coexists with a vigorous market economy and, above all, with intellectual freedom. For Fang, Marxism and the Communist party have become little more than surrogates for the traditional feudal structure of China, Confucianism and the conservative scholar-bureaucrats who ran the empire. Reform requires the genuine acceptance of the values of science, which, he argues, are innately democratic and pluralist in nature.

However, in what many see as a quixotic campaign to promote democratic values in China (not unlike the "Mr Science and Mr Democracy" movement of the 1920s) he is clearly up against a powerful body of conservative Party technocrats whose proposals for reforming China are truly Orwellian, as the following extract from an article by Dr Qian Xuesen entitled "From Social Science to Social Technology" shows:

"We definitely must set up the field of moral education, which is a social science. Moral education belongs to modernized social science and ought to be on the agenda of modernization of social science. Given this science of moral education, we can organize the use in socialist propaganda work of modern science and technology. The executive leadership in propaganda work needs a communications network for liaison with all regions, to give an up-to-date picture of the ideological tendencies of the popular masses. This intelligence must on the one hand be stored in an information bank and displayed on command display screens. Propaganda staff officers use the theory of moral education to analyze the situation, and may also use electronic computers and similar instruments with analytical models to estimate the effects and functioning in the thinking of the masses of various propaganda activities. The staff officer corps following propaganda-executive decisions transmits these to lower level units, and at the same time to newspapers, periodicals, radio and television transmitters all the way to cultural and artistic units for implementation. The conditions of implementation are reported back to the propaganda executive via the communications network. The executive is thus just like a military command. It commands operations in ideological and political work, and the entirety of workers in the propaganda departments are staff members of an operational command. Is not this then another field of engineering for the reconstruction of society. Hence ideological and political work can become a social technology."

they worked or not, had led to serious overstaffing.

It was at this point that the Director of the state factory, Wu Wendian, and the Communist party Secretary Wu Yongxin came up with an entirely new system of operation, which has transformed the factory and its productivity. They broke the workforce up into six teams that operated as independent enterprises, buying materials and renting the facilities, such as kilns, owned by the factory. Each unit was expected to pay 10 per cent of its profits to the government as tax, the rest was divided among members of the unit on the basis of their work and productive output. The units were given considerable freedom to seek markets outside the province and overseas. The factory's overheads were also drastically reduced and the pre-1984 managerial staff of 60 was reduced to 17. In 1984 the factory's output was worth 700,000 yuan ($188,066). By 1987 it had more than tripled to 2.4 million yuan ($644,797).

The profits and new wealth from this production explosion were plowed back into the community in the form of a building boom. One of the new legal code's provisions, which was to fundamentally change the standard of living of many of the most industrious of "Stove City's" ceramics entrepreneurs, was the right to own property and to pass it on to children. This concession to the Chinese family system means that the wealth of the region is now beginning to show itself in the large and spacious stone houses being erected all over the city. These houses are richly decorated with the source of their wealth — gaudy porcelain tiles. "Stove City" is taking on the appearance of a boom town similar to those in Australia or California.

The people of Lin Banchen village were organized as a production brigade in

Courtesy Film Australia

Ten years ago "Stove City" had one state-owned ceramics factory; now there are over five hundred private producers.

Mao's times, now the village is a prosperous suburb of "Stove City." Across the river from the rows of elaborate three-storied stone mansions are the ancient step-kilns that have brought the new-found wealth. The families that make up the old brigade now have rights to, but not ownership of, the surrounding farm land; rights that can also be passed on to family members. Their houses are richly furnished, with televisions, videos, refrigerators and other luxuries, which one would not expect to find in rural areas. It is this wealth in the hands of such communities that is creating the demand for the consumer electronics being produced, in increasing volumes, in the factories of Shanghai. Here there is none of the jaded cynicism about materialism common in the west. The new freedom to make money and to spend it on the items most people in the west take for granted is a powerful driving force in the new Chinese economy. Like the postwar boom in domestic consumer demand, which fuelled the remarkable growth in the United States, European and Japanese economies, China with a population of more than one billion people has now discovered the dynamic economic benefits of consumerism. Already there are widespread fears among the older members of the Communist party that the Pandora's box opened by Deng in the late 1970s cannot be controlled. This issue of control is of central concern to those senior cadres, in Beijing and in the provinces, who now find that the market mechanism — "the idol" of economic rationalism — might well displace them from their once commanding role over the direction of China's social, political and economic life. Expectations as to what is possible within the system have clearly been raised and these expectations are a potent reality that neither ideology nor rhetoric can easily force back into Pandora's box.

*   *   *

Courtesy Film Australia

China's new consumerism — a "ghetto blaster" takes pride of place before the more traditional gods.

Courtesy Film Australia

The wealth generated by the ceramics industry has led to a building boom. Fine stone houses are going up all over the area, as a consequence of the government's policy of allowing property to be passed on to heirs.

Stuck on the wall of a small nondescript building, facing a dusty street some ten minutes walk from the center of Beijing, there is a brass plate, which in English and Chinese reads "Scientific and Technological Entrepreneurs' Association of the West City District." This is the umbrella organization for a number of independent consultants who operate completely outside the state system. They own their own companies and pay taxes to the Chinese government, but apart from that they are free to go about their business. Their role is to bridge the gap between China's growing scientific-research capacity and industry.

The problem for the new industrial entrepreneurs of China is not just to gain access to overseas technology but to tap the creativity and talent of their own young and highly trained scientists and engineers. Although there remains a large hole in the education curve as a result of the "ten lost years" of the cultural revolution — when scientists were despised and technological knowledge dismissed as bourgeois — an increasing number of Chinese students are now returning from overseas training with advanced knowledge. What is in question is whether this knowledge can be effectively applied.

270

The Academy of Sciences and the universities and ministries that employ trained scientists and engineers have a limited relationship to industry, except for the large-scale state enterprises. The problem in the past has been that academic research was operating at a much higher level of sophistication than most of Chinese industry. Even where industry saw the need for scientific consultants from research institutions, there were too many bureaucratic obstructions and little real incentive for such relationships to work effectively.

There was one celebrated case in the early 1980s when a scientist was attacked by colleagues for acting as a consultant and gaining what they jealously believed were inappropriate financial benefits. The scientist was charged and threatened with dismissal from his university post. Had it not been for the issue being taken up publicly he would probably have lost his job.

Following this case it was agreed by the new State Science and Technology Commission and the Academy of Sciences that consultancies, for which academic staff were paid by state and private enterprises, were not only legitimate but highly desirable. They decided, there and then, to set up the Scientific and Technological Entrepreneurs' Association under the joint direction of Fang Yi, the retired head of the Academy of Sciences, Zhang Jingfu the Deputy Director of the State Economic Commission and the eminent sociologist Professor Fei Xiaotong. This body was to act as an official organization to encourage engineers and scientists who were prepared to set up as independent consultants. Although extremely small in scale the Scientific and Technological Entrepreneurs' Association is beginning to have an impact.

Zhou Hongji is an engineer who, until a few years ago, worked for the Iron and Steel Institute in Beijing. Zhou is an enthusiast and a man of considerable initiative. When the opportunity presented itself he decided to set up on his own, giving up his job, along with the fringe benefits and security that come with bureaucratic and institutional position in China. (A position in a research institute or in one of the large ministries had, in the past, offered the only career path for engineers.) Despite this Zhou set up his own consultancy — the Hua Ye Company — and began business in 1986.

His first major project was to take the research on smelting techniques on which he had been working at the Iron and Steel Institute and convince industry of its benefits. At the State-run Iron and Steel Company plant in Hubei he was able to save the company an average of 1.5 million yuan ($402,998) a year by introducing a better smelting technique. From this his reputation has grown into that of a major independent "trouble shooter." In a country where the old Soviet ministerial and academic structures still inhibit the easy flow of information, the role of consultants like Zhou is going to be increasingly important. He is, however, not alone. At any meeting of the Association an unusual mixture of well-qualified enthusiasts, who have responded to the option of independent consultancy, attend.

But it is not only in the private sector that efforts to break down the institutional barriers to the flow of knowledge are taking place. The entrepreneurial spirit is being fostered in most state factories where rewards, in terms of bonuses, are going to innovations introduced by employees at all levels. This system was first introduced into the Japanese company structure in the 1950s. In both countries workers aim to spend a lifetime of employment committed to the collective goals of their companies. These institutions continue to act more like extended families than like western firms. In Japan the input of shop-floor workers was an essential component in quality control and in productive efficiency, and the more innovative of the new Chinese companies have introduced similar systems. This fact is still not fully appreciated by managers in the west.

At the Shanghai No. 20 Radio Factory a young trainee engineer Wu Ketong was able to earn 1,500 yuan ($403), more than double his yearly income, for inventing a new water purification system he set up for the factory. It has been so successful that it is now being introduced to other factories by the municipal government, which is concerned with the high levels of industrial pollution in Shanghai. In developing his system Wu collaborated with industrial chemists at the local institute of technology where he studies.

What is obvious from this brief review of some of the consequences of China's reforms is that, given sufficient freedom and incentives, technological innovation is possible even within a centrally planned economy like that of China.

However, without innovation within the dominant political and economic organizations, no amount of technological change will induce economic growth — for all the tinkering on the margins of power. While the cases presented here have been selected to demonstrate what can and is being done outside the more traditional institutions, they remain like vulnerable flowers that have poked their heads up between the cracks in the concrete of an otherwise inflexible bureaucratic state.

In 1987 a Shanghai firm offered a sale of shares in their company, the first case of stocks being sold in China for at least fifty years. People queued up all night so as to be able to invest in the firm. By 9 A.M. on the day of the sale the offer — more than 3 million yuan ($805,997) worth of shares — had been sold out. This specter of capitalism rearing its head in China would have had Mao leaping from his mausoleum. However, the ideal of the moral society, controlled and ordered around a single unifying ideology, does not die easily, whether it be the Confucian imperial state or the Maoist revolutionary state. There were still many senior officials within the Communist party who would happily shut out the materialistic western world and return China to its rightful concerns with social order and economic self-reliance, as the Ming emperors did in the fifteenth century and Mao tried to do in the 1960s.

In May 1989, the Communist party's ability to contain the demands for reform finally broke down. Students in Beijing, like their contemporaries in Eastern Europe, took to the streets demanding not just greater economic freedom but cultural and political freedom as well. Earlier in the year the Central committee of the party had decided not to allow the establishment of a free labour market. Graduates would continue to be allocated jobs by the state and sent wherever they were needed. With frustration amongst the young rising as fast as expectations, confrontation was almost inevitable. As the tanks rolled into Tiananmen Square on June 4th the color of Deng's Cat seemed well and truly Red.

SUPERCOMPUTERS

In March 1980 Richard Anderson, a general manager at Hewlett-Packard, one of the largest computer firms in the United States, announced at a Washington conference the findings of a comparative survey on the reliability of computer chips: the best American products had a failure rate six times that of the lowest quality Japanese product.

In the late 1970s the Japanese began their assault on the global computer market, the last bastion of American technological dominance. It seemed set to be a repeat story of the rise of the Japanese automobile industry a decade earlier. By 1983 the Japanese had not only gained 70 per cent of the world market for 64k RAM (random access memory) chips, an American invention, but had embarked on a most audacious project designed to leapfrog a generation of computer technology and to come up with a supercomputer to challenge the most powerful American machines. With the support of Japan's influential Ministry of International Trade and Industry, a $100 million National Superspeed Computer Project and a $500 million fifth generation Computer Institute (ICOT) were set up in 1981–82. Involving 40 researchers from government research laboratories and eight leading computer firms — Fujitsu, Hitachi, Nippon Electric (NEC), Mitsubishi, Matsushita, Oki, Sharp and Toshiba — this 13-year project is an example of the long-term planning approach to technological development that has allowed the Japanese to dominate in a number of key high-technology fields.

Japanese computer firms belong to *kieratsu,* an association of interlinked companies ranging from semiconductor producers to robot manufacturers. Unlike American firms, the Japanese companies also had access to relatively cheap long-term finance, which made it easier for them to invest in new technology and new production processes. In the United States, because of the differences in the operation of the money market, the need for short-term return on investment made long-term technological planning more difficult. In other words the Japanese could "hold their breath for a long, long time."

The announcement of Japan's supercomputer and fifth generation project brought a new response from both government and the private sector in the United States. They began to look seriously at what the Japanese were doing and how they were doing it. The tables had finally turned. In 1982 a number of leading American semiconductor and computer companies came together to form a non-profit consortium, the Semiconductor Research Corporation. With a $30 million annual budget the Corporation was designed "to assure long-term survival in the market", according to its first director Larry Sumney. A similar research and development group — the Microelectronics and Computer Technology Corporation (MCC) — was established by Control Data and 12 other companies to follow the Japanese model of pooling resources for long-term planning.

It was the military who were most concerned about the possibility of losing dominance in such a strategically sensitive area. This led to the Pentagon announcing its $1 billion Strategic Computing and Survivability Project, which set out to do everything the Japanese had done and more. However, by late 1988 Japan's lead in the application of micro-electronics and computer systems was such that the world's most advanced fighter aircraft — the FSX — will be built at Mitsubishi's Nagoya aircraft and armaments factory. The United States will supply the body and frame but Japan will supply the remaining 65 per cent, including the engine, and the sophisticated radar and electronics. Both countries will have access to the technology developed in the final product. What is perhaps most ironic is that it was at the same Mitsubishi Nagoya plant that the Zero fighter was developed. Built from components taken from American designs and initially using American parts, it had played a decisive role in the destruction of the Pacific fleet in Pearl Harbor in 1942.

THE PRICE OF PROGRESS

The dilemma now facing the Chinese Communist party is acute. Having raised expectations by the success of Deng's economic reforms throughout the 1980s, the question remains whether it is possible to retain the party's old ideological values and power and still encourage the sort of innovation needed to cope with the country's enormous technological and environmental problems. (As a consequence of the repression following June 4th, 1989 many of the most innovative of China's intellectuals and entrepreneurs, such as the founder of the highly successful Stone Computer company, have been forced to leave the country or face persecution. It's a loss they can ill afford.) This is heightened by the expectation that China should be able to catch up, or at least not fall further behind her rapidly growing east Asian neighbors in Japan, South Korea, Taiwan, Hong Kong and Singapore.

Despite much rhetoric to the contrary on the part of senior Communist party officials, China since 1983 has started on a path of fundamental restructuring of its economic institutions — restructuring that, in the long term, will allow for the adoption of business practices common throughout the rest of east Asia. There is an interesting analogy here to the international arms race. Whether they like it or not, countries are forced to achieve technological parity in conventional arms if they are to defend themselves; in a similar way, the economic pragmatists argue, it is necessary to adopt the most efficient international system of industrial production if one is to compete effectively. For this reason the Chinese have welcomed joint ventures with the Japanese as have the Americans and Europeans (for example, the laser-controlled compact disk was jointly developed by Philips of Holland and Sony of Japan).

It is also interesting to observe the speed with which Japanese management approaches have been tried and in many cases adopted in the United States in the hope of regaining its lost manufacturing lead. The capacity to adopt the Japanese approach has obviously been limited by cultural and economic differences. However, there is every reason to believe that competition within the United States market from Japanese-run firms will begin to change the American industrial ethos. The Japanese have brought to industrial production new international standards of efficiency and quality control that other countries are forced to match or risk going out of business.

One has only to look at the number of failing firms in Europe and the United States that have been taken over by Japanese companies and turned around to become profitable to realise that their approach is not limited to the Japanese environment. The Dunlop tyre company in Great Britain was bought by the giant Sumitomo corporation in the early 1980s. Within 18 months, and after a major injection of capital, a net annual loss of about $40 million was turned into a modest profit. The firm had been run on traditional British class lines for decades. There were six different dining rooms, with managers and staff eating separately. Worker incentives were low as was morale. This, however, was to change radically. Under the new management 300 middle managers and ancillary staff were redeployed. There was only one canteen for everyone; there was standard dress, which eliminated the distinction between managers and workers; employees were encouraged to come up with suggested improvements in the production process and were given bonuses for doing so; levels of participation in the goals of the company increased as did bonuses based on increases in productivity and on improvements in quality.

A General Motors plant in California had an industrial relations record so bad that it was basically undermining the plant's viability. It was taken over by Toyota in the early 1980s and, by changing the production process and system of management, it was to become one of the most profitable factories in the United States. Deming's ideas were finally to be accepted back home, but via a most unexpected route.

The problem for the older industrial powers is that they, in turn, have become ossified around the institutional structures that gave them their early success. In this sense, the success of the United States in the first part of this century, like that of Britain in the previous century, provided them with little reason for change or need to innovate until a latecomer like Japan set new standards of efficiency and productivity, which challenged their domestic and overseas markets. Now change has become imperative. The only question is whether there is sufficient flexibility or pragmatism to allow the old ideological assumptions and priorities to be discarded and new approaches to be taken.

In an economy as large and complex as that of the United States there is evidence of an insularity reminiscent of the Middle Kingdom. In this respect, China and the United States face parallel problems in coping with a new international economic order in which Japan and other smaller countries (such as South Korea, Sweden and Germany) are taking the lead in key industrial fields (such as electronics, shipbuilding and automobiles). The consequences of falling behind Japan in electronics, in particular, could mean that industries in the United States have limited access to new systems of production affecting both the quality and cost of goods manufactured there. This happened to Great Britain in the late nineteenth century when Germany virtually took over the chemical industry, undercutting British firms and thus reducing the stimulus for industrial research and development. The military in the United States are particularly concerned about Japan's dominance in the electronics industry. There is a fear that the United States could fall behind and, if so, the lack of industrial innovation could affect the quality of military technology. The economic threat from Japan is not imaginary: by 1985 Japan accounted for 10 per cent of the world's economic output and in the same year average annual income in Japan was $17,000 compared with $16,000 in the United States.

The claims that the Japanese and other Asian cultures were merely imitators and could never really threaten the scientific and technological lead held by the west has encouraged complacency for more than a century. It is true that Great Britain and the United States still gain the majority of Nobel prizes and Japan, considering its present industrial power, has a woeful record in making major scientific breakthroughs. Asian cultures, many western commentators have observed, have not nurtured great or original thinkers. The emphasis on conformity and collective endeavors, it is often argued, gives east Asian cultures advantages in industrial production or process innovation, but not in invention or product innovation. In this latter area it is the more individualistic and intellectually orientated cultures of the west that will come up with original scientific and technological developments as they have done so successfully over the past two centuries.

However, as this study has, I hope, shown, such arguments take too short a historical perspective. China, long before the rise of the capitalist economies of Europe and the United States, proved itself capable of high levels of innovation, within a very different culture and economy. Also invention, although important, is not necessarily the crucial issue if one is looking for wealth and power. Many early Chinese innovations, such as mechanical spinning, had no significant economic impact in China, while in Britain with the development of the factory system it was one of the basic stimuli for the Industrial Revolution. Micro-electronics and computer-controlled production lines, although developed in the United States, were to be taken up in Japan with such success that within a decade the Japanese were to dominate the world in their use and application. Such examples prove that the benefits of invention and discovery do not necessarily accrue to the inventor.

Despite their cultural homogeneity the Japanese have proved sufficiently flexible to change their cultural institutions in the past. If greater freedom and encouragement of originality is clearly perceived to be in their economic interests, there is no reason to believe that they will not be developed. This may well be the virtue of Japanese pragmatism. An interesting issue is whether the United States, Europe and China can demonstrate similar levels of pragmatism. The cost, however, is that culture becomes subservient to economic priorities.

This is not a dilemma for the Japanese alone. The values and demands of the global market place now set the economic priorities for all countries, from the most highly developed to the smallest third-world nation. Although it was possible because of its vast size for Mao, like the Ming emperors, to insulate China from the polluting effects of the capitalist world, in the long run even China has been drawn into the global economy in order to acquire the technology it so desperately needs to keep up with its capitalist neighbors.

It would appear that, whether we like it or not, a degree of cultural and political convergence is taking place at a global level. As giant multinational corporations and international joint ventures extend national interests to a global perspective, leaders in countries as ideologically opposed as the Soviet Union, the United States, China and Australia are forced to confront the requirements of efficient industrial production and economic planning based on international demand. Modern science and technology are clearly a major force in this process. The universality of science and its embodiment in commonly used technology link human societies as never before. As basic literacy in science becomes the educational heritage of people throughout the world, it will come to represent a strong countervailing force against the traditional religious and cultural values that have fed racial and cultural bigotry for most of human history.

All this is not, however, before time, as the noted Canadian biologist and commentator on science, Professor David Suzuki, has pointed out. The price of progress, which the European economic and scientific revolution fostered, has been a double-edged sword. While progress has allowed a massive increase in our capacity to exploit the global environment and to lift standards of living to unprecedented levels, we are now, for the first time, confronted with problems that transcend the powers and capacities of individual nation-states to deal with them. The biological diversity of the globe is fast disappearing, as world population rises, demanding increased economic growth and leading, in turn, to vastly increased consumption of energy and resources. As the remaining small areas of the earth's tropical forests in the Amazon, Africa and Southeast Asia are being destroyed, and the pollution of the biosphere threatens the earth's subtle climatic balance, the idea of unlimited economic and industrial growth becomes a dangerous myth.

The global economy increasingly homogenizes consumer tastes, supposedly offering to the developing world standards of consumption achieved in the west. If this is to be successful, unprecedented levels of scientific and technological innovation will have to be achieved. While the competitive efficiency of industrial and agricultural production within a world market will determine the technology, products and cultural artifacts that are promoted or discarded, there is also the need for balance and ecological harmony, as traditional Confucian China was concerned to promote. The dynamic mechanism of the market and consumerism can, as the Chinese have recently discovered, stimulate the economy and individual initiative, but unchecked economic growth can, in an extreme case, look more like the growth of a cancer than a road to Xanadu.

In this respect the success or otherwise of China — representing as it does one-fifth of the world's population — is crucial. Considering where they were starting from, their achievements since 1949 are as impressive as Japan's, but the task of managing this vast and growing population without crushing the individual, and thus destroying the essential wellspring of innovation and creativity, is no mean task.

There is clearly not any one road to Xanadu, as many economic planners of varying ideological persuasions have tried to argue. Each country discussed in this study has been able to exploit its unique cultural and economic potential, which at different times throughout history has given it enormous economic power and influence, but this does not last, for success is so often its own worst enemy.

As we all move towards a global society, perhaps the Xanadu we should be heading for is not some place of static perfection, dreamed of in the past, but a more dynamic balance between the need to provide maximum freedom for creativity, industrial innovation and growth, and the need to preserve the earth's finite resources and natural wealth. This will require the acceptance of continued technological change, but equally important will be the capacity to accept change within our cultural, economic and political institutions. If we do not achieve this balance the price of continued growth will be a world impoverished by nationalistic greed and environmental short sightedness.

NOTES ON CHINESE NAMES

Unfortunately, there is no simple way to indicate the sounds of the Chinese language faithfully in English. In *Roads to Xanadu* we have adopted the contemporary standard offered by the People's Republic of China, known as pinyin. The older form of the name is indicated in brackets after the pinyin when it first occurs in the text, for example, Li Hongzhang (Li Hung-chang).

However, a number of names and expressions, entering English from a variety of sources, have become so familiar to generations of readers — Confucius, Chiang Kai-shek, Taoism, Yangtze and so on — that these have been retained.

ENDNOTES

THE PRICE OF HARMONY

THE CELESTIAL EMPIRE

14   Marco Polo's quotes were taken from Marsden's revised translation in Manuel Komroff, ed., *The Travels of Marco Polo (The Venetian)* (New York: Liveright, 1986), xiii.

18   For a useful article on China's early water control systems, see the article by Song Zhenghai in Chinese Academy of Sciences, ed., *Ancient China's Technology and Science* (Beijing: Foreign Languages Press, 1983), 239.

21   For more information on the Chinese iron and steel industry see Joseph Needham, *Science and Civilisation in China* (Cambridge: Cambridge University Press, 1954–62), vols. III and V. For the military implications see William McNeill, *Pursuit of Power* (Oxford: Blackwells, 1984).

22–3   For further information on Chinese agriculture see Francesca Bray, "The Chinese Contribution to Europe's Agricultural Revolution: A Technology Transformed," in *Explorations in the History of Science and Technology in China* (Shanghai: 1982) and Francesca Bray, *The Rice Economies: Technology and Development in Asian Societies* (Oxford: Blackwells, 1986). Also see Needham, *Science and Civilisation in China*, vol. VI. There is an extremely interesting chapter on China's agricultural revolution in Mark Elvin, *Patterns of the Chinese Past* (Palo Alto, Calif.: Stanford University Press, 1973). In addition, see Dwight Perkins, *Agricultural Development in China 1368–1968.* (Chicago: Aldine, 1969).

26   The quote on the rice field as factory was taken from Fernand Braudel, *Civilization and Capitalism,* vol. 1 (London: Collins, 1984), 151.

28   William McNeill, *Plagues and People* (Oxford: Blackwells, 1976) provides a good comparative account of the impact of parasitic diseases on the development of European and Asian societies. Elvin, *Patterns of the Chinese Past,* gives a useful account of the economic and social impact of the agricultural revolution in the Song dynasty.

SCHOLARS AND BUREAUCRATS

29   Renzong's poem as quoted in Ichisada Miyazaki, *China's Examination Hell* (New Haven, Conn.: Yale University Press, 1981), 17.

30–1   For a more detailed account of the Chinese examination system see Miyazaki, *China's Examination Hell.* For an interesting discussion on the impact of this examination system on China's intellectual culture see Shiheru Nakayama, *Academic and Scientific Traditions in China, Japan and the West* (Tokyo: University of Tokyo Press, 1984).

36   The extract from *Xia xiao zheng* is found in Cao Wanru, "Phenological Calendars and Knowledge of Phenology", in Chinese Academy of Sciences, *Ancient China's Technology and Science,* 230.

37   For a more detailed account of the Chinese calendar see the article by Chen Jijin in Chinese Academy of Sciences, *Ancient China's Technology and Science.* See also Needham, *Science and Civilisation in China,* vol. III.

38–9   For further details on the links between astronomy and astrology see Ho Pengyoke's article in *The Proceedings of the 4th International Conference on the History of Chinese Science* (Sydney: University of Sydney, 1985). For a review of Chinese astronomy see Nathan Sivin, *Cosmos and Computation in Early Chinese Mathematical Astronomy* (Leiden: E.S. Brill, 1969). In addition, a good general work on Chinese science is Nathan Sivin, ed., *Chinese Science: Explorations of an Ancient Tradition* (Cambridge, Mass.: MIT Press, 1973).

39   For the reference to secrecy see the quote by Christopher Cullen in John Merson, *Culture and Science in China* (Sydney: Australian Broadcasting Commission, 1981), 25.

42   The second century quote on a water-driven armillary sphere is from Robert Temple, *China: Land of Discovery and Invention* (London: Patrick Stephens, 1986), 37. For a more detailed account of the Su Song clock see David Landes, *Revolution in Time* (Cambridge, Mass.: The Belknap Press, Harvard, 1983); The article in Joseph Needham, *Clerks and Craftsmen in China* (Cambridge: Cambridge University Press, 1970); and the article by Bo Shuren in Chinese Academy of Sciences, *Ancient China's Technology and Science.*

SELF CULTIVATION AND THE COSMOS

42   The quote from Li Chuan and the Chinese alchemic verse are from Needham, *Science and Civilisation in China,* vol. V.

44–5   Joseph Needham, "Progress in Science and its Social Conditions", in *Nobel Symposium 58* (Pergamon Press, 1983) provides a good short review of how imperial priorities set the agenda for science in China. More details on this issue can be found in Needham, *Science and Civilisation in China.*

48   The quote from *Inner Writings of the Jade Purity* is cited in Needham, *Science and Civilisation in China,* vol. V: 4, 235.

BOMBARDS AND CATHAYAN FIRE ARROWS

51   The quote on the properties of sulfur and saltpeter is from a useful short account of the development of gunpowder in Temple, *China: Land of Discovery and Invention.* See also Zhou Jiahua's article on gunpowder and firearms in Chinese Academy of Sciences, *Ancient China's Technology and Science.* For a more detailed investigation see the sections on alchemy and gunpowder in Needham, *Science and Civilisation in China.*

52–3   Zhao Yurong's quote from *Xinsi qi qi lu,* written in 1221, is found in Chinese Academy of Sciences, *Ancient China's Technology and Science,* 188.

MERCHANTS, ARTISANS AND BUREAUCRATS

55   Marco Polo's quote comes from R. Latham, trans., *The Travels of Marco Polo* (London: 1958), 180 and is cited in Elvin, *Patterns of The Chinese Past.*

56   Wang Chen's poem describing a spinning machine is quoted in Elvin, *Patterns of the Chinese Past,* 198. Elvin also provides a good discussion (pp. 194–99) on why the development of water-powered spinning in thirteenth century China did not have the same impact that it did in Europe. This is further developed in Elvin, "The High-Level Equilibrium Trap: The Causes of the Decline of Invention in the Traditional Chinese Textile Industries", in W. Willmott, ed., *Economic Organization in Chinese Society* (Palo Alto, Calif.: Stanford University Press, 1972).

56–7   Jacques Gernet, (H.M. Wright, trans.) *Daily Life in China on the Eve of the Mongol Invasion 1250–1276* (London: George Allen and Unwin, 1962) provides wonderful insights into social life in Song China.

57   The quote on merchants and artisans in ancient China comes from Han Fei, *Five Evils (Han Fa-Tzu Chi-Shih)*, vol. 2, 1075–76 cited in Theodore de Berry, ed., *Source of Chinese Tradition* (New York: Columbia University Press, 1960).

The quote extolling the virtues of the farmer compared with those of the merchant is from Wang Chen, *Nong shu* cited in de Berry, *Source of Chinese Tradition.*

60   For a fascinating and detailed discussion of the emergence of China's international trade and maritime commerce during the Song, see Jung-pang Lo, "Maritime Commerce and its Relation to the Sung Navy", in *Journal of Economic and Social History of the Orient,* Part 1, 1969, 57–101. See also the chapter "The Revolution in Money and Credit", in Elvin, *Patterns of the Chinese Past.*

61   For further details on the elevation of merchants during the Southern Song dynasty see *Song shi (History of the Song Dynasty),* as quoted in Lo, "Maritime Commerce," in *Journal of Economic and Social History of the Orient.*

64   For a more detailed discussion of the growth of the European economy in the medieval period see the three volumes of Braudel, *Civilization and Capitalism;* E.L. Jones, *The European Miracle* (Cambridge: Cambridge University Press, 1985); and Henri Pirenne, *Economic and Social History of Europe* (London: Routledge and Kegan Paul, 1972).

POWER, PROFIT AND THE ARMS RACE

65   Marco Polo's description of Quanzhou is from Komroff, *The Travels of Marco Polo (The Venetian),* 254–55.

70   Leonardo da Vinci's letter comes from Carlo Maria Franzero, *Leonardo* (London: W.H. Allen, 1969), 54–56.

72   Daniel Boorstin, *The Discoverers* (U.S.A.: Dent, 1984) contains an excellent general discussion on Henry the Navigator and the impact of European voyages of discovery from the fifteenth century. For a more detailed account of the impact of Asian commodities and ideas on medieval and Renaissance Europe see Donald Lasch, *Asia in the Making of Europe* (Chicago: University of Chicago Press, 1970).

ZHENG HE AND THE LAST OF THE TREASURE SHIPS

73   The quotes from Zhou Chufei and Ibn Batuta come from Needham, *Science and Civilisation in China,* vol. IV:3.
For an interesting discussion on maritime expansion see Jung-pang Lo, "The Emergence of China as a Sea Power during the Late Sung and early Yuan Periods", in *Far Eastern Quarterly,* vol. 4:14, 1955, 489–503.

75   The quote referring to the gifts of pepper and sapanwood is taken from Tian Rukang, "Zheng He's Voyages and the Distribution of Pepper in China", in *Journal of the Royal Asiatic Society,* No. 2, 1981.

77   The quote by Emperor Gaozong and the quote (following) on the levying of duties are from Tian Rukang, "The Causes for the Decline in China's Overseas Trade between the Fifteenth and Eighteenth Centuries", in *Papers in Far Eastern History* (Australian National University), vol. 25, 1982, 38. See also the chapter "China and the Ming and Manchu Empires", in Jones, *The European Miracle.* For a more thorough analysis, the chapter "The Turning Point in the Fourteenth Century", in Elvin, *Patterns of the Chinese Past,* should be consulted.
See John Maynard Keynes, *A Treatise on Money,* vol. 1 (London: 1930) 156–57, and J.B. Black, *The Reign of Elizabeth 1558–1603* (Oxford: 1952), 210. These are both cited by Tian Rukang in "The Causes for the Decline in China's Overseas Trade", in *Papers in Far Eastern History.* The consequences of the contraction of trade and commerce during the Ming dynasty is dealt with in the chapter on China in Jones, *The European Miracle.*

THE INVENTION OF PROGRESS

82   The quote by Mencius' is taken from Immanuel Hsü, *The Rise of Modern China* (Oxford: Oxford University Press, 1977), 95.

82–3   Francis Bacon's quote comes from Elizabeth Eisenstein, *The Printing Revolution in Early Modern Europe* (Cambridge: Cambridge University Press, 1983), 12.

86   For an excellent discussion on the re-emergence of Greek science in medieval Europe and the importance of the Crusades in opening up Europe to new ideas see Lynn White, Jr., "The Medieval Roots of Modern Technology and Science", in Warren Scoville and J. Clayburn, La Force, ed., *The Economic Development of Western Europe — The Middle Ages and the Renaissance* (Lexington, Massachusetts: Heath and Co., 1968).

87   The quotes on education are taken from Nakayama, *Academic and Scientific Traditions,* 63–64. Also see the Maurice Keen chapter "Universities and the Friars" in *History of Medieval Europe* (Middlesex, England: Pelican 1986).

The quote from *Great Learning,* one of the principal works to be studied by Confucian scholars, is from John Fairbank, *The United States and China,* 4th ed., (Cambridge: Harvard University Press, 1983), 77. For a succinct argument on why China did not develop modern science see Fairbank's chapter, "The Confucian Pattern".

For a detailed account of the religious origins of European development and use of clocks see David Landes, *Revolution in Time* (Cambridge: Harvard University Press, Belknap Press, 1983) Chap. 3. Note that Joseph Needham, the famous historian of Chinese science, would argue that the idea for the mechanical clock passed to the west from accounts of the famous Su Song clock. However, the Harvard historian David Landes argues that there is no necessary relationship between the two.

88   For an interesting book on the notion of the millenium and its influence on western thought see Norman Cohn, *The Pursuit of the Millenium* (Oxford: Oxford University Press, 1970). For a scholarly discussion on the relationship between Protestantism and Capitalism see Max Weber, *The Protestant Ethic and the Spirit of Capitalism* (London: Unwin Paperback, 1985) and R.H. Tawney, *Religion and the Rise of Capitalism* (Middlesex: Penguin, 1972).

91   The quote from Leonardo da Vinci is taken from the excellent chapter "Painting and Perspective," in Morris Kline *Mathematics in Western Culture* (Middlesex: Pelican, 1972). Samuel Edgerton "The Renaissance Artist as Quantifier," in Margaret Hagen, ed., *The Perception of Pictures* (New York: Academic Press, 1980), 179–212, provides an interesting comparison to China where neither perspective nor plan drawing was used.

92   For an account of the impact of paper and printing on western culture see Eisenstein, *The Printing Revolution.* On the issue of the impact of increasing literacy in Europe see Carlo Cipolla, *Literacy and Development in the West* (Middlesex: Pelican 1969).

94   The quotes from the Qing dynasty treatise and Jesuit missionary Verbiest come from Jonathan Spence, *To Change China: Western Advisers in China 1620–1690* (Middlesex: Penguin, 1980).

The quote ". . . to garner into the granaries . . ." is from Matteo Ricci as quoted in Boorstin, *The Discoverers,* 56.

95   A good historical account of the early establishment of foreign relations between China and the West is to be found in Hsü, *The Rise of Modern China.*

96   Francis Xavier's quote is taken from C.R. Boxer, "The Christian Century in Japan," cited in *Kagoshima: a Brief History of Overseas Exchange* (Kagoshima: Public Relations Division, Kagoshima Prefectual Government, 1984), 14.

The quote on Jesuit impressions of Asia are taken from Endymion Wilkinson, *Japan versus Europe: A History of Misunderstanding* (Middlesex: Penguin, 1983), 32–33. As the title suggests this book reviews the relationship between Japan and Europe in contemporary economic terms. The earlier chapters however, provide a good social history of this relationship.

99–101   The quotes from Ricci appear in Boorstin, *The Discoverers,* 333, 57. For an excellent short review of the efforts of the Jesuit mission to China see the first chapter in Spence, *To Change China.*

102   Schall's petition as quoted in Spence, *To Change China,* 3.

104   The quote from Kangxi's journal is taken from Jonathan D. Spence, *Emperor of China: Self-Portrait of K'ang-Hsi* (New York: Vintage Books, 1975), 72.

105   The quote on the uses of western learning is taken from Carlo Cipolla, *Clocks and Culture, 1300–1700* (New York: Norton, 1979), 89.

106   "Lines in praise of a self-chiming clock," as translated in Spence, *Emperor of China,* 63.

106-09   Like the chicken-and-the-egg argument, or the nature versus nurture debate, the issue of whether Protestantism led to capitalism, or vice versa has absorbed economic historians since Tawney and Weber. The argument will no doubt absorb many student seminars but need not concern us here.

113   The quote on the instrument-maker George Graham comes from Olivia Brown, "The Instrument-Making Trade," in *Science and Profit in 18th-Century London* (Cambridge: Whipple Museum of the History of Science, 1985).

117-18   The account of De Beladoir is drawn from Mark Elvin's remarks in Merson, *Culture and Science in China,* 55.

119   There is a good discussion of the role of the new high priesthood of science as put forward by Bacon, in I.F. Clark, *Patterns of Expectation* (London: Jonathan Cape, 1978).

121   The quote on tribunals is from Ssu-yu Teng "Chinese Influence on the Western Examination System," in Ssu-yu Teng and Biggerstaff *An Annotated Bibliography of Selected Chinese Reference Works.* (Cambridge: Harvard University Press, 1950). This work provides a very good review of the history of the adoption in the west of civil service exams.

123   The quote from "Essay on Tea" is taken from Richard Thames, *Josiah Wedgwood* (Shire, Albums–Aylesbury, 1972), 6–7.

125   For an extremely instructive and entertaining account of industrial imitation see David Halberstam, *The Reckoning* (New York: Bantam Books, 1986).

129   This account of Wedgwood is drawn from two very useful small books: Thames, *Josiah Wedgwood* and Alison Kelly, *The Story of Wedgwood* (London: Faber and Faber, 1975). Additional insights have been drawn from Gaye Blake Roberts, *Mr Wedgwood and the Porcelain Trade,* paper delivered at the English Speaking Union, 1983.

130–1   The two quotes from Wedgwood can be found in Kelly, *The Story of Wedgwood,* 16, 18.

140   The advertisement in the Derby Mercury is taken from Richard Hill, *Richard Arkwright and Cotton Spinning* (Wayland, Hove, England: 1973), 41. This is an excellent brief biography.

141   John Wesley's quote on religion is cited in Thompson, *The Making of The English Working Class,* 391.

143–4   The quotes on the factory system in industrial England and the moral economy of the factory system are taken from Thompson, *The Making of the English Working Class,* 395, 397.

145   Van Braan's quote is cited in Landes, *Revolution in Time,* 49.

146–9   These figures on the East India Company and the rules of behavior for foreigners are taken from Hsü, *The Rise of Modern China,* 200, 202.

151   Qianlong's poem and the edict addressed to George III are as translated by J. L. Cranmer-Byng in "Lord Macartney's Embassy to Peking," in *Journal of Oriental Studies,* vol. IV, 1–2, 117–83. They are also quoted in Hsü, *The Rise of Modern China,* 210, 183.

153   Coleridge's famous poem comes from *The Penguin Book of English Verse* (Middlesex: Penguin, 1958).

154–5   Commissioner Lin's statement to Queen Victoria comes from Teng and Fairbank, *China's Response to the West: Documentary Survey 1839–1923* (Cambridge: Harvard University Press, 1954), 24–27.

156   A very good outline of the American involvement in the opium trade is found in Jonathan Goldstein, *Philadelphia and the China Trade* (Philadelphia: Pennsylvania State University Press, 1978).

157   The cause of the Opium War is as quoted in Brian Inglis, *Opium War* (London: Hodder and Stoughton, 1976).

DREAMS OF WEALTH AND POWER

'ON THE WINGS OF CHANGE'

160   Mori Ogai's quote is taken from Wilkinson, *Japan versus Europe,* 117. Otto von Bismarck's quote is cited in Peter Mason, *Blood and Iron* (Melbourne, Penguin, 1984).

161   The comment by Commander Rodgers is quoted in Noel Perrin, *Giving Up the Gun* (Boulder, Shambhala, 1980) in which Perrin provides an extensive review of the history of the Japanese use and abandonment of the gun 1543–1879.

163   For a good general account of Tokugawa Japan see Edwin Reischauer, *Japan: The Story of a Nation* (New York: Alfred A. Knopf, 1981) and Richard Storry, *A History of Modern Japan* (Middlesex: Pelican, 1960).

164   Donald Keene, *The Japanese Discovery of Europe 1720–1830* (Palo Alto, Calif.: Stanford University Press, 1969) deals with the impact of the west on Japan and provides a good account of the development and impact of Rangaku or "Dutch learning."

168   The statistics on population and productivity come from Hsü, *The Rise of Modern China,* 178. An additional general reference that covers this period is John K. Fairbank and Edwin O. Reischauer, *China: Tradition and Transformation* (Sydney: George Allen and Unwin, 1979).

175   The quote from Zeng's diary is cited in Hsü, *The Rise of Modern China,* 345.

      Hart's code of behavior is taken from Hsü, *The Rise of Modern China,* 339.

176   The quote from Li Hong Zhang is cited in Hsü, *The Rise of Modern China,* 347.

177   Wo-Jen's restating of the Confucian attitude comes from Hsü, *The Rise of Modern China,* 349.

178–9   A good general explanation of the complex issue of *fengshui* is found in Ernest Eitel, *Fengshui: The Science of Sacred Landscape in Old China* (London: Synergetic Press, 1985). This book, however, was first published in 1873 around the time of the Shanghai-Wusong railway controversy.

STRONG ARMY, RICH NATION

181   Shibusawa's quote is from Kyugoro Obato, *An Interpretation of the Life of Viscount Shibusawa* (Tokyo, Bijutsu Insatsusho, 1937, 48).

183   To get some insight into Fukuzawa's thinking see Kiyooka Eichi, ed., *The Autobiography of Fukuzawa Yukichi* (Tokyo, Hokuseido Press, 1981). Fukuzawa's most influential book *Things Western* is also well worth reading.

      Fukuzawa's quote comes from Wilkinson, *Japan Versus Europe,* 107.

184   Fukuzawa's quote on western customs is from his essay "Western Clothing, Food and Homes" written in 1866 and cited in Julia Meech-Pekarik, *The World of Meiji Print* (Tokyo, Weatherhill, 1986), 70.

      See Johannes Hirschmeier, "Shibusawa Eichi: Industrial Pioneer", in William W. Lockwood, ed., *The State and Economic Enterprise in Japan* (Princeton, N.J., Princeton University Press, 1969), 209–47.

185   A good account of how foreigners were employed in Japan can be found in Hazel Jones, *Live Machines* (University of British Columbia Press, 1980).

185–6   For a very readable account of the transformation of Meiji Japan see Reischauer's biography of her grandfather, Finance Minister

Matsukata Mosoyoshi, in Haru Matsukata Reischauer, *Samurai and Silk* (Cambridge, Mass.: The Belknap Press, Harvard, 1986).

187–8 Okura Kitvachiro's description of western dance is from Meech-Pekarik, *The World of Meiji Prints.*

190 *Shibusawa's quote on a moral economy is from Marshall Byronk, Capitalism and Nationalism in Prewar Japan: The Ideology of the Business Elite, 1868–1941* (Palo Alto, Calif.: Stanford University Press, 1967), cited in Gregory, "The Logic of Japanese Enterprise," in the *Institute of Comparative Culture Business Series,* Bulletin No. 92.

190–1 For a good short review of Meiji Japan and, specifically, Shibusawa's approach to the fostering of private enterprise, see Gregory, "The Logic of Japanese Enterprise," in the *Institute of Comparative Culture Business Series,* Bulletin No. 92.
For a more detailed account of the impact of technological innovation on the industrial development of Europe in the nineteenth and early twentieth centuries see David Landes, *The Unbound Prometheus,* (Cambridge: Cambridge University Press, 1968).
The quote comes from Yamamura, "Success Illgotten?" in *Journal of Economic History,* 117.

WINDOWS ON THE WORLD

193 Belloc's quote is cited Mason, *Blood and Iron.*

195 The quote from Carnegie's letter was taken from Nathan Rosenberg and Birdzell, *How the West Grew Rich* (New York: Basic Books, 1985). This is a very accessible account of the role of economic institutions in fostering technological change and the application of science to industry in the nineteenth and early twentieth centuries.

197 This quote is from Rosenberg and Birdzell *How the West Grew Rich,* 213.
There are numerous accounts of the events surrounding the Shanghai Wusong railway controversy and Li Hongzhang's Chinese Merchants' Steam Navigation Company, however, Hsü, *The Rise of Modern China,* and Fairbank and Reischauer, provide good general reviews. Jardine Matheson's own recent history ed., Maggie Keswick, *The Thistle and the Jade* (London: Jardine Matheson & Co. Ltd, 1982) gives a good picture of the treaty ports and their economic impact on China in the late nineteenth century.

CARVED UP LIKE A RIPE MELON

198 The quote from Liu Xihong is taken from J.D. Frodsham, *The Chinese Embassy in the West* (Oxford: Clarendon Press, 1974, 136).

203 The quote by Baron Von Falkenegg comes from Wilkinson, *Japan versus Europe,* 59.
The quotes by Rene Pion and Anatole France are both taken from Wilkinson, *Japan versus Europe,* 59 and 61. This book offers a very good and moving account of the complex relationship between Japan and the west.

204–5 One of the best biographical studies of Yan Fu and his efforts to adapt western ideas to Confucian China is Benjamin Schwartz, *In Search of Wealth and Power* (Cambridge, Mass.: The Belknap Press, Harvard, 1964).

206 The dialogue between Kang and Emperor Guangxu, and Kang's comments on institutional reforms come from Hsü, *The Rise of Modern China,* 452, 455.

207 Marina Warner, *The Dragon Empress* (London, Weidenfeld and Nicolson, 1972) provides a good account of court life in China during the final decades of the Qing dynasty.

COMPRADORES AND WARLORDS

209 Chen Duxiu's quote on Mr Science and Mr Democracy comes from Fairbank and Reischauer, *China: Tradition and Transformation,* 434.

210 For a discussion on the issue of western influence on education in China see Merson, *Culture and Science in China,* chapts. 4 and 5.

212 Hu Shi's thoughts on liberation are as quoted in Fairbank and Reischauer, *China: Tradition and Transformation,* 436.

ZAIBATSU AND THE ZERO-SUMGAME

213 Tokutoini's comment on the Japanese in the eyes of the world is as quoted in Meech-Pekarik, *The World of Meiji Prints.*

214 Reischauer, *Japan: The Story of a Nation,* 186, provides details of the development of the idea of "Asia for the Asians".

217 For an account of how the Zero Fighter was built Jiro Horikoshi its, designer, provides a good account in Shojiro Shindo and Harold N. Wantiez, *Eagles of Mitsubishi* (London: Orbis, 1981).

THE COLOR OF THE CAT

THE DRAGONS AWAKE

220–1 For a good account of United States policies in Japan after 1945 see Reischauer, *Japan: The Story of a Nation.* Reischauer was United States Ambassador to Japan in the early 1960's and provides a very perceptive account of United States-Japanese relations in his autobiography, Edwin Reischauer, *My Life between Japan and America* (New York: Harper and Row, 1986).

223 Chalmers Johnson, *MITI and the Japanese Miracle* (Palo Alto, Calif.: California University Press, 1982) provides one of the best studies available in English of the role of MITI in Japan's postwar development.

224 For a personal account of the history of Sony see Akio Morita, *Made in Japan* (London, Collins, 1986). For Ibuka's account of the company's meteoric rise see *Sony Challenge, 1946–1968,* (Tokyo: Sony Corporation, 1986). Makoto Kikuchi, the present chief of research at Sony provides a perspective on the Japanese approach to research and development in Makoto Kikuchi, *Japanese Electronics* (Tokyo: Simul Press, 1983).

PERMANENT REVOLUTION

225 Mao Zedong's quote is from *Miscellany of Mao Zedong 1949–1968* (Arlington, 1974), 269.

227 For further details on Sino-Soviet relations in the 1950's see Bill Brugger, ed., *China: Liberation and Transformation 1962–1979* (London: Croom Helm, 1981). Also see Wang Gungwu, *China and the World since 1949* (London: Macmillan, 1977).

229 The quote by Professor Cao Zongxun is taken from Merson, *Culture and Science in China,* 126.

232 The quote on the "four pests" campaign comes from Mikhail Klochko, *Soviet Scientist in China* (Hollis and Carter, 1964), 72. This book provides an excellent account of the experiences of a Soviet scientist sent to China in the 1950's.

233 For further statistics on the "great leap forward" see Hsü, *The Rise of Modern China,* 787.

234 Re the Box "Let A Hundred Flowers Bloom" – Thomas Malthus (1766–1834) was the economist who first put forward the theory that poverty was the result of population growth outpacing the rise in food production. A natural check on this population increase was the regular occurrence of natural disasters, war and disease. It was largely Malthus who earned for economics the title of the "dismal science."

MADE IN JAPAN

236 Morishima's quote comes from M. Morishima, *Why Japan Succeeded,* 117.
For a good general account of the west's misunderstanding of Japan, see Wilkinson, *Japan versus Europe.* Robert Christopher,

The Japanese Mind (London, Pan Books, 1984) is also worth reading on this subject.

238   For a good popular history of the development of computer technology Stan Augarten, *Bit by Bit: An Illustrated History of Computers* (Unwin Paperbacks, 1984) is worth reading.

On the issue of American failure to realize fully the potential of computer technology in manufacture see Seymour Mellman, "How the Yankees lost their Know-How", in *Technology Review,* October 1983. (Mellman is Professor of Engineering at Columbia University, New York.) Also see David Noble, *America by Design: Science, Technology, and the Rise of Corporate Capitalism,* (New York: Knopf, 1977).

239   For a detailed account of the rise of the Japanese electronics industry see Gene Gregory, *Japanese Electronics Technology: Enterprise and Innovation* (Tokyo: Japan Times, 1984).

240–1   Halberstam, *The Reckoning,* provides a good short account of the impact of Deming's ideas on the Japanese. It also provides an excellent account of how the Americans lost out to the Japanese in the automobile industry.

242   Nakane's arguments about the group orientation of Japanese society are found in Chie Nakane, *Japanese Society* (Middlesex: Pelican, 1974).

The quote by Morishima is taken from M. Morishima, *Why Japan Succeeded.* The Confucian character of Japanese society is also dealt with in some detail.

243   The quote on Japanese interdependence is taken from Jane Devitt, "Changing Social Values in Contemporary Japan," unpublished paper, (Japanese Economic and Management Centre, University of New South Wales, Sydney.)

The quote by Yasuo Kato comes from *Business Week,* 14 December, 1981. On the issue of creativity in Japan see J. Bester, *Heidiki Yukawa Creativity and Intuition: A Physicist looks at East and West* (Kodansha International, 1973). Heidiki Yukawa was one of Japan's early Nobel prize-winning physicists.

243–4   Richard Pascale and Anthony Athos, *The Art of Japanese Management* (London: Allen Lane, 1981) was one of the popular books that showed American audiences just why the Japanese were doing things better than they were. Ezara Vogel, *Japan as Number One* was also written as a warning to American industry. Lester Thurow, ed., *The Management Challenge: Japanese Views* (Cambridge, Mass.: MIT Press, 1985) is a more recent work providing the Japanese perspective on how and why they have been so successful. For a critical study of the relevance of Japan as a model for other countries see Ian Inkster, *Japan as a Development Model* (Brokmeyer Bochum, 1980).

BETTER RED THAN EXPERT

247   The quote by Professor Cao Zongxun comes from Merson, *Culture and Science in China,* 157.

248   The account of violence at a school in Xiamen comes from Ken Ling, *The Revenge of Heaven: Journal of a Young Chinese* (New York: G.P. Putnam, 1972).

Liang Heng and Judith Shapiro, *Son of the Revolution* (Aylsbury, Bucks: Fontana, 1983) is one of a number of books written by witnesses of the cultural revolution. Others worth reading are Bao Ruowang, *Prisoner of Mao* (New York: Coward McCann and Geoghagen, 1973) and Ken Ling, *The Revenge of Heaven.*

251   An interesting perspective on the events of the cultural revolution and its links to China's past is found in Donald Munro, *The Concept of Man in Contemporary China.* (Ann Arbor, Mich.: University of Michigan Press, 1977). Bill Brugger, ed., *China: The Impact of the Cultural Revolution* (Canberra: Australian National University Press, 1978) also provides a good review of the events and the consequences of the cultural revolution.

For a detailed account of the new emphasis given to science see Tong B. Tang, *Science and Technology in China* (London, Longmans, 1984).

259   The quote from the play *The Impostor,* was translated by Danny Kane and comes from Merson, *Culture and Science in China,* 174.

THE OPEN DOOR

260   For an account of the massive transfer of technology now going from the west to China, and its consequences see E.E. Bauer, *China Take Off: Technology Transfer and Modernization* (Seattle: University of Washington Press, 1986). Fingar et al., "Science and Technology in China," in *Bulletin of the Atomic Scientists,* October 1984, provides a detailed review of China's efforts to catch up with Japan and the west. See also Simon, "The Challenge of Modernizing Industrial Technology", in *China Asian Survey,* vol. XXVI, No. 4, April 1986.

TROUBLE IN STOVE CITY

265   On the issue of demands for greater intellectual freedom and democracy called for by Fang Lizhi see David Kelly, "The Chinese Student Movement of December 1986 and its Intellectual Antecedents", in *Australian Journal of Chinese Affairs,* March 1988.

269   On the more general issues of world history and the reasons for the shift in centers of economic power and creativity there is an excellent study in Kennedy, *The Rise and Fall of the Great Powers* (New York, Random House, 1988).

NOTES ON ILLUSTRATIONS

THE PRICE OF HARMONY

Pages 12 & 13: Guiseppe Castiglione (1662–1722), *L'emperor ouvre un siffon a l'occasion de la fête de l'agriculture* (The Emperor uses a plough at the agriculture fête) from "Voyages de L'emperor Kangxi". Code 72E239 Musée Guimet, Paris (Photo: Cliche des Musées Nationaux).

Page 15: *The Catlan Map* from a fourteenth century manuscript. The Mansell Collection Ltd, London.

Page 16: Attributed to Liu Kuan-Tao, *Kubla Khan Hunting,* (Yuan dynasty — 1279–1368). Collection of the National Palace Musuem, Taipei, Taiwan, Republic of China.

Page 17: "The Ocean Going Junk" in the *Liu-Chhiu Kuo Chih Lueh* of 1757. This is one of the best pictures of a Chinese ship in the Chinese style to be found in the literature. Courtesy of Joseph Needham, *Science and Civilization in China,* Vol. V1:3, (Cambridge, Cambridge University Press, 1971) 405, Fig. 939.

Page 19: Guiseppe Castiglione (1662–1722), *Southern Inspection Tour by Emperor Kangxi of the Building of the Dykes,* scroll number 4 (Mulan IV) from seventeenth century scroll titled "Tour of The South." Musée Guimet. (Photo: Cliche des Musees Nationaux, Paris).

Page 19: A late Qing (1840–1911) representation of river conservancy work from *Chin-Ting Shu ching Thu Shou* (Imperial illustrated edition of the "Historical Classic") 1905, ch 6, Yu Kung. Courtesy of Joseph Needham, *Science and Civilization in China,* Vol.IV:3, 233, Fig 865.

Page 22: Woodblock of iron foundries from a Chinese encyclopedia. Courtesy of Canton University Library, Canton (Guangzhou).

Page 24: Woodblock of salt drilling from a Chinese encyclopedia. Courtesy of Canton University Library, Canton (Guangzhou).

Page 26 (*left*): "Rice paddies" woodblock from a Chinese encyclopedia. Courtesy of Canton University Library, Canton (Guangzhou).

Page 26 (*right*): "Dragon's back bone pump" from *Thien Kung Khai Wu* (1637), Ch 1, 19a. Courtesy of Joseph Needham, *Science and Civilization in China,* Vol.IV:2, 340, fig 579.

Page 27: Paul de Limbourg and Colombe (1415–16), October *Très Riches Heures,* fol. 10v. Musée Condé, Chantilly.

Page 29: *Portrait of Emperor Renzong,* Song Dynasty (960–1279). Collection of the National Palace Museum, Taipei, Taiwan, Rupublic of China.

Page 30: Chou Wen-Chu (active 940–975), *Scholars of Liu-Li Hall,* Song Dynasty (960–1279), hand–painted scroll, detail 5 — right hand side: three scholars; two servants and Buddhist monk in front of raised platform. Ink and colors on silk. Metropolitan Museum of Art, Gift of Mrs Sheila Riddell, in memory of Sir Percival David, 1977.

Page 32: (*left*): "Compositors setting a book in wooden movable type." Illustration from *Chin Chien Wu ying tien chu chen pan ch'eng shih,* a manual on movable type printing written in 1777 by Chin Chien.

Page 32 (*right*): *The Return of Lady Wen,* (28.62–65), Museum of Fine Arts, Boston.

Page 36: "Eighth century star map," Hong Kong University Press, Hong Kong.

Page 38: (*left*): "Painting of Armillary Sphere," Qing Dynasty (1644–1911). Collection of the National Palace Museum, Taipei, Taiwan, Republic of China.

Page 39: A late Qing representation of the measurement of the sun's shadow using a gnomon. From *Chin Ting Shu Ching Thu Shuo,* chapter 1, Yao-Tien Karlen 12, 3. Courtesy of Joseph Needham, *Science and Civilization in China,* Vol.III, 285.

Page 45: (*right*): Woodblock of ginseng. From a Chinese encyclopedia. Courtesy of the University of Canton, Canton (Guangzhou).

Page 47: "Chinese of all ages standing around the ying and yang symbol," seventeenth century painting. British Museum, London.

Page 48: (*left*): "Washing the heart and storing inwardly (the secretions)" From a nei tan alchemic text: *Hsing ming Kuei Chih. Hsi Hsin Thui Tsang (1615).* Courtesy of Joseph Needham, *Science and Civilization in China,* Vol.IV:2.

Page 51: Woodblock of wall and battle. From a Chinese encyclopedia. Courtesy of the University of Canton, Canton (Guangzhou).

Page 53: Gunpowder map drawn by Mike Gorman. Details courtesy of Joseph Needham, *Science and Civilization in China.*

Page 55: Chang Tse-Tuan, *Chhing-Ming Shang Ho Thu (Returning up the River to the City at the Spring Festival),* (1125), Su Song scroll.

Page 57: Woodblock of silk weaving loom. From a Chinese encyclopedia. Courtesy of the University of Canton, Canton (Guangzhou).

Page 58: "Merchants," Art Institute of Chicago, Chicago.

Page 59: Printing block for a Mongol bank note of the Chih-yuan period. Courtesy of Denis Twitchett, *Printing and Publishing in Medieval China* (London, Wynkyn de worde Society, 1983).

Page 60: The Battleship (Lou Chhuaan) in 1510 edition of *Wu Ching Tsung Yao* (1044). Courtesy of Joseph Needham, *Science and Civilization in China,* Vol.IV:3, 426, fig 949.

Page 66: "Venetian merchants Trading Bolts of Silk". from Marco Polo, *Book of Marvels, P.N. Paris MS 2810. Bibliothèque Nationale, Paris.*

Page 67: "Medieval siege of a stronghold in Africa" from *Chroniques de Froissart,* fourteenth century manuscript. British Museum Library Board, London.

Page 68: "The Taking of Rouen by Henry V (1418–19)" from *Vigiles de Charles VII,* fifteenth century manuscript. Bibliothèque Nationale, Paris.

Page 70: Leonardo da Vinci, *Chariot with Scythes,* Courtesy British Museum, London.

Page 71: Vittore Carpaccio (1460–1526), *Return of the Ambassadors* from the Cycle of the Scuola di Sant'Orsola. Accademia, Venice. (Photo: Scala).

Page 72: Prince Henry the Navigator from Gomes Eanes de Zurara (1410–1473) (*Cronica da Tomada*). Biblioteca Nacional, Lisbon.

Page 74: Illustrations by Mike Gorman.

Page 76: Shen Tu, *The Giraffe of Bengal,* (copied by Ch'en T'ing-pi), from the book *T'oung Pao* Vol. XXXIV, 5. Courtesy of the Australian National University Library, Canberra.

THE INVENTION OF PROGRESS

Page 83: Gentile Bellini, *Audience d'une ambassade Venitienne dans une ville orientale,* (1512), Venice, school of Bellini. Musée du Louvre, Paris.

Page 84: Hans Holbein the Younger, *The Ambassadors* (1533). National Gallery, London.

Page 86: Peter Apian, *Introductio geographica Petri Apiani in*

Doctissimus Verneri Annotationes, Inglostadt (1533). British Library, London.

Page 88: *Solomon and the Clock,* Flemish mid-fifteenth century, Fr 455, fol 9. Bibliothèque Nationale, Paris.

Page 89: (*left*): "General views of Su Sung's clock tower", from Hsin I Hsiang Fa Yao (1092). Courtesy of Joseph Needham, *Clerks and Craftsmen in China and the West,* (Cambridge, Cambridge University Press, 1970), Figs. 62a and 62b, 211.

Page 89: (*right*): Stradanus of Antwerp, *Horologia Ferrea.* Courtesy of Sydney College of the Arts, Sydney.

Page 90: Jan Vredeman De Vries, perspective diagram. Engraving from *Perspective* (Leiden 1604–5), plate 28.

Page 91: Albrecht Dürer, "Perspective Device," wood-cut from *Underweysung der Messung,* (Nuremberg 1525).

Page 92: Andreas Vesalius, *Quinta Musculo,* from *Fabric of the Human Body* (De Humani Corporis Fabrica), (Basel 1543).

Page 93: Matteo Ricci, "A world map using Mercator's projection." Kobe City Museum.

Page 95: *St Francis Xavier* (1506–1552), by a Japanese Jesuit at Macao (1623). No 36 in the catalog. Kobe City Museum.

Page 97: Kano Naizen, *Nambon Screen,* late sixteenth century–early seventeenth century, six fold screen. Musée Guimet, Paris (Photo: Cliche des Musées Nationaux).

Page 98: (*top*): A Beauvais tapestry, *Die Astronomen,* (The Jesuits as Astronomers), Late seventeenth century. Bayerische Verwaltung der Staatlichen Schlösser, Garten und Seen, Munich.

Page 98: (*bottom*): "Matteo Ricci, Adam Schall and Ferdinand Verbiest", from Jean Baptist Du Halde's *Description of the Empire of China and Chinese Tartary* (London, 1738–1741, translated from 1708 work). Staatsbibliothek Preussischer, Kulturbesitz, West Berlin.

Page 100: Jean Baptist du Halde, "Pere, Adam Schaal", from Du Halde's *Description of the Empire of China and Chinese Tartary.* 269. State Library of New South Wales, Sydney.

Page 102: Jean Baptist du Halde, "Observatory on the City wall in Peking," from *Description of the Empire of China and Chinese Tartary.* State Library of New South Wales, Sydney.

Page 104: (*left*): Zonca, "Trombe Da Rota per Cavar Aqua" from Zonca's engineering treatise of 1607. It appears first in the mss of Francesco di Giorgio (1475). Courtesy of Joseph Needham, *Science and Civilization in China,* Vol IV:2, 214.

Page 104: (*right*): "The eighth diagram" from *Chhi Thu Shuo* (1627). Courtesy of Joseph Needham, Ibid.

Page 107: V.C. Vroom (1566–1640), *Return from the Second Voyage to the East Indies* (1599). Amsterdam Historical Museum.

Page 108: Job Berkcheyde (1630–63) *The Courtyard of the Amsterdam Exchange* (1668). Amsterdam Historical Museum.

Page 109: Sieuwert van der Meulen, *The Planks Rise all around the Ship* (etching). State Library of New South Wales, Sydney.

Page 110: (*left*): *Dionysius Papin M.D., Anno 1689.* From George Williamson, *Memorials of the Lineage, Early Life, Education, and Development of the genius of James Watt,* (Thomas Constable, London, 1856).

Page 110: (*right*): James Watt and one of his steam powered beam engines. Courtesy of Powerhouse Museum, Sydney.

Page 112: Jan van Kessel, *Asien,* (1664–66), oil on canvas. Alte Pinakothek, Munich.

Page 113: Thomas Sprat, frontispiece to *The History of the Royal Society of London for Improving Natural Knowledge,* (1667).

Page 114: "Octagon Room at Greenwich Observatory" (engraving). National Maritime Museum, London.

Page 115: Unidentified Artist, "Greenwich Observatory from Croom's Hill" (about 1860). National Maritime Museum, London.

Page 116: Gerrit Paape, "Operations in a Delft faience factory" (copperplate). Courtesy of Gröninger Museum, The Netherlands.

Page 117: *Gate Crashing at the Tuileries* (1783) Montgolfier brothers' demonstration of the hot-air balloon. Courtesy of Colonel Richard Gimbel, Aeronautics History Collection, US Airforce Academy Library, USA.

Page 118: Joseph Wright of Derby, *An Experiment on a Bird in the*

Airpump, (1767–1768). National Gallery, London.

Page 120: Painting by Cu Liu Peng. Sydney L. Moss Ltd, London.

Page 123: Catterson Smith, *Anna Maria, Seventh Duchess of Bedford.* Courtesy of Woburn Abbey, Bedfordshire.

Page 124: "Emperor's Audience in the Imperial Garden," late eighteenth century. Hong Kong Museum of Art, Hong Kong.

Page 127: A contemporary painting illustrating the manufacture, transport and sale of export porcelain in China during the eighteenth century. "Perfecting the Interior" from Walter A Staehelin, *The Book of Porcelain* (1965). Collection from the Benteli Publishers, Switzerland.

Page 128: "Scene in a porcelain factory: painters; muffle-kiln; preparing the paste; repairers, from de Milly's *L'Art de la Porcelaine,* (1771). State Library of New South Wales, Sydney.

Page 129: George Stubbs, *Josiah Wedgwood and his Family* (1780). Josiah Wedgwood and Sons Limited, Barlaston, Stoke-on-Trent, England.

Page 130: Staffordshire potteries (engraving). Mary Evans Picture Library, London.

Page 131: Photo of Josiah Wedgwood's 3,000 trials carried out when trying to develop his jasper-ware. Josiah Wedgwood & Sons Limited, Barlaston, Stoke-on-Trent, England.

Page 133: Engraving of Piedmontese throwing mill", (1607). Macclesfield Sunday School Heritage Centre Silk Museum.

Page 135: (*top*): M.J. Starting, *John Lombe's Water Powered Silk Spinning Factory built in Derby in 1720.* Mary Evans Picture Library, London.

Page 136: Diagrams courtesy of Macclesfield Sunday School Heritage Centre Silk Museum.

Page 138: James Gillray, *Scientific Researches! – New Discoveries in PNEUMATICS! – or – an Experimental Lecture on the Powers of Air.* British Museum, London.

Page 139: I.M. Booth, *Arkwright's Cotton Mills, by Night,* (1782–83), 34 x 45 inches. Derby Art Gallery.

Page 142: Cotton mill (engraving). Mary Evans Picture Library, London.

Page 145: James Gillray, *The Reception of the Diplomatique and his suite, at the court of Peking,* (1792). British Museum, London.

Page 146: Idealized picture of the production of tea (1780). Number 6 or 7 of the catalog Craig Clunas *Chinese Export Watercolours.* Far Eastern Series, Victoria & Albert Museum, London.

Page 147: Canton waterfront and the European factories in 1794 (chinese scroll). Hong Kong Museum of Art, Hong Kong.

Page 148: A Chinese representation of the bringing of astronomical instruments as gifts by the embassy of Lord Macartney (1793), silk K'o-ssu. National Maritime Museum, London.

Page 149: William Alexander, *Approach of the Emperor of China to his tent in Tartary, to receive the British Ambassador* (September 1793). British Museum, London.

Page 150: William Alexander, *Portrait of Qianlong, Emperor of China in the Eighty Fourth Year of his Age, and Fifty Seventh of his Reign.* British Museum, London.

Page 152: George Chinnery (1774–1852), *Hauqua II* (1769–1843). Jardine Matheson & Co. Ltd, Hong Kong.

Page 154: Thomas Allom, "China Opium Smokers," from *China in a Series of Views,* (1843), 55. State Library of New South Wales, Sydney.

Page 156: Thomas Allom, "The Hon. East India Company's steamer *Nemsis* and the Boats of Sulphur, Calliope, Larne and Starling," *The Chinese Empire Illustrated* (1858). National Library of Australia, Canberra.

DREAMS OF WEALTH AND POWER

Pages 158–159: *The Prosperity of an English Trading Firm in Yokohama.* Yokohama Archives of History, Yokohama.

Page 161: "One of the Black Ships" as seen by a Japanese artist (1853). Yokohama Archives of History, Yokohama.

Page 162: A photo of the telegraph brought from the United States. Tokyo Communication Centre, Tokyo.

Page 163: "Samurai watching a model train." Courtesy Saga Prefectual Museum, Saga.

Page 164: Anonymous, *The Battle of Nagashino,* (Edo period, seventeenth century), six fold screen, ink and color on paper. Tokugawa Art Museum, Nagoya.

Page 166: Woodblocks from Yokohama Archives of History, Yokohama.

Page 169: Anonymous, *The Taiping Rebellion.* A painting commissioned by the Qing dynasty court (1860s). Courtesy of Wango Weng, New Hampshire.

Page 173: "The European–style Warship." Courtesy Saga Prefectual Museum, Saga.

Page 174: Photo by John Thomson of Li Hongzhang. From Thomson, *Illustrations of China and its People 1868–1874,* Vol.4. Royal Geographical Society, London.

Page 176: "The Jiangnan arsenal" from *Tien-Shih Chai Huo Pao* (Shanghai Picture Magazine), (1884–1894). National Library of Australia, Canberra.

Page 179: Photo by John Thomson of Nanking Arsenal (1868–1872). From J. Thomson, *Illustrations of China and its Peoples 1868–1874,* Vol.3. Royal Geographical Society, London.

Page 180: "Early Chinese railway." Mary Evans Picture Library, London.

Page 181: (*left*): Photo of Emperor Meiji in Court Robes (1860s). Albumen print. Yokohama Archives of History, Yokohama.

Page 181: (*right*): Uchida Kuichi, *Emperor Meiji (1872).* Albumen print. Collection of H. Kwan Lan, New York.

Page 182: Hashimoto Sadahide, *Picture of the Salesroom in Foreign Business Establishment in Yokohama,* (1861). The Lincoln Kirstein Collection, Metropolitan Museum of Art, New York.

Page 183: Fukuzawa Yukichi as a young samurai in Paris (1862). Albumen print. Keio University Library, Tokyo.

Page 186: "Silk spinning factory at Tomioka." Tomioka Museum.

Page 187: Utagawa Yoshitora, *An Imported Silk Reeling Machine at Tsuuiji in Tokyo* (1872). Lincoln Kirstein Collection, Metropolitan Museum of Art, New York.

Page 188: Hashimoto Chikanobu, *A Concert of European Music* (1889). Lincoln Kirstein Collection, Metropolitan Museum of Art, New York.

Page 189: Photo of samurai. Courtesy of University of Nagasaki Library, Nagasaki.

Page 190: "Yokohama Station" (woodblock). Yokohama Archives of History, Yokohama.

Page 191: "Large European–style buildings" (woodblock). Yokohama Archives of History, Yokohama.

Page 194: "Les Ponts Roulants in the Galerie des Machines, Paris 1889" from *Illustrated London News* (1889).

Page 196: "The First Electric Street Light in Tokyo's Ginza Street" (1883 woodblock). Courtesy of the Ministry of Foreign Affairs, Tokyo.

Page 199: George Bigot, "China and Japan fish for control of Korea" (1890s). Yokohama Archives of History, Yokohama.

Page 200: Anonymous woodblocks. A contemporary recording of the Sino-Japanese War, (1894).

Page 203: George Bigot, "Japan is excluded from the Club". Yokohama Archives of History, Yokohama.

Page 207: Yu (court photographer), *The Empress Dowager Posed as Goddess of Mercy,* Yuan-Yin, Peking, (1902–08). Freer Gallery of Art, Smithsonian Institution, Washington.

Page 209: "Dr Sun Yat-sen in exile in Japan." Radio Times Hulton Picture Library, London.

Page 217: Contemporary painting of the zero aeroplane. Courtesy of United States Army.

THE COLOR OF THE CAT

Page 221: The hypocenter of the atomic bomb and Mitsubishi steel works seen from a hill in Matsuyama-machi. Nagasaki International Culture Center. (Photo: Yosuke Yamabata, August 1945)

Page 224: (*top*): Ibuka standing next to a stereo speaker. Photo courtesy of Sony Corporation, Tokyo.

Page 224: (*bottom*) Photo taken in the Sony factory 1946. Courtesy of Sony Corporation, Tokyo.

Page 225: Soviet troops remove heavy industrial equipment from a Manchurian factory in 1946. Library of Congress, Washington D.C.

Page 226: Mao Zedong and the People's Liberation Army entering Peking, January 1949. (Chinese wall poster). Granger Collection, New York.

Page 227: Mao Zedong in the Soviet Union with Soviet leaders Bulganin and Stalin. Popperfoto.

Page 237: The *Eniac* was an enticing recruitment asset. *Popular Science.*

Page 240: Motoman from Kuni Sadamoto, "Robots in the Japanese Economy — facts about robots and their significance," *Survey Japan,* (Tokyo, 1981).

Page 241: From Richard Tanner Pascale and Anthony G. Athos. *The Art of Japanese Management,* (Allen Lane).
(Photo) Paul Fusco, Magnum/John Hillelson Agency.

Page 256: "Trucks awaiting despatch at Changchun No. 1 Motor Vehicle Factory in late 1970s." Society for Anglo- Chinese Understanding, London.

ACKNOWLEDGMENTS

This book has evolved over some years, and its history is inexorably intertwined with a television series produced at the same time. This is not however a "book of the series." It was written with the intention of exploring a great deal more than was possible in a four-hour television series.

Many of the ideas for both the book and the television series grew out of discussions with my friend and colleague at the University of New South Wales, Professor Ian Inkster, whose encouragement and criticism were invaluable. I am also indebted to Professor Wang Gungwu, Dr Stephen Fitzgerald, Professor Nathan Sivin, Professor Ho Peng Yoke, Professor Shigeru Nakayama, Dr Mark Elvin, Professor Ko Tsun, Professor Eric Jones, Dr Tim Cheek and Dr David Kelly for the help they have given me. Above all I am indebted to the Needham Institute in Cambridge, and Dr Joseph Needham whose monumental work *Science and Civilization in China* first raised many of the issues of world history that this book attempts to address. I would also like to thank my colleagues at the School of Science and Technology Studies, University of New South Wales, and the Australian Broadcasting Corporation's Science Unit for their encouragement and support.

This book has also benefited greatly from access to photographs and illustrations gathered for the television series, and for the new insights that were gained in the process of making that series. For this I owe a great deal to Film Australia and, in particular, to Robin Hughes for the support she has given to this project over its long, and sometimes tortuous, history. Thanks are due also to the film production team whose capacity for demanding simple answers to problems that one would rather ignore kept me honest — in particular to David Roberts, Geoff Barnes, Tom Levenson, and Dick Gilling. For photographic material taken on location I am indebted to Tony Gailey, David Roberts, Greg Low, and Jane Castle. A special thanks to Emma Gordon whose help in picture research and in getting the manuscript ready for the publisher were essential, and to the book's editors Lesley Dow and Kim Anderson for their patience and enthusiasm.

INDEX